Praise for *Starfish Pier*

"With its nicely interwoven faith elements, Hannon's multifaceted return to Hope Harbor focuses on how forgiving oneself is as important for healing as forgiveness from others. Series fans will be overjoyed by this complex, stirring tale."

Publishers Weekly

"The restful location and quirky townsfolk are sure to be soothing to those who enjoy Christian romances set in small towns."

Library Journal

"A pitch-perfect contemporary romance novel by a gifted author who is a complete master of the genre."

Midwest Book Review

Praise for *Driftwood Bay*

"Readers will delight in this pleasant romance. Hannon's take on loss and survival is simpatico with Debbie Macomber's Blossom Street series."

Booklist

"Full of faith and characters that readers will want to root for until the end."

Publishers Weekly

"Character-driven, thought-provoking, and highly recommended for connoisseurs of the genre."

Midwest Book Review

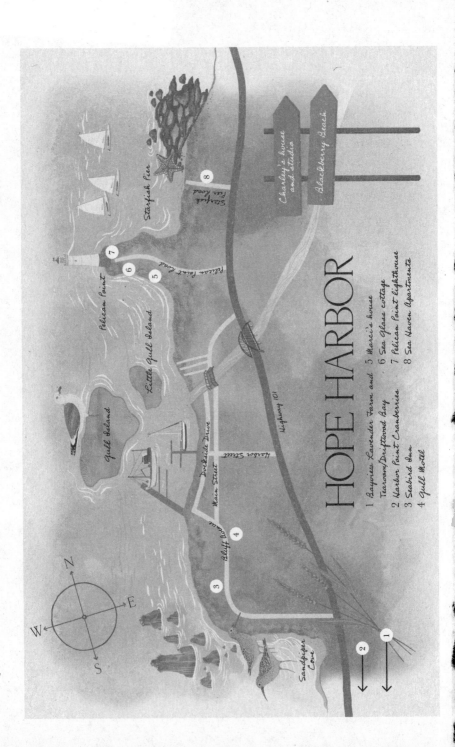

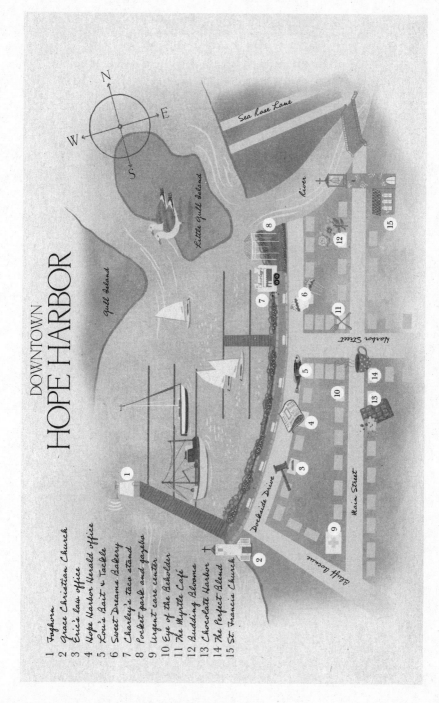

Books by Irene Hannon

Blackberry Beach

A Hope Harbor Novel

IRENE HANNON

Revell

a division of Baker Publishing Group
Grand Rapids, Michigan

© 2021 by Irene Hannon

Published by Revell
a division of Baker Publishing Group
PO Box 6287, Grand Rapids, MI 49516-6287
www.revellbooks.com

Printed in the United States of America

Library of Congress Cataloging-in-Publication Data
Names: Hannon, Irene, author.
Title: Blackberry Beach / Irene Hannon.
Description: Grand Rapids, Michigan : Revell, a division of Baker Publishing
    Group, [2021] | Series: Hope Harbor
Identifiers: LCCN 2020035396 | ISBN 9780800736156 (paperback) | ISBN
    9780800739683 (casebound)
Subjects: GSAFD: Love stories.
Classification: LCC PS3558.A4793 B57 2021 | DDC 813/.54—dc23
LC record available at https://lccn.loc.gov/2020035396

21 22 23 24 25 26 27   7 6 5 4 3 2 1

To my niece, Maureen Hannon,
as you graduate from high school.

I am so proud not only of your academic achievements
but also of your kind heart and sweet, gentle spirit.

Whatever path you follow in the years to come,
I wish you success beyond your wildest dreams.

But most of all, I wish you a future filled with
joy, love, and endless possibilities—
as well as the gifts of wonder and enthusiasm
that keep life always new.

1

The mystery woman was back.

Zach Garrett poured the steamed milk into the coffee mixture, creating his signature swirl pattern with the froth—all the while keeping tabs on the female customer who'd paused inside the door of The Perfect Blend, dripping umbrella in hand.

As she had on her first visit two days ago, the lady appeared to be debating whether to stay or bolt.

Wiping the nozzle on the espresso machine, he assessed her. Early to midthirties, near as he could tell—though the oversize, dark sunglasses hid most of her features. A curious wardrobe addition, given the unseasonably heavy rain that had been drenching Hope Harbor for the past seventy-two hours.

He handed the latte to the waiting customer and angled toward his Monday/Wednesday/Friday assistant barista. "Bren, you waited on her Monday, didn't you?" He indicated the slender woman with the dark, shoulder-length blunt-cut hair who continued to hover near the threshold.

Bren spared her a quick once-over as she finished grinding another batch of the top-quality Arabica beans Zach sourced from a fair-trade roaster in Portland. "Yeah."

"Do you remember what she ordered?"

"Small skinny vanilla latte."

"Did you get a name?"

"Nope. I asked, but she said she'd wait for her order at the pickup counter."

In other words, the woman wanted to remain anonymous.

Also curious.

While it was possible she was one of the many visitors who dropped in to their picturesque town for a few days during the summer months, his gut said otherwise.

And since his people instincts had served him well in his previous profession, there was no reason to discount them now.

So who was she—and what was she doing in Hope Harbor?

Only one way to find out.

"I'll take care of her."

"That works. I've already got customers." Bren inclined her head toward the couple waiting for their pound of ground coffee.

Zach called up his friendliest smile and ambled down to the end of the serving counter. "Let me guess—a small skinny vanilla latte."

The woman did a double take . . . took a step back . . . and gave the shop a quick, nervous scan. As if she was scoping out potential threats.

No worries on that score. There was nothing in The Perfect Blend to raise alarm bells. While several of the tables tucked against the walls and cozied up around the freestanding fireplace in the center were occupied, no one was paying any attention to the new arrival. The customers were all reading newspapers, absorbed in books, or chatting as they enjoyed their drinks and pastries in the Wi-Fi–free environment.

The door behind the woman opened again, nudging her aside.

Charley Lopez entered, his trademark Ducks cap secured beneath the hood of a dripping slicker.

"Sorry, ma'am." He flashed her a smile as he touched the brim of the cap, pushed the hood back to reveal his gray ponytail . . . and gave her an intent look. "I didn't mean to bump you."

"No problem." She dipped her chin and moved aside, putting distance between them. As if his perusal had spiked her nerves.

"Are you coming in or going out?" Charley maintained his hold on the half-open door.

"Coming in," Zach answered for her. "I'm betting she's in the mood for a skinny vanilla latte."

"Excellent choice." Charley closed the door.

"Bren will handle your order as soon as she finishes with her customers, Charley." Zach kept his attention on the stranger.

"No hurry." The taco-making artist who'd called Hope Harbor home for as long as anyone could remember moseyed toward the counter. "I doubt I'll have much business at the stand, thanks to our odd weather. August is usually one of the driest months on the Oregon coast."

"Any day is a perfect day for a Charley's fish taco."

"I may steal that line. It would be a great marketing slogan."

"As if you need one. Your long lines are proof that word of mouth generates a ton of business."

"That it does." He winked, then directed his next comment to the woman. "I hope you'll pay me a visit. My truck is on the wharf. Next to the gazebo."

"I may stop by."

"Please do. First order for newcomers is always on the house." He continued toward Bren.

Zach frowned after him. Everyone in town knew about Charley's welcome gift of a free lunch for new residents . . . but this woman hadn't moved to Hope Harbor.

Had she?

What did Charley know that he didn't?

She edged toward the exit, and Zach shifted gears. He could pick the town sage's brain later. In the meantime, why not try to ferret out a few facts himself?

Unless his skittish customer disappeared out the door first.

He hiked up the corners of his mouth again. "My assistant barista told me you ordered a small skinny vanilla latte on your last visit—but I'll be happy to make a different drink for you today."

Hesitating, she gave the room one more survey . . . then slid her umbrella into the stand by the door. "No. That's fine."

She was staying.

First hurdle cleared.

"Can I have a name for the order?" He picked up a cup and a pen.

Silence.

He arched his eyebrows at her.

She extracted a five-dollar bill and set it on the counter. "Keep the change. And it's Kat. With a K." She eased away.

Second hurdle cleared.

"Got it." He jotted the name. "I'll have this ready in a couple of minutes."

She nodded and escaped toward a deserted table in the far corner—out of conversation range.

Blast.

Thwarted at the third hurdle.

He wasn't going to find out anything else about her.

But what did it matter? Just because he was beginning to crave feminine companionship—and the pool of eligible women in town was limited—didn't mean he should get any ideas about the first single, attractive female who walked in.

Yeah, yeah, he'd noticed the empty fourth finger on her left hand.

He mixed the espresso and vanilla syrup together, positioned the steam nozzle below the surface of the milk until the liquid bubbled, then dipped deeper to create a whirlpool motion.

Charley wandered over while Bren prepared his café de olla, watching as Zach poured the milk into the espresso mixture, holding back the foam with a spoon to create a stylized K on top of the drink. "Beautiful. You have an artistic touch."

"Nothing like yours." He set the empty frothing pitcher aside and reached for a lid as he signaled to the woman in the corner. "I wish my coffee sold for a fraction of what your paintings bring in."

"Life shouldn't be all about making money. My stand isn't a gold mine, but I enjoy creating tacos as much as I enjoy painting. Customers for both can feel the love I put into my work. Like they can feel the love you have for this shop. It seeps into your pores the instant you cross the threshold. A person would have to be über-stressed not to find peace and relaxation here."

The very ambiance he'd hoped to create when he'd opened a year and a half ago.

"You just made my day."

"That's what it's all about, isn't it?" Charley motioned toward the foam art. "Why don't you show that to your customer? Brighten *her* day."

Not a bad idea. Perhaps it would elicit a few words from her—or initiate a conversation.

He set the cup on the counter as she approached and offered her his most engaging grin. The one that usually turned female heads. "Your personalized skinny vanilla latte."

Lips flat, she gave his handiwork no more than a fleeting perusal. "Thanks."

Not only was the lady immune to his charm, she had no interest in extending their conversation.

Fighting back an irrational surge of disappointment, Zach put a lid on the drink. "Enjoy."

"Thanks." She hurried toward the door, pulled her umbrella out of the stand, and disappeared into the gray shroud hanging over the town.

"I think my attempt to brighten her day was a bust." He folded his arms as the rain pummeled the picture window.

"Oh, I don't know. Sometimes the simplest gestures of kindness can touch a heart in unseen ways."

Zach didn't try to hide his skepticism. "Assuming the lady's *willing* to let her heart be touched. She didn't exude much warmth."

"She may be hiding it behind a protective wall. Could be she's dealing with a boatload of heavy stuff. That can dampen a person's sociability."

Zach's antennas perked up. "You know anything about her?"

"Nothing much—though she seems familiar." He squinted after her. Shook his head. "It'll come to me. Anyway, I spotted her on the wharf Monday, sipping a brew from your fine establishment. She was sitting alone on a bench during one of the few monsoon-free interludes we've had this week. I got gloomy vibes. Like she was troubled—and could use a friend."

Zach wasn't about to question the veracity of Charley's intuition. The man was legendary in these parts for his uncanny insights and his ability to discern more than people willingly divulged.

Present company included.

How Charley had realized there was an unresolved issue in his past was beyond him. He'd never talked about it to anyone. But the man's astute comments, while generic, were too relevant to be random. As a result, on more than one occasion he'd been tempted to get Charley's take on his situation.

Yet as far as he could see, there was no solution to the impasse short of returning to his former world and toeing the line—and that wasn't happening. The new life he'd built these past two and a half years suited him, and now that he was settled in Hope Harbor, he was more convinced than ever his decision to walk away had been the right one.

"You still with me, Zach?" Charley's lips tipped up.

"Yeah." He refocused. "You think she's a visitor?"

"I'd classify her more as a seeker."

What did that mean?

Before he could ask, Bren appeared at his elbow. "Here you go, Charley." She popped a cinnamon stick into his drink, snapped on a lid, and handed the cup over the counter.

"Thanks. It's a treat to have authentic Mexican coffee available here in our little town."

"We aim to please." The door opened again to admit what appeared to be a family of tourists, and Zach lifted his hand in welcome. "Everyone must be in the mood for coffee today."

"Count your blessings." Charley raised his cup in salute. "I'm off to the taco stand."

"I'll try to send a few customers your direction."

"Always appreciated. Maybe Kat will stop by."

"You know her last name?" He kept an eye on the newcomers as they perused his menu board and examined the offerings in the pastry case.

"No. But I may find out if she visits my truck. Or she might come back here again and you can take another crack at breaching that wall she's put up. See you soon." He strolled toward the door.

The new customers began to pepper him with questions about the pastry selection, but as he answered, the image of the mystery woman sitting alone on a bench at the wharf—and Charley's comment that she could use a friend—remained front and center in his mind.

If she *was* dealing with a bunch of garbage, he ought to cut her some slack for her lack of sociability today. Been there, done that—and it was a bad place to be.

Yet thanks to grit, determination . . . and the kind people of Hope Harbor, who'd welcomed him into the community he now called home . . . he'd survived.

Hard to say if the woman hiding behind the dark shades had similar fortitude . . . and if she was merely passing through, he'd never find out.

But if she stuck around awhile, perhaps in Hope Harbor she'd discover an answer to the worrisome situation Charley thought she might be wrestling with.

Mistake, mistake, mistake.

As the accusatory refrain looped through her mind, Katherine

Parker sipped her excellent latte and watched the boats in the harbor through the rain-splattered windshield of her rental car.

The drops on the glass looked like tears.

How appropriate.

Throat tightening, she set the drink in the cupholder, fisted her hands in her lap, and willed the waterworks behind her eyes to dry up.

She should have stayed holed up in her cottage above Blackberry Beach. That was the safest place for her, as today's excursion had confirmed.

Yet the cozy, comforting atmosphere in the coffee shop on Monday had been seductive. How could she not succumb to the temptation to visit again?

Especially since four days into her flight from chaos, she was as unsettled as ever. Her appetite had vanished, sleep was elusive, and her mind churned with questions . . . doubts . . . second thoughts.

But what else had she expected? Running away didn't solve anything.

Except . . . she hadn't run away. Not exactly. This trip was more about sanctuary than escape. A quiet interlude to rethink her goals in solitude, away from the raucous craziness that had become her life.

And Hope Harbor had seemed the perfect location for that.

So far, though, the peaceful ambiance she remembered hadn't managed to permeate her soul.

But it was possible she was expecting too much too soon. A few days of peace weren't going to counteract five years of constant stress and pressure. She ought to give herself a chance to acclimate to a slower pace. To let the tranquility of this place work its magic.

Fingers trembling, she picked up her latte. Took another sip as she gave the view a slow sweep.

Nothing much had changed in the past six years.

Overflowing flower boxes rimmed the sidewalk along crescent-shaped Dockside Drive, benches interspersed for the pleasure of passersby who could spare a few minutes to sit and enjoy the view. Beyond the harbor-hugging sidewalk, a sloping pile of boulders led down to the water, where bobbing boats were protected by a long breakwater on the left and two rocky islands on the right. On the other side of the street, shops with colorful awnings and window boxes faced the distant horizon.

She shifted sideways. At the far end of the crescent, where the frontage road dead-ended at the river that emptied into the sea, a gazebo graced a tiny pocket park containing a picnic table and what appeared to be a historic cannon. The latter hadn't been there on her last visit.

And perched on the edge of that park? Charley's taco stand. The white truck with his name emblazoned in colorful letters over the serving window hadn't budged an inch—nor changed one iota.

Neither had the owner—or those perceptive eyes of his.

She set the latte down again, the quiver in her fingers more pronounced.

Despite the passage of years and a disguise that would fool most people, that tiny flare of recognition in Charley's dark cocoa irises at the coffee shop suggested he'd seen through her disguise. That he'd realized they'd met.

Whether he'd put a name to her face wasn't clear. If he had, he'd kept her secret. If he hadn't—who knew what he'd do once he did? Worst case, he'd mention it to someone . . . who'd mention it to someone else . . . and her attempt to remain under the radar would be a bust.

Sighing, she watched a boat on the horizon disappear into the mist—as she'd hoped to disappear in Hope Harbor.

Why, oh why, had she run into the one person she'd befriended during her previous stay? The one person most likely to recognize her?

Her plan to lay low and avoid his stand, despite the fabulous fish tacos he concocted, should have protected her—but how could she have known he'd frequent the new coffee shop in town she'd popped into twice for a handful of minutes?

A shop that had managed to suck her in with its low-key, welcoming atmosphere.

She picked up her latte again and took another sip of the cooling brew, spirits dipping.

Too bad the coffee shop was now off-limits. On her first visit, it had appeared to be a relatively safe haven. The customers, most of whom were no doubt transient summer tourists, had shown more interest in the twentysomething female barista with the triple-pierced ears and spiky, rainbow-hued hair than in her.

No surprise there. While the woman wouldn't have drawn a second glance in Katherine's world, she had to be a bit of a novelty here in quiet, sedate Hope Harbor.

But Charley had ruined the shop for her.

Not fair, Katherine. Charley isn't the only reason you can't go back.

In the distance, the light from the buoy at the end of the breakwater pierced the gloom, and the sonorous blare of a foghorn dispatched a warning across the expanse of water.

A warning she'd do well to heed.

The truth was, the tall, midthirties guy behind the counter also posed a risk—perhaps a bigger one than another unexpected meeting with Charley.

She took the lid off the remains of her latte, visualizing the fanciful K the man had created on top of her drink.

He'd been there on Monday too, but other customers had kept him occupied.

Today, however, he'd given her his full—and unwanted—attention.

Katherine's fingers tightened on the disposable cup as the rain beat a staccato rhythm on the roof of her car.

In any other circumstances, the spark of interest in his deep brown eyes would have been flattering. With his dark hair, confident air, and lean, toned physique, he had the looks to rival any Hollywood heartthrob.

But romance wasn't in her plans for this trip.

The taste of the latte grew bitter on her tongue, and she set the cup back into the holder. No more coffee shop visits for her. She couldn't risk another run-in with Charley—or another attempt by the guy behind the counter to chat her up.

And unless her instincts were failing her, that's what would happen if she showed up again at The Perfect Blend. All the signs of male attraction were there.

She twisted the key in the ignition, released the brake, and backed out of the spot she'd claimed on the south end of the wharf.

As she drove north on Dockside Drive, she surveyed Charley's truck. Despite the dismal weather, a line had formed—and the savory aroma of grilling fish infiltrated her car.

A rumble from her stomach reminded her she'd skipped breakfast.

She ignored the message—and the temptation to stop. Her kitchen was fully stocked, and preparing a meal would keep her occupied on this rainy afternoon.

Her hands, anyway.

Her mind was a different story. It would be free to wander—and that wasn't smart. Not yet. It was too soon to sort through the tangle in her brain. She needed a few days . . . or weeks . . . of long hours on a secluded beach to decompress first.

That's why she'd rented a cottage perched above an isolated stretch of sand.

Now if only the weather would cooperate.

She hung a right, toward Highway 101 and the short trip north to her secluded hideaway, giving the taco stand one last glance.

Charley's gaze connected with hers, and as he smiled, warmth radiated toward her.

Not the kind of sizzle she'd felt from the coffee shop guy. That had been more . . . adrenaline stirring.

No, this felt . . . peaceful. As if the taco maker was trying to comfort her. Tell her everything would be okay. Encourage her not to worry.

As she rounded the corner and the stand disappeared from view, Katherine frowned.

That had been . . . weird.

How in the world could she have read so much into a connection that had lasted . . . what? Three seconds? Four?

Huffing out a breath, she tightened her grip on the wheel. She was losing it. Grasping at straws. Conjuring up far-fetched sources of the consolation and encouragement she craved.

Good grief, the man may not even have been looking at her. It was impossible to be certain from that distance.

Picking up speed, she left the town center behind.

Yet the soothing, uplifting feelings engendered by that fleeting connection with Charley—real or imagined—lingered.

So why not enjoy the brief boost to her spirits, whatever the source?

For as she'd discovered over the past few years, most moments of happiness were short-lived—and few of them offered the lasting gratification she'd assumed success would beget.

2

. . . .

"You about finished, Frank?" Zach called out the question to his Tuesday/Thursday/Saturday barista as he moved the thought-for-the-day sign from the sidewalk in front of The Perfect Blend into the shop.

"Almost." The silver-haired man surveyed the crumbs littering the floor. "The toddler in the family group that claimed this table was apparently more interested in shredding his cake than eating it."

"You want me to take over?" Zach folded up the A-frame sign and leaned it against the counter. Frank was spry and fit—but he was sixty-three. Not ancient by any means . . . but from the perspective of his own thirty-four years, it seemed old—even if the man had the energy of someone half his age.

"No thanks. I can handle it. This type of mess is much easier to deal with than some of the ones I ran into during my career as a mail carrier." He motioned to the sign. "What's tomorrow's saying?"

"Haven't decided yet." Zach pulled out the eraser for the dry-erase board and wiped off the quote he'd featured on this August

Tuesday. "Which do you prefer—'Keep your face to the sun and you'll never see shadows' or 'A diamond is merely a lump of coal that did well under pressure.'"

"I like them both—and they're in keeping with the encouragement theme that's been running through the sayings for the past few days." Frank gave the mop one last swirl and rested his hand on top of the handle.

Zach furrowed his brow. Had there been a theme to his recent adages?

He scrolled through the last few in his mind.

Yeah, there had—and he knew who to blame for his rare thematic tangent.

The mystery woman.

She hadn't come back to the coffee shop again, but since her visit six days ago she'd been on his mind. As had Charley's comments about her mental state.

Apparently his subconscious had been selecting sayings that would boost her spirits if she happened to drop in—or pass by.

He plucked a marker from the box behind the counter. "I didn't realize I'd fallen into a rut."

"I wouldn't call it a rut. Feels more like you're trying to cheer yourself—or someone else—up. Everything okay?"

"Couldn't be better."

"Glad to hear it." Frank picked up the mop. "Personally, I think funny sayings catch people's eye too. Like the one you used last week about coffee helping you stay grounded. Clever."

"Message received. I'll go with humor tomorrow."

"Sounds like a plan. It's never a bad idea to mix things up—but there's nothing wrong with the sayings you've been using either. Maybe they lifted someone's spirits."

Frank disappeared into the back room, and Zach considered the blank board, tapping the marker against his palm.

Seconds later, inspiration struck and he penned tomorrow's message.

If pro is the opposite of con, what's the opposite of progress?

As he finished, Frank rejoined him and inspected his handiwork. Chuckled. "Clever. Political sarcasm always gets a laugh."

"I'm half serious." Zach set the board on the floor.

"I hear you."

"Sometimes I wonder if those folks in Washington live in the same—" His cell began to vibrate, and he pulled it out. Skimmed the name on the screen.

Uh-oh.

There was only one reason he could think of for Aunt Stephanie to contact him—and it wasn't good.

"I have to take this, Frank."

"Go ahead. I want to get an order of Charley's tacos for lunch—unless his muse called and he went off to paint. See you Thursday."

As Frank let himself out, Zach braced for bad news and answered the call.

"Take a deep breath, Zach. No one died and there's no medical emergency."

At his aunt's wry greeting, he exhaled. "You about gave me a heart attack, you know."

"That's why I ditched the social niceties and got straight to the point. I knew you'd panic when my name popped up—and I take full blame for that. If I called more often, as any proper aunt would do, you'd be less inclined to jump to wrong conclusions when you hear from me."

"How long has it been?" Pulse moderating, he dropped into a chair at the closest table. Near as he could remember, other than birthday and Christmas cards, he hadn't heard from his paternal aunt in three or four years.

"Too long. I called you a few years back during a brief stopover in Chicago, but you were away on a business trip."

"I was always away on business trips in those days."

"I can relate."

"I bet." Thanks to her executive-level position with one of the world's largest accounting firms—and a client roster that spanned the globe—her greeting cards often came with exotic postmarks. Why she kept the small but pricey New York apartment she rarely occupied was a puzzle. "So how are you?"

"Fine—and I have news. My firm is offering an early retirement package to anyone sixty or older with more than twenty years' service. I qualify on both counts—barely on the first one, since I turned the big six-o a mere two months ago, but I hit the tenure minimum long ago. The deal was too lucrative to pass up."

"You're retiring?" He stared at the empty pastry case, trying to process her bombshell. Like his father, Aunt Stephanie had devoted her life to her job. She had no husband, no children, and no hobbies he was aware of. What would she do without work to fill her days?

"Wrong tense. It's a done deal. And that brings me to the other purpose of my call. You and your father are all the family I have, and I've neglected you both shamefully. Not that your father minded, of course. He's more of a workaholic than I was."

No kidding. The fast track was the only track as far as Richard Garrett was concerned—which was no doubt why he'd been the youngest man ever to reach partner status in the law firm he now headed.

"That description fits Dad." A sardonic note slipped into his voice.

If his aunt noticed it, she didn't comment. "I know he's busy, but I'd like to launch my new life by reconnecting with you both. I spoke with him earlier. He's in the middle of a big case, but he invited me to visit for a long weekend. I'm flying down to Atlanta Friday."

"I'm sure Dad will be happy to see you."

"I'm sure he will be too—once he gets over the shock about my news and reassures himself I haven't lost my mind. I think he assumed I'd work till I dropped."

"That wouldn't surprise me. I imagine that's what he plans to do." Zach smashed a stray crumb against the tabletop with his finger.

"I do too—and I intend to have a heart-to-heart with him about that very subject."

"Don't expect him to be receptive." Unless pigs had started to fly.

"You never know. Coming from me, it may have more impact. We've always been like-minded on the subject of work."

"There's more to life than work."

"I agree. I always have. But after a while, you get caught up in the climb-the-ladder game, and everything but work falls by the wayside."

"I thought you loved your job."

"I did—and I don't have a single regret. However . . . given the opportunity to bail without putting my future security at risk, I grabbed it. It's time for the next chapter in my life to begin. I want to see what I've been missing and put more energy into bolstering family connections."

He stood, crossed to the fireplace, and extinguished the logs. "I assume that means Hope Harbor is on your travel agenda in the near future."

"It is. I want to hear all about the new direction *your* life has taken. Unless a visit from me would be too much of an inconvenience."

"You're welcome anytime."

"Wonderful. Can you recommend a local inn or B&B?"

"I have a spare room at my place that's yours if you want it. I can't offer the luxurious five-star accommodations you're accustomed to from your business travels, but my modest digs do have a world-class view."

"Trust me, after working fourteen-hour days during those trips, a high-end hotel room was nothing more than a place to fall into bed at night. The luxury was lost on me."

"I hear you."

"I do recall a beautiful hotel in Paris, though, where I stayed on my last birthday. I spent the whole day in a windowless meeting room and ordered a late room service dinner. The view of the Eiffel Tower from my window while I ate was my sole chance to enjoy the City of Lights." A beat passed. "Eating alone had never bothered me, but that night . . . I felt lonely. So staying with you, sharing a few meals, will be a treat."

He flicked off the lights in the shop. "Believe it or not, I've become a decent chef. Don't expect Le Cordon Bleu fare, but you won't go hungry."

"I'll look forward to whatever you concoct—but I'd also be satisfied with sandwiches or takeout. Don't go to any trouble on my behalf. And I promise not to overstay my welcome. If I decide to extend my visit, I'll find other accommodations. You know what Ben Franklin said—after three days, guests, like fish, begin to smell."

Zach's lips twitched. Typical Aunt Stephanie. On the rare occasions they'd connected through the years, she'd been a hoot. Blunt, funny, and adventurous, radiating an almost palpable *joie de vivre* and spouting a live-and-let-live philosophy.

Too bad his dad hadn't inherited a few of those qualities. While he shared her bluntness, he was too opinionated for his own good . . . or the good of parent-child relationships.

"I doubt that will be a problem. Text me the details of your arrival once your plans are set."

"Will do."

He hesitated, propping a shoulder against the wall in the shadowed shop. Did she know about the situation between him and his dad?

Unlikely.

While brother and sister had always talked by phone on a regular basis, his father tended to keep difficult topics close to his vest.

In person, however, it was possible he'd be tempted to vent.

Without a heads-up, she could stumble into a hornet's nest

26

with an innocent comment or question—putting both her and his father into an uncomfortable position.

"Aunt Stephanie . . . there's something you ought to know before you visit Dad."

"You mean about the rift?"

So she *did* know.

But how much?

"Um . . . yeah. I wasn't certain he'd clued you in."

"Clued me in would be stretching it. After he stopped mentioning you during our phone conversations three years ago, I realized there must have been a falling-out. He never offered any details, but I assumed he was disappointed about your career switch."

Disappointed?

Far too mild a term.

More like shocked. Angry. Bitter. Confused. Distraught.

And his attitude hadn't softened in the intervening years.

"At the very least." Zach let his gaze linger on the poster-sized photo on the wall across from him. The shot of a tiny seedling growing in the crack of a boulder, pushing toward the sky as it struggled for a foothold on the inhospitable surface, never failed to encourage and uplift him.

"Family conflicts are difficult."

"Also avoidable, if people are willing to let each other live their lives as they see fit."

"I won't argue with that." His aunt's tone remained conversational. "Yet there can be extenuating circumstances. A person's history can skew their view of the world."

He straightened a crooked chair and pushed it under a table with more force than necessary. "I know all about the bankruptcy that upended your world when you and Dad were kids—and I get how an experience like that can make a person crave security. But it doesn't justify shutting out people who choose a different path. That's not what love's supposed to be about."

"Again . . . no argument. And I appreciate the heads-up, though

I'm not certain the subject of your relationship will come up. He was never one to discuss feelings."

"I know."

"Do you?"

Frowning, he planted a fist on his hip. "What do you mean?"

"I was just curious about whether the two of you have tried to talk through the issue." Her tone remained mild. Nonjudgmental.

That didn't keep his blood pressure from spiking.

"*I* tried. He shut me out. By his definition, a conversation means he talks and you listen. If you don't agree with his opinion, end of discussion."

A soft laugh came over the line, defusing the tension. "That's Richard. He was pigheaded as a kid too. Maybe he'll eventually mellow."

Zach snorted. "That would take a miracle."

"They do happen. In the meantime, watch for a text with my travel plans. It's been great to talk with you, Zach."

"Likewise. Enjoy your visit with Dad."

After they exchanged good-byes, he did one final circuit of the modest shop that gave him more satisfaction than any of the multimillion-dollar deals he'd negotiated in his previous career.

This business wasn't going to make him rich—but as Charley had said, life shouldn't be all about accruing money. He'd devoted himself to that goal for eight long years, and while his sixty-hour weeks had put him on the fast track to success and padded his bank account, they hadn't fed his soul as this shop did.

He paused at the door, fished out his keys, and gave the welcoming space a scan. There was nothing more satisfying than creating a place that gave all who entered a brief respite from their cares and worries. That left them refreshed and reenergized.

Well . . . all except one customer, whose image continued to strobe through his mind with annoying regularity.

He hadn't learned anything more about the mystery woman, despite a fair amount of subtle digging with his regular clientele.

No one had seen her, other than Charley—and she hadn't stopped by the taco-maker's stand either.

For all he knew, she'd already left town.

He secured the door and wandered down Main Street toward his car, absorbing the warmth of the sun.

This was the kind of day that put a sparkle on Hope Harbor and drew tourists from far and near during the summer months. The kind of day meant for leisurely pursuits. And The Perfect Blend's six-days-a-week, seven-to-one hours gave him ample opportunity to enjoy each and every one.

Another perk of his new life—and he intended to relish every second of this glorious weather.

Too bad he didn't have a special someone to share it with.

Once again, the image of the woman hiding behind sunglasses flashed through his mind.

He expelled a breath and mashed down the unlock button on his key fob.

Letting a stranger get under his skin was stupid. He should forget about her and whatever troubles Charley had concluded she was dealing with. She—and they—were none of his concern.

Yet as he slid behind the wheel and started his Jeep, he couldn't help but wonder where his mystery customer was—and what she was doing on this beautiful day.

3

The sun was shining at last—and the beach was beckoning.

Katherine pulled the roomy, long-sleeved T-shirt down over her denim-clad hips, shoved her feet into her sand shoes, and exited onto the deck of her rental cottage. Brilliant blue sky greeted her, and she paused to inhale a lungful of the briny air.

Bliss.

Under the radiant solar warmth, the tension melted from her shoulders. It had taken ten days, but the peace of this coastal haven was finally beginning to permeate her psyche.

Even the annoying phone calls from Simon, initiated three days into her trip and now a daily irritation, were losing their ability to stress her out. And she was done answering them, as she'd told him yesterday. Until she settled on a direction going forward, there was no point in talking to him.

Whether he would honor her request for radio silence remained to be seen—but as long as they were separated by more than eight hundred miles, the odds were minuscule he'd drop in unannounced. Hope Harbor wasn't the easiest place to get to, and Simon's aversion to driving long distances should keep him at arm's length.

For the immediate future, her solitude ought to be secure.

Settling her sunglasses on her nose, she stepped onto the small plot of manicured lawn that extended to the edge of the bluff. From there, according to the property management agent, a path led down to the trail for the beach. Since the secluded stretch of sand was only accessible from a handful of cottages, she should have it to herself most of the time.

As Katherine traversed the perimeter of the bluff, seeking a trailhead, the unbroken tangle of natural flora suggested that few renters ventured down to water's edge, preferring instead to admire the view from on high.

She did a second pass.

Aha. There. That was sort of a path, tucked in among the brambles—wasn't it?

She moved closer.

Yes.

As she prepared to plunge into the undergrowth, she gave her surroundings one more appreciative survey.

Below her, the glittering expanse of water stretched to the far horizon, where indigo sea and turquoise sky melded. Sea stack sentinels flanked the far edges of the sweeping curve of hillside that formed the cove below. In both directions, overlapping fingers of steep headlands jutted progressively farther out into the water. On the southernmost one, hazy in the distance, Pelican Point light presided.

The sheltered crescent of beach below was mostly hidden from this vantage point, but it was easy to visualize from the multitude of photos the agent had provided—and now that the weather was cooperating, she was itching to explore it in person.

Giving the edge of the property on either side of her a quick scan, she let out a slow breath. While there were a few other houses on this stretch of coast, the insulating layer of Sitka spruce, pine, and hemlock trees between them gave her absolute privacy.

Heaven.

Lips curving up, she pushed through the thigh-high foliage and began her descent.

Within fifty feet, the rough track dead-ended at a wider, more discernible trail.

Wind ruffling her newly shorn locks, she hung a left. As she strolled along, two gulls wheeled overhead and a chipmunk scampered across the path a few feet in front of her, a . . . blackberry? . . . in his mouth.

While the critter disappeared into the brush, she gave the brambles on either side of the narrow trail a closer inspection.

Good heavens.

There were blackberries everywhere.

In light of the name of the beach, their presence wasn't a surprise—but this was a mother lode.

She stopped to examine one of the bushes laden with ripe, juicy-looking berries. Plucked one. Popped it in her mouth.

Oh.

My.

Word.

Intense flavor, amplified by an infusion of solar warmth, exploded on her tongue, sending sweetness ricocheting through her taste buds.

Store-bought berries never came close to offering such a sensory overload. And there were hundreds . . . thousands . . . here for the taking.

On her next beach visit, she'd have to bring a bowl and claim a small portion of the bounty.

In the meantime, why not eat her fill during the trek down?

Ten minutes later, fingers stained with berry juice, she emerged onto an empty stretch of beach that was utterly quiet save for the gentle lull of the placid surf in the protected cove and the occasional caw of a gull.

She stopped to drink it in.

Yes.

This was what she'd come to Hope Harbor for.

Striking out across the sand toward the water, she glanced toward her left. Jolted to a stop.

Well, crud.

She wasn't alone after all.

Farther down the beach, a solitary man was sitting on a piece of driftwood, his back to her.

Katherine hesitated.

It was possible he wanted seclusion as much as she did—and if she walked the opposite direction, they could both enjoy their solitude. The expansive stretch of sand was plenty big for two people. They didn't have to interact or invade each other's space.

And on the off chance his presence wasn't as innocent as it seemed? That he was the type who might be inclined to prey on a lone woman in this isolated location?

Katherine felt her pockets.

Cell in one, pepper gel in the other.

Check.

Her arsenal was in place.

It was always wise to be prepared, even in a peaceful place like Hope Harbor—a lesson learned after one too many dicey encounters in the world she'd fled.

Paranoid, perhaps—but better safe than sorry.

Pulling out the small canister, she continued to assess the baseball-cap-wearing man who remained oblivious to her presence.

He appeared to be harmless. No bad vibes were wafting her direction.

So she'd stay. Explore the intriguing flotsam that lined the surf line. Let the aerial acrobatics of the pair of gulls swooping overhead and the antics of a belching silver-white harbor seal on the rocks offshore entertain her.

But in case the guy perched on the sun-bleached log had more on his mind than innocent relaxation, she kept her finger on the trigger of the pepper gel.

And if he made one wrong move . . . if he came one inch too close . . . he was going to be sorry he'd ever ventured onto Blackberry Beach on this bright Tuesday afternoon.

The mystery woman was on his beach.

Zach stared at the slender figure in the distance as he did the math.

Since he knew the handful of other residents in this neck of the woods . . . and the house next door to him was the only rental property in this area . . . and there wasn't any evidence of a boat indicating Kat had accessed the beach by water . . . that meant she was his temporary neighbor.

It also meant she didn't have any money problems. The Clark house occupied the prime location above the beach, and its expansive views and amenities merited top dollar.

At least that's what Charley, who lived farther up on this curving stretch of coast, had told him.

He propped his hands on his hips as he watched her peer into one of the pools that formed in the rocks at the far end of the beach during low tide.

Was the proximity of her accommodations to his home due to benevolent providence—or plain old good luck?

Based on her skittishness and attempts to remain anonymous, it wasn't likely she'd consider the coincidence to be either.

Should he disappear back up the trail and leave her to her solitary endeavors . . . or try again to breach the wall she'd erected around herself?

In view of Charley's conclusion that she was in need of a friend, there was no question what the renowned artist would recommend.

But in all likelihood, she'd rebuff an approach. She must have noticed him when she'd arrived at the beach—yet she'd walked the other direction.

Not a positive sign she'd welcome company.

On the other hand, she may have thought he was a stranger. It would have been difficult for her to identity him from the back.

If she'd realized they'd met, it was possible she'd be receptive to an overture.

Or not.

He took off his cap and scratched his head. Either option could be the wrong one. There was no way to predict the outcome.

So instead of standing around debating his strategy, why not say hello? Give her an opening to display the latent sociability Charley was certain lay under her frosty surface.

Decision made, he tugged his cap back on and strode her direction.

She continued to explore the tide pool, giving no indication she was aware of his approach.

Ten feet away, he stopped. Should he wait until she noticed him, or call out a greeting?

Whichever approach he chose, she was going to be startled—and if he waited for her to spot him, she might not be happy to find him standing here gawking at her.

Best to take the initiative.

"We meet again."

She gasped and swung around, arm extended, finger on the trigger of a canister aimed at his face.

"Hey." Pulse surging, he held out his hands, palms forward, and took a quick step back on the hard-packed sand. "Sorry. I didn't mean to scare you. I was just trying to be neighborly and welcome you to the area. No harm intended. My name's Zach Garrett—and we happen to share this beach."

Several slow, silent seconds ticked by as she inspected him from behind her dark glasses.

The canister never wavered.

Was it possible she didn't recognize him from the shop?

If he didn't remind her of their encounter last week—fast—he could end up with burning eyes and balking lungs.

"We've met, you know. At The Perfect Blend, in town."

After a few more beats passed, she lowered the canister. "I remember."

"You must be renting the Clark house."

She didn't respond.

Geez.

Either Charley was uncharacteristically off base in his assessment and this woman was more cold than cautious—or she was super freaked out and gun-shy for traumatic reasons.

"If you're wondering how I know that, I live next door." He hooked his thumbs in the pockets of his jeans, keeping his posture casual and nonthreatening. The tension radiating from this woman was almost palpable. "It's also the only house with access to Blackberry Beach that's rented out. I know all the other residents."

Her rigid stance relaxed a hair. "Thanks for the explanation. Sorry if I overreacted."

"No worries. It never hurts to be too careful these days. We live in a crazy world."

Her throat worked. "Yes, we do."

He waited for her to put the canister away.

She didn't.

Find a more innocuous subject, Garrett.

"Is this your first trip to the beach?"

"Yes."

"I see you sampled the namesake berries during your descent." He smiled and tapped the corner of his lips.

She lifted a hand, as if to scrub off the offending stain, but paused as she spotted more telltale blemishes on her fingers. "Guilty as charged. I can't dispute the evidence."

"It's no crime to pick the berries. We all do. You're fortunate to be here during peak season. Depending on the length of your stay, you may be able to enjoy them for your whole visit." Not the most subtle attempt to find out the duration of her trip—but it did give her an opening to offer additional information.

She didn't take it.

"I plan to bring a container in the future and fill it."

The woman was as hard to pin down as a burrowing razor clam.

"Join the crowd. I have a bowlful in the kitchen myself, waiting to become blackberry cobbler. It's one of my late-summer specialties."

She cocked her head. "You bake?"

"Yes. Among other leisure pursuits."

She slid the canister into her pocket. "I know a few men who enjoy cooking, but most prefer to let their wife or girlfriend do the baking."

While her body language and inflection implied her comment was inconsequential, it wasn't. She was digging for background information too.

That was promising.

And unlike her, he didn't mind disclosing a few personal facts. Perhaps that would encourage her to reciprocate.

"If I had either, we'd have to share the kitchen now that I've been bitten by the culinary bug."

It was difficult to judge her reaction with her eyes hidden, but his gut told him she was relieved by his answer.

Or was that wishful thinking?

Maybe she was just glad he was a relatively normal guy rather than a serial killer who stalked women on secluded beaches.

"Well . . ." She rubbed her palms on her jeans. "I think I'll explore the other end of the beach."

The conversation was over.

He held on to his smile despite his disappointment. "And I'm heading home. If you watch for it, you can spot the turnoff to my place from the main path on your walk back, a couple hundred feet before you reach yours—unless you're too busy eating blackberries."

Her mouth bowed a few degrees. "I've had my allotment for today."

"So have I—but that won't stop me from picking a few more

on the hike up. I tend to overindulge while they're in season." He swept a hand over the beach. "Enjoy yourself down here. It's a little piece of heaven—and a great place to touch base with the Almighty, if you're so inclined."

As the comment tripped off his tongue, he frowned.

Where had *that* come from?

Given his present relationship with God—or lack thereof—dispensing that sort of advice was disingenuous at best.

Besides, while it appeared she could use *someone* to talk to, a fair number of people were turned off by any reference to God. Until he learned this woman's story, it would be wise to refrain from doing or saying anything that would shut her down.

As if she could be any more shut down than she already was.

Again, the glasses masked any clues to her reaction, and her tone remained neutral. "I agree that the quiet and space and fresh air and solitude are a little piece of heaven." She emphasized *solitude*.

His cue to leave.

"It's all yours. In case you're wondering, very few residents trek down here—especially during working hours."

"Except today."

She meant him.

"My hours are different from most people's. I'm at the shop from six to two. The rest of the day is my own. That's why I'm down here at"—he twisted his wrist—"four."

"I'll remember that." Keeping as much distance as possible between them, she skirted around him and struck off toward the other end of the beach.

It didn't take a genius to read between the lines of her last comment.

In the future, she'd visit the beach while he was at the shop—eliminating the possibility of any more meetings.

Shoving his hands into his pockets, he watched her recede.

Give it up, Garrett. She wants nothing to do with you. Write her off.

Sensible advice supported by a preponderance of evidence—including her continued reticence. In general, two people exchanged information during initial meetings. In their case, while he'd given her a bit of personal background, she'd offered zilch.

Instead of wasting his time and energy on his reclusive neighbor, he ought to go home and bake a blackberry cobbler.

Also sensible advice.

He slogged through the shifting sand that led to the back of the beach and began his ascent up the winding path.

At the first bend, he glanced back.

Kat was still walking away from him, two seagulls circling above her. As if they were trying to keep the woman who seemed so alone company.

At that fanciful thought, he blew out a breath.

More likely they were hoping for a handout.

Whatever had prompted their interest, however, they continued to stick close. And she didn't try to shoo them away, as she had him.

Lucky birds.

Zach resumed his trek up the bluff, losing sight of both Kat and the gulls.

Yet she remained front and center in his mind.

Meaning he wasn't going to be able to dismiss her as easily as he'd like.

So, smart or not, he might have to make one last attempt to break through her wall.

Since he wasn't likely to run into her again on the beach, and she hadn't returned to The Perfect Blend, those locations weren't options for a future rendezvous.

However . . . now that he knew she was living in close proximity—and they shared an affinity for blackberries—a gift of homemade cobbler would give him an excuse to orchestrate one more encounter.

If that didn't work?

He'd fold his tent—and accept that the mystery woman would forever remain a mystery.

4

CALL ME!!!!! BIG NEWS!!!!!

Grimacing at the third text message that had pinged her phone in the past half hour, Katherine plunked the cell on the granite island in the kitchen of her rental house.

Typical Simon. Everything with him was urgent. High drama. Life and death.

But very little was life and death in Tinseltown—least of all the type of stuff that sent her agent into a tizzy.

She slammed her arms across her chest and glared at the phone. Simon was the last person she wanted to talk to—but ignoring his messages was useless. He'd keep sending them, with increasing frequency, until he wore her down and she responded to shut him up.

He knew her well.

Too well.

And he'd become an expert at pushing all the buttons that would maneuver her into making decisions he assured her were in her best interest.

Not to mention his.

Another incentive for her to take a break from a life that was spiraling out of control.

Her control, anyway.

Heaving a sigh, she gritted her teeth and picked up the cell again. She wasn't anywhere near ready to leave Hope Harbor. So no matter how hard he tried to convince her to come back, she'd have to stand firm.

She jabbed at his number and girded for a fight.

"Finally!" Simon didn't attempt to hide his exasperation.

"Hello to you too."

"Sorry, but you're talking to a frantic man. Blame my lack of manners on stress."

"You're always stressed." She rotated her head, trying to relieve the kink in her neck. "I got your message. What news couldn't wait until I initiated a call?"

"Are you sitting down?"

She rolled her eyes. "Please. Cut the theatrics."

"You should sit."

"Simon."

"Fine, fine." Apparently her don't-mess-with-me inflection had sunk in. "There should be a drumroll here, and a bottle of champagne cooling—but we'll celebrate when you come back. Guess who wants you to star in his next picture?"

Her breath hitched.

Star?

Star?

As in playing the lead role, rather than her usual supporting parts?

That *was* news.

Unless he was exaggerating—a very real possibility. Hyperbole was Simon's middle name.

Plus, despite his continued expressions of confidence that she could jump from TV to the big screen, up to this point all he'd been able to land her were secondary roles in low-budget cable flicks.

"What kind of picture—and who's the director?"

"Hold on to your hat, baby."

At his pithy, two-sentence answer, she groped for the edge of a stool and sank onto the seat.

Major director.

Major picture.

Major leap in her career.

This was the break she'd dreamed of her whole life. While her gig on a popular TV series over the past four years had allowed her to build a hefty nest egg, a major film with an award-winning director could catapult her into the stratosphere on both a professional and financial level.

If that's what she still wanted.

The very question that had prompted her to flee LA for Hope Harbor.

"Did you faint?" Simon sounded amused.

"No. I'm . . . digesting the news."

"You should be jumping up and down with joy, like I am."

Yes, she should.

So why wasn't she?

Another question to wrestle with later.

She popped one of the blackberries she'd picked on today's foray to the beach into her mouth. "What did you tell them?"

"What do you think I told them?" A touch of irritation sharpened his words.

"Simon—I'm not committing until I see the script."

Silence.

She waited him out. She would *not* let him intimidate her—or push her to move too fast.

"It's on my desk."

"It needs to be on mine."

"Your desk is in LA—where you should be."

The lingering hint of sun-kissed sweetness on her tongue evaporated.

"I had to get away. You know that. Especially after everything that happened."

"I get that, babe. Everyone does. But how long is this break going to last?"

"I don't know." She stood, paced over to the two-story wall of glass in the living room that offered a panoramic view of the deep blue sea—and summoned up her courage. "All I know is that I'm nowhere near ready to come back . . . or if I ever will be."

There.

The truth she'd been dancing around and had never voiced was out.

Silence greeted her announcement.

Wrapping her free arm tight around her midsection, she swallowed as she waited for Simon's explosion.

But he surprised her.

"That isn't what I expected to hear." For a man given to histrionics, his calmness was almost more unsettling than his usual frenzy.

"I know. It's not what I expected either." Not after all the years she'd invested in her career, building the foundation block by block, role by role, with copious amounts of blood, sweat, and tears.

"Okay. Let's take a step back." He exhaled. "I can see now that the incident with Jason had a much bigger impact than I realized. So take more time. Don't make any rash decisions. I can send the script there for you to read, and I'll talk to the director. Explain the situation. Buy you a bit of breathing space. Would that help?"

Pressure built behind her eyes, and the scene in front of her blurred.

A pox on Simon for throwing her a curveball with his sudden empathy. Why wasn't he ranting and raving at her for not jumping on this opportunity? What was with his sympathetic, understanding act?

Act.

As the left side of her brain kicked in, her vision cleared.

Yeah, that fit.

Simon knew how to read people, and he was a master at manipulation. It was difficult to distinguish his rare sincere moments from his usual performance mode.

He was the one who should be on the silver screen.

"Katherine?"

At his prompt, she snagged a tissue from the half-empty box on a side table and swiped at her nose. "Breathing space would be appreciated."

"Anything else?"

Peace. Rest. Direction. Guidance. Genuine caring.

Simon, however, wasn't wired to provide any of those.

The guy from the coffee shop, on the other hand? Zach Garrett? He seemed capable of offering a friend true kindness and consideration, no strings attached. The sort of person who possessed a deep wellspring of compassion.

But what did she know? Her instincts about people had tanked in recent months. And judging a man's character after two meetings was foolish—as was letting thoughts of him creep into her consciousness.

She sniffed and dabbed the tissue at her damp lashes.

Besides, he was history. After rebuffing his overtures of friendship twice, it was doubtful he'd seek her out again. Why would he set himself up for a third rejection? Unless he had an ironclad ego, he'd keep his distance in the future.

And that was fine by her. She couldn't handle any more complications.

Yet if that was true, why did the possibility that she'd never see him again add another dark layer to the shroud of dejection cloaking her life?

"Katherine?"

At Simon's prod, she refocused on his question. "No. I don't need anything else. Just send the script and buy me as much time as you can."

"I'll take care of both today. Have you been following the rags?"

Her stomach tightened. "No."

"They're on your side."

Like that mattered, when someone was dead.

"I don't really care."

"You will down the road."

Only if she went back to her old life.

But what other life did she have? If she didn't go back, what would she do?

Another question that continued to torment her.

"Anything else?" She wadded up the tissue.

"No—but stay in touch."

"I'll call or text if I have anything to say."

A tapping noise came over the line.

He was drumming his pen on his desk, a definite sign he was miffed.

"You know, Katherine"—a chill wafted across the miles—"we've come a long way together. There are responsibilities on both sides."

Classic Simon. The one who knew how to play guilt to his advantage. Who never failed to remind her she owed him.

But that debt had been paid long ago.

"I realize that. I also realize you've profited significantly from our partnership."

"As have you—thanks to my negotiating skills."

No acknowledgment that her acting ability had also contributed to their success.

She let the omission pass.

"We both have much to be grateful for."

"Agreed—and together, we can take your success to a new level. Add millions of admirers to your fan base."

"And millions of dollars to our bank accounts."

"That isn't a sin." The tempo of the tapping quickened.

"It also shouldn't be the main goal in life."

"That's not how you felt five years ago when you signed with me."

"People learn. Grow. Change. And money wasn't my only motive for wanting to succeed."

After a moment, the drumming ceased. "Why don't we table this discussion for today? You've earned a vacation. Walk on the beach. Eat fattening food. Take scenic drives. Sleep late. In between all that, read the script." His chair squeaked, as if he'd leaned forward. "I've got another call coming in. I'll text you after I talk to the studio."

The line went dead, and Katherine set the phone on the side table. Wandered out to the deck and dropped onto a chaise lounge, letting the sun's warming rays percolate through her pores.

So many questions—so few answers.

Too bad she didn't have someone to talk to about her predicament. Someone like Charley, who'd once listened to her dreams of fame and riches over tacos on a bench by the wharf.

All at once, a bit of wisdom he'd offered that day surfaced from the recesses of her mind.

"I expect most dreams are reachable, if a person's willing to pay the price. The question is whether the goal is worth the cost—and whether the return on investment is positive or negative."

In those days, she'd assumed he'd meant price in terms of hard work and sacrifices—and that had been a no-brainer. You didn't get anywhere in any field without those.

Yet only now was she beginning to understand the return on investment part of his comment.

Because the negatives were starting to outweigh the positives.

But after all the sweat and sacrifice she'd put into achieving her dream, how could she walk away—even if parts of it had become a nightmare?

Was his neighbor asleep?

A generous dish of blackberry cobbler in one hand and a pint of French vanilla ice cream in the other, Zach halted a few yards from the deck of the Clark cottage and assessed Kat, who was stretched out on a chaise lounge.

Eyes closed. Respiration steady. Posture limp.

No question about it. She was sound asleep.

Bummer.

He was going to have to work on his timing if he ever wanted to connect with her again.

Consigning today's attempt to the bust category, he swung around and set off for home.

And then the heavens smiled on him.

A drop of water plopped against his cheek, released by the dark gray clouds that had scuttled over the sun in the past ten minutes, blotting out much of the blue sky. It didn't appear they were in for more than a brief burst of rain—but it ought to be sufficient to rouse his neighbor.

Or give him an excuse to interrupt her slumber and save her from an unscheduled shower.

As he pivoted back, she sat up and swung her legs to the deck.

The instant she spotted him, she jumped to her feet and edged toward the sliding door.

No smile.

No hello.

No encouragement to linger.

Not the warmest welcome he'd ever received.

Nevertheless, he hiked up the corners of his mouth, strolled closer, and lifted his offerings. "I come bearing gifts. Fresh blackberry cobbler and ice cream. I thought you might enjoy sampling my culinary efforts."

She stopped at the door. Caught her lower lip between her teeth.

While he waited for her verdict, he tried not to stare at the vivid blue eyes on full display today. Fringed by lush lashes shades lighter than her dark hair, they were a striking sapphire hue. And the addition of model-like high cheekbones vaulted her into the classic-beauty category.

Why did she hide such a stunning face behind dark shades?

"I don't often indulge in desserts, but I appreciate the offer."

She was turning him down . . . yet behind her refusal, was there a hint of yearning? As if she was tempted to accept but wasn't certain she should?

Could he exploit that ambiguity?

"Not even on a special occasion?"

Her brow puckered. "What's the occasion?"

"When's the last time you had blackberry cobbler filled with fresh Oregon berries and made by a suave, sophisticated—dare I add decent-looking—guy?" Perhaps humor was the key to knocking a few chinks in her armor. Nothing else was working.

The subtle twitch of her mouth suggested his tactic had been spot-on.

"I can't say I've ever had that pleasure."

"Voilà—special occasion."

Her lips bloomed into a full-fledged smile.

Whoa.

She was gorgeous with a poker face, but that smile transformed her into a breath-stealing stunner.

He reined in the sudden surge in his pulse and ignored the jolt of testosterone that rocketed through him.

"I suppose I could make an exception for such a unique opportunity. And I have to admit I've had a yen for blackberry cobbler for the past two days, ever since you mentioned it at the beach."

He took that as an invitation to join her on the deck.

As the rain picked up, he erased the space between them in a few long strides. "I could dish this up if you want to sample it now."

She examined the generous portion. "You're tempting me."

That went both ways—except he didn't have cobbler on his mind.

"Is that a yes?"

"I . . . I guess so. You brought a lot."

"Enough for two servings. You can save half for later . . . or we could both forget about calories and divvy this up inside before the skies open and it becomes blackberry soup."

A gust of wind whipped past, and she tucked her hair behind her ear. Fumbled for the sliding door behind her. "Let's share it."

Yes!

He followed her into the soaring, glass-walled great room and gave a soft whistle. "Nice digs. This place lives up to its reputation."

"The location is what sold me." She continued toward the kitchen at the other end of the open floor plan, motioning toward an island with stools. "Make yourself comfortable."

"Won't be hard to do in a place like this." He set the ice cream and cobbler on the granite surface but remained standing. "How can I help?"

"I'll dish up the cobbler. Would you like coffee?"

"Is the pope Catholic?"

She gave a soft laugh. "I suppose that's a silly question to ask someone who works at a coffee shop."

"Actually, I own The Perfect Blend." Why not be up front? If she stayed around awhile, she'd find out anyway.

"Yeah?" She set two small bowls on the counter. "How long ago did you open?"

"A year and a half." He wandered over to the high-end coffee bar and surveyed the pricey single-serve coffeemaker. A stand filled with pods offering a variety of flavors stood beside it. "Impressive setup. Would you like a cup?"

"No thanks. It doesn't compare to the drinks at your shop."

"You should come again." He selected a pod and put it in the coffeemaker.

Rather than respond, she busied herself dividing the cobbler.

Change the subject, Garrett.

"I see you've been keeping a supply of blackberries on hand." He motioned toward a bowl on the counter.

"Uh-huh. I refill it every day." She scooped ice cream from the container he'd brought and topped off the two bowls of cobbler. "Let me get napkins and spoons and we'll be set."

She finished the prep, popped the remaining ice cream into her freezer, and met him at the island, a glass of milk in hand.

"That's my favorite drink with chocolate chip cookies." He indicated the glass tumbler. "Not a typical adult beverage, though."

She settled onto a stool and picked up her spoon. "I've always liked milk, and I didn't get much of it as a kid."

"Why not?"

After hesitating for a split second, her spoon resumed its journey toward the cobbler. "Long story."

One it was clear she didn't intend to share.

Yet.

But even if all they did today was eat cobbler and indulge in small talk, that was progress. For the rest, he'd have to be patient. Not his strong suit—but it appeared he'd be honing that virtue with this woman.

He dived into his own cobbler. "My mom always bought multiple gallons of milk. My brother and I could guzzle a half gallon each at one sitting. She used to kid my dad about buying stock in a dairy."

"Did you come from a large family?"

"No. Just my brother and me." Not a subject *he* wanted to talk about. "How about you?"

"Only child."

"Where do you come from?"

"Nebraska farm country. You?"

"Atlanta."

"Hope Harbor's a long way from there."

"Yeah—but it's home now."

"Do you have family back in Atlanta?"

For a woman who didn't share much about herself, she asked an awful lot of questions.

"My dad's there. My mom's been gone for eight years. Are your parents still in Nebraska?"

"No." She lifted a spoon of cobbler and examined it. "This is delicious. My compliments to the baker."

She was done talking about her family.

"Accepted with thanks."

"Tell me about your shop—and what you did before you opened it."

The first part of her request was no problem. The second he'd skirt. Two could play the evasion game.

"I'd always wanted to have a place like The Perfect Blend, but it was one of those dreams I'd put in the category of someday—until it hit me that if you wait too long, someday may never come. So I changed gears, learned everything I could about the coffee business, found the perfect location . . . and here I am."

"Did your dream end up being everything you hoped it would be?"

Some nuance in her question told him it was more than a casual inquiry.

"Yes—and more. I'm exactly where I'm supposed to be." Despite what his father thought.

"It must be wonderful to be that certain about your place in the world."

"I haven't always been. It took serious angst and soul searching to get here."

"I envy the comfort level you have with your life." A touch of melancholy wove through her comment.

Apparently Charley's assessment that she was troubled—and searching—had been accurate.

"You don't have that?"

She shrugged and remained silent.

Don't push, Garrett. Comment—don't question.

"For the record, getting here involved hard choices on my part."

Distress darkened the blue of her irises to cobalt. "And you never regretted them?"

"No—but that doesn't mean life is perfect. My choices did

51

cause other issues. But since there's nothing I can do about those, I don't let them bother me." Not much, anyway.

Kat scraped up the last of her cobbler and stood. "That was a treat. Thank you."

He rose more slowly. "I'll help you clean up."

"There isn't much to clean. I'll add our dishes to the ones already in the dishwasher. Let me get the rest of your ice cream."

"Keep it. Maybe we can have another cobbler party in a few days."

He held his breath until she gave a slow nod.

"That might be a possibility. I'll, uh, show you out." She detoured to retrieve the bowl he'd brought over, which she'd already rinsed out, and headed for the back of the house.

Their impromptu get-together was over—and again, she'd told him very little about herself. Left with no other option, he followed her to the sliding door. The brief shower had passed, and blue sky was peeking through the clouds.

"Ya gotta love Oregon coast weather. If it doesn't suit you, all you have to do is wait five minutes."

"I enjoy the variety." She pulled open the door and held out his bowl. "Thank you again."

"My pleasure." He took it, and as his fingers brushed hers, a sizzle of electricity surged through him.

She jerked her hand back, as if she'd felt the same high-voltage charge.

"You know . . . you never did tell me your full name." He lightened his tone and tried humor again. "I'm beginning to think you're a fugitive on the lam—or in the Witness Security Program."

His tease earned him a brief lip flex.

"Nothing that exotic. I just prefer to maintain a low-key presence. I'm here on vacation, and only a few people know where I am. I'd like to keep it that way."

"Why?"

"A story for another day. For those who are curious, I rented this house under the name Kat Morgan."

Meaning that wasn't her real name.

But it was all he was going to get today.

"Well . . . enjoy the rest of your day, Kat Morgan. And if you're ever in the mood to visit, there's a path through the trees that leads to my house." He motioned toward it. "My place is much smaller than yours, but the door's always open to friends."

"We're new acquaintances."

"That's how friendships begin. See you around." He lifted a hand in farewell and retraced his steps across the small patch of manicured grass that dead-ended at more natural flora, which in turn led to the needle-carpeted ground in the copse of trees dividing the properties.

There, he stopped to look back.

The deck was deserted. Kat must have retreated inside—taking with her all of her secrets.

Slowing his pace, he continued toward his house, for once ignoring the majesty of the trees towering above him.

So what exactly had he gleaned from the impromptu tête-à-tête with his neighbor?

He ticked off the crumbs she'd thrown him.

She had no siblings. Nebraska had been her childhood home, though it didn't sound as if she had any family left there. There'd been a dearth of milk in her young life. She was using the name Kat Morgan—but he'd be willing to bet that wasn't the one on her birth certificate.

Her questions and tone hinted that Charley had had her pegged from the get-go.

But instead of clearing up any of the mystery surrounding her, those random pieces of data led to more questions.

Pausing on his own much smaller deck, he gave his unpretentious, contemporary one-story house a once-over. Nothing as glamorous as the Clark place, with all its high-end finishes, but it was simple and comfortable and met all his needs.

Or most of them.

The truth was, much as he loved the home he'd created in Hope Harbor, it was beginning to feel a tad empty.

He rested his forearms on the damp railing and leaned forward, watching the few dawdling clouds pick up their pace and scoot toward the horizon.

If he wanted to fill the emptiness in his house—and his life—he should be proactive. Pick up the pace socially. The lack of eligible women in his adopted town didn't have to be a detriment. Online dating was an acceptable method of meeting people these days, if you stuck with reputable sites—and surely there would be a few appealing women within a manageable driving radius.

Not as close as the woman next door—but perhaps far more willing to explore a friendship.

It was worth thinking about—after Aunt Stephanie's visit. That had to be his priority for the immediate future. And during her stay, he wouldn't have to worry about loneliness. If she was the firecracker he recalled from their infrequent visits and phone conversations, a fair number of lively exchanges were on the horizon.

And maybe, if he introduced her to his reclusive neighbor, the two women would hit it off. Kat's walls would erode. He and his neighbor would discover they had much in common. Love would blossom. Happily-ever-after would follow.

Yeah, right.

Zach straightened up and entered his house, shutting the door behind him with a firm click.

He'd been listening to too many romantic stories from his baristas—one who continued to believe Mr. Right would come along despite a series of Mr. Wrongs, the other a veteran of a thirty-seven-year marriage to a woman now gone but who lived on in his heart.

Unlike their rose-tinted view of the world, real life tended to be fraught with difficulties—and relationships came with all sorts of complexities that could lead to choppy seas.

Lissa would attest to that.

As would his dad.

And getting involved with a temporary resident who came pre-loaded with problems would be like setting sail straight into a storm.

He didn't need that headache.

Detouring to the kitchen, he caught sight of a blackberry stain on his finger. After replacing the bowl in the cabinet, he flipped on the faucet and scrubbed at the spot. The stubborn pigment from the juice faded—but refused to vanish.

Kind of like how thoughts of Kat kept flitting through his mind, no matter how hard he tried to eradicate them.

Because a beautiful woman with an aura of intriguing secrecy and poignant aloneness was impossible to ignore—even if further attempts to circumvent her no-trespassing signs could be a recipe for disaster.

5

What on earth had Simon been thinking?

Katherine exhaled, closed the script he'd overnighted, and set it on the table beside the chaise lounge on the deck.

Had he even read this?

And if he had, why—

Her cell began to vibrate, and she picked it up from the table.

Speak of the devil.

He'd said he would text, not call—but while a conversation with him wasn't high on her Saturday priority list, the two of them did need to have a heart-to-heart.

She pressed talk and greeted him.

"You answered." He sounded surprised.

"The script came late yesterday. I finished it this morning."

"And?"

"Did you read it?"

"I skimmed through."

"Did you happen to notice there's a nude scene?"

"It's short—and it's not a nude scene."

"Close enough. You know I don't do that stuff."

"Katherine—the script is Academy Award material. A first-rate director will be in charge. We can trust him to handle the scene with taste and discretion."

She swung her legs to the deck and began to pace. "The point of that scene is to portray emotional vulnerability. I can do that with my clothes on. It's called acting."

"I'm not going to debate that. I'd rather hear what you thought about the rest of the script."

"It has language I'm not crazy about."

"I'm talking big picture here, Katherine, not nitpicks. What was your overall impression?"

She massaged the bridge of her nose. "It's a great screenplay ... or it would be, with a few modifications. The language and nudity are unnecessary."

"In your opinion."

"Fine—but I'm not comfortable with those elements."

He started to tap his pen. "We're not in a position to make many demands. You're not a proven commodity yet on the big screen. Once you are, we'll have more clout."

"The nude scene is a deal breaker."

Tap, tap, tap.

"They may be willing to consider a body double."

"No. The audience will think it's me."

"So what?"

"It's a matter of personal integrity—and boundaries."

"What's wrong with stretching your boundaries?"

"Boundaries are there for a purpose. Mine aren't budging."

Tap, tap, tap.

"I can talk to them. See how much they're willing to bend. But I'm not going to waste time, energy, and equity on negotiation unless you're on board with this project."

She watched the dark clouds gathering on the horizon, fighting a sudden wave of panic.

He wanted a commitment before going to bat for her—and she couldn't blame him.

But despite the powerful script . . . despite the appeal of the part, absent the nude scene and language . . . despite the fact that this could be her ticket to superstardom . . . it wasn't filling her with anything close to the breathless excitement she'd felt after winning her first tiny part in a low-end TV sitcom.

What was wrong with her?

Why couldn't she get past all the garbage that accompanied success and focus on the positives?

Because Jason died.

She closed her eyes. Exhaled slowly.

Seeing up close and personal what could happen to someone who'd succumbed to the lure of fame and lost his compass had been chilling.

But that alone hadn't tarnished the luster. The constant manipulation, relentless paparazzi, and privacy-invading tabloids were also getting old.

"Katherine? Are you willing to sign on if we work out your concerns?"

"I don't know." She sank back onto the lounge chair. "I need more time to think—and decompress."

"I can't hold them off forever."

"What happened to buying me breathing space?"

"I did."

"How much?"

"One month. They were willing to cut you slack because of the scandal. Also, they're still finalizing funding and wooing the leading man."

"Who are they trying to get?"

"They asked me to keep that confidential."

"Come on, Simon. Who am I going to tell here? My main social contact has been a pair of seagulls." She watched her two regular visitors strut around the manicured section of lawn.

He sighed. "If it helps convince you to give me a green light, I suppose I can share it—but keep this to yourself."

Her jaw dropped as he revealed the name of the megawatt star.

"I'm hoping your stunned silence means that news persuaded you."

"I *would* like to work with him." The hint of a headache began to pulse in her temples. "I've always admired his talent."

"Is that a yes?"

She gritted her teeth. Simon wanted answers, but she would *not* succumb to pressure tactics. That's why her life had spiraled out of control in the first place.

"Not yet."

"Fine." But it wasn't, based on his inflection. "You've got a month. That's it. If you drag your feet, they'll move on. I don't have to tell you that any actress in Hollywood would kill for this opportunity."

"No, you don't."

"I just want to be certain you're clear about what's being offered here."

"I'm clear, Simon. I'll call you."

He hung up without saying good-bye.

Her stomach clenched, as it always did when he got miffed at her. And that wasn't healthy.

Over the past five years, she'd given him too much control over her life. As her sole ally on the rocky road to stardom, he'd become her go-to person for everything—career guidance, contract negotiations, emotional support.

It was a pattern that had to change, or it would become locked into stone.

That insight had been the one positive to come from the tragedy.

Katherine picked up the script and wandered back into the house, toward the kitchen. If she didn't find an activity to engage her mind, the dull ache in her temples was going to morph into a raging headache.

As she filled a glass with water and scrounged through a drawer for her bottle of aspirin, the other FedEx delivery from yesterday registered in her peripheral vision.

Ah. The perfect diversion.

A supply of the finest quality chocolate . . . a huge bowl of fresh blackberries . . . a dozen recipes culled from the net for inspiration—those were the ingredients for a soothing afternoon.

And soothing was high on her priority list after her phone conversation with Simon.

Besides, there was also a practical excuse to indulge in her candy-making hobby. She owed her neighbor a thank-you for the cobbler, and handcrafted blackberry truffles would be perfect.

Plus, it would give her an excuse to visit the man who'd been showing up uninvited in her dreams.

A man she knew was available—thanks to her not-so-subtle probing about his marital status during their encounter on the beach.

A man who seemed interested in her despite her reticence and her imitation of a skittish sandpiper dodging waves whenever he encroached into her space.

She pulled out the bars made from 65 percent dark West African chocolate—her favorite for truffles—and got to work.

Whipping up fancy candies wasn't going to solve her problems or help her reach any important decisions, but it was guaranteed to clear her mind of static and calm her.

And maybe, as she dipped and smoothed and rolled, a few of the elusive answers she'd been seeking would come to her.

It couldn't hurt to add prayer to the mix either.

After all, where better for an appeal for divine guidance to produce results than in a town named Hope Harbor?

"You sure you don't mind closing up alone today?" Zach handed Frank the bag of coffee a waiting customer wanted ground.

"Not at all. We're in the home stretch, and the last couple of hours on Mondays are always quiet, as I recall from last time I switched shifts with Bren. You hear from your aunt yet?"

"No." Zach checked his watch. "She was supposed to call from North Bend after the flight from San Francisco landed, before she drove down. That should have been an hour and a half ago."

"She could have been delayed in San Francisco. The fog can wreak havoc with airline schedules."

"Yeah—and I've been too busy to get an update on her flight status." He pulled out his cell. "If you could handle the customers for a few minutes, I'll—"

The door opened, and Aunt Stephanie swept in, beaming a smile his direction as she held out her arms. "My favorite nephew!"

Grinning, he returned the phone to his pocket, circled the counter, and pulled her into a hug. "My favorite aunt."

"Also your only one—but let's not quibble over details." She returned his squeeze, then eased back to give him an assessing scan—and an approving nod. "Your new life agrees with you."

"Yes, it does. And retirement agrees with you." He gave her a once-over too. His aunt had always been trim and fashionable, and that hadn't changed. Though dressed casually in form-fitting jeans and a wrap top, she exuded class and sophistication—along with her usual energy and enthusiasm. "Welcome to Hope Harbor."

"Thank you. I'm glad to be here."

"Why didn't you call from the airport?"

"I decided it would be more fun to surprise you at your shop." She gave the space an appreciative sweep. "I like this. It's cozy and welcoming."

"That's what I was after. As long as you're here, why don't you sit for a few minutes and have a drink and a snack—unless you're too tired from the trip."

She waved his comment aside. "I'm used to traveling across multiple time zones in a day. Try flying from New York to Tokyo if you want to see jet lag. Atlanta to Oregon is a piece of cake. Food and drink would be most welcome after the cross-country airline fare—or should I say, lack of fare?"

"I feature snacks and desserts here, so a hearty meal will have to wait. But see if anything in the case tickles your fancy." He led her over to the glass display unit.

She leaned closer to peruse the offerings. "Mmm. My taste buds are already tingling. Tell me about everything."

"The packaged snacks are fair-trade sourced." He indicated the selection. "Everything else is local. Cranberry nut cake and scones from Harbor Point Cranberries, lavender shortbread from Bayview Lavender Farm and Tearoom, and Eleanor Cooper's famous fudge cake. She's ninety-three, bakes the cakes for me in the Grace Christian Church fellowship hall kitchen, and donates all the proceeds to Helping Hands, a local charity sponsored by our two churches."

Stephanie straightened up. "Fudge cake, no contest. I can't resist chocolate—or the opportunity to support a worthwhile cause. The other offerings sound yummy too, though. I'll have to sample them all while I'm here."

"That can be arranged. What would you like to drink?"

"Do you have a house specialty—or a customer favorite?"

"The café viennois is popular. And we also have café de olla. You won't find either at any of the popular chains. The viennois is—"

She held up a hand. "From France—light espresso, whipped cream, and chocolate powder. The Mexican coffee is made with cinnamon and piloncillo—that would be raw dark sugar for the uninitiated."

"The lady knows her coffee." Frank joined them and offered Stephanie a smile.

A dimple appeared in her cheek. "As a coffee lover, I've tried brews all over the world. After decades of sipping from Rio to Rome to Riyadh, I've become somewhat of an aficionado." She extended her hand. "Stephanie Garrett."

"Frank Simmons. I'm one of the baristas here." The man gave his palm a quick swipe on his jeans and held it out. "A pleasure."

"Likewise."

The clasp lasted a bit longer than protocol demanded, and Zach inspected them.

A slight flush had tinted his aunt's cheeks, and Frank was grinning as if he'd won the lottery.

Zach's mouth quirked at the interesting vibes wafting from the pair.

As the handshake continued, he cleared his throat. "Sorry. I should have taken care of the introductions."

"We managed." Frank released his aunt's hand—but not her gaze. "Welcome to Hope Harbor."

"Thank you. I expect I'll have a wonderful visit."

"We'll see to that."

We?

Zach studied Frank. If the man was thirty or forty years younger, he'd peg that look as serious interest—and attraction.

But wasn't the immediate zing phenomenon reserved for the younger crowd?

"I appreciate that."

At his aunt's response, he transferred his attention to her—and picked up the same spark in her irises.

Similar to the one that had momentarily flashed in Kat's on the beach as they'd shaken hands.

If this kept up, Hope Harbor was going to be in the midst of an electrical storm.

"So . . . Aunt Stephanie, what's your pleasure?"

The flush on her cheeks deepened as she continued to fixate on Frank.

"Aunt Stephanie?"

She blinked and broke eye contact with his right-hand man. "Yes?"

"What would you like to drink?"

"Oh. Um . . . whatever you think goes best with the fudge cake."

"I'd keep it simple and stick with an Americano. A flavored drink could affect the taste of the cake."

"Sold."

"Find a seat and I'll bring everything over."

"Perfect. Thanks." She angled back toward Frank. "It was a pleasure to meet you."

"The pleasure was all mine."

She acknowledged his comment with a nod and strolled across the shop.

"You want me to cut the cake?" Frank continued to watch his aunt.

"Sure." Zach went about preparing the Americano, keeping tabs on the other barista . . . who, in turn, was keeping tabs on Stephanie.

It appeared the ember of attraction could burst into flame at any age.

Wouldn't it be a kick if Frank and his aunt connected?

But a relationship between them had about as much chance of developing into anything serious as the one between him and Kat. In both cases, the woman involved was only a visitor to Hope Harbor, and as far as he knew, neither had any intention of uprooting herself.

He finished the Americano and took the plate and fork from Frank. "Thanks."

"You have any idea how long your aunt is staying?" Frank's tone was nonchalant as he swiped a rag over the spotless counter.

"No. I don't think she has a definite timetable in mind. I know she bought an open-ended return ticket. Now that she's retired, she doesn't have to adhere to any fixed schedule."

"You think she'll be stopping by here on a regular basis during her stay?" He leaned down to scrub at a stain Zach couldn't see, giving the task more attention than it deserved.

"I expect so. You heard her—she loves coffee, and this is the only game in town. She'll try to pay, but if you wait on her, tell her you've been instructed that her drinks and food are on the house—boss's orders."

"Is she going to be okay with that?"

"No. From what I know about Aunt Stephanie, she's not the type to accept favors or preferential treatment."

"An admirable trait."

"Unless it morphs to stubbornness."

Frank ran out of counter to scrub and straightened up, folding the cloth into a neat square. "How come you've never talked much about her?"

"We haven't stayed in close touch."

"That's a pity." He flicked her another glance. "She strikes me as a woman worth getting to know."

"I don't think she'd object to making a few friends while she's here, if you have the inclination."

"I'll have to consider that." He tucked the cloth under the counter. "On a different subject—are you attending the Helping Hands meeting tomorrow night about the foster home?"

"That was my plan, but it depends on how Aunt Stephanie settles in. I hate to leave her alone on her first full day in town."

"I can bring you up to speed if you can't attend, but a large turnout would be helpful. Personally, I think it's a fine idea if all the hurdles can be overcome. The concept of keeping foster children from the same family together, in a more permanent home environment, has a lot of merit. So much of what we become later in life is influenced by our youthful experiences of home. I'd like to think the town will throw its full support behind this."

"I would too. The steering committee has been doing a ton of legwork to generate support. I'll try to be there."

"You want me to carry any of that over to the table?" Frank tipped his head toward the cake and coffee.

"I can manage. And thanks again for closing up today. We'll be taking off after my aunt finishes her snack."

The door opened, admitting an older couple with two teens in tow. Zach greeted them as he circled the counter and wove through the tables toward Stephanie, who'd chosen the same corner spot Kat had selected on her second visit.

He set the cake and coffee in front of her and claimed the empty chair. "Enjoy."

"No worries on that score. Chocolate and coffee are an excellent pairing." She picked up her fork and used the edge to cut off a piece of cake.

"How was your visit with Dad?"

"Too fast—and he was preoccupied with his case. We had a few significant conversations . . . but if you're wondering whether we discussed the rift, the answer is no. I mentioned I was flying here from Atlanta, but he didn't comment other than to wish me a pleasant trip."

"That's more or less what I expected." Despite his assurance to Kat that he didn't let the repercussions from his decision to pursue a different course affect him, his father's lack of interest in his life remained a canker on his otherwise placid existence.

Stephanie forked another bite of cake. "If you want my opinion, I think he's lonely."

"He has no one to blame for that but himself."

"That may be true—but overtures can come from either direction."

"I tried, Aunt Stephanie."

"That was a while back. People change. I have. Three, four years ago, if someone had asked me whether I was lonely, I'd have denied it. But that night in Paris on my birthday, I'd have given anything to have someone to share it with. Mind you, I didn't dwell on it or wallow in self-pity. I long ago accepted that the parade had passed me by in the romance department."

Subtle though it was, Zach caught the look she darted toward Frank.

"Maybe not. Aren't you the one who told me not less than a week ago that miracles happen?"

"Touché." Lips curving, she continued to eat her cake and transitioned to less serious subjects.

Twenty minutes later, as they prepared to leave, his aunt touched his arm halfway to the front door. "Give me a minute."

She detoured to the counter.

Her exchange with Frank was too muted to hear, but as it ended and Stephanie turned to rejoin him, both were smiling.

And the slight flush was back on his aunt's cheeks.

He pulled open the door and moved aside to let her exit, assessing his barista.

Frank was always upbeat, but in the past half hour he'd gone from cheerful to chipper. As if someone had given him a shot of effervescence.

From behind the counter, Frank winked at him.

Geez.

Between him and Bren, the romance meter in the coffee shop was going to zoom off the charts.

Too bad Kat had decided to boycott this place. If she showed up, maybe a bit of the buoyant, fizzy ambiance would rub off on her. Soften up that hard shell she'd wrapped herself in.

Because absent that sort of catalyst, should any new romance be in the cards, it seemed slated to happen among the older set.

And for a thirtysomething guy who couldn't connect with the woman next door even after baking her blackberry cobbler, that was pretty darn depressing.

6

This could be another mistake.

A big one.

Bigger than her second trip to The Perfect Blend.

Pulse picking up, Katherine halted at the edge of the trees that separated her property from Zach's.

For heaven's sake, Katherine—just do it!

Despite the dictate from her subconscious that had brought her this far after a forty-eight-hour debate over the pros and cons of such a visit, she held her ground and crimped her fingers around the rim of the plate containing a dozen blackberry truffles.

For someone who professed to want privacy and was determined to remain incognito, initiating contact with the man next door didn't make sense.

Except . . . the two seagulls who liked to loiter in her yard and follow her to the beach weren't much company—and being around someone who seemed to have his act together, who respected her back-off signals when their conversation moved onto shaky ground, was appealing.

As was the man himself.

Who could have guessed that a hot—and available—guy like Zach would live on the adjacent property?

She tugged down the loose tunic that was flapping in the breeze over her leggings, trying to rein in her nervousness.

If she followed the prods of her subconscious, she'd be stepping into a danger zone. While Zach hadn't recognized her the other day as they'd indulged in cobbler, her luck could run out if he got another close-up gander.

But her sunglasses hid most of her face, and the rest of her disguise was solid. A new hairstyle and color, along with the absence of her usual theatrical makeup, gave her a whole different look. Even an avid fan would have difficulty recognizing her—especially out of context.

Maybe the risk of being unmasked was lower than she feared.

Besides, she didn't have to linger during the delivery. She could hand off the treat at the door and beat a hasty retreat. A few minutes in Zach's presence to absorb a tiny bit of his warmth and calm would be sufficient.

She straightened her spine.

Yes. A quick visit was worth the gamble.

Forcing her feet to carry her forward, she continued toward his house, following the short path through the small grove of trees.

As she emerged, she paused to examine Zach's home.

It was smaller than her rental unit, as he'd indicated, but attractive and welcoming. Constructed of redwood and stone, with several rooflines at various angles and large expanses of glass, it fit the image of coastal contemporary architecture to a T. Unlike her property, there was no manicured lawn. The structure was nestled into the landscape, as if it was a natural outgrowth of the terrain. The sea view wasn't quite as expansive from here either, thanks to an abundance of trees, but the house felt private and cozy.

It was a perfect complement to the man who lived here.

She continued forward . . . but stopped again at a movement in her peripheral vision.

A slender woman dressed in jeans and a sweater rose from a chair tucked into a shadowed corner of the deck.

Kat clutched the plate tighter, remaining as still as the deer that froze at the slightest hint of danger back in Nebraska. If she retreated, the woman would notice her. If she stayed where she was, it was possible Zach's guest would go inside.

Guest.

Her spirits tanked.

While he'd intimated there was no one special in his life, that didn't mean he never dated. A guy like him would have no difficulty securing a companion for dinner . . . and perhaps more.

Man, this was awkward.

Neither he—nor his date—would be thrilled by the appearance of a gift-toting single neighbor in the middle of their tryst . . . or whatever it was.

If only the earth would open and swallow her up.

Since that wasn't going to happen, all she could do was hope the woman angled away so she could—

Drat!

Zach's lady friend emerged from the shadows and walked toward the railing at the back of the deck.

Any second now she'd notice—

Wait.

Kat squinted at the woman as she strolled through the late afternoon light. Despite her slender build, youthful aura, and chic russet hair, she was too old to be Zach's date—unless he was into May-December romances.

Not likely, if the electricity that had sparked between them during their previous encounters was any indication.

It wasn't his mother either. Zach had said she'd died eight years ago.

So who was—

The woman turned toward her, as if she'd sensed someone was nearby. "Hello!" Smiling, she lifted a hand in welcome and ambled over to the edge of the deck.

Busted.

Short of following the flee-and-vanish example of the mole crabs that populated Blackberry Beach, Katherine had no choice but to return the greeting.

"Hi." She forced her stiff legs to carry her forward. "I'm renting the vacation house next door. Sorry to interrupt. I didn't know Zach had company."

"No apology necessary. And I'm not company. I'm family." She extended her hand and descended the two steps from the deck. "Stephanie Garrett. Zach's aunt. I arrived this afternoon."

Question answered.

She continued forward and returned the woman's firm handshake. "Kat Morgan."

"Nice to meet you." The older woman inspected the plastic-covered plate. "Those must be for Zach."

"Yes. They're sort of a . . . thank-you."

"Let me tell him you're here. Come on up to the deck." Without waiting for a response, Stephanie ascended the steps.

What else could she do but follow?

"Would you like to come in?" Stephanie called the question over her shoulder.

"No, thanks. After I give these to Zach, I'll leave you two to visit."

"You don't have to rush off. I'll be here awhile. He and I will have ample opportunity to renew our acquaintance."

"If this is your first night here, though, I'm sure he'd appreciate having you to himself."

"Hmm." Stephanie inspected her. "I'll let you two work that out. Give me a sec."

She pushed through the sliding glass door that led to what appeared to be a great room. Like the one in the rental house next door, it had a vaulted ceiling—but the space was much smaller, and the floor plan wasn't as open. She could only follow Stephanie's progress a short distance before the woman disappeared around a wall.

Left on her own, Katherine surveyed the deck. A glass-topped table set for two, with placemats and cloth napkins and a small vase of wildflowers in the middle, hugged the railing.

Zach had planned a welcome dinner for his aunt.

Thoughtful.

She wandered over and set her offering on the far side of the table.

Was he doing the cooking?

If so—and if it was half as tasty as that blackberry cobbler—his aunt was in for a treat.

As if she'd tuned in to Katherine's musings, Stephanie re-appeared. "He's putting the finishing touches on dinner, but he'll be out in a minute or two." She strolled over and gave the horizon that was visible through the trees a slow sweep. "This is a beautiful spot."

"Yes, it is."

After a moment, she swiveled around and leaned back against the railing. "Zach says you're here on vacation."

Katherine fidgeted.

What else had he said? Like, had he mentioned how reticent she was? Or how spooked she got whenever people were around?

Best to proceed with caution.

"Yes."

"I can see the appeal. In all the traveling I've done, I've never had such positive vibes about a place so fast. I've been here barely six hours, and I can already feel my stress level plummeting. I bet you've noticed that too."

The woman hadn't asked a single question, but her open-ended statements invited responses.

Katherine caught her lower lip between her teeth. Maybe if *she* asked a few questions, she could shift the spotlight.

"Yes. It's very peaceful. Tell me about your travels. Are they job related?"

The tiny twinkle that appeared in the other woman's irises indicated she recognized the diversionary tactic. But she didn't fight it.

Apparently everyone in the Garrett clan had the know-how-to-take-a-hint-and-back-off gene.

"Yes, my job took me all over the globe. It was quite glamorous . . . on the surface."

Katherine's ears perked up. This woman had also had a job that appeared exciting to the world but wasn't quite as glitzy in reality? Was it possible they were kindred spirits?

Before she could explore that question, Zach opened the sliding door and joined them, wiping his hands on a dish towel. Not a traditional symbol of masculinity—but the snug T-shirt that showcased his muscular chest and broad shoulders, worn jeans that hugged his lean hips, and chiseled jaw more than compensated.

His pulse-quickening smile warmed her from her toes to the tips of her ears as he approached, and she almost groped for the railing to steady herself.

Thank heaven she wasn't holding the blackberry truffles or they'd be melting into a gooey puddle.

Like she was.

And the man hadn't yet uttered a word.

"This is a pleasant surprise." He flipped the towel over his shoulder. "I'd do the introductions, but Aunt Stephanie says she's already taken care of that." He shot the older woman a teasing look. "That's twice in one day."

A tiny hint of color crept over his aunt's cheeks.

Must be an inside joke.

"What can I say? I'm a take-charge kind of woman." His aunt shrugged.

Hmm.

She and Stephanie may not be kindred spirits, after all. In Katherine's world, *others* took charge—and she was prone to let them.

Or she had been until she'd walked away to try and regain control over her life.

"More like a woman who knows her own mind," Zach

countered. "Guys respect that, you know. At least the ones worth having do."

What was this conversation about?

Clueless, Katherine remained silent.

"I agree with you." Stephanie motioned to the table and changed the subject. "Kat brought you a present."

Zach leaned closer to examine the plate of perfectly formed truffles, and the musky scent of his aftershave wafted toward her. "No one's ever given me candy."

"They're my specialty." Somehow she managed to find her voice despite the heady fragrance that was playing havoc with her concentration. "I, uh, wanted to thank you for the cobbler."

"You *made* these?"

"Yes—using the local blackberries for flavoring."

"Blackberry truffles?" Stephanie joined him, lifted the plastic wrap, picked one up, and examined it. "This is beautiful."

"If you touch it, you have to eat it. House rule." One side of Zach's mouth rose.

"No hardship, trust me—and I doubt one will suffice." She directed her next comment to Katherine. "I have to confess—I'm a chocoholic."

"And how." Zach chuckled. "She inhaled Eleanor Cooper's fudge cake today."

Katherine raised her eyebrows. "Who's Eleanor Cooper?"

Zach filled her in. "You should stop by the shop and try a piece. On the house."

"No." She shook her head. "I just repaid one debt. I don't want to go back into hock."

"It will be my treat," Stephanie said. "I'm going back tomorrow for another piece myself. Come with me."

Katherine fought the temptation to accept. "I only go into town for supplies."

"In that case, pencil a trip to The Perfect Blend on your calendar during your next shopping trip. We'll go together."

Zach's aunt really *was* a take-charge woman.

But while Simon's high-handedness rankled, Stephanie's came across as more benevolent.

"I'll think about it. Thank you for the offer. I hope you enjoy those." She waved toward the plate and eased back.

"Why don't you join us for dinner?" Zach tugged the towel off his shoulder. "I always double recipes and put the leftovers in the freezer for future meals. Our menu tonight is garlic-pepper marinated salmon with green beans amandine and au gratin potatoes."

Her mouth began to water. Much as she enjoyed chocolate-making, cooking wasn't her forte. Omelets and salads were about the extent of her repertoire.

Stocking up on takeout dinners from the Myrtle Café in town had been inspired, but the local eatery's excellent fare didn't compare to the menu Zach had planned for tonight.

The longer she was around these people, however, the higher the probability she'd let an identifying nugget slip—or one of them would recognize her.

Not worth the risk.

"Thank you, but I wouldn't want to intrude. I imagine you and your aunt would like to catch up."

"It was her idea." Zach nudged the older woman.

"That's true. I told him in the kitchen we should invite you." Stephanie swept a hand over the table. "All we have to do is add another place setting. And I for one would love to hear how you learned to make such exquisite truffles. If they taste as delicious as they look, I have a feeling you're in the wrong business—whatever business you're in."

The last comment cinched her decision.

If she succumbed to temptation and stayed, the subject of her background would come up. Those were the sorts of topics new acquaintances chatted about. While she could deflect queries and redirect the conversation during a short visit like the cobbler break she and Zach had shared, playing dodgeball over the length of a leisurely dinner would be difficult—and stressful.

She had to go.

"I can't stay tonight—but welcome to Hope Harbor, Ms. Garrett."

"Stephanie."

"Stephanie. Enjoy your meal. You have a perfect night for outdoor dining."

"You're certain we can't convince you to stay?" Zach sent a distracted glance toward the two amiable seagulls who'd followed her over and were sitting side by side a few yards away, their unblinking stare riveted on the trio on the deck.

"Not tonight."

"I'll return the plate from the truffles."

"No hurry. Have a pleasant evening."

With that, she escaped.

Not until she was safely back on the other side of the insulating stand of coniferous trees did she slow her pace.

That had been close.

Too close.

It wasn't that Zach or his aunt posed any danger. Every instinct in her body told her she could trust them to keep her secret if they happened to discover it.

No, the danger next door was of a different sort.

It was named Zach.

Stifling a sudden surge of longing, she stepped onto her deck as the two seagulls soared back and landed on her lawn with a flutter of wings. A moment later, the faint peal of female laughter drifted her direction from next door.

It appeared Zach and his aunt were having fun.

No surprise there. The two of them seemed to share a zest for life and a ready sense of humor.

She braced her hands on the railing and watched the sun descend toward the horizon.

Too bad she couldn't have joined them for what would no doubt be a lively, engaging dinner.

And too bad she hadn't met Zach under different circumstances. The spark between them could have had serious potential.

But their lives were on different trajectories, and until she decided whether a course correction was in her future, it wasn't fair to either of them to get involved in anything more than a casual, next-door-neighbor friendship. If she ended up going back to Hollywood, a relationship with a coffee shop owner in a tiny Oregon coast town would never work.

One more incentive to get her act together and decide what she wanted to do with the rest of her life.

Fast.

Because living in limbo stunk.

7

. . . .

"Beautiful presentation." Stephanie draped her napkin over her lap as Zach set her plate in front of her. "And it smells divine."

He put his own plate down and slid into his chair. "These are all tried-and-true recipes. There shouldn't be any unpleasant surprises, like the ones my early culinary efforts produced. I have blackberry cobbler for dessert—but I have a feeling chocolate is going to trump my offering." He folded his hands. "Shall we say a blessing?"

"By all means." She motioned for him to proceed.

After offering a brief prayer of thanks, he lifted his head to find Stephanie watching him. "What's wrong?"

"Nothing." She picked up her fork. "Just wondering."

"About what?"

"Your neighbor. She intrigues me."

That made two of them.

"Why?"

"I don't know. There's an aura about her that awakens the motherly instinct in me—not that I've had much opportunity to be maternal in my life, so it's possible I'm misreading the cue." His aunt speared a piece of salmon. "What do you know about her?"

"Not much. On the few occasions we've talked, she's told me very little about herself."

"Curious. How long will she be here?"

"Also a tidbit she hasn't passed on."

"Well, whatever her story, I like her."

"How can you tell after such a brief meeting?"

"How long did it take *you* to like her—or more?" A dimple appeared in his aunt's cheek as she appraised him.

Dang, she had excellent intuitive abilities.

He concentrated on scooping up a forkful of potatoes as he composed his answer. "I noticed her the first day she came into the shop."

"And I bet it didn't take long for the spark of attraction to ignite."

"Can I plead the Fifth?"

"You can—although the evidence is compelling. I may not have much personal experience with romance, but it's easy to recognize. And in your case, it's mutual."

Also his conclusion—but how had his aunt picked up on it in a handful of minutes?

Whatever her technique, why deny his interest?

"You're a perceptive woman."

"Thank you. Reading people was an asset in my business—as I expect it was in your former career. I learned to spot and interpret subtle cues . . . and not-so-subtle cues, in the case of you two. Your body language spoke volumes."

"I'm not going to dispute your conclusions—but I doubt there's much future in them. For all I know, Kat could pack up and leave tomorrow."

"Unless you give her a reason to extend her stay."

"Hard to do when she goes out of her way to avoid me."

"Not tonight."

"But she didn't linger. Besides, an extended stay doesn't solve the long-term problem. Eventually she'll go back to her real life, wherever that is. Getting involved with someone like that is a recipe for heartbreak."

"Unless both people are willing to consider a few compromises."

A muscle in his jaw clenched. "I've made too many of those already in my life."

"Mmm." She cut a green bean in half. "In that case, you could have an impasse."

"That's why it would be smarter to walk a wide circle around her."

"Yet you invited her to dinner."

"It was your idea."

"I'll concede I *voiced* it first."

He shifted in his seat. "It was the polite thing to do."

"Uh-huh." Stephanie continued to eat, but her tone implied she wasn't buying his explanation. "She strikes me as someone I'd enjoy getting to know. Would you mind if I paid her a visit while you're at work?"

"Not at all." If Kat wouldn't open up to him, perhaps she'd find another female more simpatico. And he'd wager a month's income from The Perfect Blend that his neighbor needed *someone* to talk to. "I think she likes to walk on the beach. If you plan to explore a bit, you could run into her while you're down there."

"I may try that approach first. A casual meeting would be less intimidating to someone who's reluctant to talk about herself."

Bumping into Kat on the beach hadn't loosened her tongue in his case—but why mention that?

For the rest of the meal, Stephanie kept him entertained with amusing stories, humorous insights, and tales of her adventures all over the world, filling his usually quiet deck with witty banter and laughter.

As she finished her potatoes and set her fork down, she exhaled. "That was wonderful, Zach."

"I'm glad you enjoyed it. I have to warn you, though—my usual dinners tend to be simpler."

"Perfect. If I ate like this every night, I'd lose my girlish figure. And speaking of usual routines, I don't want you to change any of yours for me. I'm perfectly capable of entertaining myself."

"Other than my hours at the shop, my schedule is flexible—and I want to spend my free time getting reacquainted with you."

"Are you certain I won't be intruding on your social life?"

He grinned. "If that's a subtle attempt to ask whether I'm active on the dating scene, the answer is no." The corners of his lips leveled off. "My heart wasn't in it after we lost Josh, and once I decided to make major changes in my life, the transition required all my energy and attention."

"Your business appears to be established now, and from what I've observed, you're settled in here at the house. It's not healthy for a young man like you to be a hermit."

"I'm not. I'm involved at church, and I'm active in the Helping Hands organization I mentioned earlier. In fact, there's a meeting I'm supposed to attend tomorrow night about a new project, but I may forgo that. I don't want you to spend the evening alone on your first full day in town."

"Why don't I go with you? Or would that be frowned upon?"

"The gathering is open to anyone who's interested—but haven't you attended enough meetings to last two lifetimes?"

"Depends. Is this one going to be as boring as listening to business managers drone on about accruals, depreciation, amortization, ROI, and EBIDA?"

He winced. "Sounds like an echo of my past life. The answer is no. Numbers may be discussed, but only in the context of the larger project."

"Which is?"

"You sure you're interested in this?"

"I'm interested in everything—in case you haven't already figured that out." She winked at him.

"Okay. I'll give you the condensed version. Aside from a paid director, Helping Hands is a volunteer organization that does exactly what the name says. If someone's in need, the group re-cruits volunteers to help. On occasion, the organization becomes more proactive if a worthwhile proposal is presented. That's what happened with Hope House—the latest project. The idea was brought forward by our police chief's husband, Adam Stone, who's an ex-con."

Stephanie's eyebrows peaked. "Talk about opposites attracting."

"Yeah—but from all indications, the matchup is working fine. Anyway, he read about an organization that purchases houses and provides houseparents so foster sibling groups can be kept intact and raised in a stable, loving home setting rather than being split up and bounced around from place to place. He hoped Helping Hands would be interested in sponsoring a house like that."

"Seems like a worthwhile project."

"The board agreed the idea was worth exploring. As it happens, one of our older residents is moving in with his son and has offered his home to the organization at a discounted price. Tomorrow's meeting is to discuss whether to accept his offer—and if so, hash out next steps."

She picked up the truffle she'd claimed earlier. "You should go."

"I know they're hoping for a big turnout—but I already told Frank I was on the fence."

"Frank's involved?"

"Yes. He's on the board."

"Admirable."

"He volunteers at the Pelican Point lighthouse too. That's an-other local nonprofit."

"Impressive." She examined the handcrafted candy. "What did he do before he became a barista?"

Her manner was conversational, but unless he was mistaken, there was more to that question than mere chitchat.

"Worked for the postal service. He retired five years ago, at fifty-eight. He and his wife dived into their bucket list, but she died suddenly two years later."

Stephanie's features softened. "How sad."

"I agree. According to Frank, after he stumbled around in a daze for almost a year, he decided his wife would want him to carry on. He ended up selling his house in Coos Bay and moving here because he'd always loved this town. When he applied at the shop, he was honest about his lack of experience but said he'd enjoy interacting with customers and was willing to learn the business. I hired him on the spot. It was one of my best decisions."

"I could tell from our brief meeting he was the amiable sort."

"He's more amiable with some than with others." He waggled his eyebrows.

She waved off his comment. "Don't be silly. You said yourself he likes people."

"I repeat . . . some more than others."

"Don't get any ideas, Zach. You may be on the track to romance, but that train passed me by long ago." She held up her truffle. "Let's try your neighbor's chocolates, shall we?" Without waiting for a response, she took a bite.

He picked one up too. "Trains can come along at—"

"Stop." She held up her hand as an expression of pure bliss swept over her face. "Don't ruin the moment. This is incredible. Wait till you taste it."

Zach studied the truffle he was holding. Professional as it appeared, it was just chocolate. How good could it be?

He bit into it—and as the creamy confection dissolved in his mouth, the cause of his aunt's rapture became apparent. The rich chocolate was infused with the essence of sun-warmed blackberries, both tastes bold but perfectly balanced and complementary.

"Wow."

"I agree." Stephanie reached for another piece. "I've had truffles from the finest purveyors in the world, and this tops them all."

Zach picked up another one too. "I'm not a chocolate connoisseur like you are, but this merits a ten in my book."

"Do you think Kat could be a chocolatier by profession?"

"Why wouldn't she tell us that?"

"True." Stephanie bit into her second piece. "But she should be."

"I won't argue with that. These put my blackberry cobbler to shame." Zach helped himself to another truffle. "At this rate, we'll polish these off by tomorrow."

"You could ask about her candy-making expertise when you return the plate. Most people are more than willing to talk about a hobby they enjoy—and that could open the door to a deeper discussion."

"I was thinking along the same lines. Great minds and all that." He motioned toward the truffle plate. "Finished?"

"For tonight." She checked her watch and attempted to restrain a yawn. "I know it's early here, but I'm still on East Coast time. Would you mind if I call it a night?"

"Not at all."

"I'll help you clean up first." She began stacking plates.

He stopped her with a touch on the hand. "I'll take care of this. Go ahead and turn in."

"Thank you. After tonight, I intend to pitch in with these sorts of chores—but I have to admit, the long day and the travel is catching up with me." She stood.

He rose too. "Sleep well."

"I intend to." She rose on tiptoe and kissed his cheek. "I think I'll dream of blackberry truffles."

He watched her until she disappeared inside, then dropped back in his chair and gazed toward the trees that separated his property from the house next door. No light penetrated the sweeping boughs, but Kat was there. From everything she'd said, aside from her supply runs and beach walks, she was *always* there.

Doing what—other than crafting exceptional truffles?

Why did she keep to herself?

What did she have to hide?

Was someone, somewhere, missing her?

Zach raked his fingers through his hair.

None of those questions would be answered tonight.

But Stephanie was right. Returning the plate gave him an excuse to see her again.

And the fact that she'd ventured over here tonight was encouraging. It suggested she was beginning to find the wall she'd built confining.

If he kept seeking opportunities to interact with her, it was possible that one of these days she'd realize she could trust him with whatever secrets she was guarding.

He didn't have forever, though. While she hadn't confided the length of her stay, it was finite. One day, she'd leave—unless, as Stephanie had said, he gave her a reason to extend her stay.

But was that wise?

Sighing, he stood again and wandered over to the edge of the deck, hands in his pockets.

Any sort of ongoing relationship would likely involve compromises on both sides . . . and he'd compromised too much already in his life.

Which left him nowhere unless Kat was willing to make the lion's share of concessions. Like uprooting herself from whatever life she'd temporarily left behind and moving to Hope Harbor.

The odds of that happening were about as high as the odds of Charley's taco stand ever going under due to lack of customers.

A faint light flickered through the trees. Disappeared.

Like Kat would do in the not-too-distant future, barring a change in the status quo.

And that left him with one more question to contemplate on this peaceful, quiet evening.

Should he continue trying to break through her wall—or would that only create more chaos for her and further disrupt his hard-won placid existence?

8

· ·

Was that a knock on her front door?

Katherine yanked the bow tight on her sport shoe, grabbed her sunglasses, and vaulted to her feet.

Who could have come calling?

Was Zach paying her another visit? Perhaps to return the truffle plate from last night?

But why would he bother to circle around to her front door? The back entry was much closer to the path.

Another knock echoed through the house, this one louder.

Her pulse accelerated.

Calm down, Katherine. It's probably another FedEx delivery.

True.

She took a deep breath.

With all her chocolate-making equipment back in LA, ordering more had been her only option now that her appetite had been whetted for her favorite pastime. Doubling up on gear was an indulgence, as her conscience continued to remind her—but she didn't allow herself many of those. She could afford to go a bit wild with her hard-earned, squirreled-away money once in a while.

At a third, more forceful knock, she tiptoed toward the door and peeked through the peephole.

Charley Lopez stood on the other side.

Stomach flip-flopping, she scuttled back.

Why had the man she'd most wanted to avoid come here? And how had he known where she was staying?

Most important—if she ignored him, would he go away?

"Katherine? Zach told me you were renting the Clark place, and I live a few houses north, above Blackberry Beach. I was on my way home from town and brought you lunch." He spoke as if he knew she was standing on the other side of the door.

Strange.

But even more alarming?

He'd called her Katherine.

She sucked in a lungful of air.

No one here was supposed to know her real name.

Was he guessing that was the longer version of Kat—or had he seen through her disguise?

No way to know for certain unless she talked to him.

Slipping on her dark glasses, she returned to the door, flipped the lock, and swung it open.

Trademark smile on display, Charley held up a brown paper sack in one hand and two bottles of water in the other. "I don't usually deliver, but since you never came to claim your free tacos and I was passing by, I thought I'd drop off an order. I hope you haven't eaten lunch already."

"No. Um . . . you didn't have to go to all this trouble."

"It was no trouble. You're on my route. As I said, we're neighbors."

And hospitality demanded that you invite a gift-bearing neighbor inside.

Besides, she had to find out what he knew and try to head any threat off at the pass.

"Would you like to come in?" She eased back and motioned toward the foyer.

"Thank you. My muse is calling, but I can spare a few minutes."
He passed her, waiting while she closed the door. "As I recall, the
Clarks have a lovely deck. Would you like to eat out there?"

"Sure."

"I'm not interrupting anything, am I?"

"No. I was getting ready to go down to the beach, but I'm not
on any schedule."

"Ah. The beauty of vacation—or a life that's not burdened by
too many commitments. After you." He waved a hand for her to
precede him.

She complied, stopping at the back of the house to push open
the sliding door.

He followed her out and deposited the bag on the table. Instead
of sitting, however, he ambled over to the edge of the deck and
gave the scene spread before them a slow sweep.

"It's quite a view, isn't it?" She remained by the table.

"Indeed it is. A sunny day in Hope Harbor is a little preview
of paradise." After a few more moments, he pivoted back and
indicated the bag. "Please eat or they'll get cold."

She didn't argue. The savory aroma had activated her salivary
glands.

As she slid into her chair and pulled out one of the bundles
wrapped in white paper, Charley joined her. He sat across from her
and uncapped a bottle of water as she dived into her first fish taco.

"I believe congratulations are in order. Katherine Parker has
achieved her dream."

The bite of taco lodged in her windpipe, and she began cough-
ing.

Charley handed the bottle to her.

After several gulps, her hacking subsided and she removed her
sunglasses. Wiped her watering eyes with a paper napkin.

"Sorry. That wasn't the best timing." Charley leaned forward
and locked gazes with her. "In case you're concerned, your secret
is safe with me."

Filling her lungs, she set the bottle on the table. "So you do remember me."

"Of course—but your disguise is quite effective. The name didn't click into place until a few hours after we met at The Perfect Blend. I kept hoping you'd stop by the stand for a chat."

"I was afraid someone would recognize me."

"You don't have to worry about that. The change in hairstyle and color alone would throw most people off—including me. And I don't fool easily." The corners of his mouth lifted. "Go on, eat."

Sixty seconds ago, eating would have been impossible—but oddly, the churning in her stomach had subsided.

She picked up her taco again and took another bite. "These are as wonderful as ever."

"The secret's in my special seasoning and sauce." He leaned back and sipped his water. "After we met, I kept up with your career. I had a feeling you were on the road to stardom."

"There have been a few potholes along the way."

"No journey is without them. But they're no more than an aggravation if the destination is worthwhile."

He hadn't couched his comment as a question, but he'd left her an opening if she wanted to talk.

And she did. Charley had proven to be an excellent listener on her previous visit to Hope Harbor.

"I'm beginning to question whether it is."

"Because of what happened to Jason?"

She froze. "You know about that?"

"As I said, I've been following your career."

"You don't strike me as the type to read the Hollywood gossip magazines."

"There are other sources for information. More accurate information."

A wave of bitterness curdled through her. "Most people are happy to believe what those rags publish."

"Their issue, not yours. I imagine that incident is what brought you here."

"It was the catalyst." She picked up a piece of avocado that had escaped from her taco. "But I also wanted space to think."

"Success wasn't what you envisioned?"

"Some parts, yes. Other parts, no." She bit into her second taco.

"Many things in life are a mixed blessing. The question is whether the good parts outweigh the bad. If they don't?" He shrugged. "A course correction may be in order."

"It's hard to do that midstream in a strong current."

"Yes, it is—but it can be done. Zach's a perfect example of that."

Her ears perked up. Maybe Charley would offer her a few insights about her charming neighbor. "I know his coffee shop is a new business, but he hasn't told me anything about what he used to do."

"It's a story worth hearing—but it's not mine to tell."

Her hopes for a few crumbs withered.

As her seagull friends landed on the railing of the deck, Charley crossed an ankle over his knee. "Well, well, well. So this is where you two have been hanging out."

Katherine looked at the birds. Back at Charley. "You know them?"

"We're old acquaintances. Katherine, meet Floyd and Gladys."

Her lips twitched. "You name seagulls?"

"These two are special. They met here in Hope Harbor."

She gave the birds another dubious once-over as she continued to chow down. They were all clones to her. "How do you tell one from another?"

"Floyd has a nick on the right side of his beak and a black spot on his head—and he's never without Gladys."

"If you say so." She opened the third taco. "They've been hanging around ever since I got here—and they always follow me down to the beach."

"Interesting." He swigged his water. "Any other regular visitors from the animal kingdom?"

90

"No—although I often see a harbor seal on my trips to the beach."

"A silver-white fellow with a doleful face and permanent indigestion?"

She chuckled at his description of the belching seal. "Yes. You know him too?"

"Casper and I go way back." He rose and walked over to the railing. The two seagulls scooted over to accommodate him but didn't fly off, as they did if she got too close. "Have you spotted a dolphin too?"

"No." She continued to plow through the last taco. "I thought they stayed far offshore and hung around in pods."

"Most do. A few wander in closer on occasion, if they have a compelling motivation." He scanned the ocean. "I see Casper down there, on the rocks." He continued to survey the water. Stopped. "And there's Trixie."

Katherine finished off the taco, wiped her hands on a napkin, and joined him at the railing. "Where?"

"She's bowing about a hundred feet offshore at two o'clock." He pointed.

As she followed his finger, a dolphin leapt out of the water in a graceful arc once . . . twice . . . again, her sleek body glistening in the sun. "Ohhh. That's beautiful!"

"The gang's all here."

At Charley's soft comment, she shifted her attention to him. "What?"

"Nothing. It's just comforting to be surrounded by friends." He inspected the table. "I think the tacos were a hit. Sorry I didn't supply dessert. I should have stopped at Sweet Dreams bakery and picked up a brownie for us to share."

"If you're in the mood for chocolate, I have another idea. Give me a sec." She hurried into the kitchen, put four blackberry truffles on a plate, and returned. "This should satisfy our sweet tooth. I made a batch for a . . . thank-you gift, and I had a few left over."

Charley remained standing but took one and bit into it. Chewed slowly. "Mmm. Another taste of heaven." He popped the rest into his mouth. "It's amazing how many small glimpses of paradise we can get here on earth if we take the time and make the effort to notice them." He indicated a second truffle. "May I?"

"Please."

He picked it up and started for the door. "I've delayed your beach walk long enough—and my muse is becoming impatient."

She trailed behind him through the house. "Thank you again for stopping by."

"My pleasure." He exited, but paused on the porch. "I hope you'll come to the truck for lunch soon. You won't have to worry about being recognized. LA is a different world—and removed from Hope Harbor by far more than distance."

"People here do watch TV, though."

"Your disguise will hold. Trust me."

There was no way he could guarantee that—yet he spoke with such conviction it was impossible to doubt him.

"I may venture out more often, now that we've talked. You were my biggest risk."

"Consider me a friend, not a risk. I won't give you away. And do come to town. Hope Harbor has much to offer." He pulled his Ducks cap out of his pocket and snugged it on. "See you soon." With a jaunty salute, he strolled over to the '57 silver Thunderbird he kept in mint condition. It didn't seem a day older than it had six years ago.

Neither did Charley.

As he drove away with a wave, she closed the door and wandered back through the house. For the rest of today, she'd stick close to her digs. Visit the beach as usual, perhaps read awhile.

But come tomorrow, if she still felt confident in Charley's assurance that her anonymity was secure, she might venture into town for shopping, another round of tacos—and a piece of that fudge cake Zach had mentioned at The Perfect Blend.

9

. . . .

"This is an impressive turnout." Stephanie surveyed the crowd gathered in the Grace Christian fellowship hall for the Helping Hands meeting.

Gentleman that her nephew was, Zach took her arm and guided her through the throng. "The people of this town never cease to inspire me. They're always willing to step in if there's a need. Not long ago, there was an outpouring of support for a refugee family from Syria."

"It must be wonderful to live in a place where everyone's so caring."

"That was one of the main draws." He lifted a hand in response to a wave from Frank, who wove through the crush toward them.

"Did you tell him I was coming?" Stephanie dropped her voice as she watched the silver-haired man approach. While Zach's part-time barista was technically a senior citizen, from his jaunty gait to his trim physique and sparkling eyes, he radiated youthful enthusiasm.

"Yes—and he was watching for us, in case you didn't notice."

Oh, she'd noticed.

Because she'd been watching for *him*.

"Welcome." The man joined them and held out his hand to her. "I'm glad you came."

As he gave her a warm smile, her pulse picked up.

Good grief.

What a ridiculous reaction for a sophisticated executive with six decades of living behind her.

She did her best to summon up the professional poise that was suddenly playing hard-to-get. "It seems like a worthwhile cause—and I didn't want Zach to miss it to keep me company. As I told him, I can take care of myself."

"I have no doubt of that. You strike me as a very capable woman."

Heat crept up her neck.

Mercy.

The man had an intensity and focus that could take a person's breath away—and a knack for infusing the most innocent phrase with deeper meaning.

A woman up front waved in Frank's direction, and Stephanie motioned toward her. "I think someone's trying to get your attention."

He gave her a quick glance. "I have to get back up there. Will you stay for a few minutes afterward?"

"Unless Zach has other plans."

"My Tuesday evening is all yours after the meeting." Zach seemed amused by their exchange.

"Wonderful. I'll talk to you both later. I think we're about ready to roll." Frank strode back toward the first row, where the board must be seated.

Stephanie commandeered Zach's arm before he could comment on her conversation with his employee. "It's filling up. Let's find seats."

He didn't protest.

As they claimed chairs, the director of Helping Hands took the mic, introduced himself, and called the meeting to order.

For the next fifteen minutes, she gave him her full attention as he filled the attendees in on the latest developments with the Hope House project—mostly because she couldn't see Frank from where they were sitting.

That would have been a major distraction.

But even if she'd been able to spot him, the subject of the meeting did interest her, and it wasn't difficult to tune in to Steven Roark.

"If we decide to proceed, there's money in the budget for a down payment, but we'll have to come up with the balance. Fundraisers are an option. We also want to be certain there are sufficient volunteers to handle necessary repairs and updates—which, after visiting the house, I can tell you are significant. Not much has been done in terms of remodeling for two decades, and maintenance issues have been neglected."

As he went on to list the more serious items that would have to be addressed, Stephanie leaned closer to Zach. "Does a town this size have people with the skills to deal with all of the issues he's identified?"

"You'd be surprised at the talent that comes out of the woodwork. But if there's anything someone here can't fix, we'll have to hire a pro."

"This is a big project for a small town to undertake."

"I know. That's why it may not fly."

She leaned back. Too bad if it didn't. The cause was more than worthwhile.

Steven looked up from his notes. "All of those nuts-and-bolts issues aside, the biggest challenge will be finding a couple to live in Hope House and care for the children. Adam's research indicates that can make or break a program. Adam . . . would you give us a few more details about what sort of qualifications and background we'd want?"

A dark-haired man with a lean, muscular build rose and took the mic, shifting his weight from one foot to the other as he pulled a piece of paper from his pocket. In light of his background, it must have taken a boatload of courage for him to stand up in front of a group like this—attesting to his passion for the cause.

"Thanks, Steven." He cleared his throat. "Finding houseparents isn't an immediate concern, since we have quite a bit to do first. In addition to the physical work on the house, there's a ton of paperwork to fill out for the state in order to get certified for the foster program. What we wanted to do tonight was lay out the parameters for the couple so if anyone is interested, or knows of someone who is, we can begin to consider candidates." He reshuffled his papers.

Stephanie leaned over to Zach again. "Do Adam and his wife have children?"

"Yes. One from her first marriage and one soon to arrive. Her mother also lives with them. Were you wondering if they'd be interested in the job?"

"Yes—but I'm guessing they already have their hands full."

"They do. Plus, his background could prevent them from being approved by the state."

"I suppose it's hard to escape the stigma of prison time."

"In terms of government agencies, yes—but it doesn't matter to anyone in town."

"Nice to hear. If a person has paid his debt to society, he ought to be able to live his life without constant reminders of his mistakes."

She settled back in her seat as Adam continued.

"The parents don't have to have college degrees, but we do want high school graduates. One of them should also have a steady job. A solid credit rating, and a demonstrated ability to manage a household budget, is important. Most of all, we want people who will love the children in their care as their own, with appropriate discipline and rules. A couple without children, or a couple with one or two children, would work. I think that's it."

Steven retook the microphone. "We have printed material on this subject for anyone who wants further information. You can see me or any of the board members afterward if you'd like a packet. Now let's open the floor to comments and questions."

Several people lined up at the mic situated in the center aisle, and as the session progressed, it seemed as if the town was behind the project 100 percent. A number of fundraising ideas were also put forward.

After the last person spoke, Steven confirmed Stephanie's conclusion.

"Given the large turnout tonight and the expressions of support, I believe this project may be one Helping Hands can tackle. But I'd ask anyone who's willing to pitch in to check out the lists of tasks in the back and sign up for any that match your expertise or interests. There's also a sheet for fundraising ideas. The board will review the volunteer response and determine whether it's sufficient to justify moving forward. Thank you all for coming."

A murmur of conversation broke out around them as people began to stand and meander toward the sign-up sheets.

Stephanie rose, as did Zach.

"You weren't bored, were you?" He edged back to let a woman exit the row.

"Not in the least. This was far more interesting than any of my meetings in the corporate world. Are you going to sign up?" She motioned toward the back of the room, where groups of people were already congregating around the worksheets.

"Yes. I'm not the handiest person, but I wield a mean paintbrush."

"Evening, Zach." A man in a clerical collar stopped beside them.

"Reverend Baker. Thanks for the loan of your fellowship hall tonight."

"It's always available for a worthy cause." He turned to her. "I don't believe we've met. Paul Baker. I'm the pastor here." He held out his hand.

Stephanie took it and introduced herself.

As another clergyman approached, Zach greeted him with a nod. "Nice to see you, Father Murphy. Since I've been tardy in the introduction department, let me take the lead on this one." He did the honors.

The jovial priest pumped her hand and offered a megawatt smile. "Welcome to Hope Harbor. I see you've already met my colleague here. A word of warning—if you spot him on the golf course, duck."

Her nephew covered a chuckle with a cough and offered an explanation. "Our two clerics have a standing Thursday golf date."

"And for the record, I'm currently up two games." The minister sent the padre a disgruntled look.

"Enjoy the lead while it lasts." The priest gave a dismissive wave. "Are you signing up for any of the work crews?"

"Yes. Are you?"

"Of course."

"Avoid anything to do with plumbing."

The priest huffed out a breath. "You're never going to let me forget my unfortunate blunder with your sink, are you?"

"No." Reverend Baker transferred his attention to her. "I had a minor leak he claimed he could fix. After he tinkered with it, I ended up with a small version of Niagara Falls in my kitchen— and a major plumbing bill."

"What I did should have worked. It was how I fixed the leak in the rectory."

"That must have been blind luck rather than expertise. Why don't you see if they're assembling a landscaping crew?"

"That's a great idea," Zach chimed in. "Father Murphy created a beautiful meditation garden behind St. Francis."

"Thank you for the compliment." The priest gave a slight bow. "I'll see if those skills are on the list. I also want to add an idea for a fundraiser. I was thinking we could hold a Taste of Hope Harbor gathering, like we did to welcome our refugee family, except charge for tickets and add a raffle."

"Seeing how you filch our donuts after Sunday service, why am I not surprised you proposed a food-related event?" Reverend Baker surveyed the padre's slightly thick midsection—but his eyes were twinkling.

Father Murphy sniffed. "I only eat your donuts if we have business to discuss on Sunday. The St. Francis homemade version is far superior. Getting back to the subject at hand—what do you think of my idea?"

"It has possibilities—but this project can't live on bread alone."

The priest groaned. "Stop with the biblical analogies."

"Just saying. It will take more than a Taste of Hope Harbor event to fund this project."

"I agree—but it would give us an opportunity to eat our food with gladness, for God approves of what we're doing."

Reverend Baker squinted at him. "That phrasing is familiar . . . but I can't place it."

"Ha. Gotcha." The priest grinned and gave the minister a good-natured elbow nudge. "It's from Ecclesiastes." He licked his index finger and drew a swipe in the air.

Stephanie slanted a glance at Zach. Her nephew was obviously amused by the amiable jibing of the town clerics—and she had to admit it *was* a hoot.

In fact, it had been entertaining enough to make her momentarily forget that Frank had asked them to wait after the meeting.

Until she spotted Zach's part-time employee winding through the crowd in their direction.

Her lungs lost their rhythm again—and she curbed an eye roll.

You'd think she was a teen in the throes of her first crush—not that she knew much about teenage romance. Her father's high academic expectations had ensured she'd been a nose-to-the-grindstone, head-in-the-books kind of girl.

"Thanks for waiting." Frank joined them.

"Our clerics and I are going to check out the sign-up sheets." Zach hooked a thumb toward the back of the room.

"Don't let me delay you. The more people who volunteer, the higher the likelihood this project will get off the ground."

"I'll be back in a few minutes." Zach touched her arm.

"No hurry on my end. I'm not the one who has to get up early for a job tomorrow."

"Neither does Frank. He's off on Wednesdays." Grinning, Zach fell in behind the still-bantering clerics. "In fact, if you two want to extend the evening, feel free. I can find my way home alone."

Stephanie stifled a groan.

She was going to have to have a serious talk later with her nephew.

"Would you like a cup of coffee?" Frank indicated a table off to the side. "It won't come close to The Perfect Blend, but if you're in the mood for java, it's decent."

"No, thanks. All coffee is off-limits for me this late in the evening—decaf included."

"Shall we sit while we wait for Zach?"

Shoot.

Frank didn't appear inclined to pick up on his employer's less-than-subtle hint.

She refused to let her lips droop. "Why not?" After they claimed adjacent chairs, she angled toward him. "Zach tells me you're retired from the postal service."

"Yes. Up in Coos Bay. That's where my wife grew up. I didn't have any family of my own, so living there was fine with me. A job with the postal service wasn't the most exciting career, but it was steady and gave us security."

"Do you miss it?"

"No—but I miss her." A shadow darkened his irises. "She passed away three years ago."

"Zach mentioned that. I'm sorry. Do you have any other family?"

"No. We were never blessed with children, and her brother passed on two years ago. He never married."

So Frank was even more alone than she was.

"That has to be hard."

"Some days have been harder than others—but after I moved here and started working for Zach, I turned a corner. Life's different now, but Hope Harbor is a wonderful place and Zach's a terrific boss."

"He's also a fine nephew. We haven't stayed in close touch—but I intend to remedy that in my retirement."

"Tell me about your job."

She gave him a brief overview of her career, touching on her extensive travel around the globe. "As I told someone recently, though, it's more glamorous in the telling than in reality."

"I expect living out of a suitcase would get old—but you've been to an impressive list of places."

"Most of which I saw only through the windows of a taxi en route to and from meetings."

"Bummer."

"Amen to that. Have you traveled much?"

"My wife and I liked to camp, and we hit most of the national parks in the western half of the country."

She tipped her head. "You know . . . for all my travels, I've never been to a national park."

"I bet you've never camped either."

"I did once, back in Girl Scouts. Sad to say, it wasn't a positive experience. I got poison ivy and chigger bites."

He winced. "Not fun. In fact, those less-than-pleasant aspects of camping helped convince my wife and me to graduate to B&Bs."

"That would be more my style."

Zach rejoined them, and Frank stood. She followed suit.

"Sorry to interrupt, but I'm ready to call it a day." He waited, as if he expected Frank to offer her a lift so they could continue their chat.

When the silence stretched too long, she quashed her foolish disappointment and summoned up a cheery smile. "I'm all set. Frank, it was a pleasure talking with you." She held out her hand.

He took it in a firm grip—and held on a fraction of a second longer than protocol demanded.

Suggesting he didn't want their evening to end either.

Yet he did nothing to prolong it.

"I enjoyed our conversation too." He released her hand. "See you Thursday, Zach."

With that he hastened toward the door.

Zach frowned after him. "I could have sworn he'd offer to drive you home."

"Your romantic inclinations are working overtime." She kept her tone cheerful as she tucked her arm in his. "Shall we?"

Without further comment, he guided her through the crowd and out to the car.

During the ride home, she kept the conversation focused on the meeting and the humorous exchange between the clerics—but once she was behind the closed door of her room, she sank onto the side of the bed. Exhaled.

What a strange twist this trip had taken.

She'd come here with two goals—renew her acquaintance with her nephew and begin to acclimate to her retiree status.

She had *not* expected to meet an attractive, available man who intrigued her.

How could this happen now, after she'd long ago sacrificed the possibility of marriage and family on the altar of corporate success?

With a sigh, she fell back onto the bed and stared at the ceiling, hugging a decorative pillow to her chest.

She did *not* need this sort of complication at this stage of her life.

Nor was she in the market for romance. Not after her deliberate and reasoned decision decades ago to forgo love as she climbed the corporate ladder.

Women might talk about having it all, but theory didn't translate very well to reality. Yes, a woman could have it all . . . but not all at the same time. Trying to juggle too many balls inevitably meant some got dropped and something—or someone—suffered. With a job that demanded constant travel and long hours, how could she have given adequate attention to a husband and children?

The answer, for her, had been simple. She couldn't. So she'd closed the door to a family—and motherhood. It had been the hardest decision she'd ever faced.

And it was too late to rethink it now.

Besides, she was used to living alone, being independent. The idea of doing as she pleased, when she pleased, in her postcareer life was appealing. Adding another person to the mix would complicate the carefree existence she'd envisioned.

But won't it be lonely, Stephanie?

She sat back up and flung the pillow against the headboard.

No!

It wouldn't be.

She wouldn't *let* it be.

Without a grueling travel schedule and long hours at the office, she'd be able to join clubs. Make friends. Volunteer. There was an abundance of opportunities like that back in New York.

Her life would be full and rich.

And it wasn't as if there was any reason to change her plans. Despite the gleam of interest in Frank's eyes during their first encounter yesterday—and the conversation he'd initiated tonight—he hadn't tried to extend their evening.

Perhaps he'd decided it wasn't worth getting to know a woman who would soon be gone.

Or he may have concluded that the memories of his cherished wife were sufficient to sustain him.

Whatever had caused him to back off, it was for the best. A relationship wasn't in her plans. Especially one here, across the country from the apartment she called home.

Suddenly weary, she rose to draw the curtains—pausing to take in the romantic crescent moon that hung in the sky outside her window.

And to tamp down the wistful, unbidden surge of longing that had no place in the future she'd plotted out.

10

Frank had been acting weird all day.

Adding a drizzle of caramel to a whipped caramel macchiato, Zach gave his barista a surreptitious scan.

While it was impossible to fault the man's diligent work or his cheery demeanor with customers, he'd been avoiding their usual small talk since he'd arrived at six thirty on this Thursday morning.

Even today's humorous saying on the board out front hadn't drawn more than a quick comment.

Zach handed over the drink, followed the customer to the door, and locked up for the day.

Now that they were alone and in cleanup mode, maybe he could get to the bottom of the man's unusual reticence.

"Busy day." He strolled back to the counter and began wrapping up the remaining pastry items.

"Yep." Frank vanished into the back room.

Zach continued the rote shutdown routine as the older man returned with a mop and began swabbing the floor.

In silence.

Oh, brother.

If Frank's mood had anything to do with Stephanie—as was likely the case—it would be wise to clear the air. In hindsight, he may have been a tad obvious in his attempt to set the two of them up the night of the Hope House meeting . . . as his aunt had indicated in no uncertain terms later.

But hey—his intentions had been good.

He circled the counter and began straightening chairs. "Any news on the Hope House project?" Best to break the ice with a neutral subject.

"The board's meeting again tonight. Steven says the number of people who signed up to help is impressive, and several viable fundraising ideas were suggested. I'm assuming we'll vote to proceed. Closing on the house should be simple, so we can dive into the work fast. In fact, the owner said as soon as we reach a verbal agreement, he'll give us authority to start." He paused. "I saw your name on the painting crew volunteer sheet."

"It was the task that required the least training or skill—not to offend professional painters. But messing up edging is less dangerous than putting two incompatible electrical wires together."

"I hear you—and painting is fine. We can use all the hands we can get on every job."

Zach returned to the counter to retrieve a damp rag—and eased into the subject that was on his mind. "Aunt Stephanie wants to volunteer too if we get underway while she's here."

That earned him an interested glance. "For real? I got the feeling she wasn't the type who'd want to get her hands dirty."

He stared at Frank. "Why would you think that?"

The man shrugged and went back to mopping. "She reeks of polish and sophistication. Dresses stylish too. I expect a woman who had such a high-level job would rather pay someone to do messy chores while she gets a manicure. Not that there's anything wrong with that."

But it wasn't the type of lifestyle Frank was used to.

Based on everything he'd shared about his marriage, he and

his wife had always saved their pennies, were big into DIY, and preferred simple pleasures.

Stephanie probably ate in more five-star restaurants every year than Frank and his wife had dined at in their entire life—a conclusion the former postal worker had no doubt reached too.

That didn't mean his aunt necessarily lived the high life off the job, however. From what his dad had said about her through the years, along with comments she'd made during their infrequent contact, she was down-to-earth and low-key.

A piece of information Frank ought to be privy to before jumping to too many conclusions.

"From what I know about her, manicures aren't her top priority." Frank kept mopping. "Still, she's a classy lady."

In other words, he didn't think a career postman from Coos Bay and a jet-setting senior executive had enough in common to have any potential as a couple.

That was baloney—and unless his instincts were failing him, Aunt Stephanie would be the first to agree.

Zach scrubbed at a glob of chocolate icing that had hardened on the tabletop. "So? You're a classy guy."

After a moment, Frank stopped mopping. "Thanks for saying that—but between the two of us, I think your aunt is out of my league. Can you imagine someone like her being content in a place like this?"

"Yeah. I can." He responded without hesitation. "I have a similar background—and I chose to live here." While he hadn't shared with Frank all the circumstances that had led to his new life, the fact that he'd taken up residence in Hope Harbor ought to be sufficient to give the man food for thought.

"You're an exception. Most people who've become accustomed to first-class treatment end up liking the high life." He went back to swabbing. "Besides, she won't be here long. What's the point of getting too friendly?"

Hard to argue with the man's logic. It was similar to the boat he was in with Kat.

"She hasn't said how long she's going to stay."

"Not long enough for anything serious to develop—if that was even in the cards." Frank put more muscle into his mopping.

He could press the issue—but this wasn't his battle to fight. Other than sharing the highlights of this conversation with his aunt, he was bowing out. Matchmaking obviously wasn't his forte . . . for Frank or himself.

Which brought him back to Kat.

He hadn't seen her since she'd delivered the truffles Monday night—but returning the plate would give him an excuse to renew their acquaintance . . . if he wanted to.

Yet Frank was right.

Like his aunt, Kat hadn't come here with any intention of staying. At least he knew Stephanie's background—and given sufficient encouragement, it was possible she'd trade her New York apartment for small-town digs.

Kat, on the other hand, remained a mystery.

He went to work on another spot on the table.

Whatever life his mysterious neighbor had left behind was waiting for her—and whatever challenges she faced were formidable. That was clear not from anything she'd said, but from her facial expressions, body language, and tone of voice.

While there was nothing tying his aunt to New York, it was obvious Kat's links to her old life were strong—and would be difficult to break.

He sighed and wandered back to the counter.

The truth was, Frank had a much better chance of wooing Stephanie than he had of winning Kat's trust, let alone her heart.

In light of that reality, it might be best to leave the truffle plate at her door with a note of thanks.

He'd have to noodle on that option.

In the meantime, there was only one antidote for the depressing cloud that had suddenly darkened his day.

As soon as they finished cleaning up and he locked the door

behind them, he'd head straight for Charley's—and an order of fish tacos with a side of the man's boundless good cheer.

Man, those tacos smelled delicious.

Katherine sniffed as the aroma from Charley's stand wafted toward the parking spot she'd claimed five minutes ago and infiltrated her car.

She may not have had the courage to tackle The Perfect Blend on this foray to town, but Charley's felt safe—especially after the taco-making artist had assured her that her disguise would hold.

Fortunately, few people were about—and the empty bench on the wharf would be the perfect spot to enjoy the view . . . and her late lunch.

She slid from behind the wheel but lingered by the car as Charley handed over an order to a family group.

The instant the coast was clear, she hurried toward the stand.

His face lit up as she approached. "Well, look who decided to pay me a visit."

"Until you brought me lunch earlier this week, I'd forgotten how much I used to crave your tacos after I went back to LA."

"And here I thought my winning personality had lured you back." He grinned, opened a cooler behind him, and removed a few fish fillets.

"That too. What fish are you cooking today?"

"Grouper." He set the fillets on the grill and began chopping cilantro. "I'm still thinking about those blackberry truffles you gave me on Tuesday. They were magnifico." He gathered the fingers of his free hand and kissed them. "Your talent extends beyond the screen."

"Thank you. Making chocolate is fun."

"And acting isn't?"

"Um . . . yeah. Of course it's fun."

Or it had been, once upon a time. Before all the craziness began to suck the joy out of performing. Before everyone wanted a piece of her. Before fame became a carrot that enticed her to do things she later lamented.

Before someone died.

Her stomach clenched.

The truth was, acting had been the most fun back in college, on a small stage with a live audience, before money and power trips and publicity stunts were involved. When she did it out of love.

But perhaps that was true of any passion.

Charley pulled out three corn tortillas and set them on the grill. Flipped the fish. "You seem sad, my friend."

His comment was more invitation than statement. If she wanted to talk, he'd listen.

Yet what was there to say—except admit the terrifying possibility that the dream she'd fought so hard to achieve may have been the wrong one?

And she wasn't anywhere near ready to do that.

"More like confused." She forced up the corners of her lips and tapped the "Cash Only" sign taped on the window. "I see you haven't yet entered the electronic age. No one pays with actual money anymore, you know."

"More's the pity." He cut up a lime and diced a wedge of red onion, throwing the latter onto a griddle as he spoke. "People have much greater appreciation for what they buy if they shell out hard cash—and it also helps them stay out of debt. Not that an order of tacos would break the bank."

She pulled out her wallet. "Your tacos would be a bargain at any price."

"Thank you. Are you going to eat here on the wharf?"

"That's my plan." She handed over a bill and motioned toward the empty bench. "That has my name on it."

"Best seat in the house—and Floyd and Gladys will keep you

company." He began assembling the tacos as two gulls landed with a flutter of wings a few yards away.

Katherine peered at them. Did one have a nick on its beak? Impossible to tell from this distance. Charley either had much keener vision than she did or he was guessing.

Didn't matter. They'd probably fly off in a minute anyway.

"Thanks for the tacos." She took the brown bag he held out.

"Enjoy."

"Goes without saying." She pocketed the change he gave her.

"Don't be a stranger."

"I won't. These are addictive—in a healthy way."

She strode toward the bench, past the gulls.

Huh.

Her step slowed.

One of them *did* have a dark spot on top of its head—and was that a chip on its beak?

She leaned closer to examine it.

Yeah, it was.

But . . . how could Charley have spotted those distinguishing characteristics from yards away?

Gauging the distance over her shoulder, she furrowed her brow. No one had vision that keen—did they?

Charley, however, was a man of many talents—so who knew?

She continued toward the bench . . . and the two gulls traipsed after her. Apparently she'd been adopted by the taco chef's avian friends.

As she settled onto the seat and opened the bag, the two birds cuddled up on the ground a few feet away. One of them cackled.

It sounded almost like a laugh.

How silly was that? Seagulls didn't laugh.

But they were cute . . . and they were company.

Not as much company as her neighbor would have been—but they didn't ask any questions either.

Meaning this little threesome was a whole lot safer than a two-some with a certain coffee shop owner.

Was that Kat sitting on one of the benches by the harbor?

Zach pulled up short a few yards from Charley's stand, his attention riveted on the woman with two seagulls at her feet.

She was angled away, and the hair falling over her cheek hid her features . . . but it looked like her.

"Afternoon, Zach."

At Charley's greeting, he continued toward the stand. "Hi, Charley."

"This must be the day for my Blackberry Beach neighbors to want tacos for lunch."

He stopped at the counter and gave the man his full attention. "Is that Kat?"

"None other."

So the mystery lady had emerged from her cave.

"How long has she been there?"

"Oh, five minutes, I'd say. I saw you coming and got your order rolling." He pivoted to remove the fish fillets from the grill and began assembling and wrapping the tacos. "You could join her. There's room on the bench."

"I don't know." He studied her again. "She likes her privacy."

"Privacy has its pluses—but too much solitude can get lonely."

She leaned down to share a bite of her taco with one of the two birds.

"She doesn't have to be lonely. Hope Harbor is a welcoming place."

"Maybe that's why she came into town today. For company." Charley finished bagging the order and set it on the counter, along with a bottle of water.

Zach dug out his wallet and handed over a few bills. "She won't meet anyone sitting by herself on the wharf."

"Unless someone takes the initiative and approaches *her*."

"If you're implying that someone could be me—we're already acquainted." He picked up the bag. "And she hasn't been any too eager to get *better* acquainted."

"No?" Charley swiped the immaculate counter with a rag. "When I dropped off an order of tacos at her house earlier this week, I got the impression she'd stopped in at your place."

"You went to her house?" Zach squinted at the man.

"Why not? After you told me we were neighbors, I thought it would be a sociable gesture."

"And she mentioned me?"

"Not directly. But she offered me a couple of blackberry truffles and said they were left over from a batch she made as a thank-you gift. If she hasn't ventured out much, who else could they be for but her neighbor?"

That felt like a stretch of logic—but what did it matter? The truth was, the temptation to join her was strong, with or without Charley's prodding.

And what could it hurt to mosey over there and say hello? She'd either brush him off or invite him to join her.

If she happened to choose the second option, how risky could it be to have lunch together on a park bench in a public place?

Plus, it beat eating alone. With Stephanie up in Coos Bay exploring today, the house would feel empty without his aunt's vivacious presence.

"I suppose I could give it a shot."

Charley dipped his chin in approval. "Wise decision. He who hesitates and all that."

Squeezing his fingers around the top of the bag, Zach left the stand behind and approached the bench, Charley's last comment looping through his mind.

That old adage could work the opposite way too.

You could also lose if you moved too fast. People could get hurt.

Who knew which was best for him and Kat?

He could only hope he didn't live to regret invading his reclusive neighbor's space yet again.

11

. . . .

"May I join you?"

At the familiar baritone voice, Katherine sucked in a breath, dropped the piece of fish she'd leaned down to give the gulls, and jerked upright.

Zach stood six feet away, holding a brown bag similar to hers.

Despite Charley's assurance that no one in town would see through her disguise, her heart stuttered—although that reaction could have more to do with unruly hormones than the fear of being unmasked.

Short of being rude, however, how could she refuse his request? She didn't own the bench, and there was ample room for two.

In response, she adjusted her sunglasses and scooted to the far end, pulling her bag along with her.

As if to accommodate the new addition to their trio, the two seagulls stood, waddled a few feet away, and snuggled up together on the sidewalk, keeping the human couple under surveillance.

Zach sat, put the water next to him, and opened his bag. "We finished your blackberry truffles yesterday. They were fantastic."

"I'm glad you enjoyed them."

"Devoured is more like it." He uncapped his water. "By the way, that piece of fudge cake is waiting for you at The Perfect Blend whenever you want to claim it—no strings attached and no repayment necessary. You can't come to Hope Harbor and not sample Eleanor Cooper's claim to fame."

She collected several pieces of purple cabbage that had spilled from her taco. "As a matter of fact, I almost came today—but I needed lunch more than cake." Plus, she'd chickened out.

"Yeah?" He dived into his first taco. "We could swing by for dessert after we finish here."

Her pulse picked up. "Aren't you closed in the afternoon?"

"Yes—but I have the keys. One of the perks of being the owner." He shot her a grin.

An intimate tea—or coffee—for two in his shuttered shop?

A delicious tingle zipped through her.

Get a grip, Katherine. Don't put yourself at risk. Keep your distance.

Excellent advice.

She quashed the zing of attraction and nibbled at her second taco. "I don't eat many sweets, as a rule."

"I remember—but I thought you made exceptions for special occasions."

The endearing dimple in his cheek was hard to resist. "What occasion would we be celebrating?"

"National spumoni day."

A laugh bubbled up inside her. Spilled out. "Seriously?"

"Scout's honor." He raised his hand.

"How do you know that?"

"I'm a font of useless information. Comes from having to find a new quote every day for the board in front of the store."

"I noticed that. It's a clever idea."

"The rest of the town agrees with you. I've had people tell me they drive by just to read the quote. I started doing it for fun, but now I'm stuck because everyone expects it."

She poked a piece of jalapeño back into her taco, her mirth fading. "I know all about how expectations can turn something that was once fun into a chore."

He stopping eating and cocked his head at her.

Too much information, Katherine.

Calling up a smile, she redirected the conversation before he could ask any questions. "What does national spumoni day have to do with fudge cake?"

He hesitated, as if he was considering whether to return to her previous comment. In the end, though, he followed her lead. "I don't have spumoni, but the fudge cake is a worthy substitute. It isn't in the same league as your truffles—not that I'd ever share that with Eleanor—but as chocolate cake goes, it can't be beat. I happened to have two pieces left today."

The appeal of sharing dessert with this man in his cozy shop, where they'd have no interruptions, continued to mushroom.

Stall, Katherine. Give yourself a few minutes to summon up the willpower to decline the invitation.

"I appreciate the offer, but why don't we wait until we're done to decide? The tacos are filling."

"True—but I can always find room for dessert. Why don't you tell me about making chocolate while we eat?"

She slanted him a look. Was his interest genuine—or was he merely trying to keep the conversational ball in the air?

"I wouldn't ask if I wasn't interested." He answered as if he'd read her mind, his tone serious as he spoke around a mouthful of taco.

"It's a hobby." She lifted her shoulders. "You like to cook, I like to make chocolate."

He arched an eyebrow. "A complementary skill set."

She had no idea what he meant by that—and she wasn't about to ask.

Instead, she gave him a brief primer on the basics of chocolate making.

Other than asking a few astute questions, he listened without interrupting until she finished.

"I'm impressed. The tempering step seems tricky." He stuffed the wrapping from his last taco into the bag. "How did you learn all that stuff?"

She washed down a bite of her second taco with a swig of water. "I've read a ton about it and taken a number of classes—both hands-on and online. Working with chocolate is actually quite challenging. Temperature, humidity, and a host of other variables can affect the outcome. I've watched hours of videos, practiced a lot, and signed up for a handful of seminars conducted by master chocolatiers during my work breaks. Those were amazing."

"I can tell. I can't see much of your face behind those glasses, but energy is crackling off you, your voice is animated, and I have a feeling your eyes are lit up." He smiled at her.

Katherine processed Zach's comment as she broke off a piece of fish and tossed it to the birds.

He was right about her enthusiasm. Chocolate making tapped into her energy and creativity far more than acting did these days.

Another worrisome reality to ponder later, in the quiet of Blackberry Beach.

Floyd picked up the morsel of fish, used his beak to break it apart, and pushed half toward Gladys.

Katherine did a double take. "That's unusual. In the animal kingdom, it's usually first come, first served."

"True—but seagulls mate for life. Maybe they take care of each other."

Like spouses did in a loving marriage.

Her lips curved up. "Whatever the motivation, it's sweet."

Zach downed the last of his water. "Speaking of sweet . . . did you save any room for fudge cake?"

She wiped her hands on a paper napkin and inspected the third taco she hadn't yet unwrapped. If she ate it, she'd be full—and have a perfect excuse to pass on Zach's invitation.

But despite the danger signal beeping in her subconscious, she wanted to spend another hour . . . or two . . . or several . . . in this man's company—even if she'd have to ditch her concealing sunglasses in the shop.

Zach had seen her without them, though. If he hadn't recognized her by now, there wasn't much risk in extending their impromptu lunch—especially in an empty coffee shop, where no one else would see her.

And didn't she deserve a few minutes of human companionship after the hermit-like existence she'd been living during most of her visit?

You're justifying, Katherine.

Tuning out the silent warning, she wadded her napkin into a tight ball and took the plunge. "If I save this one for later"—she tapped the bundle—"I think I can manage a piece of cake."

"You won't be sorry. I'll put your leftovers in the fridge at The Perfect Blend while we have dessert." He stood at once, as if he was afraid she'd have second thoughts and back out.

Smart man.

Doubts were already assailing her.

But she didn't have to stay long . . . and in the quiet of the coffee shop, with a few careful queries, perhaps she could find out the story behind Charley's cryptic comment about how Zach had changed course midstream—and glean a few insights that could apply to her own situation.

She tucked her last taco back in the bag and fell into step beside him, glancing at the white truck as they walked toward Dockside Drive.

Charley gave her a thumbs-up.

That was encouraging.

Yet as Zach took her arm while they crossed the street, she hoped she didn't live to rue this impromptu date with the man who'd been starring in her dreams since the day they'd met.

"Welcome back to The Perfect Blend." Zach twisted the key in the lock, pushed the door open, and eased aside to let Kat enter.

She slipped past him but hovered near the threshold. As if she was thinking about bolting.

He could relate.

This detour for dessert might not be wise, for all the reasons he'd already identified—and Kat no doubt had a list of similar concerns.

But they were here, and he owed her a piece of cake.

Relocking the door, he called up a smile. "Let me get the lights. Hang tight for a minute."

She waited while he crossed the room and flipped the switch, fingers crimping the top of the bag containing her remaining taco.

Zach motioned toward a booth for two tucked into the back corner that would shield them from the view of curious passersby. "Why don't you have a seat while I get the cake and put your taco on ice?"

"Okay." She met him halfway across the shop and handed over the bag.

The top was damp.

She was as uptight as he'd been during the weeks he'd been wrestling with the decision about whether to leave his old life behind.

"Hey." He gentled his tone and touched her shoulder. "I promise not to bite."

"Sorry." She rubbed her palms down her leggings. "I'm a little spooked about venturing out in public."

She didn't say why.

He didn't ask.

"No one can see us back there."

"I realize that—and I appreciate it."

119

"I know you like skinny vanilla lattes, but may I recommend straight coffee with the cake? You don't want to mask the flavor."

Forehead wrinkling, she scanned the equipment behind the counter. "Isn't everything cleaned up and shut down?"

"The commercial side is—but I keep a small French press in the back so I can get my java fix while I'm here working on the books in the office."

"In that case, straight coffee would be fine."

"Have a seat and I'll be with you in a few minutes."

As she wandered toward the booth, he ducked into the back room, stowed her taco in the fridge, and pulled out the cake. A quick zap in the microwave would bring the slices back to room temperature pronto.

In five minutes, the coffee was brewed and their dessert was plated and ready to serve.

After putting everything on a tray, he returned to the public area.

Instead of hiding in the booth, as he'd expected, Kat was examining one of the poster-sized photos.

She swung toward him as he entered, waving a hand over the gallery of close-up nature shots on the walls—the beak of a bird pecking through an egg, tips of daffodil leaves pushing through the snow, a tiny plant growing in the crack of a boulder and beating the odds of survival despite the adverse environment . . . and a half dozen others. "These are wonderful. I noticed them on my previous visits. They're so . . . hope filled."

"That's why I put them up. They add to the feel-good vibe of the shop." He continued to their booth and unloaded the tray.

She followed him over. "Did you take them?"

"No." He motioned her toward the bench seat, waited until she slid in, and claimed the opposite side. "My brother did."

"He's a very talented photographer." Kat's inquisitive blue eyes studied him.

"Yeah." That response was sufficient—yet more tumbled out. "He was."

Zach frowned.

Where had *that* come from?

He didn't talk about Josh with friends, let alone strangers. Rehashing the trauma stirred up too many painful memories.

"Was?"

Of course Kat would follow up on the past tense.

He shifted in his seat.

Now that she'd finally ditched her sunglasses, he almost wished she hadn't. Under her empathetic gaze, it was harder to sidestep her question.

Why not dole out a few facts?

"He died three years ago."

Shock flattened her features. "I'm so sorry. Was it an accident?"

"No." He sipped his coffee, taking care not to scald his tongue. "He had pancreatic cancer. Since that tends to be an older person's disease, it took longer than usual to diagnose his condition. But the survival rate is dismal anyway. He was gone in five months." The last two words rasped, and he cleared his throat.

Some of the color drained from her face. "I don't know what to say . . . except how tragic and awful that had to be—for him and your family."

"It was. It is." He swallowed. "He was only twenty-nine—two years younger than me."

She moved her cake aside, folded her hands on the table, and leaned closer, radiating compassion. "Would you tell me about him?"

Stomach clenching, he took another slug of coffee and forced himself to keep breathing.

No one had ever asked him to talk about Josh. The few people he'd spoken to about his brother had respected his back-off signals and dropped the subject after expressing their condolences.

Why hadn't Kat?

Except . . . maybe he hadn't sent those signals to her. Instead, his manner may have invited discussion.

If so, it hadn't been a conscious decision.

But why not follow through? Tell her a bit more. Bottling up all the hurt wasn't helping him heal. And talking about Josh, sharing the qualities that had made him special, could also help keep his brother's memory alive.

It was worth a try.

Besides, if he got cold feet midstream, he could always shut down.

As the silence lengthened, Kat edged back a hair. "Sorry. I didn't mean to barge into personal territory—but the images captivated me, and I was curious about the man who created them."

"It's okay. I don't talk about Josh often, but tell me what you'd like to know."

She hesitated for a fraction of a second . . . then picked up her mug. "Was photography his business or a hobby?"

"Hobby. He used the images to illustrate a weekly blog he wrote. But he was beginning to submit his work for publication and he'd had a few strong nibbles."

"I have to believe he could have built a career doing this."

"I do too—although I think he was content to keep it as a hobby. He always said there's a certain purity about things you do solely for love. Once money enters the picture, the complexion changes."

A shadow flitted across her face. "Have you found that to be true with The Perfect Blend?"

"No . . . but I had a comfortable financial cushion going in. This business was never about money."

"I can see where that would make a difference." She sipped her coffee. "What did your brother do for a living?"

"Freelance web work. He had enough clients to put food on the table and keep a roof over his head, and he was content with that. Josh never wanted to be part of the rat race or claw his way to the top of the corporate world. His priority was people, travel, photography, writing—and space to breathe."

"Seems like a healthy attitude to me."

"Looking back, I agree—but at the time we clashed philosophi-cally. Neither I nor my dad could understand why he lacked ambi-tion in the traditional sense. In fact, he and my dad had a serious falling-out over it."

As that admission slipped out, he throttled a groan. That was another can of worms he hadn't intended to open.

What was with his sudden case of motormouth?

Twin furrows appeared on Kat's brow. "Did they mend their rift?"

A logical question—and he owed her an answer, after introduc-ing the subject.

"Yes—but Dad never did understand how Josh could be con-tent living a bare-bones existence instead of using his engineering degree to earn a decent income. He was supersmart and aced all his college courses, but his heart was never in engineering. The degree was a concession to Dad. He had a different vision for his life—and after graduation he had the courage to pursue it."

"Despite family opposition and pressure."

"Yes."

"That took guts."

"Yes, it did." As he'd later learned firsthand.

"Were the two of you close?"

"As close as two brothers on different tracks can be."

"Yet you went rogue too."

"Yes—but it took me much longer to see the light. In the begin-ning, I was as driven as my dad. After college, I joined an investment firm in Chicago, where I discovered I had a knack for brokering mergers and acquisitions. I was on the fast track and successful beyond my wildest dreams by the age of thirty."

"Wow." She leaned back in the booth, cradling her mug in her hands. "A coffee shop in Hope Harbor is one-eighty from that world of movers and shakers."

"True—but the changes have all been positive. Josh had always encouraged me to slow down and smell the roses, but I brushed him off . . . until he died. That was a game changer."

"Death can definitely alter your perspective." Her soft comment was filled with angst and heartache.

There was a story there—and he wanted to hear it.

But pushing would be a mistake. All he could do was share his own history and hope she'd reciprocate.

"After he died, I read his blog. Looked through his photos. Both were a reflection of what he'd always believed—that beauty and hope can be found everywhere, even in the smallest places people tend to overlook. He noticed—and appreciated—everything." Zach stared into the dark depths of his coffee. "In hindsight, it almost seems as if he sensed his time here was limited and was determined to suck every drop of joy from every single moment."

Her features softened. "Not a bad philosophy, no matter how long your life."

"I agree. That's why I decided to leave the fast track behind and pursue my dream of running a coffee shop somewhere near the ocean. I did my homework, worked at a small coffee chain to learn the business from the ground up, and opened The Perfect Blend."

The corners of her lips tipped up. "Now I see the deeper meaning behind the name. You've found a life that gives you a perfect balance between work and leisure."

"Bingo."

"How did you end up in Hope Harbor?"

"Josh lived in Oregon, and several years ago he suggested we meet here for a short vacation after I finished a business trip in San Francisco. Three days in, I got called back to Chicago to handle an emergency. But I had fond memories of this place and came back to check it out when I was trying to decide where to relocate. It didn't take me long to realize how special Hope Harbor is."

"I feel the same way. That's why I came back too."

"You've been here before?" That was news.

"I spent several weeks in the area once for work."

He waited, but she didn't offer more.

"Where is home now?"

Instead of dodging the question as he'd half expected, she surprised him by answering. "LA." But then she put the spotlight back on him. "I expect your dad was disappointed about your decision to leave the rat race behind."

A muscle ticced in his cheek. "That's an understatement. We rarely communicate these days."

"I'm sorry."

He gave a stiff shrug. "I've learned to cope. I'm sure he has too. What about you? Any close family connections?" Other than telling him she had no siblings, she'd evaded that question the day he'd delivered the cobbler—but it didn't hurt to try again.

"No. My mom died when I was a freshman in college."

No mention of her father—which must mean the man was out of the picture.

Sad.

While he and his dad were on the outs, in a pinch the older man would come to his assistance.

He also had his aunt—and after renewing their acquaintance, he didn't intend to let her be a stranger going forward.

Unless his instincts were failing him, the woman sitting across from him had no family connections at all.

But friends could fill the gap—and he'd be happy to step into the latter category, if she gave him the tiniest opening.

He broached that subject with caution. "It's tough not to have much family—but a close-knit community helps . . . or a group of friends."

"True friends aren't easy to come by—and it can be hard to distinguish sincerity from selfishness." She forked a bite of cake with more force than necessary, put it in her mouth, and chewed. "Mmm. You weren't exaggerating. This is to die for."

He tamped down a surge of frustration.

The personal discussion was over.

Whatever her issues . . . however much she might need a friend . . . Kat wasn't taking the hand he was extending, despite his repeated attempts to breach the wall Charley had mentioned and his own soul-baring today.

It could be time to throw in the towel.

He followed her breezy conversational lead as they ate their cake and drank their coffee, and then he walked her to the wharf, said good-bye, and watched her drive away.

As her car turned the corner and disappeared from view, he shoved his hands in his pockets and wandered back toward the shop to fetch his Jeep.

He ought to forget about Kat Morgan—or whatever her name was. Instead of wasting his energies on a woman who appeared to have zero interest in the kind of mutual sharing necessary to lay the groundwork for a relationship of any kind, he should focus on finding female companionship in more appropriate places. Like a reputable dating site. Lots of people paired up through—

"Zach! Hold up a minute."

As Charley's voice rang across the wharf, he swiveled around.

The man hurried toward him. "I'm glad I caught you. Could you do me a favor?"

"Sure."

"I miscalculated with Kat's taco order. I gave her change for a ten instead of a twenty. I'm surprised she didn't notice. Since you live next door, I wondered if you'd mind passing this on." He held up a flat, taped-up packet made from the white butcher paper he used for tacos, a dollar amount written on the outside.

Zach smothered a sigh as his plans to avoid his neighbor disintegrated.

"No problem." He extended his hand.

"Thanks." Charley passed it over. "You two enjoy your cake?"

Zach narrowed his eyes. "What do you mean?"

Eyes twinkling, Charley pointed to his hand. "The evidence speaks for itself."

Zach examined his thumb. A tiny smudge of chocolate icing clung to the nail.

Sheesh.

Another example of Charley's powers of observation and deductive reasoning.

"The cake was excellent. Kat enjoyed it."

"Your brother was partial to it too."

He squinted at him.

Why would Charley bring up Josh today of all days? Especially in light of the fact that they'd only talked about him once, not long after Zach had put down roots in town.

"How do you know that?"

"He liked to hang out in Hope Harbor. I think he'd have moved here one day if the Lord hadn't called him home at such a young age. I shared a piece of Eleanor's cake with him on several occasions, sitting on the very bench where you and Kat had lunch."

"How come you never told me that?"

Charley adjusted his Ducks cap. "I didn't get the feeling you wanted to talk about him."

"Why do you think that's changed?" Yes, he'd shared Josh's story with Kat today—but Charley couldn't know that.

"Call it intuition." A drop of rain splattered on the pavement, and Charley gave the sky a sweep. "We appear to be in for unsettled weather. I'll let you get home. But as long as we're talking about Josh—you might want to know he found great strength in prayer."

"That doesn't surprise me." His brother's faith had always been strong.

"I think he'd be pleased with the outcome of his appeals to the Almighty."

A hard, cold knot formed in Zach's stomach. "He died, Charley. That's not a positive outcome."

The man's demeanor—and tone—gentled. "He didn't pray for himself, Zach. He prayed for you. Those prayers could be why you're here."

Zach clamped his jaw shut.

No.

Prayer had nothing to do with his decision to move to Hope Harbor.

He was here because after his own desperate pleas to God to save his brother had gone unanswered, grief had forced him to rethink his life.

But Charley, with his indefatigable optimism and rock-solid faith, wasn't likely to be receptive to that line of thinking.

"I'll see that Kat gets this." He lifted the packet.

"I appreciate that." Charley pulled out the keys to his car. "Tell her I expect to see her at the stand again soon. If she gets out and about more, she may begin to realize good can often come from bad." With that, he struck off down the wharf.

The rain intensified in the wake of his departure, and Zach jogged the opposite direction, tucking Kat's change into the inside pocket of his jacket—and mulling over Charley's parting comment.

It was hard to argue with the idea that good could come from bad. He was proof of it. If Josh hadn't died, he'd be in Chicago today, caught up in the corporate survival of the fittest battle—and married to a woman who was all wrong for him.

But the price for his escape from that fate had been too high. He'd rather still be a rat in the race and have Josh in his life.

As for what good could come from the bad situation Kat faced—who knew? If Charley was privy to details of her dilemma, he wasn't sharing them . . . and neither was she.

If ever a person could benefit from divine guidance, however, it was her.

And since none of his attempts to extend the hand of friendship had worked, it couldn't hurt to give prayer another shot on her behalf.

And hope the Almighty took more pity on her than he had on Josh.

12

. . . .

"Whatever we're having for dinner smells divine." Stephanie sniffed the delicious aroma wafting through Zach's house as she entered and followed the scent to the kitchen, where her nephew was stirring the contents of a large pot.

"Welcome back. Did you have fun exploring today?" He called the question over his shoulder.

"Fantastic. Your corner of the world has much to recommend it."

"I think so—and I'm glad you agree. What's all that?" He indicated the two overstuffed grocery bags she hefted onto the counter.

"A few provisions. If you're going to cook for me, I intend to provide some of the ingredients—plus a few extras." She dug through the bag and extracted a wedge of cheese. "I found a wonderful gourmet food shop in Coos Bay, and they had one of my favorite treats—Cotswold cheddar with chives. Have you ever tried it?"

"No."

"You have no idea what you've been missing. Trust me—you'll love it." She began emptying the sacks.

"What did you do, buy out the store?" He watched as she removed fillets, pork tenderloin, crackers, veggies, and assorted other items.

"Not quite—but I *will* be going back. I also found a fabulous hair salon . . . and I splurged on this." She wiggled her fingers his direction to display her fresh manicure.

"Nice."

At the disconnect between his compliment and his expression, Stephanie cocked her head. "What does that look mean?"

He shifted his attention back to the pot. "What are you talking about?"

"I'm talking about your that-reminds-me-of-a-subject-we-should-talk-about-but-I-don't-know-how-to-bring-it-up look."

He snickered. "You have a vivid imagination."

"Uh-huh." She let the subject rest while she stowed the perishables, then leaned back against the counter, folded her arms, and tackled it again. "Okay. Spill it. You have something on your mind. Are you trying to figure out how to unload your houseguest? Am I beginning to stink, like Ben Franklin's fish?"

That earned her a grin. "You don't stink, and you're welcome to stay as long as you like. You liven up the place."

"Thank you—I think. But that doesn't explain your look."

His Adam's apple bobbed, and he stirred more vigorously. "I, uh, had an interesting conversation with Frank this morning."

Huffing, she rolled her eyes. "You're not back in matchmaking mode, are you? We had that discussion already."

"I know, and I've hung up my cupid bow and arrow. As you made clear after the Hope House meeting, *I* stink at *that*."

"I don't recall being quite that blunt."

"Nevertheless, I got the message. But your name did come up while Frank and I were shutting down for the day."

"In what context?"

"I mentioned you might be willing to help paint at Hope House, and he was a bit taken aback."

Not what she'd expected.

"Why would that surprise him?"

Zach put the lid on the pot and faced her. "Can I be honest?"

"By all means. It's easier to tackle situations if all the data is on the table."

He rubbed the back of his neck, as if he was uncomfortable. "I don't want to butt in here, but I'm pretty certain he likes you. Problem is . . . he thinks you're out of his league."

Stephanie did her best to maintain an impassive expression as Zach gave her his take on Frank's concerns—including the man's manicure comment—along with a smattering of personal background that helped explain them.

After he finished, she examined her freshly polished nails. "He's wrong about me, you know. I'm not averse to rolling up my sleeves and getting dirty. In fact, I did most of the renovations in my apartment myself."

Zach's eyebrows rose. "Are you serious?"

"Yes. After the mental gyrations I went through in my job, I found working with my hands relaxing."

"Can I be honest again? You've never struck me as the prima donna type, but I can't quite envision you dressed in overalls and brandishing a wrench."

"Let's not get carried away. I don't gut bathrooms or fool with major electrical issues. Those are out of *my* league. But I'm a whiz at drywall mudding and taping, I wield a mean paintbrush, and I know how to use a miter saw and install crown molding."

"I'm impressed—and Frank would be too." He gave the contents of the pot another stir. "The issue he has may go beyond what he said, though. A fair number of men can be intimidated by high-powered, successful women."

"Only if they're insecure—in which case they're not worth my time. I don't think Frank falls into that category. I get the feeling he's comfortable in his skin and with his place in the world."

"That's a fair assessment."

"Factoring in everything you've told me, I suspect he has a couple of concerns. First, he's afraid I'm a high-maintenance woman who expects to be waited on hand and foot, and second, he's worried our different backgrounds and experiences are in-compatible."

"I'd say that's spot-on."

"Well, it's garbage." She propped her fists on her hips, her de-livery growing more impassioned as she warmed to the subject. "I don't believe the world revolves around me, nor do I have to run every show. And as long as two people are in sync on the levels that matter—intellectual, emotional, spiritual, philosophical—background and experience are secondary."

"Hey—don't kill the messenger." Zach grinned at her. "If you can toss a smidgen of that sass in this pot, I won't have to add any hot sauce."

"Ha-ha."

But he was right.

She was getting too riled up.

And for a woman who'd held on to her cool in every conceiv-able corporate situation, from hostile clients to tense negotiations to unwanted personal advances, this was out-of-pattern behavior.

She needed to calm down.

"Personally, I like a feisty woman." Zach's tone was tinged with humor.

"I prefer the term spirited." She managed to conjure up a smile. "And I do appreciate the insights on Frank."

"I thought it was only fair for you to know the obstacles he's put in the path—assuming you're also interested." He stopped stirring and looked over at her. "And now I'm fading into the background and letting you take it from here. Or not. We're eat-ing in half an hour."

"Works for me. What are we having?"

"Cioppino, featuring shellfish and halibut straight off the wharf. I picked up the ingredients after the boats came in."

"I'm glad I had a light lunch. Give me a few minutes to freshen up and I'll set the table." She grabbed her purse and escaped to the guest room.

Once behind her closed door, she walked over to the bed, dropped onto the edge, and took a slow, calming breath.

This was nuts.

She was getting all worked up about a man she barely knew. Acting like an adolescent schoolgirl in the throes of her first crush.

But she wasn't an adolescent—and neither was Frank. If they were attracted to each other, they should behave like mature adults and address the situation.

Scratch *if*.

She was definitely attracted to Frank—and she'd be willing to bet a hefty chunk of her lump-sum retirement package the feeling was mutual.

Yet so far, neither of them were handling this in a way that reflected their age and experience. Frank was backing off due to incorrect assumptions—and she was letting him.

That wasn't her style.

After all her years in the business world, she'd learned how to take control of a situation and get results. If she wanted to test the waters with Frank, she ought to dive in. Make the first move.

The real question was whether that was wise.

She flopped back on the bed and stared at the ceiling.

If she did pursue Frank, what would be the point? A brief vacation romance held no appeal, and the geographic challenges to a longer-term relationship were formidable. Frank had found his niche in Hope Harbor, and after living in small towns for most of his life and enjoying the wide-open spaces of national parks on vacations, a move to New York wasn't likely in his future.

Meaning she'd be the one who'd have to upend her life to accommodate a relationship.

Hope Harbor was terrific, and the Oregon coast was magnificent, but living here? That would require major alterations to the plans she'd laid out for retirement and a seismic shift in mindset.

Nevertheless . . . it seemed foolish to pass up what felt like a heaven-sent opportunity without doing due diligence. Men like

Frank didn't come along every day. And while *she'd* long ago written off romance, perhaps God hadn't.

Was it possible he'd been saving it for a stage in her life when she had the time to give a man her full attention?

She rose and began to pace as she pondered that question—and tried to come up with an action plan.

Strange how she'd been so definitive in the business world but couldn't decide what to do about Frank.

Best strategy?

Do what she'd done during her executive career while dealing with an especially thorny dilemma.

Give it a few days. Sleep on it. Let the pros and cons percolate in her mind.

And hope an answer came to her before she wore out her welcome with Zach and had to return to New York, leaving Hope Harbor—and Frank—behind.

Perfect.

Katherine gave a satisfied nod as she examined the tray of blackberry truffles. This batch was even more professional-looking than the first. And now that FedEx had delivered her candy molds, she could begin experimenting with the recipe she'd found for caramel-filled sea salt chocolates.

She assembled her ingredients and equipment, but just as she was preparing to dive in, the doorbell rang.

Could it be Charley again, stopping by on his way home with another taco delivery?

Not likely at three thirty on a Friday afternoon. Too late for lunch, too early for dinner.

Besides, on his last visit he'd announced his arrival with a knock, not by pressing the doorbell.

And it wouldn't be Zach—much as that possibility appealed

to her after their cozy tête-à-tête at the coffee shop yesterday. The back door was more his style.

She snagged a dish towel and wiped her hands as the bell rang again.

Probably another FedEx delivery with more of her favorite West African chocolate.

But when she peeked through the peephole, her lungs locked.

Simon was *here*?

Good heavens.

What on earth could have compelled him to leave his LA comfort zone behind and venture into the wilds of Oregon?

She unlocked the door and pulled it open. "Why are you here?"

"Hello to you too." He pressed the lock on the key fob for his rental car and brushed past her into the house, irritation buzzing in his wake.

Crud.

This was not going to be jolly.

Katherine didn't hurry as she closed the door, locked it, followed him into the great room—and repeated her question. "Why are you here?"

"So this is where you've holed up." He surveyed the surroundings with disdain, stopping short of a snooty sniff—and ignored her query.

"I don't think you came up here to evaluate my accommodations." She wadded the dish towel into a ball.

"No. I didn't. You have anything to drink?"

"If you mean alcohol, no. I can offer you soda, water, orange juice, or milk."

He wrinkled his nose. "Is the water bottled?"

"If that's what you want—but the tap water is fine."

"I'll take the bottled."

He followed her to the kitchen like a cougar stalking its victim.

"I asked for space, Simon." She pulled a bottle out of the fridge and set it on the island between them with more force than necessary. "For the third time—why are you here?"

He uncapped the water and inspected the tray of candy. "Is that how you've been spending your days?"

"Making candy relaxes me."

"So you've told me." He took a swig of water and sniffed. "Do you have the air-conditioning on?"

"No. The sliding door to the great room is open to catch the breeze off the ocean."

"My allergies are kicking in."

Good. Maybe he'd leave fast.

She squared her shoulders and held her ground. "I don't expect you'll be here long enough for that to matter."

"Boy, are you in a bad mood."

"I was in a fine mood until you showed up."

"You're my client. We're supposed to stay in touch—and you don't return my calls."

"I asked you to respect my request for a break. Instead, you phone constantly. Now you show up at my door."

"We have a major deal on the table we didn't have when you left. That changes the rules."

"You said you bought me a month to think about it."

"I did." He flicked a glance at the truffles. "But instead of focusing on a once-in-a-lifetime opportunity, you're playing with chocolate."

"My brain can think while my hands work—and barging in here to remind me how important this decision is wasn't necessary."

"I disagree. This is an isolated spot, removed from the reality—and urgency—of LA. I didn't want you to let this chance slip through your fingers without having a face-to-face discussion. Can we sit somewhere?"

In other words, he wasn't leaving until he said his piece.

Fine.

She'd listen to his spiel. Let him rant and rave. Promise to take everything he said under advisement.

But she wasn't committing to anything today, if that's what he was after.

And if he'd left his glitzy world behind to brave a trip into the hinterland, that had to be his goal.

He was right about one thing, though. Being away from LA for two-plus weeks *had* diminished her sense of urgency—along with the pressure and stress that had been part of her life for the past several years—and the break was giving her a fresh perspective. Talking to Charley again, her interactions with Zach and the background he'd shared yesterday in the coffee shop, the peaceful ambiance of Hope Harbor—all of that was helping her grapple with the choices confronting her.

Truth be told, this tiny town on the Oregon coast was beginning to feel more grounded in reality than the world she'd left behind. And one of these days, all of her conflicting thoughts would coalesce. The road ahead would be clear.

Today, however, wasn't that day.

She followed Simon into the great room, claimed a seat near the sliding door—leaving him no choice but to do the same, despite his theatrical sniffling—and braced for one of his rants.

But no matter how hard he pushed, she wasn't going back with him to LA.

Who was talking to Kat?

Truffle plate in one hand, Charley's packet of change in the other, Zach halted a few yards from her deck as voices drifted out the open sliding door. One was Kat's. The man's was unfamiliar.

"Having a part like this under your belt will give you leverage, Katherine."

"Spoken like the agent you are."

"I'm speaking for both of us. This is what you've been working toward. You've told me yourself you've always wanted to be a star. You're solid with the TV series, but the leap from small screen to big is huge."

"I've already made the leap."

"Not in a leading role. There's nothing wrong with the supporting parts I've lined up for you, but this could help you get past the scandal and make Katherine Parker a household name."

Brain firing on all cylinders, Zach backed away. Listening to a private conversation was wrong.

But in that handful of sentences he'd learned more about his neighbor than he had since the day he'd spotted her in the coffee shop.

Her name, her profession, the decision she was wrestling with—and hints at a skeleton in her closet.

Now the rationale behind the dark glasses and her preference for solitude became obvious.

He retreated to the woods separating their properties, running her name through his mind.

Nothing clicked.

No surprise, given how little TV he watched. And his movie viewings were few and far between. Other than the megastars, he couldn't tell one actress from another.

Yet it seemed as if Kat—Katherine—had achieved a fair amount of success and was on the pinnacle of fame.

So why would she be hiding away here, if that was her dream?

Did it have anything to do with the scandal her agent had mentioned?

Zach stepped up onto his deck and headed straight for his laptop, depositing the plate and change on the edge of his desk as he sat.

Listening in on a private conversation wasn't ethical, but there was nothing wrong with researching a Hollywood celebrity who lived in the public eye. Whatever was out there about Katherine Parker on the net was fair game.

He booted up his laptop, typed in her name . . . and noticed two things immediately.

First, the photos of her bore no resemblance to the fresh-faced brunette woman with the low-key persona who was his temporary neighbor. The Hollywood version of Katherine Parker was a stunner with long, wavy blonde hair, dramatic makeup that enhanced her eyes and lush lips, and a figure shown to perfection by the body-hugging gowns she appeared to favor.

The second startling piece of information was the huge number of hits that popped up—and the subject matter dominating all the recent ones, captured by the very first headline.

Hollywood Star Questioned by Police in Death of Fellow Actor

Zach scanned the Associated Press story that had appeared six weeks ago.

> Katherine Parker, one of the stars of the hit TV series *Masterminds*, has been named a person of interest in the death of actor Jason Grey, with whom she was linked romantically.
>
> Grey was pronounced dead at the scene after a wrap party at the home of producer Louis London to celebrate the completion of his latest movie, in which Parker and Grey appear in supporting roles.
>
> Toxicity results aren't yet available, but according to police reports, fentanyl was found at the scene. Friends of Grey have also reported he was a fentanyl user.

The rest of the article went on to discuss the propensity of illicit fentanyl to cause pulmonary distress and death, and the rumors Grey was addicted to narcotic painkillers.

There was no further mention of Katherine.

But another story, dated four weeks ago in a Hollywood tabloid, said the pills in Grey's possession had been identified as a counterfeit version of Vicodin laced with fentanyl. Katherine remained a person of interest, and the publication threw out the possibility that she was also a user—and could have supplied the drugs that killed him. If so, she could face a mandatory prison sentence under federal law, along with state murder charges . . .

even though it was expected the death would be ruled an accidental opioid overdose.

The final hit he opened from just ten days ago absolved her of culpability, indicating that while the source of the pills hadn't been discovered, no one would be held criminally liable for Grey's death.

Exhaling, Zach leaned back.

No wonder Katherine was skittish.

And no wonder she'd fled Hollywood to regroup in a quiet place like Hope Harbor.

But once the scandal blew over and she regained her equilibrium, it was doubtful she'd ditch that life long term.

For as he scrolled past the most recent hits and began to find articles and reviews of her work, it was evident she was a talented actress. She'd won several awards, and the conversation she was having with her agent suggested her star was about to soar.

Yet in the few short encounters they'd shared, she hadn't seemed all that excited about taking her career to the next level.

Zach stood and began to pace.

From everything he'd heard and observed, she was in a tough position—standing on the cusp of a dream, being prodded by her agent . . . yet suddenly unsure what her future should be.

Been there, done that—in a different context.

And if she'd been in love with the man who'd died, that would only exacerbate her dilemma. Losing a significant other could tear you apart.

His stomach clenched as an image of Lissa strobed through his mind.

Been there, done that too—minus the physical death.

It wasn't the best situation in which to make rational choices.

He paused beside the truffle plate and change. He still had to return both.

But how was he supposed to handle the next encounter with his neighbor, now that he knew at least a few of her secrets? It would be disingenuous to pretend he was in the dark about her identity. Yet he didn't want her to think he'd been eavesdropping.

Talk about a conundrum.

And he wasn't going to solve it by pacing back and forth in his home office.

Why not catch up on email, get dinner in the oven, and take a walk on Blackberry Beach, where the bracing breeze and salt-laced air usually greased the gears in his brain?

If that didn't work?

He'd have to wing it during their next encounter—and hope for the best.

13

Zach was on her beach.

Katherine halted as the path from the bluff merged onto the broad expanse of sand.

Of course Blackberry Beach wasn't *her* beach—even if she'd come to think of it in those terms after her many walks on the deserted stretch. Only once had she run into someone down here—the very man following the surf line today, his back to her, head bowed as if he was deep in thought.

Also the man she'd taken pains to avoid by confining her beach excursions to the hours he was at The Perfect Blend.

But after fending off Simon's attempts to wrangle a commitment out of her for the past two hours, she'd lost track of time.

It was also hard to think while your head was pounding and your stomach was churning.

A walk on the beach had seemed like the perfect stress reliever after he stalked out of the house in a huff and sped away, spewing gravel in his wake.

Katherine drew in a lungful of air . . . exhaled . . . and tried to psyche herself up for the trek back to the top of the bluff. Much as she'd come to enjoy Zach's company, playing dodgeball if he asked any questions about her past or her career would be too exhausting.

Before she could turn away, however, he paused. As if sensing her presence, he swung around and lifted a hand in greeting.

Well, shoot. Now she was stuck.

Without budging from her spot at the end of the path, she returned his wave. Maybe he'd get the message that she wasn't in the mood for conversation and continue his walk.

No such luck.

After a brief hesitation, he struck off toward her across the sand.

Sighing, she started forward. If she met him halfway, she could discreetly suggest they go their separate ways on the beach.

Fifteen seconds later, as the distance between them shrank, she forced up the corners of her lips. "This is a surprise. I'm used to having the beach to myself. It's spoiled me."

Not supertactful—but her message ought to be plain.

"Sorry to intrude. I didn't expect to see you down here at this hour." For once, Zach was the one wearing emotion-camouflaging sunglasses.

"I'm a bit out of pattern today . . . but I wanted a quiet place to think."

"You couldn't find a more perfect spot for that than here."

Yet he made no move to leave her to her musings—or continue his solitary walk.

If he was going to ignore her less-than-subtle hints, she'd have to be more blunt.

"That's true." She felt around for her own sunglasses, but they were MIA. Drat. In her haste to get down to the beach, she must have left them on the counter in the kitchen. "I don't want to interrupt your stroll. I'll leave you to it." She swung around and took a step in the opposite direction he'd been walking.

"Katherine."

She froze.

He'd used her full name. Not Kat.

Had he recognized her? Could Charley have revealed her identity to him? Had someone in Hope Harbor spotted her, realized who she was, shared the news with Zach . . . and perhaps the rest of the town?

Stomach sinking, she slowly pivoted back.

Zach removed his sunglasses. Tucked them in his pocket. Raked his fingers through his hair.

He appeared to be as uncomfortable—and distressed—as she was.

But rather than jump to conclusions about what he knew, she ought to let him speak. As Simon had always told her, the less you say, the less likely you are to put your foot in your mouth—or supply the tabloids with fodder.

Not that Zach was one of those obnoxious tattle-sheet reporters, but following Simon's advice couldn't hurt.

He didn't leave her guessing long.

"I know who you are."

Suspicion confirmed.

Shoulders slumping, she massaged her temple. "Who else knows?"

"No one that I'm aware of."

"Did Charley tell you?"

He frowned. "Charley knows your real identity?"

That answered one question—but raised another.

"He saw through my disguise. How did *you* find out?"

She listened to his brief explanation.

"I didn't hang around to hear details, Katherine. As soon as I realized it was a personal conversation, I left—but there are stories about you all over the net."

A wave of nausea rolled through her. "And you read them."

"Not every one. That would have taken hours. But I skimmed a few. Enough to fill in the big picture of your career and get the gist of what happened a few weeks ago."

Meaning he knew not only who she was, but also the particulars about her so-called romance with Jason and the questions surrounding his death.

At least he didn't make any snide comments or bombard her with questions, which was kind.

Far kinder than anyone other than Charley had been who knew her identity. To a person, the Hollywood crowd had pressed for details.

And despite Simon's attempts to deflect as much of the prying as possible, the paparazzi had been everywhere, all hungry for the latest update and every intimate detail.

"I'm sorry for all you've been through."

At Zach's quiet expression of empathy, her vision misted. No one had spoken to her with such concern, such caring, in longer than she could remember.

"And if you ever want a sounding board, I'm available."

No demands. No browbeating. No hint of judgment as he added that offer.

Just compassion.

Moisture brimmed on her lower eyelids. Spilled over her lashes. Tracked down her cheeks.

Not good.

She had to get a grip. Temper emotions that could cloud her judgment. Zach had been through enough trauma with his own family. Dumping her woes on him would be selfish—even if she was desperate to talk with someone who would listen without criticizing or dictating.

Fisting her hands at her sides, she gritted her teeth and fought the impulse to cave.

"Hey." He closed the distance between them. Touched her arm. "I meant what I said. I'm here if you need a friend." He motioned to the sun-bleached log where he'd been sitting on her first visit to the beach. "You want to join me there for a few minutes? You don't have to talk if you'd rather not, but sometimes just being around a person who cares can help."

"I don't want to ruin your day. I'll be f-fine." But the catch in her voice belied her assurance.

"You won't ruin my day. I like being with you, no matter the circumstances. And I know all about facing trauma and life-changing decisions alone. It's not fun."

No, it wasn't.

Katherine caught her lower lip between her teeth and eyed the log on the isolated stretch of beach, a wave of longing sweeping over her.

Wouldn't it be wonderful to sit there in the sunshine with Zach, pour out her doubts and fears and questions? Talk through options? Find answers?

The latter was a tall order.

Too tall.

Resolution was far too much to expect from an unplanned encounter on the beach.

But as long as he knew who she was . . . had boned up on her history . . . was willing to talk . . . what could be the harm in taking him up on his offer? She could fill in the gaps in her story, bounce a few thoughts off him, get his take.

The answers to her dilemma would have to come from within, but as Zach had said, he'd faced a similar quandary—minus the scandal. It was possible he could offer a helpful insight or two.

Go for it, Katherine. You've been craving a confidant. This may be the answer to a prayer.

Charley could be a candidate for that role too—but as far as she knew, his experiences didn't parallel hers as much as Zach's did.

Yet if she trusted Zach with her story . . . if she took a leap of faith . . . would she be sorry later?

Maybe.

Call her cynical, but after being burned by dispensing trust too freely on the early road to stardom, her self-defense skills were well honed.

Zach waited while her internal debate raged. He didn't push. Didn't cajole. Didn't try to argue his case.

He was leaving the choice up to her.

And she had to make it now.

Keeping his posture relaxed, Zach watched the play of emotions on Katherine's face.

The verdict was still out on her decision about whether to accept his offer.

Understandable.

If even half of the stories about Hollywood backbiting, undercutting, and ruthless ambition were true, she'd be more than justified in questioning the wisdom of opening up to a man with whom she'd spent a mere handful of hours.

Yet all at once, the tension in her features melted away. "If you can spare a few minutes, I wouldn't mind company. After going twelve rounds with Simon, I'm a bit battered and shaky."

That analogy didn't sit well—and it added yet another question to his growing list.

For the moment, though, he back-burnered that concern. "I have nothing on my agenda for the afternoon other than tending to a beef tenderloin in a little while. We can always resume our conversation after that if we run out of time."

Hoping he wasn't making a major tactical error, he gave in to the urge to twine his fingers with hers.

Despite her sudden, sharp intake of breath, she didn't pull away as he led her toward the log.

The temptation to hang on to her hand was strong—but pushing his luck would be foolish. Instead, he released it as soon as they were seated. But he stayed close, leaving no more than a few inches between them.

Angling toward her, he addressed the concern that had risen to the top of his list. "I'll admit I have dozens of questions I'd like to ask, but I'm not going to pry. There *is* one I'd appreciate an answer to, though. You used a boxing analogy for the visit from your agent—and from what I overheard, I got the impression he's the forceful type. He didn't use any . . . physical . . . pressure to try to convince you to fall in line, did he?"

Her startled expression, followed by a short burst of laughter, eased his mind on that score.

"Simon, get physical? Perish the thought. He might damage one of his designer shirts or jackets." Then her humor faded. "His methods are all psychological—a much more sophisticated . . . and effective . . . approach to pressuring someone to bend to your will. He's a master manipulator."

Zach narrowed his eyes. "You pay this guy, right? He works for you?"

"In theory. But certain Hollywood agents—including Simon—have God complexes. They believe they've saved you from the hell of anonymity and are primarily responsible for your success. They use this misguided conviction to create guilt and self-doubt in susceptible clients, many of whom have fragile egos. Yours truly included."

Katherine Parker had self-esteem issues?

Not from what he'd read online.

"I wouldn't have pegged you as someone with a fragile ego."

She called up a sad smile and drew a curved line in the sand with the toe of her shoe. "I'm an actress, remember? We're experts at putting up a convincing front. But Simon knows my story, as well as my dreams and insecurities and fears. He long ago learned my hot buttons."

"Why do you stay with him?"

"He has excellent connections and knows how to line up jobs. I didn't begin to get decent parts until I signed with him. If you read my career history, you know I've had a role on a TV series for several years. He got me that gig, which is the role that gave me financial security . . . and is opening the door to bigger op-portunities."

"Like the one he's dangling in front of you now."

"Yes." She stretched her legs out in front of her and hunched forward. "How much of that did you hear?"

"Very little—but I got the feeling it was a major movie."

"It is."

"I also got the impression you're dragging your feet about signing."

"I am."

Hoping she wouldn't bolt, he tiptoed into what could be restricted territory. "It can be hard to think straight in the midst of grief."

At her blank look, his spirits took an uptick. Apparently her relationship with Jason Grey hadn't been as serious as the articles had implied.

"Oh." The confusion on her face cleared. "You mean Jason?"

"The stories I read said the two of you were a couple."

She shook her head. "Not true. Our relationship was a stunt Simon dreamed up to get us both more media attention. Jason was his client too. He thought spicing up our images would generate more press, and a romance fit the bill. I went along with the plan under pressure, but I never liked the whole setup. Jason had a number of serious issues—including a drug problem—and I was about to back out of the arrangement. In fact, Jason, Simon, and I had an argument about it at the wrap party." She swallowed. "Six hours later, Jason was dead."

"And you were in the spotlight because the two of you were linked—leading to insinuations about *your* potential connection to drugs."

"Yes. Talk about irony. I wouldn't touch drugs for a million dollars."

Reassuring to know she'd never succumbed to one of the vices rampant among the Hollywood set—and in society in general.

"But you were cleared."

"By law enforcement. Speculation continues to flourish in the gossip rags, however. That's one of the reasons Simon wants me to accept the role in this picture ASAP. He thinks it will shift attention away from the negative situation with Jason and get me a more positive spin in the media."

"You don't agree?"

"I agree his argument has merit, but . . ." Her voice trailed off. *Careful, Zach. Let her set the pace or she'll close up tight as a threatened sea anemone.*

"You have other concerns?"

Her throat worked, and when she turned toward him there was a sheen over her blue irises. "This has to stay between us."

"Goes without saying."

Her respiration grew shallow, as if she was on the verge of hyperventilating, and a few tiny beads of sweat popped out above her upper lip. "I've never told this to anyone, but I'm . . . I'm not certain anymore about . . . that the dream I've spent my life pursuing is . . . that it's the right one."

The admission came out so soft and shaky, he had to lean close to catch the words before the wind snatched them away.

Ignoring the keep-your-distance warning strobing across his brain, he took her hand again. Locked gazes with her. "I've been there, Katherine. I know what you're going through."

"That's why I-I told you. I don't think anyone else would understand—especially Simon. I want time to think, but show business doesn't work that w-way. Deals don't stay on the table long. As he reminded me, the clock is ticking. If I do sign on for this movie, though, I'll be plunged back into all the craziness. That isn't . . . it's not . . ." She sucked in a ragged breath. "That wasn't the kind of life I wanted when I set my sights on an acting career."

"What *did* you want?"

"Affirmation and security."

Based on her swift response, it was obvious she'd given the question a lot of thought.

But her reply raised other questions.

He stroked his thumb over the back of her hand. "You seem very certain about your motivation."

"I am." She watched a sandpiper scuttle along the surf line, dodging waves. "It doesn't take a psychologist to figure out that growing up dirt-poor can have a lasting impact on your life." Dipping her chin, she scuffed out the smiley-face line she'd toed into the sand earlier.

"Define dirt-poor."

"I was always hungry. Our apartment was hot in the summer and cold in the winter. All my clothes came from thrift shops—and my classmates took great delight in ridiculing them." A flash of remembered pain echoed in her eyes.

His heart hurt for her. "Kids can be cruel."

"Yeah—and I wasn't their only target. They also made fun of my mom's job. She had dyslexia and never finished high school, so she spent her life cleaning office buildings. I know she loved me, but with her evening and weekend work schedule, I didn't see much of her. It was hard, exhausting physical labor—yet her wages were barely sufficient to provide us with the bare necessities."

"Like milk." Now her comment last week made sense.

"Yeah. Among other things."

"I take it your dad wasn't in the picture." He waded carefully into what could be murky waters.

Her features hardened. "He was for a while—but he drank too much and couldn't hold a job. Mom supported us. He walked out when I was ten. We didn't miss him."

Given her terse reply, it was no wonder she hadn't mentioned the man during their conversation at The Perfect Blend.

He didn't press for more details.

"Tell me how you got interested in acting."

The tension around her mouth diminished a fraction. "I discovered theater in middle school, realized early on I had natural talent—and decided acting would be my ticket to improving my lot."

"An ambitious goal, considering how difficult it is to succeed in that profession."

"I know—but I was convinced I could do it. I worked hard to get a scholarship to college, earned my degree, and moved to LA. My goal was to win the adulation of millions and prove to the world I was somebody." She sent him a sidelong glance. "Shallow, wasn't it?"

"Not in light of your background."

"Thanks for saying that—but it *was* shallow." She watched the sandpiper dash away from an encroaching wave. "I've learned that the sort of adulation you get in Hollywood is empty and fleeting. Without substance. And I don't like the flashy, ostentatious lifestyle."

"Doesn't that go with the territory?" He was no expert on Hollywood, but most show business folks appeared to be all about drama and flamboyance on *and* off stage.

"I didn't think it had to. There are a few stars who manage to stay under the radar in their personal lives, mostly by avoiding controversy and scandal."

"Unless those land on your doorstep."

"Yeah." She exhaled. "The tragedy with Jason changed everything—although to be honest, I was beginning to lose control of my privacy anyway. I live in a small, unpretentious condo, and I've had more than a few overzealous fans and media types finagle their way through our minimum security. It's been much worse since Jason died." A slight shiver rippled through her.

"Why don't you move to a more secure place?"

"According to the gossip magazines, I'm cheap. But the truth is, I never had any desire to live in a mansion. All I wanted to do was acquire a sizeable nest egg so I'd never again have to worry about going to bed hungry or wearing secondhand clothes. Thankfully, I've achieved that. The TV series is lucrative, and I've saved most of my salary."

"In other words, you have options. You could walk away tomorrow if you wanted to and not have to worry about money."

"Yes—in theory." She rubbed the bridge of her nose. "But after almost twenty years of single-minded effort to get an offer like the one Simon came here to discuss, throwing it away seems wrong."

"I hear you."

"Did you feel the same way?"

"In the beginning—but after losing Josh, my perspective changed. The luster on my career began to fade, and the dream of opening a coffee shop kept getting stronger. In the end, it wasn't difficult to walk away. I'd grown tired of deal brokering and power plays. The day I resigned felt more like a beginning than an ending."

He gave her hand a squeeze. "Are you tired of acting?"

"No—but I enjoy stage work more. And being in front of the camera is only a small piece of a career in Hollywood. I'm not liking the other parts . . . especially the lack of privacy. I hate having to hide behind a disguise in public." She waved a hand over herself. "I hate having to keep looking over my shoulder to see if paparazzi are lurking in the shadows. I hate having my life dissected in the media."

Her situation was far more complicated than his had been. There'd been no paparazzi camped on his doorstep.

He cranked up the analytical side of his brain. "Would it be easier to break your decisions into smaller chunks? The movie appears to be the highest priority for now."

"It is."

"Does the project interest you?"

"Yes. I've always wanted to work with the costar, and the director is stellar—but I'm not thrilled with parts of the script."

He listened as she explained her reservations.

"I applaud you for sticking to your principles."

She sighed. "You're the only one who does. Under duress, Simon agreed to take my concerns forward—but he thinks I should fold if they balk. As he pointed out, dozens of actresses would be more than happy to prance around naked and spew vulgar language to star in a picture like this."

"That's one of the problems with movies these days—and why I avoid most of them."

"Sad to say, you're in the minority."

"I know. As an actress, you are too. That's one more trait we have in common." He let her mull over his comment as he gave his watch a discreet scan.

Of course she noticed.

Tugging her hand out of his, she stood. "You have to get home and take care of that tenderloin."

Yeah. He did.

But he didn't want to.

Too bad he hadn't kept it for another day.

He pushed himself to his feet. "I'd rather stay here with you—but if my smoke alarm goes off, I'll be hosting the Hope Harbor fire department for happy hour."

That earned him the ghost of a smile. "And charred tenderloin will be on the dinner menu." She waved a hand toward the path. "Go ahead. I'm going to walk for a while." She started to turn away.

"Katherine . . ." He touched her arm again, and she angled back toward him. "For what it's worth, when I was deciding what to do about my own future, I didn't rush the process."

"I wish I had that luxury." She shoved her hands into the pockets of her jacket.

"The movie decision may have a short deadline, but your career plans are a different story."

"Not necessarily. Simon is convinced if I pass this offer up, very few others will come in. He claims no sane actress would hesitate to accept the role, and directors will walk a wide circle around me in the future."

Could that be true?

Not in the world of mergers and acquisitions where he'd spent his corporate years, but show business was a different animal. It was impossible to know whether her agent was being candid or blowing smoke in an effort to pressure her into a decision.

And he wasn't about to offer advice that could be all wrong.

"I don't know enough about Hollywood to evaluate the truth of that. I wish I did."

"I don't expect anyone else to take on responsibility for my dilemma. I'll work through it. Go ahead." Again, she motioned toward the bluff.

Yet she didn't walk away.

Nor did he want her to. Not after all she'd shared. Somehow he had to communicate how much her willingness to trust him with her secrets—and doubts—meant to him.

How much *she* was beginning to mean to him.

And he knew exactly how to do that.

It was a risk, yes—but with the air between them sparking like fireworks on the Fourth of July, it was worth taking.

Pulse accelerating, he erased the distance between them, until he was so close she had to tip her head back to see his face.

Wow.

At this proximity, a man could drown in the blue depths of those expressive eyes.

Slowly, he lifted his hand. Stroked his knuckles across her soft cheek.

Her breathing hitched, and a pulse began to throb in the hollow of her throat—but she didn't back off.

Inch by unhurried inch he bent down, signaling his intent, giving her every opportunity to change her mind and back away.

She didn't budge.

So he touched his lips to hers.

They were soft, lush . . . and far more receptive—and responsive—than he'd expected.

In a heartbeat, the simple kiss he'd intended as a gentle affirmation of his affection became much more.

And unless his instincts were failing him, it was generating megawatts of electricity on both sides.

How long it continued, he had no idea. The world around them faded away, the distant thunder of the waves breaking against the sea stacks and the caw of the gulls overhead nothing more than a faint soundtrack for their embrace.

In the end, he was the one who eased away. Not because he wanted to, but because he wanted much more—and even a man with well-honed willpower had his limits.

Katherine stared at him, eyes wide and slightly glazed, clinging to his arms as if she needed support—and balance.

He could relate.

"That was"—she swallowed—"unexpected."

"I hope not unwanted." Unless he'd read her signals all wrong, there was no danger of that.

"No—but it feels . . . premature."

"Not to me. I care about you—and I think we have potential."

"No." With a vehement shake of her head, she stepped back. Wrapped her arms around her middle. "That would complicate everything."

"Or simplify it."

She studied him. "What do you mean?"

Excellent question.

Trying to influence her decisions by hinting at promises that might be difficult to keep would be wrong. Despite the connection between them, it was too soon to let her make choices about her life and career based on instincts or intuition.

"I'm not sure." That was a cop-out. He knew exactly what he'd meant, but it was too early to have this discussion. "All I know is I like you. A lot. But I don't have the gift of prophecy."

"Nor do I—or a crystal ball. Who knows what the future holds?" She motioned toward the path again. "You should get going."

"Yeah." He couldn't ruin the tenderloin Stephanie had thoughtfully provided. "Why don't you stop by The Perfect Blend tomorrow?"

"I'll think about it." Without waiting for him to respond, she strode away.

Fighting the urge to call to her again, he filled his lungs. What could he say, after all? Pass on the movie role? Ditch Hollywood? Move to Hope Harbor? Find a new path? Give us a chance?

None of those were appropriate at this stage of their relationship.

All he could do was hope she stayed in town long enough for them to find out if they had a future—and pray for guidance.

For both of them.

156

14

··

Frank—Zach gave me your email address. Thought you might be interested in the attached. I plan to go. If you'd like to join me, we could share a ride and keep a few greenhouse gases out of the atmosphere. Stephanie

Frank reread the message and clicked on the attachment.

A photographer who'd published a book about exploring the hidden corners of America's national parks was giving a talk at the community college in Coos Bay on Tuesday night. In three days.

Leaning back in his chair in the spare bedroom that doubled as an office/study, he swiveled toward the window, where dust motes were dancing in the sunbeams streaming through the glass.

How about that?

Catching a woman's eye was no small ego boost at any age— but at sixty-three?

It was downright amazing.

And not just any woman's eye, either.

Stephanie Garrett was in a class by herself. With her toned, youthful figure and radiant vivaciousness, she faced the world with a sparkle of enthusiasm in her green eyes and a can-do attitude.

Zach's aunt was proof that age was a matter of attitude rather than years. She was young—and would always remain so.

He rocked back in his chair and linked his fingers over his stomach.

It was flattering that she'd contacted him about a date—but her initiative wasn't surprising. Stephanie seemed like a woman who was used to taking charge and going after what she wanted.

Apparently she wanted him.

Or at least she wanted to get to know him.

A tiny quiver fluttered to life in the pit of his stomach, taking him back to the long-ago days when he'd been an insecure teen who got sweaty palms and a racing heart whenever he called a girl to ask her out . . . and a rush of thrilling euphoria if she said yes.

It wasn't the only trip down memory lane Zach's aunt had induced either.

His first encounter with her had also tapped into a buried trove of emotions, reminding him how he'd felt during his junior-year crush on the lead cheerleader at his high school. How he'd yearned for her to notice him, and experienced a buoyant sense of optimism and hope whenever he'd passed her in the hall.

Except his hopes had gone unfulfilled. For all he knew, she'd never even known his name.

Stephanie, however, had done more than notice him.

She'd invited him out.

His smile widened as he watched a fluffy white cloud drift past the window against the deep blue sky.

Who could ever have predicted that such a smart, successful, spirited woman would be interested in him?

Trouble was, she was out of his league.

His delight dimmed a few watts, and he leaned his head against the back of his chair. Stared at the ceiling.

As he'd told Zach, they were from two different worlds. Asking him to join her at a national park–themed event was thoughtful, but would she go by herself if he declined her invitation?

Doubtful.

More likely, she'd seek out a new art gallery opening or ballet performance or a talk by a business leader.

Besides, while she might enjoy watching a presentation of photos from the great outdoors, what were the odds she'd relish hiking in an actual forest or canoeing on a mountain lake, far from civilization?

Not that it mattered.

Straightening up, he brushed a shortbread crumb off his sleeve, a leftover from his shift at The Perfect Blend.

He wasn't in the market for another romance. Jo Ann had been all the woman he ever needed. Full of pep, always ready for the next adventure, a true companion whose interests and passions and priorities had been in sync with his from day one.

Having her by his side for thirty-seven glorious years had been the greatest blessing of his life.

His vision misted, and he sniffed. Dug out a handkerchief.

Carrying on after she died had been hard, but with frequent prayer and countless pep talks, he'd managed to carve out a new life here in Hope Harbor.

And he was as content as he could be without her.

Or he had been, until a certain New York executive walked into his peaceful world and stirred the pot.

Swiveling away from the sunshine, he blew his nose and stowed the handkerchief. Skimmed the flyer again. Reread her note.

Despite all his misgivings and internal naysaying, a tiny part of him wanted to accept the invitation.

But that could be easily explained. He was flattered by her interest. What man wouldn't be? The little buzz riffing along his nerve endings was nothing more than normal male reaction to attention from a beautiful woman.

He drummed his fingers on the arm of his chair as he called

up an image of her. Why no one had ever managed to convince her to stroll down the aisle was a mystery. Surely there had been plenty of men in her jet-setting world who would have been worthy candidates for her affection.

Heck, if he'd been in her orbit—and if he'd never met Jo Ann—he'd have been first in her suitor line.

But he hadn't been.

And ifs didn't change reality.

He'd been a postal worker for his entire career, content to run the same route day after day, with no ambition to rise in the ranks. Being able to leave the job behind at the end of the workday and spend his evenings and weekends with Jo Ann had been enough.

An ambitious woman like Steph, who'd fought her way to the top in a male-dominated industry, would be unimpressed with such an unenterprising attitude.

Why belabor a decision that was obvious?

He positioned his fingers on the keys of the laptop, struggling to compose a reply that wouldn't hurt her feelings. The invitation had been kind, and it had taken courage to send it with the attendant risk of rejection.

But accepting was pointless.

Assuming they somehow managed to find common ground beyond the hum of attraction even his boss had noticed, she wouldn't be staying around long.

And getting romantically involved with a short-timer . . . letting her infiltrate his heart . . . would be foolish.

Losing one woman he'd loved had about killed him.

Watching a second one vanish from his life would finish the job.

So despite the sizzle that had sparked between them the day she walked into The Perfect Blend, it was safer to keep his distance while she was in town—and forget about her the minute she left.

For both their sakes, that was the prudent course.

Now all he had to do was summon up the willpower to follow it.

The Perfect Blend was closed?

Frowning, Katherine twisted the knob again.

No question about it. The door was locked.

Cupping her hands around her face, she peered inside. The place was dark and empty.

How bizarre was that?

Hadn't Zach said he was open every day from seven to one?

Stepping back from the door, she scanned the front of the building. There. The hours were posted on a placard inside the plate glass window beside the entrance.

She moved closer.

Huh.

The hours *were* seven to one—but the shop was closed on Sunday.

Seriously?

Who closed on Sundays in today's world—especially a coffee shop? Wouldn't that be one of the busier days?

So much for her skinny vanilla latte . . . and another chat with her neighbor.

Down the street, a bell began to chime the noon hour, and she angled toward the sound.

Must be from St. Francis. If all the cars in the parking lot she'd passed on her drive into town were any indication, they had a full house for the service that was either already underway or beginning. Giving up weekly church attendance to protect her identity had been difficult—but now that Charley had deemed her disguise solid, maybe she could slip into the back of Grace Christian next Sunday. An hour in God's house might help stabilize the crumbling foundation of her world.

The sun disappeared, and she shivered as a spiral of mist curled around her. A momentary dreary spell—or was the capricious fog about to sock in the town?

You never knew in Hope Harbor. One minute could be sunny, the next gray.

Kind of like life.

Shoulders slumping, chin down, she trudged back toward her car.

"Kat!"

At the summons, she halted and raised her head.

Stephanie stopped her rental car at the curb and called across the passenger seat, through the open window. "I thought that was you. I've been hoping you'd take me up on my offer to come into town and share a piece of Eleanor's fudge cake, but I understand Zach beat me to it."

So his aunt knew about their impromptu get-together.

What else had Zach told her?

"It was an unplanned stop. We ran into each other at the wharf."

"So I heard. What are you doing in town today?"

She motioned toward the shuttered shop. "I was hoping for a latte, but I'm out of luck."

"So is everyone else in town. I told Zach closing on Sunday wasn't a smart business move, but he says it should be a day of rest—and that not every decision should be about money."

Admirable—even if it left her latte craving unsatisfied.

"It's not a big deal. I can stop in another day—and the coffee bar at the house I'm renting will satisfy my urge for caffeine." If not for companionship.

"I have a counteroffer. Do you like tea?"

"Not as much as coffee." Best to hedge until she saw where this was going.

"Well, unless you can't stomach it or have other plans, why don't you join me for afternoon tea? Zach and I were supposed to go, but he got roped into an emergency Helping Hands project as we were leaving church. His reservation will be wasted if you turn me down—and I'll have to drink tea and eat scones and fancy cakes all by myself." Stephanie grinned.

Afternoon tea.

That would be fun, but . . .

She examined her leggings and belted tunic. A bit more upscale attire than she'd been wearing during most of her stay—not that her trip to The Perfect Blend . . . or seeing Zach . . . had anything to do with her wardrobe choices today—but it wasn't exactly formal.

"I'm not dressed for that sort of event."

"Nonsense." Her neighbor's aunt waved the excuse aside. "You're fine. I'm not wearing my tiara either."

It was hard not to cave under the woman's infectious good humor and down-to-earth manner.

And it wasn't as if she was all that excited about the long, empty afternoon stretching ahead. Her brain was fried from constant thinking, and she couldn't make any more candy until the next order of chocolate arrived.

Plus, from what she'd gleaned, Zach's aunt had led a fascinating life. Listening to her stories for a couple of hours could be the break she needed to refresh her mind.

"You've convinced me. I haven't been to a tea in ages."

"Wonderful! Hop in."

"Um . . . I could follow you." She motioned toward her car, parked a few spots down.

"Why waste gas?"

"Are we going far?"

"Only a few miles. Bayview Lavender Farm and Tearoom is south of town. I met the owner at Zach's church. A charming young woman. And the place gets rave reviews. It will be a perfect outing on a day that appears poised to turn gray."

As if to confirm Stephanie's prediction, a drop of rain splashed onto Katherine's nose.

Since there was no logical excuse not to ride with Stephanie, she crossed the sidewalk and slid into the passenger seat.

The woman's lively, nonstop chitchat lifted her spirits, and by the time they arrived at their destination, Katherine's mood was much more upbeat.

"Is this a real lavender farm?" She scanned the cars in the small parking lot in front of the low-slung building.

"Yes. I believe the flower beds are in the back. Jeannette West, the owner, moved here several years ago and ended up marrying the doctor from the urgent care center in town." Stephanie shut off the engine. "Shall we?"

Katherine fell in beside her as they walked toward the entrance, where a woman with long, wavy brown hair greeted them. "Don't tell me Zach chickened out."

"He had a legitimate excuse to bail—or so he told me." Stephanie's eyes began to twinkle. "I assume from your comment that male customers are in the minority."

"A vast understatement. The few who do get roped into coming generally finish eating in fifteen minutes flat and stop for a burger en route home. Most women, on the other hand, linger for a couple of hours and leave with a box of leftovers."

Stephanie huffed out a breath. "How stereotypical. Eating isn't the main goal of tea. It's more about taking a respite from the hectic pace of our crazy world."

"Amen to that." Jeannette held out her hand and introduced herself as Katherine returned her firm shake.

"Sorry." Stephanie completed the formalities, and after a few more pleasantries were exchanged, Jeannette showed them to a table beside a large picture window.

"We're at the height of the bloom season." She handed them tea menus. "I'll be back to take your tea order in a few minutes. In the meantime, enjoy the view."

"This is gorgeous." Katherine scanned the lush beds filled with purple flowers.

"I agree. As lovely as Provence."

After another sweep of the gardens, Katherine focused on her companion. "From what you said the day we met, I take it you've traveled a lot."

"Enough for two lifetimes. I've been to every continent, and most of the big cities in the world." Her comment was matter-of-fact. No trace of bragging.

"Your job must have been exciting."

"More in theory than in reality."

She'd made a similar comment the day they'd met—but Zach's appearance had sidetracked that conversation.

Jeannette came by for their tea order, but as soon as she retreated, Katherine returned to their previous topic. "So there was a disconnect between the reality and the theory?"

"A huge one." The older woman's lips tipped up. "Let me put it like this. My job was like going to a carnival as a kid. At first, the fast rides and games of chance and unhealthy food are exhilarating. But if you did that day after day, every day, the thrill would fade. While there were parts of my career I loved—like working one-on-one with clients—the endless meetings and constant travel and corporate politics got old."

"I hear you."

"Your career has a similar downside?"

She was saved from having to answer by Jeannette, who delivered a three-tier stand filled with scones, finger sandwiches, and pastries. After giving them a description of each offering, she left them with a promise that their tea would be ready soon.

But Stephanie repeated her question as soon as the woman walked away.

Katherine smoothed a crease in the linen napkin in her lap, scrambling to come up with a reply that wouldn't give too much away . . . or shut down this topic.

"To some degree. That's why I'm taking a break to reevaluate. It's been very stressful—and I can't tell you how much I appreciate this relaxing interlude to temporarily leave it all behind."

Once again, Zach's aunt proved to be as astute as her nephew. You didn't get into the executive ranks of a global company without learning to read signals and discern messages hidden within diplomatic phrasing.

Including ones that said back off.

"Then I'm extra glad we ran into each other today." She helped herself to a cucumber sandwich. "I always start with these. Dig in."

Katherine followed her lead. While Stephanie had respected her message that her own situation was off-limits, would she be willing to share more about *her* experiences? A woman who'd remained in a profession that appeared to have had as many downsides as acting, albeit of a different nature, could have a few insights to offer.

"May I ask you a question about *your* career?" Katherine took a dainty bite of her sandwich.

"Of course."

"If there were parts of your job you didn't like, and the travel got old, why did you stick with it?"

Before she could respond, Jeannette approached with a teapot, poured their Earl Grey into delicate cups, and again retreated.

Around them, the tinkle of silver against china, the muted conversation, and the strains of classical music created a soothing ambiance, and the tension that was always present in her shoulders—except while she was making candy—eased.

"That's a question I asked myself often early in my career, when I was working sixty-hour weeks, living out of a suitcase, and had no personal life." Stephanie took a sip of tea and selected another sandwich. "The answer finally came to me. I didn't want to disappoint my father."

Katherine stared at her.

That wasn't what she'd expected to hear.

"You're surprised, aren't you?"

Katherine fiddled with her cup. "Honestly? Yes. You come across as a strong, independent woman."

"I am—thanks in large part to my father. He was an early proponent of equal opportunity in the workplace and believed women had been given short shrift in many industries—including mine. From day one, he pushed me to excel and break barriers.

He also encouraged my brother, but he always felt it was tougher for women to get noticed and rise in the ranks."

Katherine spread lemon curd on a scone. "To tell you the truth . . . you don't strike me as the type to make major life choices in order to please someone else."

"Love is a powerful motivator." Stephanie dropped a sugar cube into her tea and stirred the hot liquid to dissolve it. "And I loved and respected my father. But I could have switched careers after he died. The truth is, I always had a hankering to change course, like Zach did. The creative fields were a passion of mine—writing in particular. Between you and me, I have a couple of fiction manuscripts under my bed, gathering dust."

"Why didn't you pursue that?"

"In the beginning, I didn't have the time or energy to juggle two careers—and as I began rising in the ranks, I enjoyed my success. I'd learned to live with the parts of the job I didn't like . . . and I'd been bitten by the ambition bug. I wasn't doing it for my father anymore. I was doing it for myself. It was all-consuming, but I liked the challenge of making my mark in a male-dominated industry." A brief shadow passed over her features. "You can put up with major inconveniences and disruptions . . . and give up a lot . . . if you're satisfied with what you've accomplished at the end of the day."

"Do you miss it?"

She shrugged. "Too soon to tell—but I don't think I will. It was a fascinating chapter of my life, but I'm looking forward to turning the page. To savoring experiences I always had to squeeze in before. Enjoying a theatrical performance or dinner out without being interrupted by urgent calls or texts. Sleeping late if I want to. Answering to no one but myself. Getting reacquainted with my brother and nephew. Broadening my horizons."

"How are you ladies doing?" Jeannette stopped beside the table and refilled their teacups.

"Wonderful." Stephanie answered for both of them. "This

lavender shortbread is divine." She lifted the delicate, heart-shaped cookie.

"Thank you. That's our signature item—although I use lavender in many of the treats you sampled. I'd like to add another chocolate item, but I haven't yet found the perfect recipe."

"Speaking of chocolate—Kat makes the most exquisite truffles. She gave Zach and me a sample from a batch she made with the berries she picked at Blackberry Beach. They were incredible."

Katherine's cheeks warmed. "It's nothing more than a hobby. I'm no expert."

"Ha." Stephanie arched an eyebrow. "I've sampled candy from the best chocolatiers in the world, and those truffles were world-class."

Jeannette shifted toward her. "Have you ever used lavender in truffles?"

"No—but it's an intriguing idea."

"A treat like that would be a wonderful addition to my sweet tier, but I have no talent with candy. I've tried, but I never get the temperature right. My end product doesn't have the glossy finish of fine chocolates."

"Chocolate is tricky. It takes a while to master tempering." Katherine sipped her tea. "You know, now that you've mentioned using lavender in candy, I'm going to have to research that. Maybe give it a try."

"We have a cranberry farm in town too. There are all kinds of local ingredients for fantastic chocolates." Jeannette acknowledged a summons from a nearby table with a lift of her hand. "I'll tell you what. Before you leave, let me cut you a bouquet of fresh lavender as inspiration—and I'd love to taste the results if you come up with a recipe you like."

The woman moved off, but already Katherine was mentally sifting through her stockpile of recipes. Nothing with lavender popped up—but there were loads of sources for ideas. And there was nothing wrong with developing her own recipe. She wasn't a master chocolatier, but after all the classes and experimenting she'd done, she ought to be able to tap into her knowledge to create a lavender truffle.

"I agree with Jeannette. A handcrafted piece of chocolate would be a perfect addition to her array of sweets." Stephanie picked up an elaborate miniature pastry and examined it. "Not that I'm complaining about the offerings on this tray. Every bite has been delicious. Zach has no idea what he missed—in terms of both the food and the company."

"Thank you." Katherine selected a tiny cranberry tart. "May I ask you one other question?"

"Fire away."

"If you *had* decided to change career midcourse—after your father died—would you have felt guilty?"

Stephanie tilted her head, cup poised halfway to her mouth. "I've never thought much about that." She set the cup back down as she considered the question. "I don't know that I'd have felt guilty, as long as I went on to another career that fulfilled me. But after investing so much of myself in my job, I suspect I would always have wondered if I could have reached my goal of being a vice president."

"So you're not sorry you stuck with it."

"No. To be honest, achieving that ambition was freeing. Once I'd proven to myself I could do it, I could have walked away satisfied if I'd wanted to."

From there, the conversation moved on to general topics, and by the time Katherine left an hour later with a sheaf of lavender in hand, a friendship had been forged. Two, based on Jeannette's parting comment that she hoped to be sampling a lavender truffle soon.

The fog had moved in while they enjoyed their tea, and as Stephanie left her at her car with an invitation to drop in at Zach's anytime, the light rain intensified.

She climbed behind the wheel, waved to her hostess, and set the lavender on the seat beside her.

It perfumed the car during the drive back to her house, the sweet scent both soothing and invigorating.

Or perhaps the energy coursing through her had more to do with a sense that the decisions she faced weren't as difficult as she'd imagined. That with prayer, reflection, and conversations like the one she'd had today—plus her exchanges with Zach and Charley—clarity would come.

Just not on Simon's timetable.

And therein lay the problem.

She drew in a lungful of the fragrant scent, trying to corral the insidious stress that was creeping back.

Constant worry wasn't going to accelerate her decision process. In fact, it could be counterproductive, tying her up in knots instead of smoothing the tangles from her mind. She needed to chill.

Despite Simon's hurried, drama-filled visit on Friday, he'd confirmed she had until September 14 to decide about the movie deal . . . and in the meantime, he was taking her content concerns forward.

That gave her three more weeks of breathing space.

And no matter how hard he pushed, she was taking every day of those weeks.

Because if she made a hasty decision that turned out to be wrong, she could end up regretting it for the rest of her life.

15

His *father* was contacting him?

Zach jolted to a stop in the woods between his house and Katherine's. Stared at his cell.

The number wasn't one he'd called in the past few years, but it was engraved in his memory.

He should answer—but after such a long gap in communication, it would be difficult to talk to his dad without significant mental prep.

Too bad Katherine hadn't responded to his knock on this late Sunday afternoon so he could return her plate and give her Charley's packet of change in person instead of leaving them on the deck. If he'd been with her, he wouldn't have paid any attention to the vibrating summons in his pocket.

As the phone continued to pulsate, he weighed it in his hand.

Ignoring the call was an option.

But what if, by some miracle, his father had experienced a change of heart and wanted to rebuild the bridge between them?

After all, what else could have prompted this out-of-the-blue call?

A wisp of hope spiraled up inside him—a reminder that despite his claim to the contrary during his conversation with Katherine, the negative fallout from his choice to walk away from his former life did still bother him. At a deep, elemental level he rarely acknowledged.

Could his dad have come to the same conclusion? Did he miss their former weekly phone calls? Was he hoping to rectify the situation?

Moving under the sheltering branches of a spruce tree, he took a steadying breath and pushed the talk button.

"Hello, Dad."

Silence.

He waited.

More silence.

Frowning, he clenched the fingers of his free hand. "Dad? Is that you?"

"Yes. Sorry. I intended to phone your aunt. I must have pressed the wrong name."

The call was a mistake. The elder Garrett hadn't reached out to him.

His spirits tanked.

And he had no one to blame but himself.

Letting that tiny surge of hope brighten his day had been foolish. If his dad hadn't softened in two and a half years, there wasn't much chance he ever would.

He squared his shoulders, struggling to maintain a neutral tone. "She went to tea and may have her phone off. I'll tell her you called after she gets back."

"I'd appreciate that." His father's voice was stiff. Formal.

But there was also a tremor in it.

Because he was annoyed he'd called his son by mistake—or was there another explanation?

In the past, Richard Garrett—deemed the courtroom sphinx by his colleagues—had never let anything disrupt his inscrutable, in-control demeanor on . . . or off . . . the job.

"Is everything okay?" The question was out before Zach could stop it.

"Fine." His father's stiffness morphed to scorn. "How's the little coffee shop doing?"

Zach bristled at the demeaning inflection.

Don't let him rile you, Garrett. It's not worth it.

He inhaled the fresh scent of the spruce and directed his gaze toward the calming expanse of open sea. "Also fine."

"Are you ready to ditch your hobby yet and return to the real world? Get back to your business career?"

He mashed his lips together and counted to five.

"This *is* my business, Dad. I'm in for the long haul."

A disgusted snort came over the line. "I'll never understand what got into you two boys. First Joshua, now you. Wasting all that education on nothing careers. I didn't send you to college to be a barista."

Zach held on to his temper. Barely. "Most of my college expenses were covered by scholarships, in case you've forgotten."

"There were other costs I picked up. For both of you. When your brother veered off track, I thought at least you'd amount to something. You were on the road to a partnership. How could you throw away success?"

That hurt.

"I didn't. I found it elsewhere. But I suppose we all define success differently." It took every ounce of his self-control to pull off a measured delivery. "I discovered a better life. And I have Josh to thank for it."

"He didn't do you any favor."

"He did me a tremendous favor—but I'm sorry it took his death to help me see the light."

"I don't want to discuss your brother."

"In that case, I'll leave it at this. Moving out here, following my dream, has been the best decision I ever made. I have a balanced life in a beautiful place and time for the important things—which have nothing to do with ambition and power plays and clawing your way to the top, in case you haven't figured that out yet."

"Don't lecture me."

"I'm stating a fact."

In the background, a ping sounded. "My dinner's ready. I have nothing else to say."

"Neither do I. I'll tell Aunt Stephanie you called."

No response.

Just a dead line indicating his father had hung up.

For several seconds, Zach remained frozen in place, fingers trembling, legs unsteady.

Why couldn't his father *try* to understand that choosing a different path than he had didn't mean his sons were ungrateful, lazy, irresponsible slackers?

It was a question without an answer.

And after tonight's conversation, it seemed unlikely the elder Garrett's attitude would ever change.

Exhaling, he shoved the phone back in his pocket.

He had to let it go. Get over it. Kill the tiny ember of hope that continued to flicker deep inside.

Except for his relationship with his dad, his life was perfect.

Well, almost perfect.

Finding a special woman to share it with would seal the deal— and there was a much higher probability of that happening than reaching a reconciliation with his father.

Even if the only potential partner who'd caught his eye in Hope Harbor didn't appear interested in playing a starring role in his life.

Katherine signed the thank-you card, slid it into the envelope, and sealed the flap.

Pen poised, she started to address it.

Stopped after writing Stephanie's first name.

What was the point of mailing a card to the house next door? Why not drop it off? Hadn't Stephanie invited her to stop in any-time?

Besides, hand delivering it gives you an excuse to see Zach.

"Oh, shut up." She quashed the smart-aleck in her head and slid off the stool at the kitchen island.

If Zach was there, fine. If he wasn't, that was also fine. Any company would do after the past two and a half solitary days of candy-making. Afternoon tea with Stephanie on Sunday and her chat with Zach on the beach last Friday felt like a lifetime ago. She'd put a hefty dent in the new supply of chocolate that had arrived bright and early Monday morning, but much as she enjoyed her hobby, a little human interaction would be welcome.

She circled the island . . . hesitated on the threshold of the living room . . . and detoured to the master bath, stopping in front of the full-length mirror to survey her attire.

Leggings with a hole in the knee and a too-big button-down shirt sporting a chocolate stain, the sleeves rolled up to her elbows, weren't exactly a go-visiting outfit.

On the other hand, dressing to impress could be a mistake. After the kiss she and Zach had shared, sending any signals that implied she wanted to pick up where they'd left off would be reckless. Her situation was too up in the air.

The chemistry between them was already potent, and getting up close and personal again could set off reactions neither of them were ready to deal with.

So if she followed through on delivering the note in person, she'd go as she was—and she wouldn't add any lipstick or mas-cara either.

But there was no rush to traipse next door. As long as Stepha-nie's rental car was visible through the trees, the woman would be available for a chat.

Why not spend a few minutes reviewing her lavender truffle notes and fine-tuning her scribbled, much-modified recipe? She was getting closer to a satisfactory outcome, but a bit more experimentation and tweaking were needed.

If she was still tempted to go visiting in half an hour, she'd consider it again.

And if she chickened out, it would cost her nothing but a postage stamp.

"Aunt Stephanie?" Zach pushed through the door from the garage into the kitchen, dropping his keys on the counter as he called out to his houseguest.

"In here."

He continued to the threshold of the living room. "Sorry again about being late. Thanks to the crumb brigade that stopped in near closing, cleanup took longer than usual. I love our kiddie customers, but they tend to leave a mess in their wake."

"Don't worry about it." She waved his apology aside. "My days of having every second of my life booked—or overbooked—are gone forever, thank the Lord."

"Give me five minutes to change into old clothes and I'll be with you."

"Don't rush on my account. My book will keep me entertained." She held up the new Irene Hannon suspense novel she was reading.

Despite her reassurance, he hustled. Being at Hope House by two, as he'd promised, wasn't going to happen—but they ought to be able to get there by two thirty.

In three minutes flat, after exchanging his work clothes for worn jeans and a paint-splattered T-shirt, he rejoined her.

"Wow." She set her book down and gave him a once-over. "What did you do, shift into warp speed?"

"Close. Listen—are you certain you're up for this? From the quick walk-through I did Sunday afternoon, we're going to have to put a ton of muscle into stripping wallpaper and drywall prep before we can paint. I know you've done your share of rehabbing and remodeling, but I hate to put you to work on your vacation." He snagged his keys off the kitchen counter.

"It will give me much-needed exercise—and be far more interesting than visiting a gym." She stood . . . but stayed in place.

Odd vibes began wafting toward him, and his pulse picked up. What was going on?

Propping a shoulder against the doorframe, he folded his arms. "Why do I get the feeling you have something you want to tell me?"

She offered him a smile that appeared forced. "Because you're a smart, intuitive man?"

"A person would have to be totally oblivious to miss the sudden tension in the air. What's up?"

Faint furrows creased her brow. "I don't know if I should tell you this or not."

He tightened his grip on the keys.

Whatever she had to say concerned his dad.

He knew that as surely as he knew his father would be furious to learn they were having this conversation. The Garrett patriarch did *not* like his personal business discussed behind his back.

"After that teaser, you can't *not* tell me." He managed to maintain a conversational manner. Even inject a teasing note. "Unless you want to be pestered for the rest of your visit."

The corners of her lips rose a hair. "You know, in many ways you remind me of Richard."

That wasn't the most flattering comparison he'd ever received.

"So what'll it be? Spill the news, or face the inquisition?"

"Put like that . . ." She lowered herself to the arm of the couch. "It's about your dad."

His instincts were batting a thousand.

"What about him?"

"He's having health issues."

Zach schooled his features, doing his best to maintain a

dispassionate expression despite the knot forming in his stomach. "What kind?"

"Shortness of breath during the few days I was there—and other symptoms as well, I expect, though he didn't share those. I insisted he visit his doctor. He got the verdict a few days ago. There's blockage in his heart that has to be addressed. He's having bypass surgery on Monday."

Zach's lungs stalled.

His father was having a major operation in five days?

And he hadn't bothered to mention that during their unexpected phone conversation on Sunday?

A stab of hurt knifed through him.

"Are you going back?" Somehow he managed to rasp out the question.

"No. He finagled a promise from me not to let his news disrupt my vacation. He said he's given everyone my number in case there's an emergency, but he's convinced he'll sail through and be back to normal after rehab."

"What do you think?"

She shrugged. "I'm not a doctor. That type of surgery has a high success rate—but there are always risks. It seems to me a family member ought to be standing by."

And if she'd promised to remain in Hope Harbor, there was only one other candidate for that job.

"You think I should go to Atlanta?"

"It's your decision, Zach."

He forked his fingers through his hair. "Did he ask you not to tell me about this?"

"Yes . . . but I didn't make any promises."

"Given the state of our relationship, I can't imagine he'd appreciate me showing up at his hospital bed. He'd probably tell me to mind my own business, that he didn't need my help, and to go back to my little coffee shop hobby." Despite his attempt to maintain an even tone, he couldn't hide his bitterness.

Stephanie rose, crossed to him, and laid a gentle hand on his arm. "The stoic front he presents to the world is more show than reality, Zach."

"No, it's not." A muscle in his jaw twitched. "I lived with him until I was eighteen. It's reality. As is his conviction that his opinion is always right. It's not easy to have a relationship with someone like that."

"I hear you." She retracted her hand but remained beside him. "However—despite his reputation as the hard-nosed, take-no-prisoners type, I remember Richard as a little boy who wore his heart on his sleeve . . . and often got hurt as a result."

Dad, wearing his heart on his sleeve?

In what alternate universe had *that* taken place?

"I don't think we're talking about the same person."

"I won't argue with that—but you're not the same person you were five years ago either. Neither am I. We're all shaped by the events of our past. If they're traumatic enough, we can change direction—as you did. Or we can develop defense mechanisms. Hide behind walls. Learn to present an image to the world that masks who we really are, deep inside. Like your dad did."

He narrowed his eyes as a niggling suspicion began to take root. "Are you referring to a specific trauma in Dad's past—other than the bankruptcy your father went through when you were kids?"

"Yes."

They were going to be very late for their Hope House commitment—but this conversation was too important to defer. "Let's sit for a minute." He motioned toward the couch and followed her over. Angled toward her after he sat. "Tell me about the trauma."

She caught her lower lip between her teeth. Appraised him. "Did you know he was fired from his first job?"

A shock wave ricocheted through Zach. "No. I thought he . . . that he'd been with his current firm his whole career."

"He's been there for most of it. But after law school, he got a

179

job clerking for a respected judge. The man took him under his wing, gave him plum assignments. Your dad was on top of the world. The two of them became friends, and Richard trusted the man implicitly. Until he was indicted for accepting bribes and tried to set your dad up to take the fall."

He sucked in a breath.

How could he not have known about an incident of this magnitude in his father's past?

"Dad never said a word about that. Neither did Mom."

"The whole family was under a gag order from your dad after you and your brother were born. He wanted to put the incident behind him. But he never forgot it. He lived in the shadow of disgrace for two years while the investigation dragged on. He took menial jobs that didn't pay squat. Our father offered to help him out financially, but he wouldn't take a dime. In the end, the truth came out and the judge took the full rap, but after that incident Richard closed himself in, doled out trust like a miser, and made security his priority."

In the silence that followed Stephanie's story, Zach attempted to digest the implications of this startling chapter in his dad's life.

A trauma like that could explain a lot.

Including his father's anger when both sons walked away from careers—or potential careers—he viewed as their tickets to financial security.

He wiped a hand down his face.

"That's a boatload of stuff to deal with in one fell swoop."

"I know. I've been debating how much to say ever since I talked to Richard. Getting in the middle of a father-son debate is tricky, and I didn't want to do anything to jeopardize my relationship with either of you."

"That's not a concern from my end. And I appreciate the insights."

"So what are you going to do about Atlanta? Richard tried to downplay the situation on the phone with me, but I heard concern in his voice."

He had too, during their brief, unplanned conversation. The tremor he'd picked up had been subtle but unmistakable.

"I don't have a—"

At a knock on the sliding door that led to his deck, he leaned sideways to see around Stephanie.

She swiveled too—and dismay etched her features as she lowered her volume. "After I had tea with Kat, I told her to drop by anytime. I'm sorry. This isn't an opportune moment."

"It's not a problem."

On the contrary. A quick chat with his neighbor could help defuse the stress of the past few minutes.

He rose, crossed the room, and pulled the door open, doing his best to force up the stiff corners of his mouth. "Hi."

As Stephanie joined him, Katherine looked between the two of them. If he appeared as shell-shocked as he felt, she was probably regretting her impulsive visit, whatever the impetus.

"I didn't mean to intrude, but I decided to deliver this in person rather than drop it in the mail." She leaned past him and held out an envelope to Stephanie.

"You're not intruding." His aunt took it. "We're getting ready to go work on the Hope House project I told you about while we were at tea. I see painting and wallpaper stripping in my immediate future."

"I won't keep you, then." She started to turn away.

"If you're not busy, why don't you join us?"

As Stephanie issued the invitation, Zach flashed her a silent *drop it* message. "I'm sure Kath—Kat—has more interesting things to do."

"Do you?" Stephanie ignored him as she directed the question to their visitor.

"Um . . . I don't know much about wallpaper stripping or painting."

"It's easy. I learned everything I know from YouTube." Stephanie gave her a bright smile. "Why don't you come along? It should be a companionable group, and you could pick up useful skills for the future. You're already dressed for the job."

Zach gave his neighbor's outfit a quick scan.

That was true—but she wouldn't want to expose herself to a group of strangers, in case someone recognized her . . . unlikely as that was in her present grub state.

"Aunt Stephanie . . . I don't think—"

"If you could use another pair of hands—"

As their comments overlapped, a soft flush bloomed on Katherine's cheeks. "On the other hand, I'm not a Hope Harbor resident. Maybe I shouldn't—"

"I don't live here either, and I'm volunteering." His aunt waved the comment aside as she cut her off. "Many hands and all that. Right, Zach?"

An elbow jab from Stephanie kicked his vocal cords into gear. "I don't think anyone will complain if we bring along another helper."

"Of course they won't." Stephanie glanced between the two of them. "And donating a few hours to a charitable project is a perfect activity for a quiet Wednesday afternoon. Doing work with the hands often frees the brain to think."

"Are you leaving now?" Katherine took a tiny step back.

"Yes. Zach's driving."

She moved farther away. "I, uh, have a few chores to finish first. I could meet you later if I get them done. What's the address?"

Zach recited it.

"I'll do my best to come." She turned and hurried back toward her house.

Hands on hips, he watched her. If he was a betting man, he'd lay odds she'd never show. Whatever had prompted her to latch on to Stephanie's invitation—loneliness, a sudden yearning to do a good deed, boredom—common sense would prevail in the end.

Given her desire to remain under the radar, immersing herself in a bunch of strangers wouldn't be smart.

But as she disappeared from view, he couldn't quell a surge of disappointment.

After everything Stephanie had unloaded on him in the past fifteen minutes, he could use the distraction of female companionship—of the romantic variety—to take his mind off the decision looming in front of him.

Should he go to Atlanta to be with his dad during the surgery and risk an abrupt and ungrateful dismissal—or stay here in Hope Harbor, where life was simpler and devoid of the tension and angst that would most certainly await him in the city of his youth?

16

. . . .

Was that *Stephanie*?

Frank set the brake on his car two doors down from Hope House and peered at the woman in safety goggles on the front lawn. Manning a miter saw, she motioned toward a piece of crown molding—as if she was instructing the people clustered around her how to cut it.

Nah.

It couldn't be her.

What were the chances a woman like Stephanie would know how to cut or install crown molding?

Minuscule.

But from this angle, it sure looked like her.

He slid out from behind the wheel and approached the small group on the lawn, the woman's voice drifting toward him.

"Corners are the hardest to cut. Remember that for an inside corner, the bottom of the molding should be longer than the top. For an outside corner, the top will be longer. A coping saw is your best friend for corners."

It *was* Stephanie.

Jaw dropping, he halted and gave her another scan as she proceeded to demonstrate how to use the saw.

She was as dressed down as he'd ever seen her, in broken-in jeans, an untucked shirt, and sport shoes.

Demonstration finished, she raised her head—and their gazes met.

Surprise registered in her eyes . . . quickly followed by pleasure, unless his skills at reading body language weren't as polished as he thought they were.

The hesitant smile she sent him, however, confirmed his take.

Close your mouth and stop staring, Frank.

Following that sensible advice, he clamped his jaw shut and returned her smile.

He waited until she finished fielding questions, then met her halfway as she walked toward him.

"I didn't expect to see you here today." She brushed sawdust off her jeans and removed her safety goggles, mussing her stylish coiffure.

She didn't appear to notice—or care.

"That goes both ways. Zach didn't mention you'd signed on for the painting crew—although it appears you've been commandeered for a different job." He motioned to the saw and crown molding.

"A temporary reassignment. The guy who was supposed to lead the woodworking team got hung up. I was doing a basic introduction to get them started until he arrives."

"How did you acquire a skill like that?"

"YouTube." She grinned. "I renovated my whole apartment in New York on my staycations."

"You stayed home and rehabbed on your vacations?" He tried to wrap his mind around that piece of news.

"Yes. I have a long-term lease, and the landlord was more than happy to let tenants make agreed-upon improvements. After all my travel, it was bliss to sleep in my own bed during my brief—and infrequent—days off."

A gust of wind whipped several strands of hair across her face, and she lifted a hand to brush them aside.

Three things registered.

Her fingers were long and graceful.

The nail polish on her pinkie was chipped.

And he had a sudden, strong urge to tuck her flyaway hair behind her ear.

The latter was totally inappropriate.

To corral that renegade impulse, he motioned to her hand and stuck his fingers in his pockets in case they decided to misbehave. "Your manual labor has already done a fair amount of damage."

She examined the chipped polish and shrugged. "The manicure was on its last legs anyway. And hurrying the process along is more than worth the fun I'm having."

Stephanie thought rehabbing was fun?

Another point of difference between her and Jo Ann.

His wife had been more than happy to pitch in on most jobs around the house, but she'd walked a wide circle around saws and drills—or any semidangerous tools.

Zach's aunt was full of surprises.

"Could you use another set of hands with the crown molding?" The offer was out before he could stop it—surprising him as much as it seemed to surprise her.

What had happened to the quick, impromptu walk-around he'd planned to do en route to the grocery store—and the quiet dinner on his patio to unwind after his busy Wednesday volunteer shift at the lighthouse?

One answer sprang to mind—but he shoved it into a shadowy corner.

Her brow wrinkled. "Are you on the list for today? Zach didn't mention seeing your name."

"No. This was an unplanned stop. But I put up crown molding at our house in Coos Bay. If you're short of experienced people, I could stay for a while."

"That would be terrific. Let's go take measurements."

Without waiting for a response—or giving him an opportunity to rethink his offer—she strode toward the house.

He followed.

Slowly.

This could be a mistake.

After turning down her invitation to the national parks lecture, he ought to keep his distance.

She hadn't said anything about that, though—nor did she appear to hold his refusal against him.

Maybe she'd simply accepted it for what it had been—an I-like-you-but-have-no-interest-in-romance message—and moved on. Her demeanor today suggested she was willing to be friends, with no expectation their relationship would ever progress beyond that.

He should be relieved.

So what was with the sudden pang of disappointment in the pit of his stomach?

You know the answer to that, Frank.

He sighed.

Yeah, he did.

It was easy to like Stephanie Garrett—and getting easier with every encounter.

But if that trend continued . . . if liking suddenly began morphing into an emotion much deeper . . . it would open another can of worms.

Several cans.

Like, how could he have loved Jo Ann as much as he had, yet find himself attracted to someone new?

And what would he do if he began to care too much for a woman whose life was on the East Coast, in an apartment with a long-term lease?

He trailed after her—waving at Zach, who brandished a wallpaper scraper at him from one of the bedrooms as he passed the doorway.

No answers to those questions came to mind.

But if his changing perceptions of Stephanie continued to break down his defenses, he'd have to get himself in gear and nail them down.

Otherwise, he could find himself falling for her—and putting his heart at risk of a very hard landing.

Of course the wallpaper didn't come off in long strips, despite the soaking he'd given it.

And of course Katherine hadn't shown.

Zach attacked another piece of the stubborn floral paper that refused to relinquish its grip on the drywall, scraping with more force than necessary.

With all the information Stephanie had dumped on him earlier, Katherine would have been a welcome distraction.

Instead, his mind was in overdrive trying to reconcile the background she'd given him with what he knew about his father—and debating whether a trip to Atlanta should be in his immediate future.

Funny how you could think you knew everything there was to know about a person, only to discover there were gaping holes in your data.

Too bad they hadn't been filled in years ago.

If he and Josh had had a fuller understanding of their father's history, it was possible they could have avoided the falling-out that had created a world of angst for all of them.

As for the trip to Atlanta—who knew how his father would react if he showed up? What if having his older son appear at his bedside precipitated the very heart attack the surgery was designed to prevent?

But if he didn't go, and there were complications . . . if his father ended up—

He couldn't bring himself to form that thought.

His dad couldn't die.

Not with so much unresolved between them.

His father may have been a hard taskmaster during his growing-up years, but he'd also been supportive, encouraging, and proud of all his older son had accomplished.

Only after Zach went rogue did the relationship disintegrate.

Now that he had more insight about why that had happened, was it conceivable he might be able to—

"Could you use a hand?"

He whipped around at the familiar voice, his scraper carving a gouge in the drywall that someone would have to repair later.

Katherine hovered in the doorway of the room, holding a foil-covered tray and wearing her usual dark glasses.

She'd actually left her hideaway and shown up?

His day brightened.

"Another pair of hands would be more than welcome. At the rate this wallpaper is coming off, we'll be working on it until Christmas. What's that?" He motioned to the tray.

"Truffles for the volunteers. I've been doing a ton of experimenting, and if I eat all the samples myself, I'll *gain* a ton. But I'd rather they be an anonymous donation."

He walked over and took the tray from her. "I can put them in the kitchen, on the counter with a few goodies other volunteers brought. And I'll tip off my aunt to stay mum about the source."

"Thanks."

"I already soaked the paper on that wall." He motioned to where he'd been working. "Pick a spot and have at it. There are more scrapers in the bucket next to the water."

"Got it."

As she walked over to the wall, he detoured to the kitchen, set her offering on the counter—and popped one of the truffles in his mouth.

Not blackberry this time. A different flavor he couldn't quite put his finger on.

But it was delicious.

He told her that after he rejoined her and went back to work.

"Thanks. They're infused with lavender and Earl Grey tea. The woman who runs the tearoom Stephanie and I went to inspired me to try incorporating those ingredients. They're not quite where I want them yet—but they're getting closer."

"I don't see how you could improve on them."

"I can—and I'll know when they're right." She propped her sunglasses on top of her head and got to work.

A companionable silence descended between them, the muffled conversation of other volunteers and the scuffing of their scrapers providing a muted backdrop, interrupted occasionally by the whir of the saw that had been set up on the front lawn.

Several minutes passed as he tried to shift into small talk mode—but much as he'd hoped Katherine's presence would distract him, he couldn't vanquish the dilemma with his father from his mind.

"You're quiet today."

He glanced over—but her focus remained on the wallpaper as she methodically scraped off one tiny piece after another.

Though Katherine's inflection hadn't reflected annoyance, as Lissa's had near the end, hearing those same words again stirred up memories of her—perhaps because that terrible period in his life, when he'd lost Josh and struggled with life-changing decisions and incurred his father's anger, was on his mind.

And Lissa had been part of that.

A major part.

Katherine peeked over at him. "Sorry. That wasn't a criticism."

"I didn't take it as one. It's just that you aren't the first woman to say that to me."

"Stephanie remarked on your reticence too?"

"No." He went back to peeling off wallpaper.

After a moment, she did too.

But unless he wanted to shut down communication between

them, he owed her an explanation. His reply had been too terse—and left too many questions hanging.

Besides, why keep his relationship with Lissa a secret? It was over. And that painful piece of his history had turned out to be a blessing.

He stopped scraping and gave Katherine his full attention. "The other woman who used to tell me that was my fiancée."

She froze. Sent him a cautious look. "You were engaged?"

"Yes. We broke up after I decided to leave Chicago. Lissa was a model, with lofty career and personal goals. I asked her to come with me, but being married to a barista wasn't part of her game plan."

Katherine's eyes softened. "I'm sorry."

"I was too—at the time. Not so much now." He wanted no doubts about that to linger in her mind. "It hurt to discover her feelings for me were based more on my position and earning power than love—but in hindsight, the breakup was a blessing. I don't think either of us would have been happy in the long term, even if I'd stayed in Chicago. After Josh died and my priorities shifted, I realized we had far less in common than I thought . . . and that what I'd classified as love was more like infatuation. It's hard to build a long-term relationship on such a shallow emotion."

"Still—a broken engagement on top of everything else. You had a lot to deal with back then." Twin furrows scored her forehead.

"Yeah." He tugged at a loose strip of wallpaper until it pulled away from the drywall—but small remnants remained stuck to the surface. Ones it would take considerable elbow grease to scrape off. "I still do."

The instant the admission slipped out, he gritted his teeth. With everything going on in Katherine's life, it wasn't fair to dump his latest issue on her shoulders.

"Does that mean a new problem has come up?"

"Sort of." He wasn't going to lie. "But I'll deal with it." He began scraping off the stubborn residue from the last piece of wallpaper he'd removed.

After a few beats of silence, she spoke again. "You listened to my story that day on the beach—and talking through the situation helped. I'd be happy to return the favor. If we close that"— she motioned to the bedroom door—"we'll have privacy—and I promise to keep whatever you tell me between us."

Her offer was tempting. An impartial, third-party sounding board—someone who could view the situation without any of the biases he or Stephanie brought to the table—might be helpful.

And he didn't have to dump the whole mess on her. He could keep it simple. Give her a top line of the current situation, let her offer a few thoughts.

Any input that could help clarify his thinking would be welcome.

Running his finger along the edge of the scraper, he turned to her. "I wouldn't mind getting someone else's read on this—and I can give you the gist of it in a couple of sentences." After closing the door, he relayed the news about his dad's medical condition— but left out the history piece Stephanie had shared. "I'm trying to decide whether to show up in Atlanta for the surgery."

Her brow puckered. "I don't want to be morbid—but how will you feel if there are . . . complications . . . during the operation, and you stay here?"

She'd homed in on the same question he'd been wrestling with.

"I don't know."

"What's keeping you from going?"

Also an excellent question—and one he hadn't yet pondered.

But now that she'd posed it, the two answers that sprang to mind didn't sit well.

The first was fear.

Fear of rejection—again. And fear that if a cross-country trip didn't mend their fences, his last embers of hope for a reconciliation would be snuffed out and his relationship with his father would forever remain broken.

The second was pride.

Putting himself in the position of having his priorities and new career belittled—again—twisted his gut.

Katherine didn't wait for him to answer before hitting him with a follow-up question.

"And whatever's holding you back, is it more important than taking this opportunity to try and end the estrangement? Traveling across the country to be with him could send a powerful message."

"Or not." Zach rolled a small piece of wallpaper into a tight ball between his index finger and thumb. "He could throw it back in my face. Refuse to talk to me."

"People can feel differently when faced with their own mortality."

He studied her. Did that subtle nuance in her tone mean she'd witnessed such a transformation in her own life?

"Is that experience speaking?"

"Not directly. But I've played a few roles that forced me to dig deep and think about those kinds of issues. When you speak the words of a character dealing with a life-and-death situation, you develop an understanding of why people do what they do, even if you don't agree with or approve of their behavior. Rifts can be mended in that environment, if both parties are willing—and want that outcome."

"That's a big if." He flicked the ball of wallpaper off his finger. "I've already tried to mend our fences. The onus to repair the damage in our relationship isn't on me at this point."

She cleaned the edge of her scraper with a rag, removing all the jagged bits. "I didn't mean to imply it was. From what you've told me, your dad was pretty unreasonable in his response to the choices you and your brother made. It was almost like he was viewing the situation through an off-kilter lens that was distorting his perspective. Or operating from a very narrow frame of reference that gave him tunnel vision."

Tunnel vision.

Narrow frame of reference.

Distorted perspective.

That nailed his father's issue.

Had Katherine listened in on Stephanie's story this afternoon? Not possible.

Which meant the lady had excellent instincts. Honed, perhaps, by her career—as she'd noted.

"That about sums up my dad—although he does have an excuse for being that way, as I recently learned." Saying any more would divulge secrets his father had gone to great lengths to protect—and at this stage of his relationship with Katherine, that would be disloyal to his dad.

To her credit, she didn't ask for details. "Maybe, armed with that new knowledge, you can give a truce one more try. Worst case, you end up where you are now. But I don't see how a son traveling across the country to be with his father during a health crisis could produce anything but positive results."

He could.

Stubborn didn't come close to describing his father. Once he dug in his heels, he was as tenacious as the barnacles that clung to the rocks at Blackberry Beach.

Yet armed with the new insights about what made his dad tick, perhaps the outcome could be different if he changed *his* approach. Instead of being defensive or confrontational, why not show a touch of empathy for all his dad had gone through earlier in his career, try to get him to acknowledge how that experience had shaped his reaction to his sons' choices? If his father did that, it might set the stage for a dialogue that could begin to smooth out their thorny relationship.

He exhaled and massaged the bridge of his nose. "I wish I had more time to think this through."

"Do you really need it?"

At her soft question, he angled toward her. "You think I should go."

"That's your decision . . . and I'm not privy to all the hurt and

heartache you've been through. But sometimes, if the clock is ticking on a decision and we don't have an answer, we have to listen
to our hearts and take a leap of faith."

Was she talking about herself—or him?

"Is that what you're going to do with the movie role?"

"I have more breathing space than you do. I'm hoping if I
continue to mull over all the pros and cons, my thinking will
clarify and the right choice will be obvious with no leaping
involved." She motioned to the wall. "We're not making much
progress here."

Deflection.

She didn't want to discuss the choices she was facing.

Fair enough.

"No, we're not—but taking a few minutes to talk this through
with you has helped."

"A prayer or two couldn't hurt either."

Huh.

She hadn't bitten when he'd thrown that suggestion out to *her*
on the beach two weeks ago, so he'd assumed prayer wasn't part
of her routine.

But she must have assumed it *was* part of his.

Better set her straight on that.

"It may not help either."

She cocked her head. "You're on the outs with God too?"

"I wouldn't go that far—but we haven't talked much since
Josh died." He plucked a sponge out of the bucket of water and
squeezed it dry.

"Because he didn't save your brother?"

His stomach clenched.

How had they gotten on *this* subject?

He swiped the sponge over the wall, dropped it back in the
bucket, and attacked an obstinate strip of wallpaper with renewed
vigor. "I realize prayer doesn't always work."

"Actually . . . it does."

He stopped scraping and frowned at her. "How can you say that? Josh died."

"What did you pray for?"

"A miracle. I wanted Josh to live."

"He *did* live. He *does* live. Just not where you can see him. And while you were thinking of a miracle in terms of Josh, God may have used your brother's trials to bring about a miracle somewhere else."

"He didn't pray for himself, Zach. He prayed for you. Those prayers could be why you're here."

As Charley's comment about Josh replayed in his mind, he tightened his grip on the scraper.

He'd refused to consider the man's theory that day, but if his brother had been praying for him—could God have used Josh to bring about a miracle? Nothing as flashy or dramatic as the multiplication of the loaves and fishes or walking on water, but a miracle that was profound in its own way?

Like the miracle of a man rediscovering what really mattered in life, realigning his priorities, and making a new start.

He took a long, slow breath.

All these months here in Hope Harbor he'd paid lip service to his faith. Followed its principles as best he could, went to church every Sunday, said an occasional prayer.

But none of it had come from the heart.

Maybe it was time it did.

Maybe it was time to stop going through the motions of his faith and begin to live it. Reconnect with God as he longed to reconnect with his father.

There was no question the Almighty would be more forgiving—and more willing to welcome him back.

"Sorry." Katherine tucked her hair behind her ear and went back to scraping. "I didn't mean to barge into your faith life. That's private territory, and I—"

"Hey." He touched her hand.

She looked over at him, her blue eyes inches from his. Her mouth a whisper away.

A mouth that had stirred sweetly beneath his mere days ago.

And it was a temptation of the first order.

But another kiss wouldn't be wise. He wasn't ready to make any promises . . . and she didn't want complications.

They were in a holding pattern until something changed.

He cleared his throat and dropped his hand. "Where you're concerned, there aren't any no-trespassing signs . . . and I'm glad you came today."

The corners of her lips tipped up. "Thank you. I'm glad I came too."

She went back to work and launched into a new, less personal topic.

Fine with him. It would be far too easy to let himself get carried away by another woman who might not share the dream he'd come here to pursue.

Until Katherine settled on a course for her future, it was prudent to play it safe.

In the interim, he had decisions to make about his own future . . . and how far out on a limb he was willing to go to try and reconnect with his father.

And his deadline was much closer than hers.

17

. . . .

"This room's ready for installation, as soon as the painting crew finishes." Stephanie leaned the final piece of crown molding in the corner, dusted off her hands, and turned to Frank. "Shall we join the mudding brigade? The master bedroom is in dire straits, and I'm ready for a quieter chore. Or do you want to call it a day? I know this wasn't in your afternoon plans."

As she waited for his reply, she held her breath. Working side by side today with the most appealing man she'd met in ages had been an unexpected pleasure, and she wouldn't mind extending their partnership for another hour or two.

His neutral expression was difficult to interpret—until the corners of his mouth rose. "I can stay awhile. Lead the way."

Mercy.

The man had a killer smile.

An invigorating surge of energy zipped through her, and she strode toward the staging area. "All the supplies are in the garage."

After collecting what they needed, they moved on to the bedroom, where she swept a hand over the walls. "Do you want to work in the same area or divide and conquer?"

Frank didn't hesitate. "Let's stick together. It'll be easier to talk."

Yes!

Not only had he stayed, he wanted to converse.

Another positive sign.

In fact, Frank had been giving her nothing but positive signs since he'd arrived.

Had he had a change of heart after declining her invitation to the lecture—or was that wishful thinking?

Wait.

Make that *foolish* wishful thinking.

What about the life waiting for her in New York? Did she really want to encourage a man who had no intention of moving? What would be the future in that—except potential heartache?

The very same questions she'd wrestled with ad nauseam while debating whether to extend the invitation to the lecture. In the end, asking him had been an impulsive leap of faith—and disappointed as she'd been by his refusal, at least that had put the matter to rest.

Yet his actions today suggested the regrets he'd sent may have engendered other regrets. That he *was* interested in exploring their mutual attraction.

However . . . it was also possible she was getting ahead of herself. Frank's sociability could be nothing more than an attempt to let her know his negative response to her invitation hadn't been personal. That he liked her as a friend and wanted to make certain she wasn't offended.

From a logical perspective, that was a plausible conclusion.

Except the spark in his eyes whenever their gazes met implied his motive for staying today went far beyond mere politeness.

"The owner must have had a bunch of pictures on the walls." Frank propped his hands on his hips and scanned the pockmarked surface. "And whoever took them off wasn't any too careful. Look at all the rough edges."

"Yep. They'll have to be sanded first." Stephanie picked up a sanding block. "What'll it be—sanding or filling?"

"Do you have a preference?"

"I've done both."

"Why don't I sand?"

She handed over the block. "Have at it."

He dived in as she opened the spackle and picked up a putty knife.

There was ample opportunity to talk in the quiet bedroom, as Frank had indicated—but all at once he seemed tongue-tied.

Not a problem.

After years of cultivating clients and running meetings, keeping the conversational ball in the air was a no-brainer.

Rule number one—ask open-ended questions.

"Tell me why you're here today. I assume board members don't get hands-on with every program the organization sponsors."

Frank picked up a paper towel and wiped drywall dust off the first hole he'd sanded. "No, but I do try to get involved in most of the larger projects we take on."

"This appears to be a big one."

"It is. Maybe the most ambitious in the organization's history. When Adam Stone brought the idea forward, the board had serious concerns. Not about the merits of his proposal or the need for a place like Hope House, but the start-up costs were significant. There are also a number of other challenges—including reams of government red tape to maneuver through in order to be accepted for the foster system."

"Yet Helping Hands pursued it." She used her putty knife to work spackle into the hole he'd sanded.

"Yes. You caught the end of the process, at the town meeting. After that, the board voted to proceed—but a few members do have reservations."

"What camp are you in?"

"Full speed ahead." He wiped off the drywall dust on the second hole and moved on.

Stephanie smoothed out her patch with the edge of the putty knife and followed him down the wall. "Any special reason you're so gung ho?"

"I like kids—and some can benefit from a leg up to help them overcome the bad stuff they've experienced. I volunteered with the Big Brother program for years, and I saw firsthand the negative results of a shoddy upbringing. Giving children from dysfunctional backgrounds a stable, loving home environment through Hope House is a wonderful addition to the Helping Hands program."

"It certainly fits with the altruistic nature of the organization."

"Yes, it does—but I have to admit I also have a bit of a selfish motivation for getting involved."

She angled toward him. While she and Frank were recent acquaintances, she'd seen nothing to indicate he had a selfish bone in his body.

"Now you have me intrigued. What could possibly be in this project for you?"

He shot her a quick, sheepish grin. "A chance to play grandpa." He went back to sanding. "Whoever we get as houseparents may come with real grandparents for the kids, but I figure no child can have enough older folks in their life who like to dote on them."

"So you intend to make a personal investment in the project." Not surprising for someone who'd volunteered as a Big Brother.

Her heart warmed a few more degrees toward the man beside her.

"Yes. It's not like having my own grandkids, but you don't have to be related by blood to have an impact on a young person's life. And seeing the world through the eyes of a child helps you appreciate things you've come to take for granted—and keeps you young."

"I suppose that's true." Not that she'd had any experience with children herself. Nor had she let herself think much about them after she decided to devote herself to her career instead of trying to juggle a family and a job.

What was the point?

That train had passed her by, as she'd told her nephew.

As if he'd tuned in to her thoughts, Frank spoke again. "If I'm being too personal, just tell me to mind my own business—but I'm curious about why you never married and had a family."

She took extra pains as she smoothed out the spackle with the putty knife, blending it in to the surrounding wall until the edges were seamless. "I didn't think I could do justice to both my career and a family. I had my sights set on an executive position, and that's where I chose to focus all my energy. If I'd had a husband and children, I'd have spent my life being pulled two directions and feeling I wasn't giving either all they deserved."

"These days, many women have both."

"But they either don't rise as high in the ranks as they could have because they're distracted by other obligations, or they delegate many of their parental duties to a nanny who becomes a surrogate mother. I believe in giving 100 percent to anything I undertake."

"Admirable." He leaned closer to the wall and picked off a flaking piece of drywall. "And I hear what you're saying. Jo Ann felt the same. She didn't have a high-level job like yours, but she always planned to cut her hours back after we had kids. A moot point, as it turned out."

"Did you ever think about adopting?"

"Yes. But we kept trying to have a child until we were in our forties, and then Jo Ann began to have a few health issues. The adoption process can be long, and she was afraid that by the time we got a child, she wouldn't have the energy to raise him or her. So I'll settle for being an adopted grandfather. Despite this silver hair, I have a superabundance of energy."

"I noticed." The man bristled with it.

That was one attribute they had in common. She was brimming with vitality too, and looking forward to many more lively, productive years.

It was too bad they wouldn't include visiting children and spoiling grandchildren—but she'd made her peace with her choice long ago.

Nevertheless, for the first time in decades, she couldn't help wondering what might have lain beyond the door she'd firmly closed.

"You okay?" Frank glanced her direction.

She called up a perky smile and tackled the next hole. "Fine."

But a change of topics was in order. "By the way, I think you would have enjoyed the national parks presentation. The photos were spectacular, and the speaker's stories about his adventures taking them were entertaining."

Although she kept her attention fixed on the wall, in her peripheral vision she saw him give her a surreptitious perusal.

Maybe she shouldn't have brought up the event he'd declined to attend, but why not chat about a subject he was interested in— and one far less personal than their previous line of discussion?

"You went?"

"Of course. I thought it would be fascinating, and it was."

"I didn't think that topic would be your cup of tea."

Ah.

He thought she'd chosen the lecture for his benefit.

Only partially true.

"I'm trying to broaden my horizons now that I'm retired. And after hearing you talk about your vacations to national parks, I realized there's a whole world out there I've never experienced. The presentation whetted my appetite to see a number of those places in person."

He went back to work without responding.

But a couple of minutes later, when she peeked over at him, there were faint furrows on his brow. As if he was surprised she'd have any interest in outdoor activities.

In truth, her Atlanta upbringing hadn't given her much exposure to the natural world. Nor had her corporate treks taken her anywhere but large metropolitan areas. She'd always been a city girl through and through.

Yet smaller towns—like Hope Harbor—had much to recommend them, as she was discovering.

And from the photos she'd seen during the presentation, nature had as much beauty to offer as any of the art museums she'd visited on her global travels.

While the back-to-nature leisure pursuits Frank and his wife had enjoyed had never been on her radar, if she was committed to expanding her horizons, why not include them?

There wasn't much opportunity to do that in New York City, but she could go see the places that had caught her eye.

However . . . it would be much more fun to go *with* someone. Especially someone who already knew how to navigate that world.

She checked out Frank again as she scooped more spackle from the container.

He could be a candidate for that role—if she was willing to alter her retirement plans, give up the lifestyle she'd envisioned.

Was she?

Too soon to say.

And how would she ever find the answer to that question unless she got to know him better?

But that wouldn't happen if he kept turning down her invitations.

Give the man a break, Stephanie. He may see no point in getting involved with a woman who'll soon be leaving. If he thought you were willing to hang around awhile—and consider a permanent move—the outcome could be different.

Hard to refute that argument.

Still . . . it would be safer to remain friends.

Yet she'd played it safe in her personal life for more than forty years.

Could it be time to listen to her heart—and entertain the notion of altering the retirement plans she'd assumed were locked in stone?

A critical question.

One she needed to work hard to answer before she wore out her welcome with Zach and found herself winging away from Hope Harbor and back to the East Coast.

Today had *not* played out as he'd expected.

Frank flipped the single piece of salmon destined to be his

Wednesday dinner, closed the lid on the small grill, and ambled over to the edge of the patio.

The house he'd purchased in Hope Harbor might be modest, but the view was world-class. From this last dwelling on the short block that dead-ended at the sea, he could take in the mouth of the river to the south, rocky Little Gull Island offshore to the west, and to the north, Pelican Point light on the soaring headland.

Breathtaking didn't begin to do the scene justice.

If he wanted a view like this at a fancy hotel, he'd pay megabucks.

Fancy hotel.

Like the kind Stephanie would have frequented during her career.

He rubbed the back of his neck and followed the progress of a pelican overhead, its orange beak a splash of brightness against a low-hanging white cloud.

Stephanie.

He sighed and wandered back to the grill.

Turning down her invitation should have sent a definitive signal that he wasn't interested in a dating relationship.

And the message had apparently been received. She hadn't done anything today to imply she intended to try again. Her manner had been amiable, nothing more.

He was the one who was suddenly having second thoughts about drawing the line at friendship.

Spatula in hand, he opened the grill lid and turned the fish again. Almost ready. Time to get the baked potato out of the oven and nuke his veggies while the entrée finished cooking.

Back inside, he went about those chores by rote while his mind churned with weightier matters.

Namely, Stephanie Garrett, and how she fit into his life.

No.

The question was *whether* she should fit into his life.

Trouble was, the image he'd formed of her early on kept crumbling.

Today was no exception. Seeing her in work attire, hair mussed, fingernail polish chipped, wielding saws and crown molding and putty knives like a pro . . . that had been a shock.

She'd also gone to the national parks lecture without him—proving she truly had been interested in the topic.

He picked up his plate, returned to the patio, and transferred his salmon from the grill to the crockery. Once seated at his table for two, he said a short blessing and began to eat.

In general, he enjoyed the view over the water.

Today, the empty chair got in the way.

And the fresh salmon he always relished lacked its usual flavor.

Or was it his life that lacked flavor?

Sure, he had a job he enjoyed at The Perfect Blend, and chatting with the regular customers gave him social interaction—as did his volunteer gig at the lighthouse. Plus, his work with Helping Hands fed his soul.

But after thirty-seven years of marriage, it was hard to come home at night to an empty house—and a solo dinner.

That, however, wasn't sufficient justification to get involved with someone.

Except . . . it was more than that with Stephanie.

A smile tugged at the corners of his lips.

From the get-go, she'd made him feel young again. Revved his engines. Added a spark to his days.

Young love was a distant speck in his rearview mirror, but near as he could recall, this was exactly how he'd felt when he'd fallen for Jo Ann.

So what was he supposed to do about it?

Mouth flattening, he put a pat of butter on his baked potato. Watched it melt.

Moving to New York wasn't an option. Heck, he'd feel like Crocodile Dundee—if anyone even remembered that old movie.

And a woman with a long-term lease wasn't likely to uproot herself without any guarantees, even if she felt the zing as much as he did.

He poked at his salmon . . . then dropped his fork onto the table and sat back in his chair as two seagulls wheeled overhead.

What a dilemma.

If he did want to test the waters, it would be up to him to initiate it. Stephanie had made the first overture, and she didn't strike him as a woman who'd push once she got a negative response. On an interpersonal level anyway.

Was it worth having a conversation with her about his dilemma? He'd been wrong on so many fronts—could he be wrong about her willingness to embrace a lifestyle far removed from New York?

Was there any harm in asking?

The two seagulls landed at the edge of his patio, cuddled up together, and stared at him.

Wanting a handout, no doubt.

He broke off a piece of salmon and tossed it to them.

They each took half—but they didn't fly away after they ate. Nor did they pester him for more.

Strange behavior for gulls, which could be annoyingly persistent.

He forced himself to eat a few bites of his meal.

Having a talk with Stephanie wasn't a bad idea. With her business background, she'd be used to frank discussions.

But that didn't solve his other issue—how to reconcile his growing feelings for Stephanie with his love for Jo Ann.

The forkful of potato he'd just swallowed stuck in his throat, and he fumbled for his glass. Took a sip of water.

Was it disloyal to think about another woman in romantic terms?

Would Jo Ann be upset?

Yet finding a new partner wouldn't diminish anything they'd shared. No one would ever take his wife's place in his heart.

He pushed more food around on his plate and lifted his face to the heavens.

Lord, I could use a little direction here. I want to do what's right—but I feel like I'm at an intersection without signs. Please show me which road to take.

At a raucous cackle, he shifted his attention to the gulls.

They ruffled their feathers, nudged each other, and in perfect harmony took flight. Within seconds they'd disappeared from view in the direction of the harbor.

Not the most talkative dinner companions—but sociable.

He went back to eating. Most of the food had grown cold, but it didn't matter. His mind wasn't on his meal anymore.

It was on whether to let what seemed like a heaven-sent opportunity slip through his fingers—or grasp this unexpected gift, which had the potential to radically alter the solitary years ahead that he'd come to accept as his lot.

18

· ·

Woo-hoo!

Katherine pressed the end button, tossed her phone on the couch in her rental house, and exited onto the deck.

A lungful of the fresh, invigorating air sent energy and optimism coursing through her on this last Saturday of August.

Or—more likely—her upbeat attitude was the result of the accolades her truffles were receiving.

According to Jeannette at the lavender farm, today's patrons had raved over the samples she'd dropped off yesterday—and the woman had asked for more for next weekend.

That meant they had to be good.

Kind as the tearoom owner appeared to be, she ran a business— and she wouldn't serve her guests anything that wasn't stellar. All of the offerings on the three-tiered stand last weekend had been top-notch.

On top of that, Stephanie had passed on the complimentary comments she'd overheard at Hope House during a break on Wednesday. From what she'd picked up, many of the volunteers had been trying to figure out who donated the truffles—and not a morsel had remained on the tray Zach retrieved for her.

Maybe she did have a knack for chocolate-making—at a higher-than-hobbyist level.

A cloud scuttled across the sun, and as the light dimmed she glanced toward the house next door, hidden behind the towering coniferous trees.

It would be fun to share this happy news with Zach—but he'd been laying low since the day they'd stripped wallpaper together. He hadn't even been at The Perfect Blend when she'd stopped for a latte yesterday on her drive back from the lavender farm, and the female barista with the multicolored hair hadn't explained his absence.

Had he gone to Atlanta?

But if he had, wouldn't he have told her?

Why would he, Katherine? It's not as if you two are anything more than neighbors.

Sad—but true.

Well . . . not sad, really. It was a mutual choice to stay at arm's length—except for that brief kiss on the beach.

The cavalcade of sensations aroused by that meeting of the lips swept over her again, and she gripped the railing to steady herself.

Zach Garrett definitely knew how to kiss. Better than most of the so-called heartthrobs with whom she'd shared an onscreen clinch.

But there was more to a successful relationship than chemistry, and until they sorted through—and resolved—all those other parts, it was important for them to keep a lid on their emotions.

Surely, though, it would be okay to share the reaction to her truffles—and follow up on their conversation from Wednesday, ask if he'd come to a decision about Atlanta. Any caring neighbor would do as much.

You're rationalizing, Katherine.

Her chin tipped up. No, she wasn't. There was nothing wrong with paying her neighbor a quick visit. She'd stay ten minutes, max.

Armed with that plan, she strode across the lawn, through the trees, and onto his deck.

The driveway was empty—so Stephanie wasn't home.

Perfect.

Much as she liked Zach's aunt, having the owner of The Perfect Blend all to herself would be the icing on this cake of a day.

She crossed to the sliding door and knocked.

Thirty seconds later, he appeared on the other side and slid it open.

"Hi. I hope I'm not interrupting anything."

"Nothing important." He returned her smile—but his was a bit weary around the edges. "Come on in."

"I'm not staying. I just had a piece of good news to share."

"That would be welcome about now."

She frowned, her cheer fading. "Is your dad all right?"

"As far as I know. I'll get the whole story soon." He motioned to the floor behind him.

A duffle bag was beside the couch.

"You're going to Atlanta."

"Yeah. I decided this afternoon. I leave tomorrow morning. What's your news?"

In light of the ordeal Zach was facing, the positive reviews on her truffles suddenly seemed inconsequential.

"It's no big deal. I just had a call from Jeannette at the lavender farm." She filled him in.

A fan of creases appeared at the corners of his eyes. "That doesn't surprise me. Like my aunt said, they're world-class. Are you going to supply more for her next weekend?"

"I haven't committed yet."

"You should. Stephanie told me the volunteers on Wednesday loved them too. In fact, I was thinking about asking you to donate a tray of them to the Taste of Hope Harbor event for Hope House. I heard earlier today it's been scheduled for September 14."

The same day she owed Simon an answer about the movie offer.

But whatever she decided career-wise shouldn't affect her ability to provide truffles for the Hope House fundraising effort.

And if she did accept the role and return to Hollywood, a truffle donation would let her exit on a sweet note.

"I'd be happy to. Let me know how many you'll need."

"I'll check and get back to you."

She'd done what she'd come to do—and her ten minutes were up. She ought to leave.

"How long will you be gone?" The question spilled out before she could stop it.

Well, shoot. Prolonging the conversation wasn't going to expedite her departure.

"It all depends on my dad. If he shuts the door in my face, I'll be back as soon as the doctors tell me he's out of immediate danger."

"I'll pray for you both."

"Thanks. I can't speak for Dad, but I'll take all the help I can get." He hitched up one side of his mouth, but stress over the upcoming reunion with his father was taking a toll. There was a new tautness to his features, and faint remnants of the crinkle lines from his smile remained embedded after his lips flattened, suggesting he hadn't slept much the past few nights.

A pang of sympathy echoed in her heart.

Hard as her career decisions were, mending a rift with someone she loved didn't hang in the balance. The personal stakes for Zach were high, the risk substantial.

You had to admire a guy who was willing to lay it on the line for love even after being spurned. That took a boatload of courage.

Pressure built in her throat. "Will you let me know how it goes?"

He cocked his head. "You mean . . . call you from Atlanta?"

"If you get a minute."

"I'll find one." He whipped out his cell. "What's your number?"

She recited it. "Very few people have that."

He finished keying it in and tucked the phone back in his pocket. "I assumed as much. I appreciate you trusting me with it."

"I've already trusted you with all my other secrets."

"Yeah." His acknowledgment came out husky, and he started

to lift his hand. Swallowed. Let it drop back to his side. "Thanks for stopping by to share your news. I'm glad the truffles were a hit—but I'm not surprised."

He was moving to a safer subject.

Because he was tempted to get up close and personal again—like with another kiss?

If only.

But he'd backed off at the beach, stopped short of making premature commitments—and a man of honor didn't mislead a woman he cared about.

One more appealing attribute to add to his growing list.

That didn't mean *she* couldn't take the lead on getting up close and personal, though. What harm could there be in a quick, innocent send-off kiss between friends?

Innocent, my foot. Get real, Katherine. A kiss is a kiss—and you know what message it will convey.

She shut off her inner voice. Later, after Zach was gone, she'd think about the implications.

Maybe.

In the meantime, she was giving him a proper good-bye.

Proper—or improper?

She quashed that rebuke too.

"Have a safe trip." She rose on her tiptoes . . . pressed her lips against his . . . lingered as long as she dared . . . then scampered across the deck and dashed through the woods.

Not until she was on her own deck did she look back.

He hadn't followed.

No surprise there.

He was probably still trying to fathom why she'd initiated a lip-lock—and what it meant.

Join the club.

Pulse hammering, as out of breath as if she'd run a competitive hundred-meter dash, she braced her hands on the railing, sucked in air . . . and admitted the truth.

Zach Garrett was getting under her skin.

Enough to become a factor in her decision about the movie role—and her career path.

Which was scary.

After all the work she'd put into achieving success, letting a surge of hormones influence her choices was a mistake.

Yes, she had a host of other reasons to rethink her goals. All the ones she'd enumerated to Zach. All of them legit.

Hormones weren't.

And it was too soon to call the sparks between them anything more than that. Electricity was potential, nothing more . . . and giving up her dreams to pursue a potential that might not pan out would be crazy. Her decision had to be based on lucid, sound analysis.

Problem was, it was hard to get the left side of her brain to cooperate with thoughts of Zach short-circuiting her logic.

Perhaps a walk on the long, empty expanse of Blackberry Beach would help whisk away the cobwebs in her head.

She stepped off the deck and marched toward the hard-to-find path through the brambles.

Until Zach returned, she'd do her best to banish him from her mind. Stop fixating on short-term decisions and think about long-term goals. Like, where did she want to be in five years? Ten?

That could help her put her more immediate choices into perspective, perhaps clarify her short-term decisions.

And until she had a rational resolution to her present situation, she would follow one important rule.

There would be no more mind-muddying kisses with a way-too-appealing neighbor who gave new meaning to the word *hot*.

Stephanie—There aren't any national parks in our backyard, but the gardens at Shore Acres State Park are beautiful. I thought I'd drive up there Tuesday after The Perfect Blend closes and see what's blooming. Should be quiet on a weekday. If you're not busy, I'd enjoy your company. Let me know. Frank

Stephanie stopped on the sidewalk outside of Grace Christian as she read the new message that had popped up in her email during the Sunday late service.

All that dithering over whether to issue a second invitation to Frank, only to have him take the initiative and force her hand.

A tingle zipped through her as the breeze lifted the end of the filmy silk scarf around her neck and sent it fluttering behind her.

She might not need a man to complete her world—but having a beau at this stage of her life was a delightful prospect.

Even if she hadn't yet decided whether to listen to her heart and consider altering her retirement plans.

"Morning, Stephanie." Charley stopped beside her. "Beautiful day, isn't it?"

She angled toward the taco man Zach had introduced her to early in her stay—and whose stand they visited often. "Yes, it is. I hope it lasts." She motioned toward the horizon, where dark clouds were gathering over the sea. "I'm wondering if those will move in."

"They may." He perused them. "But cloudy days serve a purpose too. They help us appreciate the sunshine."

His positive take was consistent with the optimism he'd displayed during each of their encounters. "You have a point."

"Is Zach with you today?"

"No. He's out of town."

"Ah. Let's hope he has a productive trip."

She studied him. That was an odd term to use—unless he was privy to Zach's destination. But as far as she knew, her nephew had only shared it with her and Kat.

Charley's adjective choice must be a fluke.

He picked up the conversation again. "How are you enjoying our quiet little haven?"

"I'm loving it."

"You aren't missing the lights and excitement of the big city?"

"No. The slower pace has helped me unwind after years of nonstop travel and packed schedules. And reconnecting with Zach has been a joy."

"I'm sure he feels the same. Strengthening family ties is always a worthy pursuit. In the end, it's the people in our lives that matter most."

"Yes." She rubbed her thumb over the cell in her hand. "Although to be honest, during my corporate days I was so occupied with my career I lost sight of that."

"Easy to do. We can all get caught up in the whirlwind." Charley watched a few leaves swirl in a vortex of air, then scatter in the breeze. "Now that you're retired, you can start with a clean slate. That's a wonderful blessing."

"I agree—and I have lots of plans."

"Ah yes. Plans. I remember those." A smile played at his lips. "Years ago, as a young man determined to make a difference in the world, I had my whole future planned out in meticulous detail."

"Is that bad?"

"Not always. Plans are necessary for many undertakings—like getting Hope House up and running. But plans do have a downside, as my abuela reminded me before I left Mexico."

"Your grandmother didn't approve of yours?"

"I don't think she had an issue with my goal. More with the process I'd laid out for getting there. But she was too wise to criticize a young man who was burning with enthusiasm. What she did say stayed with me, though."

He paused, and Stephanie's lips twitched. The man certainly knew how to milk a story. "Are you going to tell me?"

"If you'd like to know. I don't want to delay you."

"There's nowhere I have to be. As I told Zach not long ago, my days of back-to-back commitments are over."

"Good for you. As for my abuela—she looked at me in that wise

216

way of hers and said, 'Plans are wonderful, *mi querido*—and it is wise to think ahead. But remember that this'"—he tapped the left side of his chest—"'can sometimes alter plans. And that is not always bad. For those who have been raised well, the heart is the best compass at any crossroads.'"

Stephanie tightened her grip on the phone. Strange how he'd mentioned listening to the heart on the heels of her debate over the merits of that very course. "Have you found that advice to be helpful?"

His mouth curved up, his countenance reflecting peace and contentment. "Very. It's what brought me here, to this lovely town that has been my home for many years." He swept a hand over the surrounding buildings and the harbor. "I thought long and hard before I followed my heart—which is always smart—but in the end it didn't betray me. It led me to my destiny."

"Charley!" A man holding the hand of a little girl called out to him from a few yards away. "Are you opening today?"

He gave a thumbs-up. "I'll be ready for business in ten minutes." He turned back to her. "My customers are calling. Stop by later for tacos if you're in the mood." He touched the brim of his Ducks cap and strolled down the street.

Stephanie watched him for a few moments, then wandered toward her car, still holding her phone as she mulled over Charley's comments.

They weren't directly relevant to her situation. She wasn't a young woman starting out with the lofty goal of making a difference in the world.

But the part about listening to the heart while pondering the choices at a crossroads applied.

Besides . . . wasn't it similar to the practice she'd followed during her career, of listening to her instincts when evaluating business prospects? Of course she did her due diligence, gathered all the facts—but she'd never discounted her intuition.

And it had rarely failed her.

So if she'd trusted her instincts as she'd navigated the corporate jungle, why couldn't she trust her heart to guide her on her personal journey?

At the very least, why not let it have its say?

She opened Frank's email and skimmed it again.

The message was simple and straightforward. The man wasn't asking her to marry him, for heaven's sake. He was asking her to visit a state park. A casual, daytime outing to look at flowers. Dates didn't get more innocent than that.

What could be the harm in going? It would give her another opportunity to learn more about him—and you could never have too much data when evaluating options.

Put in that context, accepting his invitation was an entirely logical, left brain decision.

Even if her heart was doing a happy dance as she lifted her phone and keyed in her response.

19

· ·

This was it.

As the cab that had brought him from the Atlanta airport pulled away from the curb and sped off, Zach pocketed his wallet and examined the two-story, Georgian-style brick house with the white columns that had been the center of his youthful world, back when harmony and happiness reigned here.

His childhood home hadn't changed—but everything else had.

And showing up out of the blue could backfire. Exacerbate the enmity between him and his dad rather than restore peace.

His stomach knotted.

Maybe he should have called first.

But after hours of debating the best approach, of considering possible outcomes from every angle, his conclusion had always been the same. Calling would have been a dead end. His dad would have told him not to come—guaranteed.

As the old saying went, it was easier to ask for pardon than for permission.

And most people would find it difficult to ignore a family member standing on their doorstep. Plus, it was harder to close a door in someone's face than to jab the end button on a cell phone.

His father *could* give him the cold shoulder—but perhaps the elder Garrett would take into account the almost three-thousand-mile journey that had brought his son to his doorstop and at least invite him in.

If he did . . . if he opened the door of the house . . . it was possible he'd also crack the door to his heart.

Or not.

Who knew how his dad would respond?

And standing out here on the sidewalk wasn't going to give him that answer.

Zach bent, picked up his duffle and laptop case, and forced himself to walk down the path and up the two steps to the veranda that ran the length of the house.

At the door, he set the duffle down, leaned forward . . . and hesitated, finger poised over the button.

Just do it, Garrett.

Taking a fortifying breath, he pressed the bell.

From deep within the house, the familiar ding-dong chimed.

Ten seconds ticked by.

Twenty.

Thirty.

Sweat began to trickle down the middle of his back under the long-sleeved dress shirt he wore year-round in Hope Harbor. Too bad he hadn't remembered how hot and muggy August could be in the South.

More beads of sweat popped out on his forehead as he pushed the bell again.

Could his dad have chosen to stay somewhere else the night before the surgery?

But why would he do that? None of the hospitals he was likely to use were more than a short drive—

The lock clicked.

The knob rattled.

The door swung open.

From the other side of the threshold, the man he hadn't seen since Josh's funeral stared back at him, looking exactly as he had that day—except for his almost palpable panic.

"Did something happen to Stephanie?"

It took a few seconds for his father's question to register.

"No. She's fine."

But it wasn't difficult to understand why his dad would jump to that conclusion. Why else would his estranged son travel across the country unless he had bad news to deliver?

Zach attempted a smile but only managed a tiny flex of his stiff lips. "I thought I'd drop in for a visit."

Comprehension dawned in his father's eyes, and his jaw hardened. "Did Stephanie put you up to this?"

As his momentary panic subsided, Richard Garrett again became the man he'd morphed into a few days after Josh's funeral, when his elder son had told him he was ditching the corporate world to follow in his brother's footsteps. Same grim expression, same parallel crevices carved in his forehead above his nose, same rigid shoulders that suggested he was primed for confrontation.

Not the most welcoming body language.

Zach tightened his grip on the laptop case.

Stay calm. Say your piece. Extend the olive branch. Give it your best shot. That's all you can do.

"No, she didn't. I make my own decisions."

"But she did tell you about the surgery."

"Yes."

His father's features tightened in displeasure. "I asked her not to."

"She said she didn't promise to keep it to herself."

"No, she didn't." A muscle clenched in his jaw. "She was always stubborn."

Must run in the family.

But Zach left that unsaid.

The sweat on his forehead began to trickle down the side of his face, and he swiped it away with unsteady fingers. "I forgot how hot it can get here in the summertime."

His father motioned toward the duffle. "You just arrive?"

"Yes. I took a cab straight from the airport."

"You have a place to stay?"

"Not yet." There were any number of hotels nearby, and he could very well end up in one of them if this reunion went downhill. But getting an invitation to stay in his childhood home would be encouraging.

"It's too hot to stand out here talking. Come in out of the sun while you make arrangements."

So much for encouraging.

His spirits nosedived.

His father pulled the door back, and Zach picked up his duffle. Stepped into the welcome coolness.

"On days like this, I'm grateful for air-conditioning—not that I have much use for it in Oregon." He did his best to maintain a conversational tone. "It was sixty-five there this morning." Perhaps a discussion about an innocuous subject like weather would smooth out the awkwardness before he tackled more serious topics.

Like heart surgery.

His dad closed the door. "The temperature doesn't matter to me. I'm not outside much. You want to freshen up, use the facilities?"

"No."

Silence.

Zach motioned toward the kitchen. "I wouldn't mind a glass of water—if it's not too much trouble."

"There's no shortage of water." His father strode toward the back of the house.

Zach left his luggage in the foyer and followed him, pausing on the threshold of the room.

Though it had been a long while since he'd been home, the kitchen hadn't changed one iota. Same high-end stainless-steel appliances. Same granite countertops. Same sleek, modern furniture.

All reflecting the remodel his father had undertaken after Mom died, when being in the homey kitchen she'd loved had been too painful a reminder of his loss.

That was an insight Zach would never have gained if he hadn't wandered down here late one night the Christmas he'd come home after her death and found his dad sitting at the table, tears streaming down his cheeks.

His father had actually spoken about his dark desolation on that quiet midnight, and not long after he'd commissioned the remodel.

That breakdown—and their discussion—had never been mentioned again.

Zach slowly filled his lungs.

He hadn't thought about that incident in years.

But after what Stephanie had told him about Dad's younger days, that night may have given him a rare glimpse of the little boy who'd once worn his heart on his sleeve.

"I have orange juice or Diet Coke if you prefer one of those over water." His father opened the fridge.

"Diet Coke would hit the spot."

His dad extracted two cans and set them on the island. "You have any food on the plane?"

"A couple of packs of pretzels."

His father shook his head. "Airplane food was never all that palatable, but it's gone straight downhill."

"Another reason I'm glad I don't have to travel anymore."

"I suppose that's one advantage to your new job."

The only one, as far as his dad was concerned.

His reluctant host didn't have to voice that for the message to come through loud and clear. His inflection said it all.

Zach opened his Coke, letting the CO_2 hiss out, and implemented part B of his if-he-got-inside-the-house plan. "I was hoping you'd let me buy you dinner." Unless his dad had broken pattern and started eating earlier than seven thirty, his evening meal should still be ahead.

The twin furrows on his father's brow deepened as he released the tab on his own drink. "I hadn't planned to eat much tonight."

"Are there dietary restrictions prior to the surgery?"

"Fast after midnight."

"That's almost five hours away."

"I'm not very hungry."

Understandable.

If *he* was facing major surgery tomorrow, Zach doubted he'd have much appetite either.

"Instead of a big meal, why don't we get a quick bite at Fetterman's? I used to love their pastrami sandwiches." And his favorite deli was still around, according to Google. If that didn't fly, there were several other options, depending on his dad's mood.

"I have business to take care of this evening."

Was that true—or an excuse to avoid prolonging the conversation with his son?

Whichever the case, the message was unmistakable. The elder Garrett wasn't receptive to sharing dinner.

Don't push, Zach. Let him come around on his own terms and timetable—if he chooses to come around at all.

"Okay."

More silence as they sipped their sodas.

"If you're hungry, I keep a variety of frozen dinners on hand."

His father's offer was grudging—but it *was* an offer.

While a microwave dinner wasn't the type of meal he'd had in mind for tonight, it was more appealing than eating alone in a hotel restaurant. The longer he could extend his stay here, the more opportunity he'd have to chip away at the wall between them.

"I can do frozen—if you'll join me. I don't like to eat alone."

"Who do you eat with in Oregon?" His dad gave him a disapproving scowl. "Have you shacked up with someone?"

That hurt.

His father, of all people, should know he'd never violate the moral principles that had been instilled in him. Maybe he only paid lip service to his faith these days, but the virtues it taught were deeply ingrained.

"Not my style. Never has been, never will be." He met his father's gaze straight on.

"Hmph." His dad was the first to look away. "Nice to know some things haven't changed."

"More than some."

His father let that pass. "If you want to check out the dinners in the freezer, help yourself."

"I'd like to talk about the surgery first."

"Nothing to talk about. Arteries in the heart are blocked. The doc's going to fix them. End of story."

"What about after the surgery? Are you going to a rehab place?"

"I'm not planning to. They can send a home health aide here. After the first week or so, I expect I'll start working from home."

"I thought the recovery took six to twelve weeks." That's what all the websites he'd scoured had said.

His dad gave a dismissive flip of his hand. "I'll be bored out of my mind in two days. Working will keep me occupied until I can go back to the office." He gave him a steely look. "There was no need for you to traipse across the country for this. Who's running your store?"

It wasn't a store. It was a business.

But that was an argument for another day . . . or not. He'd come here to build bridges, not rehash old fights.

"I have two excellent part-time employees who are working extra hours to cover the gap while I'm gone."

"Your staff consists of two part-timers?"

"Any more would be unnecessary overhead—and I'm there every day. It's a lean, efficient operation."

"I bet you work longer hours now than you did in your corporate job."

"During the start-up, yes. Not anymore. And even when I'm working, it doesn't feel like work. I love what I do."

"It can't be all that profitable."

"It pays the bills."

"And you're satisfied with that?" The corners of his father's mouth turned down.

"I had a nest egg saved from my corporate career that provides a comfortable cushion and all the security I need. Anything on top of that is gravy. I'd rather have flexibility and the leisure to enjoy what's important in life than an extra zero on my bank balance."

"You won't scoff at that zero if your business ever goes under or the cushion you have gets eaten up by an emergency."

Zach swigged his soda. Now might not be the best time to bring up what Stephanie had told him about his father and the judge—but would there ever be a good time?

Besides, his father's comment was the perfect lead-in to the discussion he wanted to have that could lay the groundwork for the olive branch he was trying to extend.

He set the can back on the island and braced. "Aunt Stephanie and I had a long talk before I came back here."

His father's eyes narrowed. "About what?"

"About your first job."

Muttering a word Zach had never heard him use, his father turned away and stalked over to the sink. Twisted the knob. Rinsed his can.

Zach waited.

"She had no right to tell you that." His voice quivered with rage. "She knows how I feel about rehashing old history."

"In her defense, I think she hoped it would help me understand why you were so upset about what Josh and I did—and why you were always guarded with your emotions. It worked. I knew your dad's bankruptcy had an impact on your view of security, but the judge story was enlightening. Had I known when Josh died what I know now, I may have broached my career change differently with you."

His father swiveled toward him and crossed his arms. "Are you saying you'd have considered staying in Chicago?"

"No—but I would have tried harder to explain to you why I was doing what I was doing instead of getting mad at your reaction."

"The outcome would have been the same. You'd still have gone off to become a barista."

"I'm more than that, Dad." He maintained a calm tone—with an effort. "I run a business. One that turns a healthy profit and brings joy to me and my customers. People come from miles around because of the welcoming atmosphere I've created."

"You'll never get rich."

"I don't care. Money doesn't buy happiness."

"Don't spout pious adages to me."

"It happens to be true. You're rich. Are you happy?"

"Of course I'm happy. I'm exactly where I always wanted to be. What more could I want?"

"A relationship with your son?"

A subtle flinch at his quiet query gave Zach his answer, even though his father sidestepped the question.

"The breach between us wasn't my choice."

"Wasn't it? You could have picked up the phone anytime and called me. I left the door open to that before I went back to Chicago after Josh's funeral."

"You wanted me to apologize. I'm not sorry for the way I feel about what you and your brother did. I thought it was foolish and reckless, and my opinion hasn't changed."

"I can accept that. But does your disapproval of my career choice have to mean we can't have a relationship? I don't agree with how much you've sacrificed for your job, but I can accept—and respect—*your* choice."

His father blew out a breath. "Tonight isn't the time for a discussion like this."

"I know it's not ideal—and I wish we'd had it sooner—but I don't like unfinished business. Losing touch with you has been my one regret. I'd like to do what I can do to resolve our differences, get back on track. Life is too short to build walls that cut you off from the people you love."

There.

He'd said the L-word.

It hung between them as the ice maker dumped a new load of frozen cubes into the holding compartment.

When his father responded, there was less animosity in his inflection. "It's not like I'm planning to check out tomorrow, you know."

"I'm not expecting you to either. But after we lost Josh, I learned not to take anything for granted. Can't we establish a truce? If you won't accept my choice, could you try to accept *me*? I'm your son. The only one you have left. Do we really want to spend the rest of our lives at odds?"

His father took Zach's empty soda can and walked over to the sink. Rinsed it. Gripped the edge of the counter and looked out the window, where day was morphing to dusk, muddying the view into the distance.

In the silence, Zach focused on inhaling and exhaling.

Prayed.

If his dad rebuffed his overture . . . refused to cooperate with this last-ditch effort to reconnect . . . it was doubtful the rift between them would ever be mended.

Should that worst case come to pass, he'd find a hotel. Tomorrow, he'd go to the hospital during the surgery. Hang around Atlanta until his father was released from intensive care. Then he'd go back to his life in Oregon.

While the gulf between them would always bother him, he could take a modicum of comfort in knowing he'd done his best to bridge it.

His father remained at the window, his back to the room as he spoke. "I'm not up to a discussion tonight. Have a frozen dinner if you're inclined. Stay in your old room if you want to save the cost of a hotel. I'll be in my office for an hour or two. After I finish, I'm going to bed. I have to get up early."

It wasn't much of a concession—but it was more promising than the silent treatment . . . or being shown the door.

"I'll stay. Thank you. What time do you have to be at the hospital?"

"Five thirty."

"I'll drive you, if you're willing to let me take your car."

"Cab's already been ordered."

"You can cancel it."

More silence.

"Fine." His father closed the blinds over the sink, straightened the soap dispenser, deposited the cans in the recycling bin inside one of the cabinets . . . and walked toward the door without ever making eye contact. "Good night."

Zach returned the sentiment as his father disappeared down the hall.

For several minutes he remained standing beside the island in the empty kitchen—until his stomach rumbled, reminding him it was long overdue for a feeding.

After the meals he'd grown accustomed to preparing in Oregon, a sodium-laden frozen entrée didn't hold much appeal. But the calories would stoke his flagging energy—and it was a notch above eating a room service meal at an impersonal hotel.

He wandered over to the refrigerator. Pulled open the door to the freezer compartment and scanned the stacks of boxed microwave dinners. Selected one with a meatloaf entrée . . . all the while processing the past few minutes.

No, he and his dad hadn't had a real discussion about their estrangement . . . but talking about feelings had never been Richard Garrett's strong suit. Except for that night here in this kitchen, he'd always expressed his emotions more with actions than words.

Unless he was displeased.

Then the words came easily.

Tonight, though, he'd been judicious with his negative comments.

That was progress.

And assuming the surgery went well, it was possible a few more chinks would appear in the wall between them over the next few days. Enough to break the radio silence and create an opening for future conversations.

Wishful thinking?

Perhaps.

But as his tenure in Hope Harbor had taught him, sometimes—despite the odds—good could come from bad . . . and happy endings weren't always just the stuff of fairy tales.

20

· ·

"Knock knock. Anyone home?"

At the summons from her deck, Katherine padded barefoot down the hall and into the great room.

Stephanie stood on the other side of the slider screen, dressed in the same outfit she'd worn at Hope House on Wednesday.

"Hi." Katherine crossed to her and opened the latch. "Come on in."

"I'm only staying a minute. With Zach gone, I was at loose ends, so I decided to join the Sunday evening rehab crew at Hope House and help paint. You want to come along? We could get tacos first, if Charley is cooking."

Mmm. A far more appealing dinner than the quick omelet she'd planned.

But her first trip to Hope House had stretched her comfort level. Without Zach by her side today, she could be assigned to assist a loquacious volunteer who'd pepper her with questions . . . especially now that Stephanie and Frank had paired up.

"Um . . . I'm not in the mood to socialize with strangers."

"I'm not a stranger."

"No—but won't you be working with Frank?"

"Not today. He's busy with a special event at the lighthouse. It would be just you and me, kid."

An evening spent with Stephanie, including tacos.

Easy decision.

"Give me five minutes to change."

"Don't rush on my account. By the way—have you heard anything from Zach?"

"No. Have you?"

"Only a text letting me know he arrived. I thought he might have called you. In case you haven't figured it out, he's smitten."

Warmth crept across her cheeks. "Let's not get carried away."

"*I'm* not the one who's getting carried away." She dropped onto the couch. "I may not have much personal experience with romance, but I know it when I see it."

Katherine went into the best-defense-is-a-good-offense mode. "No personal experience? What about all that high-voltage electricity pinging around on Wednesday at Hope House while you and Frank were patching walls? I was afraid I'd be electrocuted whenever I walked by the door of the room where you two were working."

"You, my dear, have a vivid imagination." Stephanie picked a piece of lint off her jeans.

"Nope. I'm an actress. Emotions are—"

Whoops.

Katherine clapped a hand over her mouth.

How in the world had she let *that* slip out?

But mistakes happened if you got too comfortable around someone, lowered your guard.

Stephanie's eyes sparked with interest. "You're an actress?"

Too late to backtrack.

Katherine walked over and sat in the chair across from her. "Yes—but I'm here incognito while I sort through some . . . career issues. Please don't tell anyone."

"My lips are sealed. Does Zach know?"

"Yes. He and Charley are the only ones in town who do—besides you."

"So where is home?"

"LA is my base—but in my business, you go where the parts are."

Stephanie's brow knitted. "A career as nomadic as mine was."

"It can be—although my ongoing role in a weekly TV series keeps me close to LA for much of the year."

"May I ask your real name?"

After Katherine shared it, Stephanie gave an apologetic shake of her head. "I'm sorry. I don't stay up with Hollywood personalities or watch much TV."

"Even if you did, I'm not a household name." That could change, however, if she accepted the movie role dangling in front of her.

Stephanie gave her a cautionary look. "You know Zach is happily settled here, right?"

"Yes." She didn't blame the woman for wanting to protect her nephew. "That's why we're being careful to keep our relationship low-key. For both our sakes, I'm not comfortable moving forward until I make several important decisions."

"Sound thinking." Stephanie's forehead smoothed out. "To be candid, I'm in the same boat with Frank. Long-distance relationships are difficult to sustain and often plagued with problems. One of us would have to make a radical lifestyle adjustment—and I can't see Frank living in New York."

"Are you willing to consider relocating?"

"If you'd asked me that a month ago, I'd have said no. Now . . . I don't know. Meeting Frank has been an unexpected blessing—and this is an appealing town. There's really nothing tying me to New York."

"I wish I could say the same about LA."

Stephanie gave a sympathetic nod. "I hear you. And I thought *I* was facing a tough choice. But I had a long, productive career, and I achieved all my goals. I imagine your star is rising, and who knows what the future could hold? Romance in your situation is far more complex than in mine—and affects both your personal life and your job."

No kidding.

Katherine rubbed her forehead. "I know—and it wasn't a complication I expected to have to deal with while I was up here plotting my course for the future."

"It wasn't on my vacation itinerary either." Stephanie twisted her wrist to expose the face of her watch. "You still want to paint, or would you rather pass after this depressing discussion?"

"I'll paint. If I sit around here, I'll—whoops. Call coming in. Give me a sec." She pulled out her vibrating cell.

"Maybe it's Zach with an update."

No such luck. Simon's number flashed on the screen.

"Crud."

"Not someone you want to talk to?"

"No. My agent can't seem to grasp that I don't want to be disturbed." She let the call roll and put the phone away. "Let's go paint. Can I get you a drink while I change?"

"No, thanks—but if you have a truffle lying around, I wouldn't object to that."

"I do have a few rejects." She told Stephanie about the batch she'd taken to the tearoom—and the reception.

"You're a woman of many talents, that's all I can say. And rejects are fine with me. They may not be as pretty as the ones you delivered to the lavender farm, but they'll taste just as delicious."

Katherine retrieved two from the kitchen and handed them to her on a paper napkin. "Enjoy."

"Every bite—even if they'll dampen my appetite for tacos."

While her guest sank back on the couch to savor the chocolates, Katherine retreated to the bedroom, changed into the same outfit she'd worn while stripping wallpaper with Zach—and mulled over Stephanie's subtle warning not to disrupt the placid life her nephew had here.

It was hard to fault.

Starting something she didn't intend to finish would be wrong—which made yesterday's good-bye kiss all the more inappropriate. Zach had been through too much turmoil in his life already, had lost too many people he cared about. For all she knew, his last-ditch effort to salvage his relationship with his dad would also nosedive.

He didn't need another broken romance on top of all that.

What he needed was a woman who had her act together, who'd found her place in the world—as he had—and was content with life in a small seaside town, away from the cameras and lights and accolades . . . and the magic of acting.

Truth was, she could do without the first three. The compulsion to prove herself to the world had diminished, and notoriety had become more exhausting than exciting.

Yet she did enjoy the magic part.

The question was, did she enjoy it enough to walk away from the most intriguing and appealing man who'd ever crossed her path?

She fingered a piece of wallpaper stuck to her sweatshirt. Pulled it off.

That wasn't a question she was going to be able to answer today.

But in two weeks, she owed Simon a decision on the movie—and that choice could have implications far beyond one starring role.

In the meantime, all she could do was pray—and hope her pleas for guidance would be answered before that looming deadline was upon her.

He'd survived.

As the world around him slowly came into focus and that reality sank in, Richard frowned.

Was that good or bad?

The answer eluded him.

Yes, he had his job to fill his days—but without the woman he'd loved . . . without the younger son he'd once doted on . . . with Zach off in Oregon—so far away in every respect he, too, might as well be dead—what was the point of it all?

But those weren't questions he should be dwelling on. They were disruptive. Unsettling. And it was important to present a strong, confident face to the world.

Even if you were shaky and uncertain inside.

"Mr. Garrett?" The summons came from somewhere to his left, and he peered that direction.

A woman in scrubs, her hair covered with a cap, mask pulled down, was watching him.

"Yes?" His reply came out scratchy, as if he were recovering from laryngitis. He tried to clear his throat.

"Don't worry about your voice. The hoarseness is from the breathing tube. I'm your surgeon, Dr. Edwards."

He frowned at her. Did she think the arteries to his brain were blocked too?

"I know."

She smiled at his gruff response. "Excellent. Sometimes it takes a while for patients to emerge from the mental fog after surgery. You're recovering fast. Right now, you're in the ICU—that's common for the first day after surgery, as we discussed. I expect to move you to a regular room later today. The surgery went fine. We took veins from your leg and redirected the blood flow around three partially blocked sections of arteries in your heart. Any questions?"

"When can I go home?"

"Let's see how you do—but if there are no complications, Friday or Saturday would be realistic."

"What day is it?"

"Tuesday."

He'd lost an entire day?

"What happened to Monday?"

"Most patients don't remember much about the first twenty-four hours after surgery. But here's someone who does." She shifted aside, and a man took her place.

Zach?

All at once, the events of Sunday night clicked into focus.

His son had shown up on his doorstep. And despite a less-than-cordial welcome, he'd stayed the night. Driven him to the hospital. Squeezed his shoulder in the moments before they'd wheeled him into surgery.

From his scuzzy appearance, he hadn't left the hospital since then either—nor clocked much shut-eye.

"Hi, Dad." He leaned down, putting them on the same level.

At this proximity, Zach looked even worse. His eyes were red-rimmed and bloodshot, his hair was unkempt, and the whiskers on his cheeks and chin had passed the stubble stage.

"You need a shave—and sleep." The words rasped past his throat.

"You could use a shave yourself." The corners of his mouth rose. "But you're on the mend. That's all that matters."

"Go home. Sleep. Eat."

"I will."

"Now."

"I'll get a meal in the cafeteria."

"You don't have to stay."

"I want to."

A wave of fatigue crashed over him, and hard as he fought to remain alert, his eyelids drooped.

"Rest, Dad. I'll be here when you wake up."

He stopped struggling. If Zach wanted to stay, he would. That boy had always had a one-track mind once he set a goal.

It was no wonder he'd caught the attention of management and risen at lightning speed through the ranks at his firm in Chicago.

If only he'd—

He lost his train of thought as his hand was grasped in a firm, comforting clasp.

The contact felt . . . odd.

No one had held his hands in years.

No one had to hold his hand now.

He could cope on his own, as he always had.

Yet the warmth of that caring, human touch seeped into his pores—and zoomed straight to his heart, chasing away the chill that had kept that defective organ in cold storage since his sons had deserted him.

No.

That wasn't quite accurate—or fair.

Both had tried to maintain contact, but he hadn't been receptive to their appeals.

Thank God he and Joshua had reconnected before his younger son's death—but Zach walking away from a promising career had been like déjà vu. Why had neither of them taken advantage of the educations they'd received to create a safe, secure future?

Not that they'd ever been slackers. Both had worked hard at school, been offered excellent positions. But Joshua had turned his offer down flat, and Zach had ultimately followed in his brother's footsteps.

Why had they bothered to get fancy degrees if they hadn't planned to build solid careers, like he and Stephanie had?

Why?

"What did you say, Dad?"

Zach spoke close to his ear, and the pressure on his fingers increased.

He summoned up the energy to repeat the question he hadn't realized he'd spoken aloud.

"Why what?" His son sounded puzzled.

"Why . . . did you . . . get . . . business degree?"

He strained to hear the answer over the various beeping monitors around him, fighting the numbing fatigue that was sucking him back down into a black hole.

Zach spoke, but the words were too faint to hear.

"What?" He strained toward his son.

"Rest, Dad." A gentle hand pressed him back against the pillow.

"Tell me."

This time, Zach spoke closer to his ear. "You said it would be a practical choice. One that would set me up for success."

"But it . . . wasn't what . . . you wanted."

"I didn't know that until later. Josh realized sooner than I did that neither of our degrees were the best fit. But we both hated disappointing you. We always wanted to make you proud."

Yet they'd failed.

Zach didn't have to say that for Richard to read between the lines, despite his half-groggy state.

And it was true. He'd been profoundly upset and frustrated after they'd each veered off the straight and narrow to take jobs that offered little of the security and prestige so critical to him after the shattering incident with his first mentor left him destitute and reviled.

Yet his firstborn's point on Sunday night, about respecting each other's choices and not letting a disagreement over that ruin their relationship, had been valid.

The very conclusion he'd been dancing around for the past twelve months himself.

But how to reach out, how to initiate a reconciliation—that had been the stumbling block.

Maybe because he had too much pride.

Scratch that.

He *did* have too much pride.

That was the stumbling block.

Admitting he may have overreacted . . . that it had been wrong to try and force his sons to live lives that conformed to his definition of success . . . that not everyone who refused to fall into lockstep with him was a failure . . . had been a formidable challenge.

One that required courage—and the kind of touchy-feely conversation he always took pains to avoid.

But now Zach had sucked it up and done the heavy lifting. The son he'd shunned and disparaged had swallowed his own pride and come to his door to try and bridge the gulf between them.

He was the one with the guts in this family.

Richard tried to raise his heavy eyelids, but they refused to cooperate.

Instead, he squeezed the strong hand that held his. "I'm proud of you."

Those were the words he tried to say—but they came out garbled.

"What?" Zach leaned close, so close he could feel his son's breath on his cheek.

He tried again—with even less success.

Muted voices spoke in the background, and Zach relinquished his grip.

Richard tried to grope for his hand—but it was gone.

"I'm here, Dad. The nurse has to check a few monitors."

His reassurance registered . . . but the world faded away.

Yet as darkness claimed him once again, his patched-up heart felt lighter.

Because while Zach didn't yet realize it, the long silence between them was about to come to an end.

21

Yes!

Zach was calling her back.

Finally.

Katherine pressed the talk button, put her cell to her ear, and sat on the log on Blackberry Beach. "Good morning."

"Morning." A trundling noise that could be a hospital cart came over the line. "Sorry—I just noticed the time. This wasn't too early to call, was it?"

"No. I'm actually down on Blackberry Beach, taking an early morning walk. How's your dad?"

"He spoke to me a few minutes ago. He was on the fuzzy side, and he's faded out again—but the surgeon says he's doing well. They're talking about moving him out of the ICU in a few hours."

"That's a positive sign."

"I know. Thanks for your return message yesterday."

"I'm sorry I missed your call after he came out of surgery." Naturally, she'd picked that ten-minute window to take a shower. "How did it go when you arrived?"

"We didn't talk much—but he did invite me to stay at the house."

"Also positive."

"That remains to be seen. His resistance may have been down

241

the night before surgery. Hard to say what will happen after he's back in fighting form."

"Maybe the surgery will be a wake-up call. Remind him how vulnerable we all are—and how fleeting life is."

"Hold that thought. How's everything with you?"

Offshore, Charley's dolphin friend Trixie bowed, her sleek body glistening in the morning sun.

"If you're asking whether I've come to a decision about the movie, the answer is no. But I still have almost two weeks. In the meantime, I'm working on truffles for the tearoom and—hold a sec. I've got an incoming call."

She checked the screen.

Simon.

Again.

His fourth call in two days.

The man ought to get a life.

She ignored the summons and went back to Zach. "Sorry. My agent is nothing if not persistent."

"Do you want to take it?"

"No. I'll call him back." Much as she'd prefer not to. A combination of multiple calls in forty-eight hours and several texts was a bit over the top even for him, so it was possible he did have an urgent need to speak with her.

"Go ahead and do that. I have a few questions for the surgeon anyway, and I want to catch her before she leaves."

"When are you coming back?"

"I'm covered at the shop through Thursday. If no issues arise, I may be back that evening."

"Call again with an update if you can."

"I'll do my best. Take care."

Psyching herself up for a less-pleasant exchange, she punched Simon's number. Why listen to all his messages? He could tell her about the latest emergency live.

One ring in, he answered. "Where are you?"

She focused on Trixie's antics, trying not to let the man's frenzy disrupt the serenity of her favorite thinking spot. "You know where I am. Hope Harbor."

"No. I mean, where are you this minute?"

"On the beach. Why?"

"How fast can you get back to your house?"

"Ten minutes." She rose, giving up the attempt to remain calm. "Where are *you*?"

"Cooling my heels on your deck."

He was *here*?

Again?

Bad vibes began to course through her as she strode toward the path that led to the top of the bluff. "What's going on?"

"If you'd answer your phone once in a while, you'd know. We'll talk after you get back."

The line went dead.

Heart pounding, Katherine picked up her pace. Despite Simon's propensity toward over-the-top theatrics, the man seemed to be legitimately rattled.

This had to be about the movie. Nothing less momentous could persuade him to leave LA behind again.

And while she wasn't all that keen to hear his news, she ascended the bluff at twice her usual speed.

True to his word, he was on her deck. Not cooling his heels but pacing.

The instant he spotted her emerging from the brambles, he planted his fists on his hips and sent her a glare that would shrivel a person with twice her confidence.

Don't let him intimidate you, Katherine. You're an actress. Play this cool.

Silently repeating the mantra, she closed the space between them, using every step to shore up her flagging composure.

Once on the deck, she stopped several feet away from her unexpected—and unwanted—visitor. "What are you doing here?"

Instead of respecting her personal space, he swooped in, bristling with rage. "You know, Katherine—you're not a big enough star to indulge in this temperamental 'I want to be alone' diva act . . . or ignore your agent."

"We had an understanding. I wanted to get away. You agreed to give me breathing room. I'm aware of the studio deadline, and I'll have an answer for you on that date."

"The date's changed."

Her stomach dropped to her toes. "What are you talking about?"

"If you'd answered my calls and read my texts, you'd know." His nostrils flared as he inhaled. "The studio wants an answer by this weekend."

"What?" Her stomach began to churn.

"You heard me. In four days—five at the latest."

An ache began to throb in her temple. "Why? What happened?"

"The shooting schedule's been accelerated. They want to begin at the end of September and wrap up location work by year-end to keep travel expenditures in this calendar year. They need to lock down the stars ASAP. I don't have to remind you there are several actresses waiting in the wings who'd sign on the dotted line tomorrow."

No, he didn't.

The pain in her head intensified.

"I'm not ready to give you an answer."

"Maybe this will help you decide. They've agreed to let you keep your clothes on, and the language you didn't like in your lines will be removed. Those are huge concessions."

Yes, they were.

Also unexpected.

Instead of making her decision easier, the director's willingness to meet her terms complicated the situation. Removed the excuse she'd been keeping in reserve if she decided to turn the role down.

She massaged the bridge of her nose. Simon wanted her to cave—but despite all he'd done to convince the powers-that-be to address her concerns, she still couldn't pull the trigger.

"I have to think about this, Simon."

He compressed his lips and tried to stare her down.

She waited him out.

At last he stalked over to one of her deck chairs and sat. "Fine. I'll wait while you do."

Her jaw dropped. "Here?"

"Yes. I'm not going back to LA until this is resolved. It's too big a deal, and too much hangs in the balance, to give this anything less than total focus. Helping you come to a decision is my top priority."

No . . . getting her to sign the contract was his top priority. There were megabucks and a healthy helping of prestige in this for him too.

"You can't stay here. I don't want any more scandal in my life."

"No one knows either of us is in town—and you have plenty of space."

"If someone finds out, you know how the media will play it."

"Nobody cares in this day and age."

"I do. And I've had enough undeserved scandal to last a lifetime."

Smirking, he stood. "I knew you'd say that. I'm already booked at a quaint little inn called the Gull Motel—their description, not mine." His mouth curled in distaste. "I just hope it's clean. The B&B that appears to be the only high-end place in town was already booked."

"You'll survive. Or you could go back to LA and I'll call you this weekend."

"Not happening. At least here, I can drive up to see you if you ignore my calls."

"I won't ignore them."

"I'm not taking that risk." He let out a slow breath, and as he continued, his manner became more conciliatory. "Look, Katherine—I know the whole nasty business with Jason and the investigation afterward were traumatic. But you have to keep the prize in sight. This role is what you've wanted since the day you came to Hollywood. It's a dream come true—and it doesn't happen for everyone."

"I know that. And I'm grateful for the offer."

"I hear a *but* in there." He motioned to the two chairs on the deck. "Let's sit for a few minutes. Talk to me about what's on your mind."

Her vision misted, and she clenched her hands at her sides until her nails dug into her palms.

It was much easier to blow off the high-handed, arrogant Simon. This kinder, gentler version was far harder to deal with—even if his empathy was an act.

He walked over to the chairs. Waited.

She brushed a few grains of sand off her leggings, mind racing. Should she have a frank discussion with him? Share her concerns, as she'd done with Zach? After all, the man *was* her agent.

Yeah. She probably ought to be more candid about her career turmoil.

Forcing her feet to carry her forward, she joined him at the chairs and sank into one.

As he sat beside her, Charley's seagull friends swooped down and landed on the deck railing a few yards down. After giving them a wary perusal, Simon redirected his attention to her. "Tell me what's holding you back."

Mustering up her courage, she poured out all her turmoil, sharing her doubts and disillusionment and dissatisfaction as she had with Zach—though not in as much detail.

Simon listened without interrupting until she finished, then leaned back in his chair, brow knotted. "I didn't realize how unhappy you were—or that your discontent predates the incident with Jason."

That wasn't the reaction she'd expected.

He hadn't yelled at her. Or berated her. Or tried to convince her that her feelings weren't valid.

Either he'd suddenly developed compassion and understanding—or fear of losing out on a deal to have one of his clients star in a prestigious film was forcing him to put a long-rusty skill set to use.

Her money was on the latter—but she'd give him the benefit of the doubt.

"I think my misgivings have been simmering for quite a while. Jason's death was . . . it forced me to confront them."

"So you're having a sort of midcareer crisis, questioning your goals. It happens." He patted her hand, oozing empathy. "But that's a different challenge than the decision about whether to accept this role. They don't have to be dealt with together. Why not take the part and defer the question about where to go from there until after the film wraps?"

He knew why as well as she did.

"Because if the critics are kind and the film is a success, more offers will come in. The pace will accelerate. I'll have even less time to think. Walking away now would be cleaner and less complicated than walking away afterward."

"Walking away." He drummed a finger on the arm of the chair. "That's a very final step, Katherine."

"I know."

"What would you do if you left Hollywood behind? Acting is all you know."

"No, it's not." Her defensive hackles rose. "I have other options."

"Like what?"

"Like . . . like making candy." The suggestion of such a radical career change appeared to surprise him as much as it did her.

He gaped at her as if she'd said she wanted to travel to Mars. "You can't be serious."

Maybe she hadn't been when that idea had tripped off her tongue—but the concept wasn't *that* bizarre.

"Why not? I enjoy it, and the truffles I've made during my stay here have gotten rave reviews."

Simon rose. Walked over to the railing and looked out over the sea. Ran his fingers through his hair, leaving his pricey salon cut in disarray as he pivoted back to her.

Mr. Empathy was gone. The shrewd, deal-making Hollywood agent was back.

"I'm beginning to worry about your mental state, Katherine. Why on earth would you give up an acting career poised on the brink of success to spend your days making chocolate?"

"I like doing it. It's satisfying. And I wouldn't always have nosy reporters in my face."

"It's not going to pay like acting."

"I've saved my money."

"I know." His lips twisted in disgust. "You live like a pauper."

"I live like someone who knows the value of a dollar—and who craves financial security. Which I have. That gives me options."

"Are you saying you don't like acting anymore? That you wouldn't miss it?"

"No. I do and I would. But I don't like what comes with it at the Hollywood level."

"So you're going to give up everything you've worked for and open a little froufrou chocolate shop."

At his belittling tone, she bristled. "I didn't say that. I said I *could* if I wanted to. You asked about my skills, and that's one I do have."

He began to pace again. "Listen—if you want to get involved in the chocolate business, take the movie role. Get famous. Then I'll go find a chocolate company that will sign you as a spokesperson. You'll have the best of both worlds."

The man just didn't get it.

"I'm interested in *making* chocolate, not endorsing it."

She could try to explain to him how she enjoyed the physical act of tempering chunks of chocolate until they were transformed into glossy goodness, experimenting with different flavors and ingredients to produce a product that was uniquely hers, inhaling the heady and comforting aroma as she worked. She could tell him how much she cherished having total control over her creative—and personal—life.

But he wouldn't understand.

The façade of sympathy he'd adopted for a few minutes had melted away.

"Come on, Katherine. Get real. The average chocolatier in this country earns a fraction of your current income. There are actors out there who would kill to be in your position. You already have a level of fame and fortune the average Joe can never hope to attain, and you're on the brink of becoming a megastar. If you want to be a recluse off-screen after you reach that stage, go for it. It could add to your mystique."

That was plausible in theory—but it didn't always work out in reality. Even if you tried to keep your nose clean and stay under the radar, scandal could find you . . . as she'd learned the hard way. And the paparazzi were relentless under the best of circumstances.

"I'll take everything you've said under consideration." She stood too.

He gave a loud huff. "Can't you make this easy on both of us and just say yes?"

"No."

He threw up his hands. "Fine. Do your thinking. But hurry it up. I'll be at the motel—but I'll be dropping by frequently."

As he stormed across the deck, one of the gulls cackled. Then the pair took off, circled above them—and left a calling card with her guest before winging toward the sea.

"What the . . ." As Simon took in the gooey mess splatted on the sleeve of his shirt, he spat out one of the expletives she'd insisted be removed from the movie script.

Hard as she tried to restrain it, a chuckle erupted.

He glowered at her. "You wouldn't be laughing if a stupid bird had ruined one of your four-hundred-dollar shirts."

"I don't have any four-hundred-dollar shirts." She tried to curb her mirth.

"Of course not."

"You want to clean that off in the house?"

"No." He unbuttoned the shirt and stripped it off, careful not to touch the bird poop. "This is going straight into the trash." He held it at arm's length.

"You could wash it."

"No thanks."

"Leave it on the deck. I'll take care of it."

And once it was washed, she'd donate it to the clothing drive bin in the parking lot at Grace Christian. At least someone would benefit from Simon's misfortune of being in the wrong place at the wrong time.

He dropped the soiled garment at his feet as if it was radioactive.

"You want to borrow one of my baggy T-shirts?" She motioned toward his bare chest.

"My luggage is in the car. I'll put on a different shirt before I leave." He continued to the steps but paused at the top. "From now on, answer my calls. Otherwise, I'm moving in here—even if I have to camp on this deck."

Without waiting for a response, he stomped down the steps, circled the deck, and disappeared from view.

Four minutes later, a car engine revved, gravel crunched—and he was gone.

Quiet descended—in the natural world around her, if not in her mind.

What a mess.

She massaged her temples.

In five days, max, she owed Simon an answer.

Yet she was no closer to a decision than she'd been the day he'd told her about the offer.

Replaying their conversation in her mind, she wandered over to the railing and rested her palms on the flat surface.

Some of what he'd said had made sense.

It was true she was facing two decisions, not one . . . as Zach had also pointed out. The movie and her future career path didn't have to be linked. Yes, it would be difficult to keep a successful big-screen role—and Simon's goading—from dictating her plans going forward, but it was possible if she mustered up her moxie. She wasn't the same desperate young woman who'd signed with him five years ago, driven to prove to the world she was somebody, hungry for the media attention she'd come to loathe.

The question was, who was she?

Or, more important, who did she *want* to be?

Those questions deserved thorough analysis—and required more than a few days of thought.

She also needed guidance.

Too bad Zach wasn't here so she could pick his brain.

But he had enough problems of his own in Atlanta.

More prayer could help—though her diligent pleas for guidance had yet to produce answers.

So how was she supposed to figure out what to do before her time ran out and Simon showed up on her doorstep again, brandishing a contract that could change her life forever if she signed on the dotted line?

22

He was as nervous as he'd been back in tenth grade on his very first date, with Mary Lou Wheeler.

And the feeling wasn't fun.

Too jittery to sit still while the gas station attendant filled his tank, Frank slid out from behind the wheel as a silver Thunderbird with a white top pulled in on the opposite side of the pumps.

"Afternoon." Charley called out the greeting through the open window as he set his brake and killed the engine.

"Afternoon to you too. You aren't cooking today?"

"Lunch crowd's thinned." Charley opened the door, got out, and strolled over while he waited his turn for service. "I think I'll paint on this beautiful afternoon—although an outdoor pursuit would be a delightful alternative. What's your plan for the rest of the day?"

Frank transferred his weight from one foot to the other and shoved his hands in his pockets. "I'm driving up to Shore Acres State Park."

"Ah. A perfect day for a walk through the gardens." Charley leaned down and peered into the empty passenger seat. "Are you going alone?"

"No." He could leave it at that—but the response seemed too abrupt in light of Charley's affable manner. "I, uh, thought I'd give Zach's aunt a tour of the place. Her being new in town and all."

"A gracious gesture. I expect she'll appreciate the company, especially with Zach gone for a few days."

"Uh-huh."

Charley leaned back against the hood of the car. "Pleasant woman, Stephanie."

"Yes, she is."

"I imagine she has fascinating stories from her travels."

"Yeah." With an effort, Frank called up a smile. "Quite a contrast to a lowly mail carrier like me. My most exciting moments involved dogs nipping at my heels."

"A different kind of excitement, no question about it." Charley flashed him a grin. "Were you ever bitten?"

"No."

"That doesn't surprise me. Most dogs are more bark than bite—though they can be intimidating. People can be too—for a host of reasons that don't involve barking."

Frank squinted at him.

Could that be a veiled message about Stephanie's jet-setting past and executive position?

Maybe.

News could have traveled around town that he and Zach's aunt had spent last Wednesday painting together—and chatting up a storm while sparks pinged around the room. There'd been a ton of volunteers at Hope House that day.

Or was that remark just one of those random philosophical comments Charley liked to throw out?

"I suppose that's true." Best to play this nonchalant.

"Count on it. In the end, most of us want to be liked—and defined—by who we are inside rather than by external trappings and stereotypes." As two seagulls fluttered in and landed at Charley's feet, he motioned to them. "Have you met Floyd and Gladys?"

Frank regarded the gulls. "You name the birds?"

"Not all of them. These two are old friends. Actually, I've known Floyd the longest. I met him a number of years ago, after he lost his wife. Did you know seagulls mate for life?"

"I don't recall ever hearing that."

"It's a fact. And Floyd was in sad straits, let me tell you. Started moping around the stand. Took to pecking at Tracy's door—that would be Tracy Hunter, from the cranberry farm—looking for company. He was one lonely bird. Then one day, he showed up at my stand with Gladys, happy as a clam."

Frank inspected the birds, which were cuddled up next to each other—close to Charley but watching *him*.

"Nice story." If only it was that easy for humans to move on.

"It's more than that." Charley studied the birds. "Instead of letting fear hold them back, Floyd and Gladys took a leap into the unknown—and now neither is lonesome anymore. I'd call them role models."

Again, Frank scrutinized the man. The remark *appeared* to be personal—but he'd never talked about his battle with loneliness. And he'd certainly never told anyone about his stomach-churning turmoil over the conflict between his devotion to Jo Ann and his interest in Stephanie.

"Easier for birds to do than humans, though. They don't have to deal with logistics . . . or loyalties." Frank sent a sidelong glance toward the attendant. Why on earth was it taking him so long to finish with the gas?

"Logistics can be worked out if the goal is worth the effort— and while loyalty is a fine trait in general, it can be a negative in the wrong context."

What was that supposed to mean?

"How can loyalty ever be bad?"

"If someone holds on to it as an excuse not to open a new door, once the need for it is gone." Charley motioned behind him. "I think you're good to go."

The attendant joined them and handed over his credit card and receipt. "All done."

Finally.

This discussion had become too unsettling—and he was already spooked enough about going on his first date in more than four decades.

"Thanks." He slid the card back into his wallet.

"What'll it be, Charley?" The attendant adjusted his cap.

"Fill 'er up. Bessie purrs along best on a full tank—like we all do. It's tough to run on fumes." Charley pushed off from the hood and tipped his Ducks cap. "Enjoy the gardens, Frank—and give Stephanie my best."

"I'll do that."

The two birds followed the man back to the other side of the pumps.

Frank retook his seat behind the wheel, twisted the key, and put the car in gear. As he pulled out onto 101, he looked in the rearview mirror.

Charley lifted a hand in farewell, as if he knew he was being watched.

But it would be impossible at that distance to detect someone peering at you through a rearview mirror.

Nevertheless, Frank waved out the window—and pressed on the accelerator.

That had been one weird conversation.

Yet as the station and Charley disappeared from view, as he picked up speed toward Zach's house, where Stephanie was waiting for him, the man's comments kept looping through his brain.

Nothing Charley said had been specific to his situation—yet it was all applicable.

Being intimidated by external trappings instead of paying attention to what was in people's hearts.

A grieving seagull who'd found a new love.

The power of fear to hold a person back.

Loyalty as an excuse to maintain the status quo.

The difficulty of running on fumes—be it gas, or a love that existed only in memory.

Frank passed the town limits and increased his speed again.

How could Charley have communicated so much in those few minutes of casual conversation?

And how much of it was personal versus chitchat?

With Charley, who knew?

Yet whether the man had intentionally brought up those subjects—or the topics of their conversation were happenstance—what he'd said offered food for thought.

And if today's outing with Stephanie was as enjoyable as he suspected it would be, he'd be putting his brain on overtime to figure out what he should do about the woman who'd come into his life out of the blue—and who could vanish just as suddenly if he didn't give her some indication he was interested in more than a stroll among roses.

Did furniture designers make hospital chairs uncomfortable on purpose?

Zach stretched out his legs, crossed his ankles, slouched down, and folded his hands over his stomach.

No improvement.

His back continued to protest, and his neck kinked. Again.

That's what he got for trying to sleep last night in a similar chair in the cardiac ICU.

The nurse assigned to his dad had tried to convince him to go home, but he'd come here to stick close until—or unless—the elder Garrett told him to get lost.

So far, that hadn't happened.

He transferred his attention to the bed, where his father had dozed off after the move from the ICU to a regular room. All the bustle of getting him settled had worn him out.

It had been a grueling day—for both of them.

He scanned the clock on the wall. Six o'clock here, three o'clock in Oregon.

Not quite the dinner hour at home—but in view of his erratic eating schedule over the past thirty-six hours, it was no wonder his stomach was growling.

Now, while his dad was sleeping, could be the best time to run down to the cafeteria and wolf down a plate of real food. His body was beginning to protest the diet of candy bars, chips, and peanuts he'd been ingesting from the vending machine in the visitor lounge.

He rose. Stretched. Rubbed a hand over his bristly chin. Grimaced.

The nurse entered and gave him a sympathetic appraisal. "Long day?"

"Long day . . . and night . . . and day."

"I hear you. Why don't you go home and catch a few z's, freshen up? We'll be watching your dad closely overnight—and you'll feel more human after a few hours of shut-eye and a shower."

That was true. Besides, they wouldn't have released his father from the ICU if there was imminent danger or any cause for concern—and the staff appeared to be on the ball and responsive.

Nevertheless, leaving didn't feel quite—

"Go."

As his father spoke, he and the nurse moved toward the bed in unison, one on each side.

"You're awake." Zach called up a weary smile. Seeing his always-healthy dad flat on his back and attached to an array of monitors and IVs was unnerving, no matter how successful the surgeon had deemed the operation.

"Yes—and feeling more like myself."

He sounded more like himself too. His voice was stronger, and a touch of his usual authoritative tone was back.

Hard to tell how much was show and how much was bravado, though.

"Glad to hear that."

"Why are you still here?"

Uh-oh.

This could be the dismissal he'd feared.

"I didn't want to leave until I knew you were out of danger."

His father turned his head toward the nurse. "Am I in danger?"

"Not that I can see. All your vitals are excellent."

His dad refocused on him. "See. Go back to the house and sleep. I bet you look worse than I do. Doesn't he?" He directed that question to the nurse too.

"I'd definitely diagnose a case of fatigue. And I imagine he hasn't had a decent meal in the past day or so." She fiddled with the IV line and grinned at him across the bed.

"Two against one." His dad waved a hand toward the door. "Go."

Zach hooked his thumbs in the pockets of his jeans. "I came to be with you."

"You've been with me for forty-eight hours."

"While you two work this out, I have another patient to check on. If you need me, press this button." The nurse demonstrated the call button to his dad.

"Got it." He tucked it beside him as she left and returned to their previous discussion. "When did you last eat?"

"I had a pack of cookies a couple of hours ago."

"I mean a real meal."

Back in Oregon, with Stephanie, in his kitchen.

That felt like a week ago.

"I'll eat later."

"Eat now. Away from the hospital. Stop at that deli you like."

In other words, his father wanted him to leave.

Why?

Was he concerned—or did he want his son out of his life?

No sense dancing around that question. If his dad didn't want him here, he may as well face that fact sooner rather than later.

"Are you sure you want me to leave?"

"Yes."

The answer was definitive, and his spirits sank . . . until his dad added a caveat.

"But I'd like you to come back tomorrow."

The coil of tension in his gut eased.

Those were the sweetest words he'd heard in two and a half long years.

Thank you, God.

"Count on it." He managed to choke out the promise.

"We should talk—but let's wait until we're both more alert." His father's voice was gruff. Not mad gruff, but as if his emotions were getting the better of him.

"I'm on board with that plan." He took his father's hand and gave it a squeeze. "Hang in until tomorrow."

"I intend to hang in for much longer than that." His father squeezed back, then gently tugged his fingers free. "Go home. Sleep."

"I'll give it a shot."

But as Zach left the room and walked down the hospital corridor toward the exit, he had no doubt he'd snooze like a baby.

For while there were fences to mend and mines to defuse, the atmosphere between them had taken a quantum leap into positive territory.

Now, like the fresh, salty air in his adopted town thousands of miles away, it was filled with hope.

The sky was blue, the air was warm, the gardens were gorgeous. All of which added up to a perfect day.

Except for one thing.

Frank was stressed out.

Stephanie peeked at her date as they strolled side by side through the rose garden. Faint creases dented his brow, his features were taut, and his lips had straight-lined.

He looked like a man in the throes of serious second thoughts.

Swallowing past her disappointment, she stopped walking.

Enough of this.

If he was sorry he'd asked her out, why prolong this outing?

He continued another two paces before he realized she'd halted.

Jolting to a stop, he swiveled toward her. "What's wrong?"

"I could ask you the same question."

His Adam's apple bobbed. "What do you mean?"

She shrugged. "You're not having fun."

A faint hint of pink crept across his cheeks. "Why do you think that?"

"Come on, Frank. Give me a little credit. A person would have to be totally oblivious to miss the tension radiating off you. I appreciate the invitation to come up here, but if you want to call it a day, I won't hold it against you. We're both adults. Sometimes reality falls short of expectations. I can accept that."

"Are *you* having fun?"

She fingered the petal of a velvety red rose beside her. Inhaled the sweet scent wafting upward as she composed her answer. "Honestly? I had more fun anticipating today than I've had since you picked me up."

"I'm sorry."

"That's life. I'll get over it." A damaged petal dropped into her hand. She examined the curled edges . . . and let it fall to the ground. "It's probably for the best anyway."

"Why?"

How to respond?

Should she save face and say that since she'd be leaving soon, getting too chummy wouldn't be smart—or tell him the truth?

Be straightforward, Stephanie. You're too old to play games— and mature enough to handle rejection.

She wiped her fingers, damp from the dewy petal, on her slacks. "I was getting too interested—and trying to figure out how to fit a relationship with you into the future I have planned has been a challenge. If the feeling isn't mutual, that solves my dilemma."

In the silence that followed, he gave a slow blink—as if her frankness had surprised him.

At last he inhaled. Straightened his shoulders. "Could we sit for a few minutes?" He motioned toward a bench off to the side.

"We don't have to talk about this, Frank—and you don't owe me any explanations. I'm a big girl. I'll survive." She was *not* going to get emotional about the end of a potential romance she hadn't been all that certain was wise to begin with. Lightening her tone, she swept a hand over the nearby Japanese garden. "Why don't we finish up there and drive back?"

"Because the feeling *is* mutual."

Her heart missed a beat, and she pressed a hand to her chest. Oh. My.

It took her a second to find her voice. "I'll say this for you, Frank Simmons. You know how to keep a woman guessing."

"That's not my intent. Shall we?" He motioned to the bench. "Please."

It was impossible to refuse his heartfelt request—or his warm, earnest blue eyes.

He followed her over, and after they were seated, angled toward her. "As long as we're being honest, I have to tell you that until the day you walked into The Perfect Blend, romance wasn't on my radar screen. And I never expected to feel like a teenager again. This whole turn of events has thrown me for a loop."

"Join the club."

"I also have the same concerns about logistics and geography as you do—plus another issue."

"We may be able to work out the distance hurdle." Especially if she decided to pull the trigger on an idea that had begun bouncing around in her head after her chat with Charley outside church Sunday. "What's the other issue?"

He rested an arm on the back of the bench, his fingers inches from her shoulder. "Jo Ann."

Ah.

He was worried that falling in love with someone else would be a betrayal of his late wife.

"I can't say I understand that feeling from personal experience, but I *can* understand you wanting to be faithful to the memory of your wife and the love you shared." She studied him. "How do you think *she* would feel about us?"

"I don't know. She was a one-man woman. I was the only boy she ever dated—and we vowed to love each other as long as we lived."

"You kept that promise."

"But I'm still alive—and I'll never stop loving her."

She fingered the edge of her sweater, where a piece of yarn was beginning to unravel, and composed her reply with care. If Frank wasn't ready to move on, pushing him that direction would be a mistake. "I can accept that—but does it mean there's no room in your heart for someone else? What about those kids who'll be living in Hope House? The ones who could use a foster grandfather? Will you be able to love them?"

"That's a different type of love."

"But don't we love everyone in our life differently? Parents who have more than one child love them all. A new arrival doesn't take away from their love for the children they already have. Each child is unique and has his or her own special place in their hearts. Couldn't the same principle be applied to romantic love?"

The question hung in the air between them as the seconds ticked by—and it was impossible to read the kaleidoscope of emotions on Frank's face.

This much was clear, however.

While prayer had guided her to a solution for the logistics part of their dilemma, Jo Ann was an obstacle Frank would have to overcome on his own.

The question was, could he?

Frank drew in a long, slow breath and watched a hummingbird flit among the roses.

The woman beside him had made an excellent point—a testament to her ability to analyze a situation and cut to the chase, a skill she would have honed in the wheeling-dealing business world.

And it raised several questions.

Could he view his growing feelings for Stephanie as equal, but different, than the love he and Jo Ann had shared—as Charley's seagull Floyd had done?

What was holding him back, really? Was it loyalty to a vow that no longer applied—or fear of taking a leap into the unknown?

Would falling for Stephanie be—

"Hey." She touched his hand and offered a reassuring smile. "I can almost hear the gears grinding in your brain. You don't have to answer that question today. I was just tossing it out for your consideration."

"I don't mind answering. It's not a question I've dwelt on, but I'm thinking the answer is yes. Every love *is* different. Loving one person doesn't take away from the love you have for someone else. The trouble is, this unexpected—sizzle, if you will—between us is muddling my mind, making me doubt my judgment. I've also been around long enough to know it's dangerous to play with electricity."

"And I've been around long enough to know I can trust my instincts—and my heart." A dimple appeared in her cheek. "That's not to suggest I'm an impetuous woman, you understand. Far from it. I wouldn't jump into anything on a whim. I do, however, believe in paying attention to the possibilities that drop into my lap—and feel right. You fall into both categories."

He inched the hand he'd laid on the back of the bench toward her shoulder. Brushed his fingers against the fine, soft yarn. "Assuming we want to test the waters, continue to get to know each other, geography is against us." He surveyed the sea, visible through the trees bordering the garden. "Believe me, I've thought about this long and hard, but I always come back to the same conclusion. I can't imagine myself living in New York."

"I can't imagine it either. So I have a proposal about how to manage the geography—at least while we're testing the waters, as you put it. I'll rent a place here in Hope Harbor for a few months. My long tenure at my New York apartment means I can invoke the early exit clause in my contract if I choose. With three months' notice, I can be out of there."

Pressure built in his throat, and he dropped his hand to twine his fingers with hers. "You'd do that for me?"

"For us."

He searched her face, seeking any sign of uncertainty or resentment at the sacrifice such an arrangement required. Saw none.

Still . . . Hope Harbor was about as far from the exciting, sophisticated world she'd occupied as a person could get. .

"Do you really think you could be happy here, after all the glamorous places you've traveled? After calling New York home?"

"Living here for a few months will help me determine that. But I can tell you this. Glamor is overrated—and it doesn't take the place of having someone to love. I wasn't ready to admit that earlier in my life, nor trade in my career ambitions for small-town living and romance. Now, both have a definite appeal—and I'm beginning to suspect that's why God brought us together at this stage of my life. He saved the best for last, if you will."

Warmth filled him, as potent and heady as a perfect summer day in Hope Harbor. "You may want to reserve judgment on that."

"I don't think that's necessary—but we can revisit this in a few months . . . if you want me to stay. And you don't have to give me an answer today. I'll be around another week or two. Zach hasn't threatened to send me packing yet." Her lips curved up.

His gaze homed in on them—and his pulse shifted into high gear. She had beautiful lips. Soft . . . supple . . . welcoming.

Tempting.

Don't be a fool, Frank. Tell her to stay. God sent a woman into your life who's put a lilt in your voice and a spring in your step. If you let her get away, you should have your head examined.

Smart advice.

It was time to tuck his treasured memories of Jo Ann into the corner of his heart that would always be hers, banish fear, and take another chance on love.

Because, to use Charley's earlier analogy, he was running on fumes—and a high-octane dose of Stephanie Garrett was exactly what he needed to rev his engine.

He brushed his thumb over the back of her hand and looked straight into her eyes. "I can give you my answer now. Stay."

A soft flush crept over her cheeks. "Done."

"I have to warn you, though—my dating skills are beyond rusty . . . and I'm not certain they were all that hot to begin with."

She offered him a wry smile. "Trust me, they're more polished than mine. I was always more interested in spreadsheets than smooches."

A chuckle rumbled deep in his chest. "What do you say we work on polishing our skills together?"

"I like that plan."

"Are you certain you don't mind paying two rents for a few months? That'll be a big expense."

"I view it as an investment. One I have a feeling will pay off handsomely." Her mouth bowed. "There's a compliment in there, in case you missed it."

"Thank you for that. And I agree about the investment. I can't see much downside to giving this a go—and the upside potential is impressive."

"Upside potential." She gave a soft chuckle. "That sounds like something one of my clients—or my boss—would have said."

"I don't feel like either." He scooted closer. "What do you say we forget spreadsheets and focus on smooches?"

"I'm in."

"Then let's try this on for size."

He leaned close . . . closer . . . until his lips touched hers. Tentative. Careful. Exploratory.

But she wrapped her arms around his neck and leaned into him, responding without reservation.

Maybe he didn't have to take this slow and easy.

He pulled her tight against his chest—and in the seconds before he deepened the kiss and the world faded away, he gave thanks.

For while he enjoyed his new life in Hope Harbor and had found a measure of peace and contentment he'd never expected to experience again without Jo Ann by his side, it had been difficult to shake the loneliness.

That seemed poised to change.

It was possible, of course, that the journey he and Stephanie had embarked on today wouldn't end as he hoped.

But if he was a betting man, he'd wager such worry was unfounded—and that his tomorrows with this woman would be filled with deep contentment . . . and grand adventures he could never have imagined in his wildest dreams.

23

Where was his father?

Heart stumbling, Zach tightened his grip on the venti Americano and scanned the empty bed in the hospital room early on Wednesday morning.

He strode over to the bathroom door, open a mere crack. "Dad?"

No response.

Now what?

He tried to shake the fuzziness from his brain, still sluggish despite a solid eight hours of sleep.

The nurses' station. Someone there would know what was going on.

He swiveled toward the door.

His father stood on the threshold, an aide by his side.

"You look more human today." His dad inspected him. "That bad-boy scruff didn't suit you."

It took him several seconds to find his voice.

"You're okay." The words scratched past his windpipe.

"Of course I'm okay." His father gave a dismissive wave. "I told everyone I'd sail through this, and I did. Is that your breakfast?" He motioned toward the cup.

"No. I had an egg and sausage biscuit too."

"My breakfast should be here soon—solid food, right?" He aimed the question at the aide.

"Yes. The doctor authorized a regular diet."

"Thank the Lord. After all those liquids yesterday, I was ready to float away. Let's sit." He indicated two chairs by the window.

The aide stayed close as he walked over. After helping him settle into the chair, she left.

"Have a seat." His father tapped the adjacent chair.

Zach dropped into it. "How are you feeling?"

"Better than I expected. I assumed I'd recover fast, but I've surprised even myself. At this rate, I may be able to go back to work much sooner than I anticipated."

"Don't rush it, Dad. The firm has sufficient people to pick up the slack while you recuperate."

"Unlike your shop."

"I'm covered through tomorrow—and I can stay longer if necessary. Frank and Bren are always willing to work extra shifts if necessary."

"It won't be. After you left yesterday, I talked with the woman who coordinates home health care. I'll be fine at the house once they spring me, and they're watching me like a hawk here. You have a business to run. You should get back to it."

His father had referred to his shop as a business.

That was progress.

"I have tentative reservations for tomorrow."

"Go today."

Uh-oh.

That didn't sound like progress.

"Trying to get rid of me?" He forced up the corners of his mouth.

"No." His father linked his fingers together and looked down at his hands. "I've been thinking about what you said Sunday night. Actually, I've been thinking about it for months. You and Stephanie are all the family I have left—and much as I love my sister, there's been a hole in my life since you and I had our falling-out. I may not agree with all of the choices you've made, but it's your life—not mine. I'd like to put aside our differences, see if we can't get back to where we used to be. Or as close as possible, given our history."

"I'd like that too. That's why I'm not in a hurry to go back."

"But I want you to go. This"—he swept a hand over the sterile hospital room—"isn't where I want us to spend our time together. They treat me like an invalid. Here's what I propose. You go home. We'll stay in touch by phone. After I'm fully recovered, I'll come out to Oregon. Stephanie's been singing the praises of your adopted town, and I'd like to see for myself why it's bewitched both of you."

His father was willing to travel across the country to visit him?

That was the answer to a prayer.

To countless prayers.

Once again, pressure built in his throat—but he tried to swallow past it. His dad's attitude may have softened, but it wasn't likely he'd ever be the demonstrative type—or be comfortable around displays of emotion.

"You're welcome anytime."

"Let's plan on November, possibly for Thanksgiving. If Stephanie can swing it, maybe she can join us—along with anyone else you'd like to invite. I expect you've made close friends out there by now."

"Yes, but they all have families. Except Frank, the retired guy who works for me."

"You don't have a girlfriend?"

An image of Katherine flitted through his mind—but that was wishful thinking. For all he knew, she'd be back in Hollywood or off making her movie come Thanksgiving.

"No."

A young man toting a tray of food pushed through the door. "Mr. Garrett?"

"Yes." His father motioned him over. "I'll eat here."

The man set the tray on the portable bed table and positioned it by his father's chair.

As soon as he left, his dad lifted the cover from the plate.

Zach surveyed the scrambled eggs, sausage, and hash browns. "That's a real breakfast—though not the most heart-healthy food."

"The doc told me to eat whatever I want for the first few days." His father put the napkin on his lap. "I don't expect this will be gourmet quality, but it's an improvement over yesterday's menu. Why don't you check on flights while I eat?"

"You sure you don't want me to stay?"

"I want you to get back to your normal life and take care of your business. I appreciate that you dropped everything to come all the way here on the spur of the moment, but I know it was a huge inconvenience." His father positioned his knife to cut into a sausage.

"No, it wasn't. Doing things for the people you love is never an inconvenience."

His dad shifted his attention to him—and unless the light was playing tricks, there was a sheen in his eyes. "Thank you for that. I don't deserve it after what's gone on these past few years."

"Why don't we forget that and just start over?"

His father nodded and dived into his food.

Once Zach booked his return flight, the conversation moved to more general topics while his dad ate. Nothing significant—but the lack of tension between them *was* significant.

And by the time he left, with a quick hug and a promise to call after his flight landed, it was almost as if there had never been any enmity between them.

Which was nothing short of a miracle.

Perhaps it was too much to wish for, but when he boarded the plane three hours later, he couldn't help but hope another life-changing blessing might await him back in Oregon with a certain chocolate-loving actress who was fast making inroads on his heart.

"Zach? Is that you?"

As Stephanie called out to him from down the hall, he dropped his duffle bag onto the floor, set his laptop on the kitchen counter, and took a deep breath. It was good to be home. "Yes."

She appeared in the kitchen doorway a few seconds later, dressed in the same getup she'd worn to Hope House the day she and Frank had sequestered themselves in the master bedroom to patch holes. "You're a more accomplished cook than I am—but I could whip up an omelet for you, if you like. You must be exhausted after traveling all day."

"I'm fine." And he had dinner packed in dry ice in his duffle. Enough for two—if he could interest his neighbor in an impromptu beach picnic.

"I hear the trip was successful." She leaned back against the island and folded her arms.

"You talked to Dad?"

"Yes."

"He told you we reconciled?"

"Yes."

"Not without prodding, I'll bet."

"I've learned how to ask leading questions as well as my attorney brother has." She smirked at him. "However . . . he was pretty closemouthed. I couldn't get many specifics, but he did say he's planning a trip out here. That told me everything I needed to know—from his end. You want to fill in the gaps?"

"We reconciled."

She rolled her eyes. "You're as bad as he is."

Zach grinned. "Dad claims he's been thinking along those lines for a while. Given how fast he extended an olive branch, I have to believe that's true."

"It didn't hurt that you traveled thousands of miles to see him because of the surgery. That sent a powerful message."

"Whatever brought about our truce, I'm grateful." He waved a hand over her attire. "What's with the work clothes?"

"Frank and I are going to put in a couple of hours at Hope House, then stop for tacos afterward if Charley is cooking."

"How goes it with you and my right-hand man?"

She shoved her fingers into the pockets of her jeans and gave him a slow smile. "It goes well. In fact, I have big news."

"Lay it on me." He opened the fridge and reached for two cans of soda.

"I'm moving to Hope Harbor."

"Whoa." He pivoted and shut the door without retrieving the sodas. "That *is* big news."

She lifted a hand. "Don't get too carried away. It's temporary. I'm not giving up my apartment in New York . . . yet . . . but it's a possibility down the road. And before you panic about inheriting a permanent houseguest—I've arranged to rent accommodations from a woman in town named Anna Williams. She has a small studio unit on her property called The Annex. Charley recommended it."

"I know Anna. Pleasant woman. But you're welcome to stay here."

"Thank you, but I don't want to wear out my welcome—and I think we may both prefer a bit of privacy." She tipped her head in the direction of Katherine's house. "Your neighbor and I volunteered at Hope House on Sunday. She's a lovely young woman."

"I agree—but she's only visiting. Her job is waiting for her elsewhere."

"I know. In LA. She told me she's an actress."

He arched his eyebrows. "That surprises me. She's trying to stay under the radar."

"So she said. I think it was a slip on her part—and she didn't offer many details. I got the impression she was rethinking her future, though."

"You have excellent insights."

"If intuition counts for anything, I didn't get the feeling she was locked into the Hollywood life."

"I'd like to believe that."

The doorbell rang, and Stephanie glanced at her watch. "That's Frank. Do you want to talk to him?"

"No. I texted him and Bren I'd be back on duty tomorrow and we could return to our usual schedule. Go. Have fun. Tell him I said hi."

"Do you have any plans for the evening, other than unwinding after a full travel day?"

"I may drop in on Katherine."

"Not a bad idea. And in that case, you have fun too." She crossed to him, rose on tiptoe, and kissed his cheek. "Welcome home."

"Thanks."

He waited until she picked up her purse and disappeared through the front door, then headed for the bathroom to freshen up.

Five minutes later, after adding two sodas to the bag of sandwiches, he exited through the back slider and strode toward Katherine's.

In twelve days, these treks would come to an end—unless she'd decided to turn down the part while he was gone.

Somehow, he didn't think she had. After their in-depth discussion on the subject, wouldn't she have texted him if she'd scratched that decision off her list?

He crimped the bag tighter in his fingers as he approached the grove of towering coniferous evergreen trees that separated their properties.

If she was still on the fence, perhaps a romantic beach picnic would remind her of all she'd be giving up should she choose to return to Hollywood . . . and the lifestyle she'd admitted no longer held much appeal.

He couldn't offer her glamor or excitement or fame or enormous wealth—but if she could be content with a simple life and a man who would always put her first, the two of them ought to see where the spark between them led.

But she had to want that as much as he did—and be willing to live with the possibility it could fizzle.

From *her* perspective, with all she had at stake, that would be very scary.

Frowning, he emerged from the woods and slowed his pace as he approached her house.

If she gave up her Hollywood career and the spark between them petered out, her life would be far more disrupted than his. He'd still have his home, his job, his routine, his friends. She'd have to start from scratch.

As he knew all too well, that was an intimidating prospect.

So trying to persuade her to take that leap, to give them a chance, if she wasn't prepared for all the possible consequences would be selfish—and unfair. He'd have to get a read on her state of mind tonight before launching a campaign to convince her to stay.

And pray he had the strength to follow the honorable course if this visit didn't go as he hoped it would.

24

Zach was back?

A day early?

Why?

Pulse leaping, Katherine vaulted to her feet as he emerged from the woods. Shading her eyes against the dipping sun, she squinted at him.

He didn't look upset.

That was reassuring.

When he drew close, she crossed the deck to meet him at the top of the stairs. "I didn't expect you back this soon. Is your dad okay?"

"Yes. He's doing well. So well there was no excuse for me to hang around."

"Did he . . . send you away?" If there was more diplomatic phrasing for that question, it eluded her.

"No—not in the sense you mean." He lifted the bag. "Pastrami sandwiches from my favorite deli in Atlanta, packed in dry ice for my trip home. If you'll join me for an impromptu dinner on the beach, I'll tell you the whole story."

"Is that a bribe?"

"Only if it worked."

"It worked. Let me grab a sweater." She retreated to the house, plucked her sweater off the great room couch, detoured to the kitchen for a few truffles from her latest batch, and rejoined him. "All set—with dessert in hand." She waved the plastic bag at him. "Shall I bring water too?"

"I've got the drinks covered."

"A man who thinks of everything." She draped the sweater around her shoulders and started toward the steps—but he caught her hand as she passed.

She turned—and her lungs stalled.

There was no missing the heat in his eyes . . . nor the silent message they were sending, even before he spoke.

"I wouldn't say that. But I did think of you while I was gone. Constantly." His voice hoarsened. "I missed you, Katherine."

He didn't ask if the reverse was true, but the question hung in the air between them.

The honest answer was yes.

Yet with Stephanie's warning echoing in her mind . . . and her own situation unresolved . . . it wasn't fair to build expectations.

"I thought of you too."

Also honest—but not what he'd wanted to hear. Though he masked it quickly, the flash of disappointment in those brown irises was telling.

"Nice to know." He released her hand and motioned toward the steps. "After you."

He followed as she descended and took the lead down the narrow path that led to the main trail. There, he fell in beside her.

"Are you certain you don't want to share your bounty with your aunt?" She indicated the bag he was holding.

"No. I had you in mind when I bought these. Besides, Frank picked her up not long after I got home. They were going to Hope House, then to Charley's for tacos."

"She went to Shore Acres State Park with him yesterday."

"Yeah?"

Katherine cringed. "Whoops. Maybe I shouldn't have said any-thing. But she mentioned it to me while we were at Hope House on Sunday. I didn't think it was a secret."

"It's not. Neither is their date tonight. She also told me she's decided to stay in Hope Harbor for a while. Much as she likes the town and our fabulous scenery, I don't think that's why she's considering a permanent change of address." He stopped and motioned for her to continue, past a blackberry bush that was encroaching on the path.

"I'm happy for her." Too bad she couldn't be as definitive about what *she* wanted. "And I envy her having that decision behind her."

"Does that mean you're still thinking about the movie?"

"Yes. There's been a new development—but I want to hear about you and your dad first."

"Couldn't we flip a coin to see who goes first?"

"Nope. You promised me an update while we ate. My news can wait until dessert."

"You drive a hard bargain."

She wrinkled her nose. "You sound like Simon."

"I don't think I like that comparison. Has he been bugging you again?"

"You could say that. But let's stick with more pleasant subjects while we walk down. Tell me about these sandwiches you carried thousands of miles, and why they're special."

She listened to his stories about Fetterman's Deli and the happy hours he'd spent there with friends as a teen, until at last they emerged from the brambles and stepped onto the beach.

"Our table awaits." He indicated the log. "Or in this case, a seat with a view. Let's use it as a backrest tonight. It will be easier than trying to juggle everything on a rounded surface."

They sat on the sand, and Zach pulled the sandwiches and sodas out of the bag. After everything was divvied up, she angled toward him. "You're on."

"First, try that." He tapped the sandwich in her lap and

unwrapped his own. "It's not quite at the level of Charley's tacos—but close. They assured me it would survive the trip. Spread this on it first, though." He retrieved a container of the topping from the bag, along with a plastic knife, and passed them over.

She unwrapped the gargantuan sandwich, removed the top piece of bread, added a generous portion of the separately packaged mixture, then took a bite.

An explosion of tangy flavors tickled her taste buds.

Wow.

"You weren't kidding. This is incredible." She examined the sandwich close-up. "What else is on this besides pastrami?"

"Swiss cheese—and coleslaw that's put together with home-made Russian dressing. They bake their own bread too."

"The deli doesn't happen to have a branch on the West Coast, does it?"

"Nope. It's a family-run business."

"It would be worth a trip to Atlanta just for this."

"There could be other reasons to visit Atlanta someday."

She peeked at him.

He was focused on his own sandwich and didn't dwell on that comment, but it wasn't hard to read between the lines.

Without pushing, he was letting her know he had a vested interest in her decision about the movie—and her career.

That made the new deadline all the more difficult to deal with.

She nibbled at the sandwich, letting the steady splash of the surf and the caw of the gulls soothe the cacophony in her mind. In a few minutes, she'd fill Zach in on her news—but first, she wanted to hear about Atlanta.

"Tell me what happened with your dad."

She continued to eat as he gave her the highlights of his trip, and her heart warmed as he wrapped up with his dad's plan to come to Hope Harbor.

At least *Zach's* story had a happy ending.

"You must be over the moon." She smiled at him as she picked up a piece of coleslaw that had escaped from her sandwich and fitted it back in.

"At the very least. Maybe over Mars. It was more than I'd hoped for. More than I'd prayed for. I would have been satisfied to be invited inside and treated civilly. For Dad to do a one-eighty . . ." He shook his head, and his Adam's apple bobbed. "It was beyond anything I could have hoped for."

"When is he coming out here?"

"Thanksgiving, if his recovery progresses as we expect. Appropriate, isn't it?"

"Very."

"I assume Stephanie and Frank will be there too—and Dad suggested I invite any other close friends." He picked up the second half of his sandwich but shifted his attention to her. "He also asked if I had a girlfriend."

The mouthful of pastrami she'd swallowed got stuck halfway down, and she groped for her soda. Took a swig. "What did you say?"

"No—but that's not what I *wanted* to say."

His answer didn't surprise her—but his candor did.

"I thought we'd decided to . . . that we were going to try to keep our relationship low-key?"

"I've been trying. It's not working."

For her either.

Despite her efforts to suppress her growing feelings for the man who lived in the house next door, he'd also begun to take up residence in her heart.

But until she decided what to do about the movie—and her career—it would be safer for both of them if they kept their feelings on a low burner and gave themselves space to see where the electricity led.

Easier said than done, though.

Yet more important than ever, in light of her news.

She set her sandwich back on the paper in her lap. Filled her lungs with the salt-laced air. "Can we switch gears for a minute?"

His eyes narrowed. "I'm picking up serious undertones here."

"More like frustrating—and nerve-wracking. Simon's here."

He frowned and set his sandwich down too. "Here, at your house?"

"Not at the moment—but he *is* in Hope Harbor. He showed up yesterday with the news that the deadline for the movie decision has been changed to this weekend."

Despite the golden light cast by the dipping sun, Zach's complexion seemed to lose a few shades of color. "Why the shortened time frame?"

She briefed him. "Of course, Simon is pushing me to accept—ASAP, now that the studio has agreed to address my reservations about language and nudity."

"Which way are you leaning?"

"I don't know. What do *you* think?"

He hesitated. "You really want to know?"

"Yes."

Several beats passed as he studied her.

Then, instead of a verbal response, he set the paper holding his sandwich beside him, leaned close, and captured her lips in a kiss that answered her question far more eloquently than words ever could.

It was the sort of kiss that made a woman forget about everything but the man whose magic touch chased every care away.

Until all at once, he jerked back and uttered four words that hurt far more than the jeers and taunts of her childhood peers.

"That was a mistake."

As the harsh, ragged declaration hung in the air between them—and Katherine's shattered expression registered—Zach's stomach twisted.

Way to go, Garrett. You know her history, know rejection is her Achilles' heel. Could you have been a bit more diplomatic—and articulate?

"I'm sorry." He touched her hand, willing her to accept his contrition. "Not about kissing you, but for my motivation. Trying to influence your decision is selfish—and wrong. You have to choose what's best for you . . . even if the idea of you leaving makes me sick to my stomach."

The shock on her face faded. "Oh. I thought—"

"I know what you thought. I'd attribute my tactless faux pas to jet lag, but a three-hour time difference isn't enough to qualify for that excuse. Forgive me?"

"Yes." No hesitation. "I have a thicker skin than I used to after living in the rejection-rife world of Hollywood, but I'm still too sensitive to snubs and put-downs. Leftover baggage from my youth, I suppose—another button Simon knows how to push."

And that brought them back to the movie offer.

If he couldn't make the decision for her, perhaps he could help her arrive at the best one—even if the outcome wasn't in his favor.

"Why don't we talk about the movie for a few minutes? If the studio has caved to your demands, what's holding you back?"

She rewrapped the other half of her sandwich, twin furrows creasing her brow. "I'm afraid if I do it, I'll be sucked back into the whole Hollywood scene and it will be harder than ever to break free afterward."

"Take that concern out of the equation. Think of the movie as an isolated decision, with no bearing on anything else. In that context, would you do it?"

"Yes." Again, no hesitation. "It's a wonderful script. Working opposite the male lead would be a dream come true. The director is exceptional. The character I'd play is a woman who would require every ounce of my skill to bring to life—but that sort of challenge is what drew me to acting in the first place. From the artistic and creative standpoint, it's a no-brainer."

The more she talked, the more radiant she became.

Zach's stomach twisted again.

Katherine might not like all the trappings that came with a career in Hollywood, but she loved the acting part—and this was a plum role. Whatever her ultimate decision about her career, if she turned this part down, she could regret it for the rest of her life.

And much as he wished she would, if he tried to push her in that direction, he'd regret his selfishness for the rest of *his* life.

"I think you have your answer, Katherine."

"How can you be so certain when I'm not?"

"I can see it in your face." He forced up the corners of his mouth. "You're glowing. You look like I did the day I opened The Perfect Blend—excited, eager, ready to dig in and create something that would feed my soul. For you, it would also be the culmination of a lifelong dream . . . even if you decide to change direction and pursue a new dream afterward."

"That's the tricky part." She brushed her hand over the sand beside her, letting the grains trickle through her fingers. "It will be much harder to walk away if the movie's a success."

"But not impossible. And while you're filming, you'll have a chunk of time to think about your future. How long will it take to shoot the movie?"

"I don't have the schedule yet. I know the major location work is supposed to be done by year-end. It may take another few weeks to finish the set work."

"So it's not a long commitment."

She tipped her head. "I'm beginning to think you're trying to get rid of me."

"You know better. If I had my druthers, you'd ditch the Hollywood life today and move to Hope Harbor."

"But if I did, what would I do? Would I miss acting? What would happen if I moved here and our electricity shorted out?"

"Only you can answer those questions—and you should before you initiate such a radical change."

"I know." She sighed and picked up the baggie. "Are you going to finish your sandwich?"

"Later." He rewrapped his too.

"You want a truffle?"

"I wouldn't mind ending this conversation on a sweet note—and since my preferred treat isn't available"—he brushed his fingertips across her lips with a whisper touch—"I'll have to settle for a truffle."

Her breath hitched, and she swallowed. "It might b-be available."

Despite the temptation, he resisted. "No. Let's not muddy your decision with hormones."

She pushed her hair back with fingers that weren't quite steady. "You're killing me here."

"Hey. This isn't easy for me either. Give me credit for taking the honorable course." He managed to conjure up another smile.

"You couldn't rise much higher in my estimation than you already are." She doled out the truffles, two each, and bit into hers.

He followed her lead, savoring the flavor of sun-ripened blackberries and chocolate on his tongue. "Mmm. I liked the lavender and Earl Grey version, but these edge them out by a hair."

"The blackberries will be waning soon. I wanted to take advantage of their availability before they were gone." She finished her first truffle. "That leads to another concern, if I decide to take the movie role. Opportunities, like blackberries, have a season. They don't hang around forever." She met his gaze. "Men like you don't come around every day, Zach—and several months is a long time. Nations have been conquered in less."

She was worried he'd meet someone else while she was gone.

That was one fear he could put to rest.

"If you're concerned another woman will come along and claim my heart, don't be. Other than you, I haven't met anyone who's interested me in two and a half years—and Hope Harbor isn't exactly a swinging singles scene. It's not like women are beating my door down."

"Romance is in the air, though. Look at Stephanie and Frank. And I've been hearing stories about other couples who met here too. Not to mention Floyd and Gladys." She lightened her tone with the last reference—but her worry was real.

He took her hand again. Wove his fingers through hers. "If you decide to do the movie, I'll be here after it's finished. You have my promise. We'll keep in touch while you're gone, and once it's over, we'll figure out the best path forward together. Fair enough?"

Her blue irises began to shimmer. "Not for you. You're putting your life on hold for me."

"No. I'm living the life I've chosen in a place I love. I'm not putting anything on hold." Except falling in love with the woman across from him.

Or, more accurately, falling *more* in love. He was halfway there already.

But giving voice to that this early in their relationship could put more pressure on her, which she didn't need.

"You know what I wish?" Her tone grew wistful.

"Tell me."

"That God would write the direction I'm seeking in the sky." She waved her hand across the blue expanse, now gilding near the horizon.

"I've been in your shoes. But subtle guidance can be less disruptive. You don't want the kind of shove *I* got." A cloud scuttled past the sun, momentarily dimming the light and chilling the world.

As Josh's death had done to his life.

"I know your peace was hard-won." She squeezed his fingers. "I'm just glad there was a happy ending with your father."

"Me too." He scanned the bluff behind them. "We ought to head back. Negotiating the path in the dark is tricky. Ready?"

"Yes."

He stood, held out a hand to help her up, and tucked his sandwich back in the bag. "Want me to carry your half for you?"

284

"No. I may not get it back." She gave him a teasing shoulder nudge. "Want me to carry your second truffle for you?"

"Uh-uh. I can take care of it." He put the whole piece in his mouth and motioned her toward the path.

He chewed as they strolled to the end of the beach and started up the bluff, the sweetness of the candy offering a pleasant finish to an otherwise stressful conversation.

Nothing had been resolved—and who knew what Katherine would decide?

If she did take the movie role, what would he do if she didn't return?

No answer came to him as they hiked up the steep trail.

At the path to his house, she stopped—but he motioned for her to continue. "I'll walk you home."

"It's not far, and after all my treks to the beach, I could walk the route in my sleep. Thank you for the sandwich—and the conversation. I'm going to sleep on everything we talked about and try to come to a decision in the next day or two."

"Stop by the house if you want to talk again."

"I will." After a nanosecond hesitation, she leaned forward and hugged him. Tight. "No matter what happens, I'll always be grateful our paths crossed." Her voice was muffled against his chest. Tear-laced.

That didn't leave him feeling warm and fuzzy.

But what was there to say?

So rather than respond, he held her close, dipping his head to brush his cheek over her hair and inhale the sweet scent that was all Katherine.

Much too soon, she eased back and hurried up the path in the waning daylight.

Despite a powerful temptation to go after her and give her a proper good-night kiss, he let her go.

Because really, wasn't that the only way to hold on to someone?

A person had to choose to stay—or return—without coercion or they could never be truly yours.

He waited until she disappeared from view, then finished the steep ascent to his house.

At the top of the bluff, he paused and surveyed the darkening sea. Nearby, a yellow-rumped warbler welcomed the evening with its distinctive, tweeting song. The boughs of the trees swayed in the gentle wind.

All was peaceful.

And he had much to be grateful for on this day. His dad's operation had been a success, and the wall between them had been breached.

It seemed selfish to want more.

Yet as he wandered toward his house, he *did* want more.

He wanted a chance with Katherine.

But could a man who ran a coffee shop in a tiny town on the Oregon coast possibly offer enough incentive for her to stay . . . or return?

God alone knew.

And as the last lingering taste of blackberries and chocolate on his tongue faded, he could only hope that if Katherine chose to make the movie, her memories of her stay in Hope Harbor—and of him—wouldn't do the same.

25

. . . .

Give it up, Katherine. You're done sleeping for the night.

As if to verify that, her cell on the nightstand beside the bed began to vibrate.

Expelling a breath, she pushed herself into a sitting position and pulled the phone out of the charger.

Simon's name flashed on the screen.

She groaned—but pressed the talk button. No sense avoiding the inevitable.

"What are you doing up at"—she angled her watch toward the pale light seeping in around the drapes—"six forty-five? You never get out of bed in LA until after nine."

"I'm not in LA, and there's nothing to do in this town on a Wednesday night. I went to bed at ten. Let's have breakfast."

"I'm still in bed."

"Get up and get dressed. I left you alone yesterday, but—"

"No, you didn't. You called three times."

"But I didn't show up on your doorstep. I gave you space. Today, we're going to talk. In person. Either you meet me for breakfast, or I'll pick up coffee and bagels and come there."

She swung her legs to the floor and pushed her hair back. "I don't have anything to talk about yet. It's only Thursday."

"What time should I be there?"

He wasn't backing down.

Fine. She'd talk to him.

But not here. This was her haven, and his frenzied presence always disrupted the calm vibe.

She stood and began to pace. "I'll meet you in town—but not for breakfast. I didn't sleep well last night, and it will take me a while to get in gear. Let's have lunch at the Myrtle Café in town."

"When?"

"Eleven thirty."

"I'll see you there."

He ended the call without a good-bye.

Typical bad-mood Simon.

She set the phone on the nightstand and glanced at the bed.

That little inner voice had been right. There would be no more sleep for her this morning. Not after Simon's brusque phone call—and the conversation with Zach last evening that had kept replaying in her mind through the long, dark hours while she'd tossed and turned.

Shoulders drooping, she scrubbed a hand down her face.

God, where can I find the answer to my dilemma?

As she sent that silent, angst-ridden question heavenward, a sunbeam infiltrated a crack in the blinds and cast a thin line of bright light on the hardwood floor. It traversed the room, climbed the opposite wall—and illuminated the simple cross that had been there when she arrived.

Odd timing—though not all that helpful.

After bending the Almighty's ear about her predicament for weeks, she was no closer to knowing what she wanted to do with the rest of her life than she'd been the day she arrived.

While her priorities had clarified, she was still at a loss how to juggle them.

And meeting Zach had complicated the situation.

Big-time.

She studied the cross again.

Should she give prayer one more shot? Perhaps somewhere different? It was possible a new setting could offer her a fresh perspective.

All at once, the perfect place came to mind. A spot designed for the very kind of communion with God she was seeking.

The meditation garden at St. Francis church.

Reverend Baker had sung its praises last week as they'd chatted after the Sunday service, and she'd been meaning to stop in. With several hours to fill until her lunch with Simon, this was an ideal opportunity.

Picking up her pace, she showered, dressed, ate a piece of toast—and within forty-five minutes was pulling into St. Francis.

At this early hour, a few cars were parked near the main entrance to the church, but back by the garden, the lot was empty.

She swung into a spot close to a rose-covered arbor, where a sign proclaimed "All are welcome." Leaving the car behind, she passed beneath the arch of fragrant pink flowers and strolled down the circular stone path. It wound through a garden as lovingly tended as Reverend Baker had promised, silent except for the soft tinkle of a water fountain in the center.

As she drank in the soothing ambiance and beautiful flowers interspersed with greenery, the tight knot of tension in her shoulders began to dissipate. Perhaps here, in the serene solitude of this tiny, tucked-away sanctuary, the elusive answers she'd been seeking—

She came to an abrupt halt as she rounded a rhododendron.

Well, shoot.

She wasn't alone.

Reverend Baker was seated on a wooden bench up ahead—and she wasn't in the mood for conversation.

Could she retrace her steps and—

As if sensing her presence, he turned toward her, smiled, and raised a hand in greeting.

So much for escaping.

Resigned to a brief, polite exchange, she continued down the path.

He rose as she approached. "Good morning, Kat. I must have done an excellent sell job on this place last Sunday when we chatted."

"You did paint an appealing picture."

"Was I exaggerating?"

"No. It's beautiful."

"I always come early for my Thursday golf game with Kevin—Father Murphy—to sit here and absorb the peace." His eyes began to twinkle. "You'd understand why if you'd ever played golf with Hope Harbor's padre. He has a right hook that brings him no end of grief, and his putting is a constant source of frustration—which he isn't shy about expressing."

"I thought golf was supposed to be fun."

"It is. And it gives us both the opportunity to practice patience and humility. To tell you the truth, I could improve my game in a few areas too." He winked. "What brings you here at such an early hour?"

"It seemed like an ideal place to sort through the jumbled thoughts I'm wrestling with. But I can come back later. I don't want to disturb your peace—or contemplation."

He waved her comment aside. "I've transitioned from contemplation to vegging. Would you like to sit with me, talk through those thoughts you're trying to sort out? Kevin always gets waylaid by a parishioner or two after Mass. I doubt he'll be out for another twenty minutes."

Katherine hesitated, mulling over the pastor's offer.

Would it help to talk to a third party about her issues? Someone who had no vested interest in the outcome? All Simon did was push her to take the role and stick with her career, and while Zach's approach had been less selfish, there was no doubt about where he hoped she'd end up.

Maybe the minister could offer a few insights.

"If you're sure you don't mind, I *am* dealing with sort of a thorny—and confidential—problem."

"Discretion is part of ministry. Whatever we talk about here will stay between us." He motioned to the bench. "Please . . . join me."

She closed the distance between them and sank onto the bench.

His expression open and kindly, he retook his seat and gave her his full attention.

Katherine knitted her fingers in her lap. Reverend Baker couldn't offer her his best guidance unless he knew her whole story—so she told him the condensed version, ending with her current dilemma.

"Now I'm faced with a very short deadline, and to be honest, I'm more confused than ever."

"Why do you think that is?"

After all the brainpower she'd invested in her quandary, that was the one question she could answer with absolute assurance.

"Because I don't know what I'd do if I left that life behind—and because I've met someone here."

"Ah. Romance." He nodded. "That can affect your priorities. I know. I've been there."

She raised her eyebrows at that unexpected revelation, and he aimed a rueful smile her direction.

"My experience in that department was long ago, but I remember it as if it happened yesterday. You see, my late wife wasn't a Christian when we met—and for a man who'd had his sights set on a career in ministry since he was a teenager, that was a challenge after we fell in love."

Speaking of thorny problems . . .

"I can see how that would be an issue."

"To put it mildly. It's not an exact parallel to your situation, but it gives me an inkling of what you're going through. I had to think long and hard about my career plans. Thankfully, my wife chose to embrace Christianity, solving my dilemma. The difference in our situations is that you were already having second thoughts about your career choice when you met this person. That should make your decision a bit easier."

"It would—if I could figure out what to do instead." She watched a chickadee land on the feeder and help itself to a morning snack as she voiced the vague but tempting idea that was beginning to gel in her mind. "I've toyed with the idea of being a chocolatier, but my agent says I'm crazy."

Interest sparked in his eyes. "Did you make those truffles that were in the kitchen at Hope House a couple of weeks ago?"

"Yes."

"I sampled one . . . or two. They were amazing." He leaned back and regarded her. "I don't suppose that sort of business pays like a Hollywood career, but if you can earn a living from it and the work gives you satisfaction—along with the privacy you're after—why would that be crazy? Not every decision has to be predicated on whether it will bring fame or wealth."

More or less the same conclusion she'd come to—until Simon had undermined her conviction.

"That's what I've been thinking."

"But will you miss being in front of the camera?"

It was the same question Zach had raised—and one she'd wrestled with mightily as she'd battled insomnia last night . . . until the answer had clicked into place.

"No. I enjoy acting—but I prefer stage work to film. And I'm also getting more interested in the directing side of the business."

"Could you somehow combine your love of theater with candy making?"

That was an interesting suggestion.

"How would I do that?"

"I don't know—but if you think about it, and pray about it, you may find a solution in God's time."

She sighed as the bell in the church tower chimed the hour. "Unfortunately, God's time isn't Simon's time."

"Then maybe for now you should focus on the movie role and let the larger issue percolate in your mind."

Also what Zach had suggested—and he'd promised to wait while she sorted through her options.

But what if another woman came along who appealed to him—and who knew Hope Harbor was where she belonged without any of the angst that had plagued his temporary neighbor? Would it be fair to hold him to his promise if that happened?

"You don't like that idea?"

At the minister's gentle prompt, she reined in her wayward thoughts.

"You aren't the first to suggest it—and it does have merit. I'd kill two birds with one stone—achieve my goal of proving to the world and myself that I have the acting chops to play a starring role in a major feature film and buy myself breathing space to think about my longer-term plans."

"I hear a *but* in there." The Grace Christian pastor's gentle demeanor encouraged confidences.

She brushed a stray leaf off the seat beside her. "But . . . I'm afraid that if I leave, the man I'm interested in will find someone else. He says he'll wait—but what if he doesn't? What if I look back and regret putting this movie role ahead of him? What if I'm sorry later that I didn't turn the part down and stay here while I decide what to do with the rest of my life?"

"Those are all valid concerns."

She waited, but he didn't offer anything more.

Where were the words of wisdom clerics were supposed to dispense to floundering souls?

"You don't have any advice?" She tried for a neutral tone, but a thread of disappointment wove through it.

"Only you can answer those questions, Kat—sorry, Katherine. But if you want my take, it seems to me the root of the problem is trust—in your friend and his promise, and in God."

Katherine filled her lungs with the spruce-scented air. Lifted her face to the heavens, where fluffy white clouds scuttled across the deep blue dome of sky.

In one fell swoop, Reverend Baker had nailed the cause of her ambiguity about whether to accept the movie role.

It was all about trust.

About having faith in the man who lived next door—and in God's promise that he had plans for her welfare, not her woe.

But trust had never come easy for her—and working in Hollywood hadn't bolstered it.

Yet deep inside, she knew God would never fail her . . . and unless her instincts were malfunctioning, neither would Zach. The man reeked of integrity, honor, courage—and dedication to the people he loved. New as their friendship was, every scrap of evidence she'd seen about her neighbor pointed to a man who was noble, principled, and trustworthy.

Doubting his promise did a major disservice to him.

Both God and Zach deserved her trust.

Maybe it was time to follow the advice she'd given Zach days ago—if the clock is ticking on a decision, listen to your heart and take a leap of faith.

She refocused on the minister, her heart lighter than it had been in weeks. "I think you helped me find the answer I've been searching for. I appreciate—"

"Paul! You ready to go?"

At the interruption, they turned in unison toward the entrance to the garden.

A late-fiftyish man, wearing a sport shirt and carrying a few extra pounds, trotted around the large rhododendron, a golf bag slung over his shoulder.

He came to an abrupt halt as he caught sight of them. "Whoops. Sorry. I didn't mean to interrupt."

Katherine rose.

"No worries." The minister stood too. "We were just chatting. I did such a great sell job on your garden, one of my new congregants stopped by to visit while I was waiting for you."

Reverend Baker introduced them as the priest continued down the path.

Father Murphy gave her hand a vigorous pump. "Wonderful

to meet you. You're welcome anytime—in the garden, or in St. Francis, if someone's sermons get too boring . . . not to mention any names." He nudged his fellow cleric.

"Very funny." Reverend Baker shot him a disgruntled look, but the twitch in his lips suggested the two of them had been through this amicable routine before. "At least my sermons include Bible quotes."

"We have three Bible readings every Sunday, in case you've forgotten—and I always reference them in my homily." The padre directed his next comment to her. "I hope if you're in town for a while you'll stop by on a Sunday. Do a little comparison shopping, find the best value."

The minister rolled his eyes. "You sound like a used car salesman."

"Nothing wrong with putting marketing principles to work for faith. I'm willing to try anything that could bolster church attendance and get people more invested in their relationship with the Lord." He turned back to her. "If it's any incentive, we also serve tastier donuts."

"Not true . . . but I'm not going to debate that point." Reverend Baker motioned toward the entrance to the garden. "Do you want to play golf or not? If we stand around here talking, we're going to miss our tee time."

"Perish the thought." The priest hoisted his bag of clubs higher and shook her hand again. "Stay as long as you like. At this hour of the morning, you should have this little piece of paradise all to yourself. Paul, I'll meet you at the car."

With that, he retraced his steps down the path.

"Kevin's giving us a minute to wrap up." The minister followed his progress, an affectionate smile tugging at his lips. "Sometimes my wisecracking Catholic colleague has more discernment than I give him credit for. To tell the truth, he's an all-around good guy—not that I'd say that to his face. I wouldn't want to be responsible for giving him an inflated ego." He shifted his attention back to her. "If you'd like to continue this conversation later, I'm available."

"Thank you for that—and for your insights this morning. I think I'll be okay now."

He extended his hand. "I'm glad I was of help. And the offer stands if you decide you want to bounce more ideas off someone."

"I'll keep that in mind. Enjoy your game."

"Goes without saying. It's one of the highlights of my week." Grinning, he took off down the path.

After he disappeared around the rhododendron, the muffled conversation of the two clergymen drifted back as they continued their banter.

Katherine gave them a few minutes' head start, then meandered back toward the entrance. Much as she'd like to linger in this peaceful spot, she had a stop to make before her lunch with Simon.

It wasn't one she relished, but now that she'd settled on a course of action, it was only fair to share her decision with the man who had a personal stake in the outcome.

26

As Katherine came through the door of The Perfect Blend, the cranberry scone Zach had pilfered from the display case for breakfast turned to a rock in his stomach.

She'd come to a decision. He could see it in her eyes.

The movie was a go.

Meaning her days in Hope Harbor were coming to an end.

"Watch the foam."

At Frank's warning, he jerked his attention back to the cappuccino he was finishing.

His signature swirl looked more like a deformed question mark than an artistic flourish.

As Katherine walked toward him, he added more foam to cover up his mistake and handed the drink to the waiting customer.

After giving the bustling shop a scan, she pulled out the dark sunglasses she'd worn on her first visit and slipped them on.

He managed to call up a smile. "Good morning. You look like a skinny vanilla latte woman."

Her lips bowed up. "I bet you say that to all the girls."

"Nope. Only the special ones. You want a small—or are you going to splurge and go medium today?"

"Small works."

"I'll have it ready in three minutes. If you want to find a seat, I'll even deliver it."

"Could you join me for a few minutes?" Twin furrows dented her brow as she gave the interior another survey. "Or is it too busy? I know coffee shops can be crazy in the morning. I should have thought of that."

"The rush hour—or what constitutes rush hour in Hope Harbor—is slowing. Frank can cover for me while we chat. Go ahead and claim a table."

She headed for the booth for two tucked into the back corner, where they'd sat the day he'd brought her here to sample Eleanor Cooper's fudge cake after their impromptu taco lunch on the wharf.

The one that offered the most privacy.

Confirming his conclusion she had news to share.

As he prepared her drink, gave Frank reign over the counter, and walked over to join her, he tried to psyche himself up for the conversation to come.

There was no question that taking the role was the right decision for her. After all the years she'd worked to reach this pinnacle, she owed it to herself to plant a flag on the summit—whatever she decided to do afterward. Coming this close to realizing her dream, only to walk away when it was within her grasp, would be a decision she'd regret the rest of her life.

That's why he'd sucked it up and played devil's advocate on the beach last night. And it was why he'd continue to support her choice, despite the risk.

The significant risk.

Katherine might think she was burned out on the Hollywood lifestyle and lack of privacy, but if the movie was a success and other similar offers began to pour in, she could succumb to the allure of fame and forget all about her idyllic time here making blackberry truffles, painting at Hope House—and walking on the beach with the local barista.

298

Being a star had to be a power trip of the first order, one that could mess with a person's head—and priorities.

But if the two of them were meant to be, it would happen.

He had to keep believing that.

After setting her latte in front of her, he slid onto the bench seat on the other side of the small table. Rather than wait for her to lead up to the news, he plunged in. "You decided to take the movie role."

She removed her glasses, studying him as she set them on the table. "How did you know?"

"Call it intuition." He hitched up one side of his mouth. "Am I right?"

"Yes. You're the first person I've told."

"Simon doesn't know yet?"

"No. I'm meeting him for lunch at the Myrtle."

"He'll be happy."

"Yeah."

"Are *you* happy?"

She sipped her latte, the creases reappearing on her forehead. "Relieved is more like it. I'm glad the decision is behind me."

"What was the tipping point?"

He listened as she told him about her conversation with Reverend Baker in the St. Francis garden.

"It wasn't as if he said anything I hadn't already thought about—or anything you and I hadn't discussed. But he did help me realize that my fear about taking the role was due to lack of trust. And for that I apologize."

He frowned at the non sequitur. "Sorry. You lost me."

"Let me back up and talk about God first." She linked her fingers on the table. "I realized I have to trust him to lead me in the right direction career-wise. I've agonized over this for weeks. Prayed about it. Weighed the pros and cons. I wish the direction I've been searching for had been written in the sky, but sometimes you have to interpret the guidance you're being given as best you can. I finally concluded that after all the work I've put into this career, I owe it to myself to finish it off with a bang."

Finish it off.

That was encouraging.

His spirits took an uptick.

"I won't dispute that—but why the apology?"

She sipped her latte, watching him over the rim of the cup. Set it down. "I also realized I have to trust your promise that you'll be here after the movie wraps. I don't come from a background that breeds trust, but you've given me no cause to doubt your word—or to be afraid you'd forget me. I'm just not used to someone being willing to wait when there aren't any guarantees."

"I hear you. And the truth is, I might not be inclined to—if I didn't think the potential outcome was worth waiting for." *Follow her lead and put your own concerns on the table, Garrett.* "As long as we're laying it all out there, I'll admit to a few fears too. If this movie is a success, it could tempt you to stay in Hollywood . . . despite all the negatives about the lifestyle."

"I hope success, if it comes, doesn't skew my perspective."

"But it could happen."

She fiddled with the lid of her cup. "I know."

That wasn't what he wanted to hear.

Despite the tension thrumming through his veins, he managed to maintain a conversational tone. "I imagine the lure of stardom would be powerful."

"Yes—but so can the lure of a life without paparazzi digging into every personal detail"—she locked gazes with him—"and the possibility of finding a real-life happily ever after with a guy who puts all the Hollywood heartthrobs to shame."

Some of the tautness in his shoulders eased. "Thanks for the ego boost—and infusion of hope. In the spirit of candor, I want you to know I'll be counting the days until the movie wraps. Only my better angels have kept me from using every possible means of persuasion to convince you to ditch Tinseltown now for Hope Harbor."

"Why didn't you try?"

"For the same reason you decided to make the movie. After all the years you've devoted to your career, you owe it to yourself to claim the brass ring."

She let a beat pass, never breaking eye contact. "Other types of rings are also worth claiming."

Whoa.

That was direct.

A soft flush tinted her cheeks at his lack of response, and she dipped her chin. "Sorry for putting you on the spot. What I meant was that down the road, maybe we—"

"Hey." He covered her fingers with his and waited for her to look up. "Don't apologize. I feel the same way. I just didn't want to say it too soon and risk spooking you."

"It *is* too soon to be thinking along those lines. We shouldn't let ourselves get carried away or jump to too many conclusions after only a handful of weeks."

That was true.

Yet the same ability to read people—the same instincts that had served him well in business relationships in his previous career—told him his feelings for Katherine weren't premature. While he wouldn't rush their courtship if she came back, he was pretty certain he knew what the outcome would be.

"Don't worry. I'm not the impulsive type. We'll take our time—assuming Hope Harbor doesn't lose its appeal for you."

"That won't happen. I've loved this town since the first day I set foot in it years ago."

Whether her affection for the town—and for him—was sufficient to bring her back, however, remained to be seen. Even if she left Hollywood behind for another career, whatever new direction she took could lead her elsewhere.

For now, all he could do was pray for the outcome he wanted—and enjoy her last couple of days here.

"I agree with you. It's a special place. So . . ." He checked his watch. "You have lunch with Simon. Are you up for a dinner on the beach tonight?"

Now that her decision was made, he intended to do everything in his power to create a few romantic memories she could call up while she was away to remind her of all she was missing . . . and all that awaited her in this small Oregon seaside town.

"That would be wonderful."

"Does six o'clock—"

"Zach—sorry to interrupt." A frazzled Frank stopped a few feet from their table, flashing her a silent apology before refocusing on his boss. "We got slammed with a tour group." He motioned behind him, where the order line snaked out the door.

"I'll be there in a minute." He slid out of the booth as Frank hustled back to the counter, then turned toward Katherine, his back to the shop to block the patrons' view of her. "Until tonight." He leaned down and kissed her, hands flat on the table, lingering as long as he could.

When he straightened up at last, her cheeks were pink again.

"I'm guessing our take-it-slow-and-easy rule has been suspended for the duration."

"Uh-huh. Unless you have any objections."

"I can't think of a single one."

"In that case, be prepared for a memorable evening."

Her eyes began to sparkle. "That sounds promising."

"Count on it." He ran a finger along her jawline with a whisper-soft touch.

"Can I . . . bring anything?" Her question came out a bit breath-less. "Like, um, truffles for dessert?"

The lady was distracted.

Also promising.

"Truffles are always welcome—although I had another sweet dessert in mind." He grinned and waggled his eyebrows.

"I think I should have ordered one of your icy drinks instead of this latte." She fanned herself.

In his peripheral vision he caught Frank giving him a desperate glance. Reluctantly, he stepped back. "I have to go."

"I know. I'll be waiting for you at six."

Calling up every ounce of his willpower, he forced himself to walk away, plunged into the fray behind the counter—and for the next twenty minutes barely had a moment to breathe.

In fact, they were so busy and the milling crowd in the shop so dense he didn't see Katherine leave.

Not a problem.

In seven hours, she'd be all his.

And from the instant he closed up shop for the day until six o'clock, he was going to put all his efforts into creating a beach picnic worthy of a big-screen chick flick.

What in the world?

Katherine jolted to a stop as she entered the great room and spotted a man on her deck.

He was off to the side, his back toward her, and she had only a partial view—but it wasn't Zach.

Their beach picnic wasn't scheduled to start for another forty-five minutes, even if she was ready to go and counting the minutes.

She detoured into the kitchen and unplugged her phone from the charger. Peeked around the corner of the wall toward the deck again.

The man was gone.

Nevertheless, a tiny quiver of fear rippled through her.

But that was silly. This was Hope Harbor, not LA. The police chief here no doubt had the easiest law enforcement job in the state. Her unexpected visitor was probably a tourist who'd wandered off a trail somewhere and—

Ding-dong.

She froze.

Maybe that guy *was* looking for her.

But why hadn't he rung the bell to begin with?

Phone at the ready in case she had to call 911, she walked to the door.

Though the peephole distorted his features, the man appeared to be normal. And from the glimpse she'd gotten of him while he'd been on the deck, he hadn't come across as a vagrant or someone with nefarious intent.

It was possible he had a legitimate purpose for being here. A friend of the owner, perhaps, who didn't know the house was currently occupied by a vacation renter.

To be on the safe side, however, she left the chain on as she cracked the door—and she positioned her thumb to tap in 911.

"May I help you?"

The man smiled at her, but his eyes were assessing. "You aren't one of the owners of this house."

Her assumption must have been correct. "No. I rented it for a few weeks."

"Then my information was correct—but I wouldn't have recognized you. Kudos on the disguise." He swung up the arm that had been concealed behind his back and began snapping photos with the camera in his hand before she could process what was happening. "I understand congratulations are in order. Any comments on your movie deal?" All the while he kept clicking.

She finally found her voice. "You're on private property. If you're not gone in thirty seconds, I'm calling the police." She slammed the door. Sucked in a lungful of air. Tried to rein in her stampeding heart.

There was only one explanation for this.

Simon.

Punching in his number, she stalked into the living room and began to pace as the phone rang.

He took his sweet time answering.

Four rings in, on the cusp of rolling to voicemail, he picked up and greeted her.

She dispensed with any pretense of politeness. "What have you done?"

"What are you talking about?"

"Don't give me that, Simon. Someone from one of those gossip rags just rang my bell."

"Goes with the territory if you're starring in a major motion picture—as you are, my dear, now that you've signed on the dotted line. I snapped a photo of the contract and sent it to the studio as soon as we finished lunch. Tomorrow I'll deliver the hard copies in person and gear up for a major publicity blitz." He could hardly contain his glee.

"The blitz has already started."

"What can I say? Leaking a few crumbs to the press stirs up interest."

"My location is not a crumb." She forced the sentence through gritted teeth.

He didn't try to deny he'd sicced the media on her. "I'm surprised someone's already shown up. They must have contacted stringers in Portland or happened to have people in the vicinity. I guess they pulled out all the stops to try and get a juicy exclusive."

Her stomach began to churn.

Once again, she'd lost control of her life.

This was what she hated most about Hollywood.

"I don't want these people on my doorstep, Simon."

"Call the police if anyone else trespasses—or fly back with me to LA tomorrow. You have to be there Monday morning anyway for a meeting at the studio."

Leave tomorrow and give up two more days with Zach?

Not happening.

Besides, she still had two dozen truffles to make for the Hope House benefit. The finished ones on the island, boxed and ready to go, weren't sufficient for the sold-out event.

"I'm not leaving until Sunday."

"Suit yourself. I'm out of here at the crack of dawn tomorrow."

"Good-bye, Simon." She jabbed the end button, already wrestling with second thoughts about her decision.

But she'd signed the contract. She'd have to see this through.

However—she wasn't going to let Simon's zeal for publicity ruin these next two days with Zach.

Phone in hand, she opened the sliding door in the great room . . . peeked both directions . . . and stepped out. She needed to calm down, and the view from the deck would help her chill. If that guy—or anyone else—ventured onto the property, she was dialing 911 without bothering to issue a warning.

She walked over to the railing and gave the sea a sweep.

Frowned.

A sleek white cabin cruiser had dropped anchor very close to shore.

Strange.

In all her weeks here, no boat had ever ventured near the beach.

A twinge of suspicion began to niggle at her.

Pivoting, she reentered the house, picked up the binoculars from the coffee table, and returned to the deck. After lifting them into position, she adjusted the focus.

One person was on the deck of the boat—but the camera with the long lens in his hands wasn't pointed at Trixie, who was prancing about in the water, giving a fine aquatic show.

It was aimed her direction.

"Crud." As she muttered the word, she swung around and stomped back into the house. Slammed the slider closed. Locked it.

Her private Hope Harbor haven was ruined.

And her beach picnic with Zach was a bust.

Heck, they couldn't even eat on either of their decks, not with that guy in the boat watching her every move.

Crud, crud, crud, crud, crud.

She set the binoculars down, rubbed at the ache beginning to throb in her forehead, and resumed pacing.

Knowing Zach, he'd insist they have their picnic and modify

the setting to accommodate this new development—but any rendezvous was dangerous. What if a camera caught them together?

She cringed as a series of melodramatic headlines strobed across her mind, all of them scandalous, shocking, lurid, sensational—and false.

But true or not, they'd be hurtful and upsetting.

Having been down that road already, she could handle the overblown hype—but subjecting someone she cared about to such nastiness would be wrong. Especially a decent man like Zach, who lived an exemplary life and ran a business that depended on the respect and goodwill of his regular customers in town.

Unfortunately, unless she took action fast, he was going to show up at her door in thirty minutes.

So as soon as she psyched herself up for the call she didn't want to make, she'd key in his number and break the news.

27

· ·

Smiling, Zach picked up the loaf of French bread he'd asked Sweet Dreams bakery to put aside for him, tucked it into the antique picnic hamper Frank had loaned him, and set the basket on the floor next to the two throws he'd retrieved from the linen closet.

"Now that's a picnic." Stephanie wandered into the kitchen and surveyed his gear.

"I hope my neighbor agrees."

"You can't go wrong with a wicker picnic hamper. It appeals to the romantic in every woman."

"So Frank told me. He said it's the one he used the day he asked his wife to marry him."

Stephanie's eyebrows rose. "Is there more to this date than you've told me?"

"No." He'd filled her in on Katherine's decision about the movie, since it would soon be public knowledge anyway. "But I thought I'd launch this courtship in style—and give her some sweet memories to think about while she's busy being a movie star."

"That ought to do the trick." She waved a hand over the accoutrements he'd assembled.

"Frank said the two of you were having dinner together too."

"We are. He wants to take me to a fancy restaurant up in Coos Bay. I tried to talk him out of it, told him we should save that for a special occasion, but he said any date with me qualifies for that designation."

Zach grinned. "I didn't know my assistant barista was such a smooth talker." He leaned back against the counter and folded his arms. "He must really be sweet on—" His phone began to vibrate and he pulled it out. "Speaking of sweet . . ." He held up the cell.

"My cue to exit. Besides, I have to finish primping." She patted her hair and sashayed out.

Zach let the phone ring again as he waited for his aunt to disappear. After the door to her room clicked shut, he put it to his ear. "Couldn't wait another twenty minutes to see me, huh?"

"I've been ready for the past half hour—and looking forward to a whole evening on the beach in your company."

Her reply should have stoked his libido.

Instead, an underlying thread of wistfulness—and a touch of emotion that could be regret—put him on alert.

"Why do I hear a *but* in there?"

One second ticked by.

Two.

Three.

She sighed.

He braced.

"Under the circumstances, I don't think getting together with you would be wise."

Suspicion confirmed. She had bad news to share.

"What circumstances?" He wrapped his fingers around the edge of the counter and held on.

As she filled him in on Simon's leak to the media, he struggled to tamp down his anger.

Didn't work.

If her agent was standing in this room, he'd be tempted to flatten the man for ruining his remaining days with Katherine.

A strong reaction from a man who abhorred violence—and a telling measure of the depth of his feelings for his neighbor.

"So rather than subject you to that sort of scrutiny and turf invasion, I think we should cancel the picnic. I'm sorry, Zach." Katherine's voice was shaky—as if she was on the cusp of tears. "I bet you went to a lot of trouble."

He surveyed the hamper packed with all the gourmet goodies he'd rounded up during a whirlwind trip to a specialty food store in Coos Bay.

This picnic was happening.

"I'll tell you what. I'll wait until after dark and sneak over with our food. You can shut all the drapes and we'll have complete privacy."

"I'd like to believe that would work, but you don't know how dogged these photographers can be. For all I know, there are a couple camped out in my bushes—or hanging from trees outside my property line, cameras pointed at the house. Not to mention the guy on the boat. They could be equipped with night vision cameras."

He jammed a fist on his hip. "Would they honestly go to such extremes just because you signed a movie deal?"

"Depends on what Simon 'leaked.' He wasn't all that forthcoming with details. But in light of what happened in LA a few weeks ago at that party—yeah, they might. And if they see you sneaking over and manage to get a picture, I can imagine the headline now: 'Jason Grey's grieving girlfriend finds solace in Oregon coast love nest.'"

A muscle spasmed in his jaw. "How can people read that type of garbage?"

"I have no idea—but I don't want to put you in the position of having to deal with the fallout if any of those rag reporters find out about us and decide to make a nuisance of themselves after I'm gone."

"I can handle them."

"I don't want you to have to."

"It's worth it to have a couple more days with you."

A moment of silence ticked by.

"I'll tell you what. Let's put the picnic on hold for today. I'll touch base with you first thing in the morning. For tonight, it's safer if you keep your distance."

"I can find a way to get over to your place without being detected, Katherine." At least he was 99 percent certain he could.

"Zach—do this for me. Please. I don't want our relationship tainted by being splashed all over the scandal sheets that pass for magazines in the show business world."

Her impassioned plea was impossible to refuse—and much as he wanted to see her, her peace of mind took priority.

"If that's what you want, I'll stay on this side of the property line tonight—as long as you call me in the morning."

"I will."

"Early."

"I promise." Her voice caught. Like she was trying to hold back a sob.

"Hey." He gentled his tone. "We'll work this out. Everything will be fine."

"I hope so. Talk to you soon."

She ended the call before he could respond.

After a few moments of silence, he lowered the cell.

Down the hall, Stephanie's door clicked, and less than half a minute later she poked her head into the kitchen. "Is the coast clear?"

"Yeah."

She joined him. "You don't look happy."

"Change in plans."

He recounted his conversation with Katherine.

Stephanie wrinkled her nose. "Bummer."

"Tell me about it."

She tucked her purse under her arm and regarded him. "For

what it's worth, I have a feeling she's in tears as we speak—and battling more than a few regrets about taking that movie role."

"It was the right choice, much as I would have preferred her to turn it down."

"In that case—if I may offer one piece of advice—follow her lead on how to handle this development. She already has more than her share of pressure and stress in Hollywood. She doesn't need any more here. And she knows the nasty side of that business better than you do."

A knock sounded on the door, and Stephanie motioned toward the front of the house. "That would be Frank. You want me to stay here tonight and keep you company?"

He summoned up a smile. "No reason two romantic evenings should be ruined. Go. Have fun. I'll give Dad a call, finish the thriller I picked up at the airport for the trip home, and make it an early night."

"Are you sure?"

"Yes." Another knock rattled the door, and he shooed her toward it. "He seems anxious. Go ahead and answer."

After a brief hesitation, she nodded. "Okay. I'll see you in the morning." She picked up her sweater from the island, rose on tiptoe to kiss his cheek, and disappeared down the hall. After a short, muffled exchange, the front door clicked shut as they headed out for their dinner date.

Leaving him alone to face the whole lonely, empty evening that stretched ahead.

After expelling a breath, he put the hamper back on the counter and began unpacking the contents. Surely if he applied a hefty dose of brainpower to the logistics of arranging a clandestine picnic, he could come up with a solution that would placate Katherine.

But the plan he formulated during the long evening and the longer, restless night came to naught.

Because at some point in the early hours of the morning, Katherine left.

He made that discovery after the fact, as the first pale light of dawn began to seep around the drapes in his room.

Finally giving up on sleep, he swung his legs to the floor, reached for his cell on the nightstand—and found an email from her waiting for him.

Zach—Please don't be mad, but I can't in good conscience stay here any longer with paparazzi on my tail. Sorry as I am to leave without an in-person farewell—and our picnic on the beach—there's nowhere safe for us to get together . . . and if we talk again, I'm afraid you'll convince me to attempt a rendezvous. So I left with Simon early this morning.

I promise to stay in touch every day during the shooting, by phone and text and email—to the point you may get tired of hearing from me. (I hope not.) Please know that you'll be constantly in my thoughts—as I hope I'll be in yours. Until we meet again . . .

Your Katherine

P.S. I finished the truffles for the Hope House benefit in the wee hours. You'll find them on the island in my kitchen. The house key is under the pot of flowers on the deck.

Gut twisting, Zach forked his fingers through his hair and stared at the screen.

Hard as he tried to be mad, he couldn't summon up one ounce of anger. Walking out without a good-bye had to have been as hard on Katherine as it was on him.

And you had to admire a woman who did what she believed was best for someone she cared about, despite the cost to herself.

Zach pushed himself to his feet and crossed to the window. Moved the drapes aside.

From here, the house next door wasn't visible through the needle-bedecked boughs of the trees.

But it was there.

Just like Katherine would remain in his heart during the weeks ahead, even if he couldn't see her.

Lifting his cell again, he tapped in a response.

I'm not mad . . . and I'll never get tired of hearing from you. As for you being in my thoughts—goes without saying. Will miss you at the Hope House benefit.

And so she'd know he'd caught the significance of her sign-off, he ended his email the same.

Your Zach

Then he geared up for the day at The Perfect Blend.

Because at this stage of the game, with the woman who was fast claiming his heart far away from Hope Harbor and once again immersed in the glamor and fast-paced life of Hollywood, the outcome of their relationship was in the hands of a power far greater than either of them.

28

· ·

"The turkey smells divine, Zach." Stephanie entered the house on a gust of chilly air and gave an appreciative sniff. "Happy Thanksgiving." She handed him a casserole dish, shed her jacket, and slid her damp umbrella into the stand by the door.

"The same to you." He leaned down and kissed her cheek. "Where's Frank?"

"Running an errand. He'll be along soon. Is your dad in the great room?"

"Yes."

"I'll go say hello—and take advantage of the fireplace. You do have a fire going, don't you?"

"Wouldn't be Thanksgiving without one. Let me put this in the fridge"—he hefted the casserole—"and I'll join you in a minute. Can I bring you a drink?"

"I'll help myself to one after I warm up, thanks."

As she continued toward the back of the house, Zach detoured to the kitchen and slid her sweet potato casserole into the refrigerator, then pulled out his cell and scanned the screen.

Nothing more from Katherine since a text at dawn—all he had to console himself on this holiday they'd planned to spend together, until the location shooting schedule in Texas had been delayed by rain and the studio honchos had decided to forge ahead and try to regain the lost ground. From what Katherine had said, they'd planned to film until last night.

He reread her brief message, sent at the crack of dawn.

Zach—Missing you. This isn't where I want to be
for the holiday. Will be in touch later.
Your Katherine

At least she'd promised to call.

But after eleven weeks with only texts, emails, and phone calls to sustain him, having to forgo their much-anticipated reunion stunk.

"You joining us, Zach?" His father called out the question from the great room.

"I'll be right there."

Taking a deep breath, he did his best to banish his negativity. After all, he had much to be grateful for this day—including the fact that he was spending the holiday with all his remaining family members.

The reconciliation with his father alone ought to lift his spirits. It was nothing short of miraculous—as was his father's attitude. Nervous as Zach had been about his dad's reaction to his business and the life he'd created here, the older man had apparently come to terms with his elder son's choices. He'd not only been interested in exploring the town and visiting The Perfect Blend since his arrival on Tuesday, he'd been complimentary about both.

To buy himself another few seconds to fire up his enthusiasm, Zach crossed to the refrigerator and pulled out a soda.

Having Katherine here as he gave thanks for all the blessings his move to Hope Harbor had brought would have made the day perfect—but if their relationship continued to progress, they'd be spending future holidays together. Christmas wasn't far off, and the location shooting would be over. The studio filming should conclude by the end of January.

Then she'd be free.

And from all indications, she was sticking to her plan to exit the movie world after this film.

She hadn't yet decided what she wanted to do instead, but as far as he was concerned, she could take as long as she needed to figure that out.

And what more perfect place to do that than in Hope Harbor?

A case he intended to argue during their next in-person visit—or sooner.

Swigging his soda, he left the kitchen and strolled toward the living room, where his dad and aunt were sitting side by side on the couch in front of the fireplace.

"You picked a cozy spot."

"Perfect for a day like this." His father waved a hand toward the deck, where tendrils of fog were engaged in a sinuous dance outside the sliding door. "You get socked in often?"

"Fog's part of life here—but in general it comes and goes fast." Zach sat in an overstuffed chair at a right angle to the couch. "You get used to it after—"

The doorbell chimed.

"Must be Frank. You want to do the honors?" He motioned toward the hall with his soda can as he directed the question to his aunt.

"To tell you the truth, I'm too comfortable to get up." As if to reinforce that, she burrowed into the cushions. "I haven't quite shaken the chill I got driving over."

Zach arched his eyebrows. "Your significant other is waiting on the porch and you aren't in a hurry to see him? Shouldn't you be flying toward the door, cheeks flushed, heart racing?"

She snickered. "That could be a quote from one of my romance novels. Don't tell me I've converted you to my favorite genre."

"Hey—if his girl is far away, a guy has to live out his fantasies where he can find them." Grinning, he set his soda on the side table and rose. "Fine. I'll let Frank in. And I won't tell him you preferred to warm up in front of a fire instead of in his arms."

"I'll hug him *after* he sheds his wet-weather gear."

"I *may* tell him that."

"Not if you want to stay in my good graces."

Chuckling, Zach strolled down the hall. It had been fun to watch the romance between his part-time barista and his aunt blossom over the past few months. If this kept up, wedding bells shouldn't be far off.

Corners of his mouth tipped up, he twisted the knob and pulled the door open.

Stopped breathing.

What the . . . ?

His jaw dropped as he took in the blonde woman holding an umbrella who stood on the other side of his door.

"Happy Thanksgiving, Zach."

Somehow he managed to find his voice. "Katherine?"

"None other. Did the blonde hair throw you?" She patted her tresses, longer now and back to their natural color.

"No." She'd been sending him production stills and selfies for weeks, so her appearance wasn't a surprise. Her arrival on his doorstep? Different story. "What are you doing here?"

Before she could respond, Frank slid out from behind the wheel of the car in the driveway, hustled over, and gave him a disgusted look. "If that's the best you can do when your girl arrives out of the blue after weeks apart, you deserve a kick in the pants. And I'm not waiting out here in the car for you to get yourself in gear and give her a proper welcome while *my* girl is waiting for me inside." He elbowed past and disappeared into the house, juggling a box in one hand.

"I guess I surprised you." The spark of excitement in Katherine's eyes flickered, and her smile dimmed a few watts. As if she was uncertain of her welcome.

Better fix that. Pronto.

"Come in out of the rain." He took her arm and tugged her inside.

"I thought it would be fun to show up unannounced, but I should have—"

"Let me take your coat and show you how happy I am to see you." He peeled it off. Relieved her of her umbrella. Grabbed her hand and towed her down the hall.

On the threshold of his bedroom, she balked. "Um . . . this might be the other extreme."

"I intend to give you the proper welcome Frank mentioned, and I don't want an audience." He pulled her inside, shut the door with his foot, and wrapped his arms around her. "You ready?"

A dimple appeared in her cheek, and she tossed her purse on the bed. Snuggled closer to him. "Lay it on me."

He lowered his lips to hers—and gave her a no-holds-barred kiss that should leave no doubt about how much he'd missed her.

She reciprocated, all in, all the way.

When they finally surfaced for air, her lipstick had disappeared and her hair was mussed.

"Wow." She leaned her forehead against his chest. "I think Frank would be impressed."

"I'm more interested in whether *you* were impressed."

"I'd rate that an A+ welcome."

He stroked her back, then eased off a few inches to see her. "So tell me how you managed to pull this off."

"We finished yesterday afternoon, ahead of schedule. Booking a last-minute flight over the Thanksgiving weekend is a challenge, but if you're willing to take a red-eye, lady luck can grant you a few favors."

All at once, the shadows under her lower lashes registered. "Define red-eye."

"I got on the plane in Texas last night at midnight. Had a long layover in San Francisco. Caught a flight to North Bend this morning. As soon as I booked everything, I contacted Stephanie. I wanted to surprise you, but I thought it best to let *someone* know I was coming."

"You've been flying all night?"

"The trip was worth it for that kiss alone."

"A mere preview of what's in store during your visit."

"Ooooh. Be still, my heart." She fanned herself. "Frank would approve."

"Speaking of my cheeky barista—how did he get involved?"

"I was planning to rent a car and drive down, but Stephanie told him I was coming, and he insisted on picking me up. Best of all? No paparazzi know where I am—not that they're following me around much anymore. Now that last July's trauma is receding into history—*ancient* history, by Hollywood standards—I'm old news."

He stroked her silky cheek. "You must be exhausted."

She inched closer. "Not anymore. That kiss was a first-rate wake-up call."

No matter what she said, she had to be dead on her feet after a sleepless night and two flights. "You need a nap."

"No way, no how. I'm not giving up a single minute with you."

He'd debate that later.

"How long can you stay?"

She made a face. "Not long enough. I have to be back on Saturday afternoon. I'm leaving super early that morning."

"So we have today and tomorrow."

"For now."

His pulse stuttered—and his hope surged. "What does that mean?"

She gave him a slow smile and played with a button on his shirt, letting the suspense build for a few moments. "It means that after the movie wraps, I'm coming back here."

The cloud of worry that had been hanging over him for weeks began to dissipate like a Hope Harbor mist under the warmth of the sun.

Thank you, God!

"That's the best news I've had in months. Years."

"I hoped that would be your reaction."

"Have you also decided what you want to do with the rest of your life?" Maybe she was only coming back here to think again.

She dispelled that worry at once. "I've decided to try my hand at being a chocolatier—and I've been watching the Hope Harbor commercial real estate from afar. Did you know the space next to The Perfect Blend is going to be available in the spring?"

"No." How had he missed that piece of news?

"Yep. The older woman who ran that shop is retiring. I've already put—"

At the soft knock on his door, she fell silent.

"Zach?" Stephanie's voice. "Sorry to interrupt, but there's a timer going off in the kitchen. We have no idea what it's for, and we didn't want the turkey to burn."

"I'll be out in a minute." His attention never wavered from Katherine. "We'll pick this up later. In the meantime, let me introduce you to my dad."

She touched her hair. "Give me a minute to get straightened out."

"Have at it." He motioned to the attached bath. "I'll baste the turkey while you do whatever you think is necessary. But I kind of like the tousled look."

"Your dad may not." She rubbed her palms down her slacks. "Can I admit I'm a little nervous about meeting him?"

"Don't be. I've done nothing but sing your praises."

"No pressure there." She rolled her eyes, retrieved her purse, and walked toward the bathroom. "I'll be out in five minutes."

After she disappeared behind the door, he slipped out of the room and took care of turkey business in the kitchen.

True to her word, Katherine joined him as fast as she'd promised.

"Ready to meet the family?" He twined his fingers with hers.

"No." She drew in an unsteady breath. "I feel rumpled from all those hours in planes and airports. Maybe I should change. My bag is in Frank's car, and it wouldn't take very—"

"You look fantastic. Trust me." He squeezed her fingers. "You already know Stephanie and Frank, and Dad's mellowed over the past few weeks. Come on. I'll be by your side for the duration."

He honored his pledge—though as it turned out, his support wasn't necessary. His dad turned on the charm, and Katherine in turn charmed him. By the time they all sat down to dinner, said a blessing, and dived into the feast, her nervousness had vanished.

Thanks in large part to the women at his table, there were no awkward conversational gaps during the meal either. The chatter was lively, the topics wide-ranging, the laughter abundant.

It was the kind of Thanksgiving he'd always dreamed of hosting in this house.

As the meal drew to a close, he set his napkin on the table. "Everyone ready for dessert?"

His query was met with groans.

"Let's wait awhile." Stephanie patted her stomach. "I'm not certain I can squeeze one more ounce in here—and I want to have a taste of pumpkin pie—plus one or two of those cranberry truffles Katherine brought."

Zach transferred his attention to his unexpected guest. "You made truffles?"

"Yes. Earlier in the week, before our shooting schedule got rain delayed. I was able to arrange to get access to a kitchen for a few hours in Texas. I'm glad they didn't go to waste."

"Heaven forbid!" This from Stephanie.

"Shall we move to the great room until we're ready for dessert?" Zach pushed back his chair, but Stephanie touched his arm.

"I'm all for heading back to that wonderful fire, but Frank and I would like to make an announcement first." She covered the man's hand with hers as she transferred her attention to him. "Do you want to do the honors?"

"It would be my pleasure." He smiled at the small group gathered around the table. "I'm delighted to announce that Stephanie and I are engaged."

Zach grinned. "Now that's what I call an announcement. If I had any champagne, I'd break it out. Congratulations to you both."

His father and Katherine added their own best wishes.

"When's the big day?" His dad aimed the question at the happy couple.

"Between Christmas and New Year's. We haven't locked in a date yet. It depends on the availability of the church." Stephanie glanced at Frank again.

"Go ahead." He twined his fingers with hers. "I'll concede the floor to you for part two."

She gave the small group at the table a sweep. "There's more news. You all know how involved Frank and I have been in the Hope House project. We realize the committee was expecting to find a younger couple to be houseparents, but we've spoken with the Helping Hands board and thrown our hat in the ring. We'll be married before all the paperwork and final approval from the state are completed, and we can't think of a more gratifying way to spend our retirement than by helping children get a solid start in life in a loving home."

Zach stared at them.

The engagement announcement wasn't unexpected.

But houseparents at Hope House?

It took him a few seconds to absorb that—and he wasn't alone. In the wake of Stephanie's announcement, there was dead silence around the table.

At last, his aunt spoke. "You think we're too old to do this, don't you?"

"Of course not." His father responded at once, God bless him. "From what I've seen, you two have more vigor than most people half your age. You just took us all by surprise."

"Convincing the board we're up to the job could be a challenge, though." Frank edged his chair closer to Stephanie's and slipped his arm around her. "But we intend to give it our best shot."

Zach's vocal cords kicked in. "If you want a reference, you can count on me. I'll attest to your boundless energy. And I think it's a terrific idea. I may go out and buy that bottle of champagne yet."

"I'll happily settle for a truffle or two later," Stephanie said. "For now, however, that fire is beckoning."

After carrying their plates into the kitchen, they all retired to the living room—where Zach stayed close beside Katherine. Happy as he was to have the people he cared about most in the world gathered together on this holiday, he couldn't help wishing he had her to himself.

As if sensing that three . . . or four . . . or five . . . was a crowd, Frank and Stephanie left not long after dessert. At the door, Frank offered to fill in for him tomorrow with Bren at The Perfect Blend—and Zach didn't hesitate to accept.

A few minutes later, his dad retired to his room, claiming fatigue.

By eight o'clock, he and Katherine were alone by his fireplace.

"I think I'm responsible for breaking up this party early." Katherine snuggled against him on the couch.

"I'm fine with that. Dad will be here ten more days, and I can see Frank and Stephanie anytime. Except . . ." He frowned. "Did Frank drive away with your suitcase?"

"Uh-huh. He's dropping it at the Gull Motel for me. I managed to snag a last-minute cancellation."

"Why don't you stay here? Dad can be our chaperone."

"But there's only one guest room—and I don't want you to sleep on the couch, which is what you'd offer to do if I stayed."

"It would be a small sacrifice to have you close. Cancel the motel. I'll call Frank and ask him to run back with your suitcase." He reached for his phone.

She grabbed his arm. "Nope. It's the motel for me. We can't be together while we're sleeping anyway." A yawn snuck up on her, too fast to smother. "Whoops. Sorry." She clapped a hand over her mouth.

Much as he'd like to spend the next few hours kissing and talking . . . and kissing some more . . . Katherine needed to sleep.

"I'll take you to the motel. You can get a full night's sleep, and we'll spend all day tomorrow together." He tried to disengage, but she tightened her grip.

"I'm not going to deny I'm tired—but can't we stay here by the fire for a few more minutes?"

As always, she was impossible to refuse.

"If that's what you want." He urged her back against him.

With a contented sigh, she nestled close again. "There's nowhere I'd rather be on this Thanksgiving Day."

He stroked her hair, corralling the desire to launch a heavy kissing session. That could wait until tomorrow, when the woman in his arms wasn't running on adrenaline. "Tell me about the chocolate shop you're going to open."

She complied, but as he asked her a few questions, she began to drift off.

He let her.

Whenever she awakened, he'd take her to the Gull so she could get some real sleep.

But for now, he was as happy as a seagull with a french fry just to hold her in his arms and give thanks on this appropriately named day. For he agreed with what Katherine had said a few minutes ago.

There was nowhere he'd rather be on this Thanksgiving Day.

And it was exactly where he hoped to be on every Thanksgiving Day to come for the rest of his life.

Epilogue

"Ready for the big day tomorrow?"

At the question, Katherine straightened up from the glass display case, polishing cloth in hand, and smiled at the man in the doorway who'd walked with her on every step of the journey from doodles on a paper napkin to hands-on renovations to tomorrow's grand opening of Chocolate Harbor.

"As ready as I can be—and more than a little nervous."

"After all the press you've gotten, you shouldn't be. And the residents are chomping at the bit to support your business." Zach continued through the door and shut it behind him, a wicker picnic basket in hand.

"What's that for?" She motioned to the antique-looking hamper. "And why aren't you at The Perfect Blend? Fridays are always super busy."

"Shop's closed for the day. Did you eat lunch?"

She twisted her wrist and gaped at her watch. "I can't believe it's two o'clock already."

"I'll take that as a no on lunch. Let's go to the beach." He lifted the hamper. "I owe you a picnic."

"Now?"

"Why not? You're ready for the opening. If you hang around here, you'll just get more nervous." He held out his hand. "Thanks to uncooperative weather, we never did get to reschedule our cancelled beach picnic from September, and this gorgeous May day is made for a celebration on the sand."

"Sold." She tucked the cloth under the pristine counter and circled around to join him. "Besides, I have another piece of news to share that also deserves a celebration."

"Any hints?"

"Not until we're at the beach."

"Then let's get this show on the road. Do you want to swing by your house first?"

"You mean *Frank's* house. It still doesn't feel like mine."

"He may own it, but it's yours as long as you want to rent it, now that he and Stephanie are ensconced as houseparents at Hope House."

"I'm glad that worked out for them. They seem to be loving it."

He switched the hamper to his other hand. "You know, it's funny. All those years Stephanie was enmeshed in her career, I never thought of her as the motherly type. But from what I can tell, she's thriving in the role—as are the kids under her and Frank's care."

"A perfect illustration of what love can do."

"Speaking of love . . ." He swung the hamper out of the way and leaned down, letting actions speak louder than words.

As always, his kiss sent a ripple of delight through her.

She put her arms around his neck and held on tight.

In the end, he was the one who broke the lip-lock. "If we keep this up, we'll never get to the beach."

"I could live with that." She didn't relinquish her grip, letting him back up only a meager few inches. "It's romantic here—or wherever you are."

"Sweet." He gave her his heart-melting, I'm-all-yours look that never failed to turn her insides to jelly. "But you could use a change of scene. You've been almost living in this shop for weeks, between the renovations and decorating and chocolate making."

"It came out nice, though, didn't it?" She pivoted in his arms to give the space a slow, three-sixty scan.

A large glass display case took center stage, with a small checkout counter beside it. Boxed chocolates were arranged on two long shelves that hugged one wall. The other wall was adorned with large photos of the various stages of chocolate production, from cacao trees and beans to tempering to the final product. The picture window in front offered passersby an enticing glimpse of the inviting retail part of the store, with its hardwood floor covered by a rug in jewel tones and a tiny table with two chairs—for patrons who couldn't wait to sample their purchases.

The back of the shop, where the magic happened, was all stainless steel and high-tech, but up here the ambiance encouraged indulgence.

"Nice doesn't come close to describing it." Zach nuzzled her neck. "Spectacular would be more accurate."

"Thank you." She refocused on him. "By the way, I like your quote on the board out front today."

"With a chocolate shop opening next to me tomorrow, I had to get in the spirit. Besides, a balanced diet *is* chocolate in both hands. Right?"

She grinned. "Right. Let's hope enough people agree with that to keep me in business."

"You already have a standing order at the tearoom. And Tracy at the cranberry farm was receptive to the idea of doing a joint promotion with her cranberry nut cake and your cranberry truffles, wasn't she?"

"Yes. I've also got two custom orders for truffles as wedding favors."

"And you haven't even opened your doors yet."

"I know."

"I predict you'll have a booming business." He took her hand. "Let's go have our picnic before you're too busy to hang out with the local barista."

She squeezed his fingers. "That will never happen."

His eyes warmed at her husky tone. "Hold that thought."

"I intend to hold more than that. Those broad shoulders of yours are beckoning."

The smoldering ember in his brown irises erupted into a blaze, and he tugged her toward the door. "We're out of here."

She followed without protest.

As she'd follow him wherever he wanted to go for the rest of his life.

That's what happened when you fell in love with a guy who always put you first and never tried to control you. Who understood that you wanted a man to hold your hand, not hold you up—or try to push you the direction he believed you should go.

A man like that was worth following to the ends of the earth.

Fortunately, she'd had to go no farther than Hope Harbor—the very place that had felt like home since the first day she'd set foot in town.

Now it was home for always.

And unless she'd been misreading every cue during the unhurried courtship Zach had insisted on, in the not-too-distant future she'd be exchanging her current residence for a house overlooking Blackberry Beach.

One she'd have no trouble at all calling her own.

This was the day.

But as Zach waited while Katherine locked the door to the shop, doubts began to assail him.

Maybe this wasn't the best timing.

Maybe he should defer his plan until after the opening.

Maybe he ought to—

"I hope that hamper is well stocked. I'm starving. What's the main course?"

At Katherine's comment, he gave her his full attention. With her infectious enthusiasm, caring heart, keen intellect, and killer sense of humor, she was everything a man could hope to find in a wife—and more.

And he wanted to start waking up next to her every single morning ASAP.

He quashed his qualms about timing. A month ago, he'd vowed to take the leap on the first day that was conducive to a beach picnic, and this was it.

"Zach." She elbowed him. "Are you paying attention?"

"Yes. To you. Everything else recedes into the background when we're together."

A dimple appeared in her cheek. "And they say men don't know how to be romantic."

"Who are *they*?"

"Popular wisdom. But you defy stereotypes."

"Thank you." He gave a mock bow and took her hand. "Come on. Our beach awaits."

"I'm all yours."

He hoped that was true.

The signs had all been encouraging these past months, but until a lady said yes, it was impossible to be absolutely certain.

Fifteen minutes later, he swung into his driveway, retrieved the picnic hamper and two blankets from the trunk, and led her toward the path that dropped to the beach from the bluff.

Within ten minutes, they were at their favorite sun-bleached log, spreading out the blankets and settling in as two seagulls wheeled overhead. Other than the birds and a silver-white harbor seal who was watching the proceedings from a rock offshore, they had the place to themselves.

"You never did answer my question about what we're having for lunch." Katherine sat cross-legged and tapped the lid of the picnic hamper.

"Goodies from a gourmet shop in Coos Bay and fresh-baked

French bread from Sweet Dreams. I recreated the menu from September."

"How did you manage to assemble this feast? Weren't you at the shop all day?"

"Yes. I got most of the food yesterday, once the various weather sites agreed on the forecast. I picked up the bread after I closed the shop."

Her dimple returned. "You must have been awfully certain I'd agree to come."

"I have great confidence in my powers of persuasion." About picnics, anyway.

She reached for the lid. "Tell me what we're having."

He gave her fingers a gentle rap. "Not until you tell me your news. Is it about the movie?" Unlikely, since she seemed glad to be free of Hollywood—but there was positive buzz about the film in the media, and a few influentials who'd reviewed the rough cut were singing its praises.

"Nope. I'm not even thinking much about that—and I won't until a few days before the premiere. I'd ditch that if I could, but my contract says I have to show up." She grimaced.

"Think of it as an opportunity to tout your new career. Orders from a few show-business types could raise your profile."

"Spoken like the businessman you are. Your previous firm lost a star when you left *that* world."

"I've never looked back."

"I don't expect I will either."

"Are you certain?" It wasn't a subject they talked about often, but knowing how much Katherine enjoyed diving into a juicy part, it remained a subtle worry.

"Yes."

Her instant reply was reassuring.

"You won't miss acting?"

Her eyes began to sparkle. "That's the perfect segue to my news. Guess who I heard from today?"

"I haven't a clue—but it must have been someone important. You're glowing."

"Important to me, in any case. The director of a professional theater in Coos Bay called. He saw the story about me opening Chocolate Harbor. He's familiar with my screen work and heard excellent reports about the movie from a contact in Hollywood. He wanted to know if I'd be willing to chat about occasionally appearing in a production or directing a show."

"Wow. I'd say you ended up with the best of both worlds."

"I agree. Stage work was always my first love, and directing appeals to me." She leaned against the log. "You know, back in August, Reverend Baker asked if I could combine chocolate making and acting. The idea intrigued me, but I didn't see how I could make it work—until now. The theater gig would let me dip my toe back into acting if I get the urge, but it wouldn't interfere too much with my candy business."

"I take it you're going to talk to him."

"Next month, after I get past the grand opening. What do you think?"

"I say go for it—but you're going to be one busy lady."

"I'm used to that."

He'd intended to wait until after they ate to bring up the main item on his agenda for this picnic, but all at once the time felt right.

Pulse picking up, he reached into the picnic hamper and pulled out a small box wrapped in white paper, a shiny bow on top. Set it on the lid. "I'm hoping you can fit one more job into your schedule."

She stared at the box.

"Go ahead. Open it."

"Is it . . . is that what I think it is?"

"Open it and find out."

She picked up the box, tore off the paper, flipped up the lid—and gasped.

The large, marquise-cut diamond in the platinum setting sparkled in the mid-afternoon sun, as impressive here as it had been in the showroom, where the clerk had complimented his excellent taste and assured him any woman would be thrilled to wear such a ring.

"It's stunning." Katherine's verdict was hushed.

"It's also exchangeable, if you prefer a different style. Or returnable, if necessary. I hope it won't be." He tried for a teasing tone, but nerves kicked in and his voice cracked.

Katherine lifted her chin. "Is there a speech to go with this?"

"If I can remember it. I'm not used to learning lines, like you are."

"From-the-heart comments are always more powerful than scripted lines."

He angled toward her and took the box from her fingers. Removed the ring. Clasped her hand in a gentle grip. "I'm not going to deliver a long monologue. I think relationships should be about dialogue. But I want you to know that after I moved here from Chicago, I thought my life was perfect. That I had everything I needed to be happy. As I came to realize, though, there was one glaring gap—and your arrival verified that. From the day you walked into The Perfect Blend, I sensed you could fill the empty place in my life . . . and that you might be destined to play a starring role in my future."

The two seagulls that had been circling above landed about thirty feet away and sat on the sand, as if they wanted an up-close-and-personal view of the scene playing out on the beach.

Offshore, the seal belched and a dolphin executed a series of perfect jumps, leaping out of the water in a graceful arc.

Zach hitched up one side of his mouth and motioned to the menagerie. "We have an audience."

"They're waiting for the finale. So am I."

"Then let's get to it." He held on tight to the ring with his unsteady fingers. "Over these past few months, everything I intuitively sensed about you has proven to be true. Your kindness, enthusiasm, clear sense of priorities, and ability to turn every day into a holiday have become the sunshine that warms my days—and my heart. I don't want to rush you, but waiting won't make me any more confident than I already am that we belong together. I love you more than I can say—and I'd be honored if you'd agree to be my wife."

In reply, she held out her left hand.

Her fingers weren't steady either.

"Is that a yes?"

She nodded as a tear spilled over her lashes and trickled down her cheek.

Throat tightening, he slid the ring on her finger. "Shall we seal this engagement with a kiss?"

When he leaned toward her, she pressed a hand against his chest. "Wait."

He cocked his head. "Second thoughts already?"

"Not even close. I just . . . I wasn't expecting this today. If I had been, I would have prepared a speech too."

"No speech necessary. I'll take a kiss instead."

"But I want to tell you how much I . . . how blessed I feel to . . . what an honor . . ." Her voice trailed off, and she exhaled. "Could I be any less articulate? *Your* speech was beautiful."

"It should be, after all my practice. And I get the gist of what you're trying to say."

"Let me try again anyway." She took a deep breath and locked gazes with him. "Zachary Garrett, I love everything about you. You're principled, caring, brave, hard-working, funny, kind—and you have your head on straight. You also respect me and never try to dominate our relationship or take control of my life. If you'd waited any longer to ask me to marry you, I might have been tempted to take the lead."

She scooted toward him and wrapped her arms around his neck, her beautiful, expressive eyes inches from his—and filled with longing and love. "Let's make this official—and then let's get married as soon as possible."

"I like that plan." Without further ado, he pulled her close and leaned down to claim their first kiss as an engaged couple.

Somewhere in the distance, a seagull cackled—but his focus was on the woman who'd become the center of his world.

And as he folded her into the shelter of his arms, his heart overflowed with gratitude.

For who could have imagined, back in his fast-paced, wheeling/dealing Chicago career, that he'd find his true calling—along with love and contentment—in a tiny town on the Oregon coast?

God's hand had to be in it.

And perhaps Josh's.

All at once, Charley's revelation about his brother from months ago replayed in his mind.

"He didn't pray for himself, Zach. He prayed for you."

The world began to fade away as the magic of their kiss sucked him in—but in the last moments before he succumbed, he gave thanks. For his new life in a charming town with the perfect name. For the gratifying reconciliation with his father. For the much-loved and much-missed brother who was cheering him on from heaven.

And for the amazing woman in his arms, who would fill all his tomorrows with love and laughter and light.

WANT MORE FROM IRENE HANNON?
Keep Reading for a Preview
of *Labyrinth of Lies*!

**Book 2 in Irene's
Latest Suspense Series**

They wanted her to take on another undercover gig?

No way.

Not happening.

But if both her boss and the head of the Crimes Against Persons unit were ganging up on her, getting out of the assignment would require finesse.

Brain firing on all cylinders, St. Louis County detective Cate Reilly crossed her legs, clenched her hands together in her lap, and surveyed the sergeant behind the desk—and the lieutenant seated beside her. Five seconds. That was all she needed to formulate a diplomatic, persuasive refusal.

Sarge didn't give them to her.

"We're aware you prefer not to do more undercover work, Cate. It's not for everyone, and we appreciate you giving it a try this year." He rested his forearms on his desk and linked his fingers. "But this is a . . . . unique . . . situation, so I'd ask you to hear us out. Lieutenant?"

The commander of the unit picked up the cue. "It goes without saying that what we discuss here stays here, no matter how this meeting ends." He locked gazes with her.

"Of course." After ten years with the St. Louis County PD, she knew when to zip her lips.

He gave a curt nod. "Two months ago, Gabe Laurent's seventeen-year-old daughter, Stephanie, disappeared from a private girls' boarding school in the far western portion of our jurisdiction, along the Missouri River. You know who Laurent is, I assume."

"Yes." In an era when badge holders were often painted as the bad guys, every County PD employee was aware of the software executive's staunch—and vocal—commitment to law enforcement. "Why haven't I heard about the girl's disappearance?"

"We were keeping it under wraps until we determined whether it was the runaway situation it appeared to be. Only the detectives assigned to the case were privy to the details."

"*Was* it a runaway?"

The lieutenant shifted in his seat. "That was our conclusion. All the pieces fit. Her backpack was gone. Her boyfriend also went missing—as did *his* backpack and car. Everyone our people spoke with agreed she was troubled and unhappy. That's why her father sent her to Ivy Hill Academy. He didn't like the crowd she was running with—or her boyfriend, slipping grades, and attitude. In addition to being a prestigious all-girl college-prep school with high academic standards, Ivy Hill is known for its rigid discipline."

"Is the investigation still active?"

Sarge leaned back in his chair. "We've been keeping an eye out for her, but it hasn't been our highest priority."

No, it wouldn't be.

Teen runaways were disturbing, but the County's heavy homicide caseload and other serious crime investigations took precedence. The detectives were already stretched thin, and the long hours couldn't expand much more without significant fallout—like a major decline in morale or a mass exodus.

"So why are we talking about it now?"

The lieutenant rejoined the conversation. "We've been asked to dig deeper."

"By whom?"

He held up a hand. "Let me back up first. Gabe Laurent wasn't satisfied with our conclusion or our promise to continue our efforts to locate his daughter as resources allowed. He ended up hiring a PI who turned up one piece of information that suggests there may be more to the story than a mere runaway situation."

Ouch.

That put County in an awkward position.

"What did the PI find?"

"Two days before he disappeared, the boyfriend had been in touch with a counselor at one of the community colleges about registering for the spring term."

O-kay.

That put a whole different spin on the case.

"In other words, he may have taken the backpack for a weekend getaway with his girlfriend, but he wasn't planning to disappear." Cate exhaled.

"That was Gabe Laurent's conclusion."

"This is starting to smell like foul play."

"I agree."

She furrowed her brow. "How did our people miss that nugget?"

"The boyfriend—Alex Johnson—lived with a grandmother who's in poor health and a father who comes and goes . . . mostly to the local bar. The PI happened to be at the apartment talking with the grandmother when a financial assistance application from the school arrived in the mail."

"She knew about his plans?"

"No—nor did the father. Based on what the PI gleaned from the counselor, Alex decided the laborer job he'd taken with a roofing company after high school graduation wasn't going to lead anywhere and intended to continue his education."

Uncovering that key piece of intel may have been a fluke—and a huge piece of good luck for the PI—but it was distressing nonetheless.

And Sarge and the lieutenant weren't the type to enjoy having egg on their face, deserved or not.

Still . . . an undercover operation? Those kinds of resources were usually reserved for larger-scale operations, like the human trafficking setup she'd helped investigate for her first—and she'd hoped, last—undercover assignment.

"So we're going back to take another look at the case. I get that." She kept her inflection neutral. "What I don't get is the undercover component."

The lieutenant stood and walked over to the window. After a few moments, he pivoted back. "Pressure is being exerted to use every available tool to expedite the investigation. Gabe Laurent wants answers." The man clasped his hands behind his back, his expression neutral save for a flare of . . . annoyance? . . . that tightened his features for a fleeting instant. "He also happens to be a big contributor to the campaigns of his state representative and the County Executive."

Ah.

The man had called in favors. Talked to friends in high places, who'd contacted County—not with demands, but to drop a few strong hints that the case might deserve renewed focus.

Yet it didn't explain the undercover angle.

"Why not just assign more personnel?"

The lieutenant scanned his watch and crossed to the door. "I'll let Sarge explain the particulars to you. I'm already late for another meeting." He swung back to her. "I hope we can count on your help with this."

Without giving her the opportunity to respond, he exited, closing the door behind him.

In the ensuing quiet, her pulse accelerated.

That hadn't been a request.

He wanted her on this job.

Why?

She laced her fingers more tightly together and redirected her attention to Sarge. "You know how I feel about undercover work." One taste had been more than sufficient to dim any allure it may have had. Who knew why it had held such appeal for—

Mashing her lips together, she severed that line of thought. It was pointless to revisit history. Her attempt to figure out what motivated a person to live a life of deception and shadows had been a bust, and it was time to move on.

Past time.

"I know, Cate—but we need you on this one."

She waved his comment aside. "There are plenty of detectives at County who like undercover work. Why not tap one of them?"

"Because you're the only one who can pass for a seventeen-year-old."

Her jaw dropped as she processed that bombshell. "You want me to go in as a *student*?"

"Yes."

"Sarge." She gaped at him. "Let's be serious here. I'm thirty-three. Seventeen is a distant speck in the rearview mirror."

"Not that distant—and age is nothing more than a number. With appropriate hairstyle and clothes, you won't have any difficulty convincing people you're seventeen."

She shook her head. "This is crazy. I could be a seventeen-year-old's *mother*."

"Cate." Sarge leaned forward again. "When were you last carded?"

Dang.

He would bring that up.

She cleared her throat and flicked a speck of lint off her slacks. "I don't drink."

"You're avoiding the question."

Okay.

Fine.

She did buy wine on occasion as a gift for party hosts—as Sarge knew, since she'd not only brought a bottle to the retirement barbecue he'd thrown last summer for one of the detectives but joked about having to produce her driver's license for the clerk.

"So I get carded now and then." Like always if she went makeup-free off duty and pulled her hair back into her usual ponytail. "So what?"

He looked at her in silence.

As seconds ticked by, sweat beaded on her upper lip. The moisture in her mouth evaporated. A wave of nausea rolled through her.

Huh.

Who knew that being backed into a corner would have the same effect on her as being trapped in a small space?

Not the best time for her latent claustrophobia to rear its head.

Chest tight, she rose and began to pace. "Maybe the school has nothing to do with this. Stephanie and Alex could have run into trouble away from the campus."

"That's possible—and we'll continue to work that angle with a conventional investigation. But given the high-level interest in this case, we want to cover all the bases—and you know firsthand how much more you can learn from the inside."

Yeah. She did.

If she hadn't befriended the key people in the trafficking case, convinced them she was on their side, the ring would still be operating.

Instead, thanks to the evidence she'd been able to amass, the operation had been shuttered and the leaders rounded up and charged.

"Look at it this way, Cate." Sarge leaned forward, using his most persuasive tone. "If Stephanie told another student where she and her boyfriend planned to go for the weekend—and you can get that girl to confide in you—we can realign our resources. As soon as we have a trail that leads off campus, we'll cut you loose. That could be as fast as a week or two."

She narrowed her eyes. "The trafficking job wasn't supposed to last long either."

"It didn't—not for an investigation like that."

That might be true . . . but it had felt like forever.

Another reason to write off undercover work.

Hardened as she'd become to violence and gore and man's inhumanity to man during her decade in law enforcement, it was a whole different ball game to live that seaminess every day from the inside.

But the lieutenant and Sarge had presented a compelling case.

She *was* the best candidate in the department to pass for a seventeen-year-old.

And if foul play *was* involved in the girl's disappearance, as the new evidence suggested, they should use every tool at their disposal to track down the truth whether there was political pressure being brought to bear or not.

She let out a long, slow breath. "You're not giving me much choice here."

"Yes, I am. We won't force you to take an undercover assignment. If this isn't a role you think you can pull off, we'll try to come up with an alternative plan. For the record, we did check to see if the school has any open staff or faculty positions. It doesn't. But even if it did, the ideal is to place someone who can talk to the girls—especially Stephanie's roommate—as a peer. A student is the best candidate for that."

His rationale was difficult to refute.

She was stuck.

Author's Note

Thank you so much for visiting Hope Harbor—where hearts heal . . . and love blooms.

Back in 2015, when I launched this series, I hoped readers would love my charming Oregon seaside town as much as I did. Seven books in, that's proven to be the case—and I'm beyond thrilled. Thank you all for helping me give life to this special place.

As you've already discovered, for the first time we've included a map of Hope Harbor with this book. I've had one for myself since book 1, but my editor agreed it was time we shared it with all of you. So a graphic artist prettied up my rough sketch and made Hope Harbor even more real for all of us. I hope you enjoy seeing this wonderful little town literally put on the map!

Because a long writing career doesn't happen without the support of numerous people, I'd like to take a moment to thank a few of them.

In my personal corner are my husband, Tom, whose support has been unfailing since the day we met, and my parents, James and Dorothy Hannon. My mom cheers me on from heaven now, but my dad is still rooting for me here in the earthly realm.

I also want to thank my incredible publishing partners at Revell—Dwight Baker, Kristin Kornoelje, Jennifer Leep, Michele

Misiak, Karen Steele, and all the other staff members who bring my books to readers. I feel blessed to work with every one of you.

Looking ahead, in October, watch for *Labyrinth of Lies*, book 2 in my Triple Threat series. And next April, I'll take you back to Hope Harbor for another uplifting story set on the beautiful Oregon coast.

In the meantime, I hope you enjoyed *Blackberry Beach*!

Irene Hannon is the bestselling, award-winning author of more than sixty contemporary romance and romantic suspense novels. She is also a three-time winner of the RITA award—the "Oscar" of romance fiction—from Romance Writers of America and is a member of that organization's elite Hall of Fame.

Her many other awards include National Readers' Choice, Daphne du Maurier, Retailers' Choice, Booksellers' Best, Carol, and Reviewers' Choice from *RT Book Reviews* magazine, which also honored her with a Career Achievement award for her entire body of work. In addition, she is a two-time Christy award finalist.

Millions of her books have been sold worldwide, and her novels have been translated into multiple languages.

Irene, who holds a BA in psychology and an MA in journalism, juggled two careers for many years until she gave up her executive corporate communications position with a Fortune 500 company to write full-time. She is happy to say she has no regrets.

A trained vocalist, Irene has sung the leading role in numerous community musical theater productions and is also a soloist at her church. She and her husband enjoy traveling, long hikes, Saturday mornings at their favorite coffee shop, and spending time with family. They make their home in Missouri.

To learn more about Irene and her books, visit www.irenehannon.com. She posts on Twitter and Instagram, but is most active on Facebook, where she loves to chat with readers.

Hate Mail Was One Thing.
This Was Quite Another...

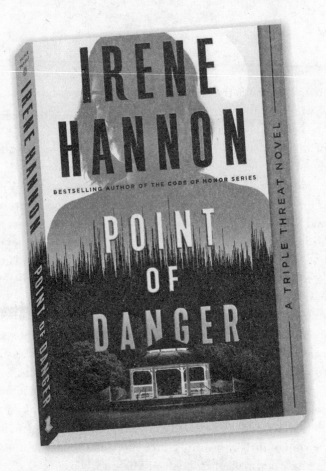

Radio show host Eve Reilly is used to backlash for her on-air commentary. But when angry online posts escalate to menacing harassment, it will be up to Detective Brent Lange to track down a dangerous foe who wants to silence the fearless woman now stealing his heart.

Welcome to

Hope Harbor . . .

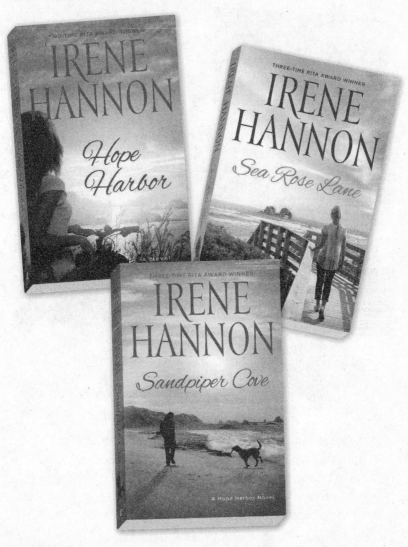

. . . where hearts *heal*
and *love blooms*